SAVAGE MOON

SAVAGE MOON

Chris Simms

First published in Great Britain in 2007 by Orion Books,
an imprint of The Orion Publishing Group Ltd
Orion House, 5 Upper Saint Martin's Lane
London, WC2H 9EA

An Hachette Livre UK Company

1 3 5 7 9 10 8 6 4 2

A CIP catalogue record for this book is
available from the British Library.

ISBN (Hardback) 978 0 7528 8929 0
ISBN (Trade Paperback) 978 0 7528 8930 6

Typeset by Deltatype Ltd, Birkenhead, Merseyside
Printed in Great Britain by
Clays Ltd, St Ives plc

The Orion Publishing Group's policy is to use papers that are natural,
renewable and recyclable products and made from wood grown in sustainable
forests. The logging and manufacturing processes are expected to
conform to the environment regulations of the country of origin.

'Bad Moon Rising' © Words & Music by John Cameron Fogerty © Jondora Music Ltd.
All rights administered by Warner/Chappell Music Ltd, London W6 8BS.
Reproduced by permission.

Extract on Post Natal Depression © Royal College of Psychiatrists 2007
Accessed via www.rcpsych.ac.uk

www.orionbooks.co.uk

To Dad –
those forced marches over Exmoor had their
uses after all.

Hope you got your things together,
Hope you are quite prepared to die,
Looks like we're in for nasty weather,
One eye is taken for an eye.

Well, don't go around tonight,
Well, it's bound to take your life,
There's a bad moon on the rise.

Bad Moon Rising
Creedence Clearwater Revival

Prologue

The quad bike bounced across the moors, headlight catching coarse blades of grass before rearing up into the infinity of the night sky. Like a rider struggling with an unbroken horse, the woman fought to control the vehicle. But rather than slow down, she kept the revs high, her knees flexed in readiness for the next jarring bump.

Way off to her right the undulating red light that topped the radio mast disappeared behind a rise in the land. Finally she dropped her speed, and the engine's angry growl subsided to reveal the same sound that had sparked her reckless dash in the first place: the terror-stricken bleating of a sheep.

'Not another,' she murmured, eyes turning to the shallow ravine that dropped away to her right. She yanked the handlebars round but the headlight's angle was too high. A turn of the key and the engine shuddered into silence. Suffocating darkness engulfed her. She groped for the heavy-duty spotlight behind the saddle and, as she set off down the slope, began playing the yellow beam before her.

Maybe thirty metres away was a cluster of large boulders. A haze-winged moth homed in on the torch like a heat-seeking missile. It landed on her cuff and she felt the frantic blur of wings against the back of her hand. Ignoring the insect, she trudged onwards, eyes fixed on a blood-stained clump of white fleece. The moth launched itself on a sharp curve, flashed across the trembling shaft and plummeted into the turf. She reached the head-high rocks, stepped round the outermost one and shone the light into the semi-circular grouping.

The sheep was lying on its stomach, its head hanging over front legs that were tucked under its chest. The rear legs were tangled up in entrails that glistened like freshly caught eels. An acrid smell stung her nostrils as she stepped closer, then crouched down. Oh no. The animal was still alive. She swung the torch towards the base of the nearest boulder. Something to put it out of its misery. A rock. Anything. The light picked out a trail of blood dripping down the steep grit surface – the implications were just sinking in when the low snarl sounded from above. As she began to swivel the torch upwards a heavy black form landed on top of her.

One

The house was pitch black as Jon Spicer shuffled, sleepy and naked, towards the mewling little cries. He stepped into the nursery where the soft glow of a nightlight barely revealed the tiny form in the cot.

She was on her back, head twitching from side to side, limbs jerking in mounting frustration. He stared down, mind slowly firing up as he assessed the situation, trying to work out what the problem was. Cold? Hot? Wet? Surely not hungry again, he thought, knowing that would involve a trip downstairs to warm a bottle of milk in the microwave.

He heard a faint plastic click as she flung a miniature fist out to the side. The dummy. Her dummy's fallen out. His movements were slow and clumsy as he patted the soft cotton sheet around her head and, at that moment, finding an object worth less than two pounds became the most important thing in the world.

A fingertip caught on the rubber teat. He picked the dummy up and held it to his daughter's lips. They immediately latched on to it and she began a greedy sucking.

He stood motionless with his eyes half shut, trying to maintain his semi-awake state, desperate to return to his own bed and fall back into the heavy folds of sleep. But the sucking noises continued with the same urgency and a tiny puff of exasperation escaped round the object in her mouth.

Shit, he thought. A dummy isn't going to be enough. She's hungry. Accepting that a feed was necessary, more parts of his brain started clicking into gear. He stepped back into the darkness and towards the stairs.

Movement from the main bedroom as his wife shifted in their bed. 'Jon?'

'It's all right,' he whispered, knowing that however tired he felt his wife was a step closer to total exhaustion. 'Holly's hungry. I'll sort it.'

The bed creaked as she fell back against the mattress. He padded quickly down the stairs.

Punch stirred in his basket as he entered the kitchen. 'Hi there stupid,' he murmured, opening the fridge. A pool of feeble light spilled out across the floor, casting a ghostly glow across the room. He took a squat plastic bottle three quarters full of the formula they used when Alice was too tired to breast-feed. Leaving the fridge door open, he placed the bottle in the microwave. Holly's whimpers were increasing in strength upstairs. Looking out the window, all he could see was the faint reflection of his head and torso floating in the expanse of black glass before him. He felt a fleeting sense of vulnerability. Anything could be lurking beyond the thinness of the window, watching him from the darkness.

Uneasily, he glanced up at the clock on the wall. Four thirty-seven in the morning. The hours before dawn and the perfect time for raiding a suspect's house. The time when people were in their deepest sleep, disoriented and slow when wrenched from unconsciousness by their front door bursting off its hinges. Or a baby bursting into cries, he thought with a dry smile.

As the microwave whirred he heard Punch's claws ticking on the lino. He looked down and saw his Boxer bathed in the glow from the fridge, the stump of his tail wagging uncertainly. 'Still getting used to these commotions, aren't you boy?' he said quietly, running a hand over the animal's head. 'Me too, me too.' The machine pinged and he took the bottle out, cupping the base of it in his hand to test the warmth of the liquid inside. 'See you in the morning.'

He pushed the fridge door shut and the darkness instantly surged back, jealously reclaiming the room.

Jon climbed the stairs two at a time, making it back into the nursery just as the dummy tumbled from his daughter's mouth. The whine of frustration was rapidly turning into a toy-like cry.

'Hey there,' he whispered, hooking his index fingers under her arms and lifting her clear of the cot, always amazed at how

4

light she was. He sat down on the padded chair and positioned her in the crook of his arm as her tiny legs kicked about.

'Here you go, greedy young madam.' He offered her the teat and she immediately took it. The squeaks were replaced by bubbling noises and she pressed her fists against the sides of the bottle.

Thank God, he thought, settling into the seat, feeling the cool material against his back. He stared down at the little thing in his arms, sifting through his feelings, searching as usual for the unbreakable bond of emotion that ought to be there.

But he couldn't find it. Of course he loved the baby and knew instinctively that he would lay down his life for her, but the tangible feeling of love that he felt every time he looked at Alice, or Punch for that matter, just wasn't there. Like an oak tree in the dark, he could sense its looming presence but, for now, he couldn't locate it.

Holly was born just over three months ago and he was only now beginning to comprehend how their lives had changed forever. At first, it had felt like she was a temporary break in their routine. The first night feeds were easy – after all, anyone can handle a few interruptions to their sleep. They'd even laughed, feeling relief at how it wasn't that hard having a baby after all.

But then the days stretched into weeks and the weeks into months and slowly it was starting to dawn on him that they were in this for the long run. Things weren't about to settle back to how they'd once been. Not ever.

He closed his eyes and leaned his head back. Almost five o'clock. An hour and a half more sleep if he was lucky, then Monday morning and back to work. Bollocks, he thought, letting out a sigh. The case he was working on seemed to be a total dead-ender. A few elderly homosexuals had been assaulted at night in car parks dotted around Manchester. No one wanted to talk about it, especially not the victims once the ambulance drivers had patched up the minor cuts and bruises to their heads. Normally the Major Incident Team wouldn't be dragged into a case of this nature, but the latest attack had moved the case up several notches in the serious crime scorecard.

The recording of the emergency call was clear in his head. A man's voice, panic making it waver and dip.

'Police? That's the police? You need to get out here, someone's being killed!'

The operator's voice, calm and steady. 'Where are you, Sir?'

'What? It's the car park. The one by the recreation ground. Silburn Grove, Middleton.'

'The public car park on Silburn Grove. Thank you, Sir. Who is being attacked?'

'Listen, I don't know! This lad jumped out on us by the shed. He's got an iron bar. Oh Jesus, I can hear screaming.'

The recording had captured it too, muffled and faint in the background. Someone in terror for their life.

'Good God, hurry. He's killing him.'

'Please stay calm, Sir. Who is being attacked?'

'Oh! I can see him now, he's come back round. He's going towards his car.'

'Who, Sir? The attacker?'

'There's so much blood!'

'Can you see the make or registration?'

'MA03 H something. It's a big estate. Jesus, I don't know where the other guy is.' Movement against the earpiece as the man must have looked desperately around. Just before he rang off an engine surged as the accelerator was pressed down.

By the time the patrol car arrived the car park was deserted. As one of Manchester's more popular sites for gay rendezvous, that was very unusual – especially since it was late evening. The attending officers had swept the area around the shed with their torches and soon found blood spatters arcing in dotted lines up a side wall. Someone had taken a serious beating.

Clusters of drops had then led them across the asphalt towards an area of undergrowth that screened a shallow, dirty stream. The water was clogged with old tyres, bags of dumped rubbish and the odd shopping trolley. No corpse was in the vicinity.

The decision was made to refer the assault on to MIT and Jon arrived at the crime scene two hours later. The powers that be saw it as an escalation of violence that could – if it hadn't already – lead to murder.

The problem was the lack of witnesses. Jon was familiar with cases where victim and witnesses were unwilling to come forward. He was left trying to investigate a case that was doomed to failure. Only when an actual body showed up would the resources needed for a breakthrough be released. Still, at least he was getting home on time each night.

Gurgling noises returned him to the present. He looked down as Holly pushed the teat from her mouth. Her arms slowly lowered then fell slackly to her sides. He held the bottle to the nightlight and saw it was almost empty. Jesus, she could bolt milk like there was no tomorrow. His mum had seen this and, unable to resist in a bit of misty-eyed reminiscing, proudly told Alice that, as a baby, Jon could sink nine ounces in a few minutes. But, Jon thought, he'd weighed almost eleven pounds when he was born. The little thing in his lap had been almost half that. Obviously making up for it.

He lifted her to a sitting position, formed a V shape with the thumb and fingers of his spare hand and then gently wedged her chin into it. Her arms hung down and he began rubbing her back, feeling the minute bumps of her spine against the palm of his hand. So tiny. So fragile. Eventually a couple of surprisingly large burps escaped her. 'Good ones, my piglet,' he whispered, planting a kiss on her soft cheek. He lifted her up and gently placed her back in the cot. He was just straightening up when a noise outside caused him to freeze.

The sound, at first low and guttural, suddenly erupted into a hideous yowl. Something deep in Jon reacted to its animal ferocity and his heart started to beat more quickly. The noise came again, dying away into a fearsome hiss.

He stepped over to the window, lifted the blind and peered out into the blackness. A crack had opened in the unseen cloud layer above and moonlight shone down. Balanced on their rear wall was a large tabby cat, back arched upward, fur jutting out in a series of spikes. Its attention was riveted on something on the other side of the wall.

Jon felt like a wildlife photographer observing the secret interplays that take place between the creatures of the night. Sightings of foxes were becoming more and more common in the neighbourhood and he felt a slight thrill that a wild animal could be just metres away, roaming the streets and alleys, using the darkness to claim an urban territory as its own.

Suddenly a tingle worked its way down his spine as he thought about what had taken place up on Saddleworth Moor not three weeks ago. A farmer's wife had been savaged to death by some creature and a frenzy of 'mystery beast' fever had gripped the nation ever since.

Jon knew from recent newspaper articles that the loss of sheep was a fairly commonplace occurrence for many farms in and around Britain's national parks. The problem had got so bad around Bodmin during the mid-nineties that the Ministry for Agriculture, Fisheries and Food had commissioned a scientific investigation to determine once and for all if a wild panther was stalking the bleak expanses of Dartmoor. The study was inconclusive and the issue had lapsed back to occasional sightings of large black cats. But ripped open and disembowelled carcasses of sheep continued to be found in the more remote parts of the countryside.

The Suttons' farm on Saddleworth was suffering particularly badly and the wife, a few years younger than her more elderly husband, had taken to going out at night and patrolling the perimeters of their land on a quad bike. On the fateful night, the husband had been away from home, staying overnight at a big sheep market in Keswick up in the Lake District. According to numerous witnesses, he'd got mightily drunk before staggering off to his hotel room at gone two in the morning. When he returned home the next day his wife was nowhere to be found. Eventually he'd gone out on to the moor, spotted the abandoned quad bike and then discovered her corpse alongside the remains of a partially eaten ewe in a nearby ravine. Both of their throats had been torn out and short strands of wiry black hair were found under the wife's nails. Laboratory analysis revealed that the hair belonged to a panther.

The cat on their yard wall was now backing away, a horrible low noise emerging from deep within its throat. Deciding there was enough distance between it and the unseen adversary below, it turned and leaped onto the adjoining wall before disappearing up and over the neighbour's garage with a frantic scrabble of claws. The gap in the cloud closed up, the scene vanished and silence returned.

From beyond the curve of the earth came a faint glow, just strong enough to separate black horizon from dark sky. Night was coming to an end.

The creature remained motionless, body pressed into the tundra-like grass of the moor. Before it the ground dropped away, clumps of gorse quickly dissolving into the gloom. Further down the slope two sheep sheltered at the base of a particularly dense bush.

The wind shifted and the long hairs that emerged from the tips of the creature's ears bent ever so slightly. This new current of air carried up from the plains of Cheshire stretched out below. Contained in it were some interesting sounds and scents. The noise of engines, the sharpness of exhaust fumes, the presence of Man.

The creature's gaze moved across the uncultivated land, settling on the outermost edge of urban sprawl leading back into the city of Manchester itself. Its eyes narrowed slightly and it examined the lights that twinkled from street lamps and cars and people's homes.

Two

Jon stood in front of the draining board the next morning, unscrewing caps of dirty feeding bottles and dropping them into the sink full of warm water. His eyes felt itchy and tired and he raised his hands to rub them. But his fingers were covered in soapy bubbles and he had to use the heels of his palms instead. It only made them feel worse.

He leaned to the side and scooped a spoonful of muesli into his mouth. As he did so his eye caught on the row of photos stuck to the fridge door by an assortment of coloured magnets. His and Alice's wedding day. Chewing on the cereal, he stared with a slight smile at an image of his wife. She'd picked a simple white off-the-shoulder dress with a gossamer shawl that shimmered in the sunlight. Unusually for Alice, she'd worn her hair up, clips carefully arranged so that a few strands hung down at the sides of her face.

They'd opted for a registry office, much to both of their mothers' disappointment, but Alice was keen to get married before the baby arrived and it was their only option at such short notice. After a brief debate during which Jon felt he was being guided to the right answers by Alice, they'd decided on a humanist wedding. He wasn't bothered whether it was religious or not, but his mum still went to her local Catholic church every Sunday and he could sense her disappointment deepen.

The day itself had been clear and crisp, pale blue May skies, blossoming chestnuts swaying in the light breeze. The sort of day when you could feel the world easing itself into the start of summer. He had been nervous before the ceremony, anticipating that the gravity of the commitments they were about to make would slam home at any moment. But the impact never came and he'd floated through the day feeling like he was playing a lead part in some sort of strange play.

For after the ceremony they'd booked a function room at the Marriott hotel, close to where Alice's mum lived in Worseley. It was meant to be a small, simple and inexpensive reception, but the guest list soon began to multiply. Jon remembered their slight argument when he'd added the names of his team mates from Cheadle Ironsides rugby club. Probably wasn't such a good move after all, he now admitted to himself, remembering the flaming sambuccas that had begun appearing towards the end of the night.

Half way through the evening, in a brief moment alone with Alice, he'd mentioned how surreal everything felt, almost as if he was at someone else's wedding entirely. To his relief she had immediately agreed, gushing that it all felt like a dream to her too. Just in time he'd stopped himself from saying that wasn't quite what he'd meant. Instead, he'd sat back and lit a celebratory cigar, grinning as Rick, his friend and colleague, expertly twirled Alice around the small dance floor.

He looked down at the silver wedding band on his finger, still finding the sight of it there slightly bizarre. Shaking his head, he turned back to the sink and scrubbed at the bottles with a small brush. Satisfied they were clean, he lined them up in the rack, shoved it in the microwave and turned the dial to three minutes on full power.

Christ, he thought, what did I actually do with my time before this baby was born?

Punch sat in his basket patiently watching Jon's every move. 'I know, I'll be ready in a minute,' he said with a self-conscious glance towards the door, aware of how Alice laughed at him for chatting to the dog. Once he'd eaten the remainder of his cereal, he crouched in front of the washing machine and started emptying damp babygrows and bibs into a plastic washing basket. Turning the key in the back door, he stepped out into their yard and began hanging the miniature items from the clothesline.

The sun was just clearing the end of the alleyway and a horizontal shaft of orange light cut across the top of the yard walls. Punch came padding out, nose to the ground, to begin his usual check around. When he reached the wooden door leading into the alleyway itself he stopped and began sniffing loudly.

Jon looked over his shoulder. 'Smell something boy? Something been prowling about, hey?' He pegged out the last babygrow and ducked into the kitchen for the dog lead and his jacet. As soon as he unlocked the wooden door, Punch shoved his way past Jon's legs and began excitedly cutting back and forth across the cobbles. Jon looked to the side. Their bin had been tipped over and the refuse sack partially dragged out. Something had ripped it open and removed the remains of the chicken they'd eaten two nights before. Bones were scattered around, pieces of vertebrae crushed and mangled. 'Bastard foxes,' Jon muttered to himself, thinking how he'd have to sweep the mess up later. Punch's head was down and he was snorting away at the base of the yard wall opposite. Abruptly he turned around and sprayed some urine over the spot.

'Something been marking your territory? Well, Punch, if it comes over into our yard you'll see it off, won't you?'

The dog heard the words 'see it off' and began to look around eagerly at the tops of the walls, tongue hanging from his open mouth. It was the phrase Jon used whenever they spotted a squirrel in the local park and it was Punch's cue for a mad dash towards the smaller animal. Jon knew his dog was doomed to eternal failure in his chases, but it amused him to see his pet frantically dancing around a tree trunk, excitedly barking up at the branches.

'Come on then, I haven't got long.' He set off towards the end of the alley, cold autumnal air clearing his head. Out on Shawbrook Road the yellowing leaves were beginning to curl and drop from the trees. Kicking aside spiky horse chestnut shells, Jon thought about how it was getting dark by seven-thirty each evening. The clocks would go back in another few days and then things would get really miserable. Bloody great.

He reached the grounds of Heaton School five minutes later, striding along the track that dissected the playing fields, Punch keeping pace off to his side like a hunting party's outrider. As he skirted the edge of Heaton Moor Golf Course he looked across the dew-covered grass at the bunkers full of damp sand. Cobwebs glistened on the clusters of gorse bushes that crouched in the still morning air and curls of steam rose where the sun's rays sliced through the trees to his side.

Ten minutes later he was back home and unlocking the kitchen door. Punch waited obediently as his wet paws were dried with an old towel, then they both stepped back into the house.

Silence.

Jon took off his coat, grabbed a bin liner and the dustpan and brush, then went back out into the alley and swept up the scattering of bones. After dumping them in the fresh bag, he placed the ripped bag inside it too and walked back into the kitchen. He made a cup of tea, then climbed the stairs and peered into their dimly lit room. Alice was lying on her side with the duvet peeled back. Holly's tiny body was alongside her, face pressed against an exposed breast. Jon could smell the slightly musty aroma of milk.

'She scoffing again?' he said, placing the cup of tea on the bedside table.

Alice smiled. She had a serene expression on her face and it was one Jon had never seen until she'd become pregnant. It carried a suggestion of peace and contentment and he was always delighted to see it. 'She woke up as you took Punch out. Did you clean his paws before you came in?'

Irritation suddenly needled him. He could sense Alice's mounting resentment of his dog – now the baby had arrived, Punch had dropped in her affection. He had even spotted her looking at the animal with obvious distaste.

'Course I did. So she's been feeding a good quarter of an hour then?'

'I suppose so, I think she's about full.'

'I should hope so. She took almost six ounces just before five this morning.'

Jon realised that, though they were talking to each other, both of their eyes were glued to the baby.

'I thought I heard you moving around. I wasn't sure if it was a dream.'

Jon sat down and passed a hand over the sheen of pale hair covering his daughter's head. Her skull was so warm and he had the urge to kick off his shoes and climb in beside them. Sod work and the bunch of dirty old men he was trying to protect.

'What are you up to today?' he asked.

Alice reflected for a moment. 'Thought I'd skip into Manchester for a spot of shopping, pop into the gym for a massage and sauna, have lunch in Tampopo then go to the cinema or theatre. Or I could sit in all day with this gum-toothed little monster latched on to my tit.'

Jon looked at her, relieved to see she was smiling.

'Actually, your mum's coming over and we're going to the park. Might stop for a coffee somewhere. I may even end up doing the feeding thing in public,' she said, raising her eyebrows and nodding down at her swollen breasts.

Jon frowned. 'That's not a problem, is it?'

She hunched a shoulder. 'Some people can be funny. You know, they reckon it shouldn't be done outside.'

Jon shook his head. 'That's totally wrong. It's the most natural thing in the world.'

Alice put on an upper class voice. 'Not very civilised though, is it?'

He let out a snort, then remembered the scene from their back yard. 'Did you hear that bloody cat screeching in the night?'

Alice was looking back down, attention almost completely absorbed by her baby. 'No.'

'God, it was a horrible noise. I can see where the word caterwaul comes from. It was on our back wall, something down in the alley was really putting the shits up it.' He paused. 'Which park are you going to?'

'I don't know. Probably Stockport Little Moor, walk along the river there.'

Jon glanced at her mischievously. 'Well, don't stray from the path, OK? What if the thing scaring the cat last night was the Monster of the Moor? It's only twenty miles away from here. It could have crept down from the hills looking for fresh meat.'

Alice glanced up, looking alarmed. 'Jon, stop it! That's horrible.'

He grinned sheepishly, surprised at her reaction. 'It's only a joke, Ali.'

'Well,' she said, hand cupping Holly's head protectively. 'It's not funny. Imagine being that poor woman. Your last memory some savage black beast lunging at your throat. What's happening with that anyway?'

Jon's eyes lingered on his wife. The outburst wasn't like her. He'd noticed a few since the birth. Brief flashes of insecurity, even tears at the most trivial of human interest stories from the news. He shrugged. 'The local bobbies out near Mossley Brow are dealing with it. Apparently they've called in some expert in charge of the panther enclosure at Buxton zoo. He's giving them advice on how best to trap it.' He grinned. 'Last I heard there was a proposal to draft in a regiment from the Paras to stake out the moor with lamb chops.'

'Oh, that's ridiculous.' Her hand moved across to Holly's crown then back to her forehead. Rhythmic, soothing, even though their daughter wasn't crying. 'There must be a better way of catching it. People aren't safe with that thing roaming around.'

Jon felt himself frowning. What had happened to her sense of humour? He thought back, trying to remember the last time he'd heard her laughing. When she was working as a beautician she'd always be giggling, relaying the gossip from the salon, recounting Melvyn's outrageous exploits in the Gay Village. Too much time in the house, that was the problem. He hooked a frizzy strand of hair from her face. 'Hey Ali, why don't you leave Holly with my mum and nip into Melvyn's for a haircut? Your work mates, they'd love to see you.'

'It's not a barber's, Jon. He'll be fully booked for days.' Suddenly she shuddered. 'You've put me off now. We'll probably end up going to the Trafford Centre.'

Jon pictured the gargantuan shopping centre on the eastern edge of Manchester. 'I'd rather take my chances with the

Monster of the Moor than the hordes of zombies shuffling around in that place. And give Melvyn a call; the treat's on me, all right?'

Three

Half an hour later Jon was grinding a cigarette out in the car park of Longsight police station.

Much to Alice's disapproval, he'd been smoking again since his involvement in the hunt for the Butcher of Belle Vue that had taken place earlier that year. It had culminated in a major clash with his SIO, DCI McCloughlin. In the pressure cooker environment of a major investigation, one such occurence might not have been problematic, but it was a repeat of a similar falling out they'd had on the Chewing Gum killer case the year before.

Nothing had been explicitly said, but it was no surprise to Jon when he wasn't among the officers named to work with McCloughlin on his next case. Insead, he'd been moved to DCI Edward Summerby's syndicate. The man was white-haired, overweight and due to retire next year. Jon wasn't that bothered – he was finding it impossible to cope with McCloughlin's dictatorial style anyway.

The only problem was that the less demanding cases were being farmed out to Summerby in the run up to his retirement. The result was that Jon found himself walking down the corridor to a side room, where he made up a team of one trying to catch the assailant of men skulking round car parks looking for casual sex. How fucking sad, he thought, knowing it was a fairly commonplace practice. A natural consequence, he concluded, of a society that, despite all its comforts and luxuries, left many feeling isolated and alone. So they jumped into their cars in search of contact with other humans.

His smoking went up and down in its frequency. Some days he hardly touched them, but on others the nicotine was a vital way of perking him up. You're just tired, he told himself, not wanting to admit that the job he so loved could be starting to bore him. Stifling a yawn, he pressed the buttons on a dispensing machine and watched as a spindly stream of black coffee fell into the plastic cup below. The liquid died away to a succession of droplets like the end of a piss. He picked up the cup and entered the side room.

As he made his way over to his desk in the corner, a few colleagues working on a fraud case acknowledged him with a lift of an eyebrow or a tilt of a head. None smiled: there was a tarred brush dangling above DI Spicer and no one wanted to get too near.

He sat down, glanced at his in-tray and turned on his computer. Increasingly this was now his routine – sitting at a desk and spending all day staring at his screen or shuffling paper.

The search of the crime scene at the car park hadn't revealed anything other than the trail of blood. A sample had been taken and tested for DNA, but there was no match on the national database. Following that, Jon had placed an incident board at the end of the car park giving the time and date of the attack and requesting that anyone with information call his number. The phone hadn't gone once.

He'd even parked there himself one evening and approached car drivers as they pulled up. It was amazing how many men had 'got lost', 'made a wrong turn' or were 'looking for a toilet' as he produced his badge.

When he decided to approach a car with his identification hidden, he'd been greeted by the sight of a fifty-year-old man sitting with his flies wide open. His penis was jutting upwards like an extra gear stick. Jon almost nicked him for gross indecency. When he returned the next night he was the only one there; word obviously spread fast within that particular community.

He wondered how his partner in the Butcher of Belle Vue investigation would handle things. DS Rick Saville was a graduate on the accelerated promotion scheme. He had a razor-sharp eye for detail and an ability to relax people when questioning them. He was also gay – perhaps he could provide a few pointers. Last he'd heard, Rick was back at the Greater Manchester Police's headquarters at Chester House on a rotation with police complaints. Maybe he'd give him a ring and suggest a beer at the Bull's Head.

He lifted the few pieces of paper in his in-tray. There was a response from the communications liaison unit letting him know that the person who'd called 999 on the night of the incident had done so from a pay-as-you-go mobile. The chance of tracing him from his phone records had just vanished.

With a sigh, Jon looked at the next sheet of paper. Confirmation from the A&E department at North Manchester General hospital that no one on the night of the twenty-fifth had been treated for injues consistent with being repeatedly hit with an iron bar. Just like every other hospital in the region.

He picked up the final piece of paper, a status report from the two civilian assistants who were helping him on an intermittent basis. Jon had got a list of vehicles with licence plates that began MA03 then had the letter H in the remainder of the registration. There were several thousand of them.

Of the vehicles registered to drivers in the Greater Manchester area, many were smaller models or saloons, some were four-wheel drives and around a third were estates. So began the aspect of police work Jon detested most – the laborious trawl through a massive list, slowly crossing off possibilities one by one.

The person who'd dialled 999 had described the attacker as a lad: so he'd gone through the list of estate drivers under the age of twenty-five checking for any with a record for violence. There were fourteen of them, but all appeared to have solid alibis for the night of the attack.

After that, he'd requested that his civilian assistants call every local car owner under the age of twenty-five from the list and ask if they could give their whereabouts on the evening the incident took place. Whenever their questions were met with vague or elusive answers the civilians flagged the call and gave the details to Jon for following up.

It was a tenuous way to go about an investigation and the process was worsened by the fact that his assistants were rarely available to actually help him. Time and time again they were being commandeered by DCI McCloughlin to provide back-up in his pursuit of an armed gang terrorising post offices around Salford.

His phone rang. 'DI Spicer here.'

'Jon, it's DCI Summerby.'

'Morning, Sir,' Jon replied, sitting up straighter.

'Morning. I have ten minutes if you're not too busy. Just wanting to see how things are progressing down there.'

Jon rolled his eyes. 'I'll be straight up.'

As he slipped the pieces of paper in his report book he thought about his boss. DCI Summerby's style of management couldn't have been more different to that of his old boss, DCI McCloughlin.

Summerby was softly spoken and led through a permissive approach, involving his officers in the decision-making process and giving them as much autonomy as he could in the investigation.

McCloughlin, gruff and bristly, was far more autocratic. He took decisions on his own then issued sets of commands to his team. And if an officer strayed from his designated role McCloughlin didn't like it – as Jon had discovered to his cost.

He climbed the stairs and knocked on Summerby's door before opening it.

'Jon, come in.'

He stepped into the room, immediately noticing that the window was wide open despite the crisp chill to the morning.

'Beautiful day, isn't it? Shame to be stuck in an office,' said Summerby, hand cutting through a ray of sunlight as he gestured to the chair on the other side of his desk. Jon had a sudden image of him pruning a garden. 'Though you look like you've been up well before dawn's rosy fingers crept over the horizon.'

Jon gave a crooked smile, aware of the dark smears of skin below his eyes. 'You're not wrong,' he replied, running a hand through the cropped brown hair on his head.

Summerby gave a sympathetic smile. 'How is the baby?'

'Fine, thanks. Eating for England she is.' He glanced at the photos on the wall of two young men, mortar boards on their heads, academic gowns draped from their shoulders. 'I bet you can hardly remember the horrors of night feeds.'

Summerby linked his fingers and looked off to the side. 'True. You only remember the good times I'm pleased to say. Anyway, how's this case going?'

Jon tried to keep his voice from sounding too negative. 'Not much headway so far, Sir. The person who reported the incident called on a pay-as-you-go phone, so that's a non-starter. No hospital in the area treated anyone for blunt trauma injuries to the head that night. I'm currently working my way through the car registrations, but progress is slow I'm afraid. My civilian assistants seem to be spending all their time on Operation Stamp.'

'McCloughlin's post office investigation?' Summerby looked slightly irritated.

Jon nodded.

'Let me make a call. We'll get you an agreed number of hours since the man seems unable to stick to an informal arrangement.'

Glad to have some support behind him, Jon smiled inwardly.

'How about the request for information at the scene?'

Jon thought about the forlorn incident board sitting at the end of the car park. 'Nothing from that, Sir.'

'And your own efforts? Didn't you visit the car park a couple of times yourself?'

'No luck there either, Sir,' he replied, cringing at the memory.

Summerby leaned back. 'Well, keep plugging away. How many more to get through on the car registration list?'

'We've almost gone through every owner aged under twenty-five. I'll open up the rest of the list today, though I think we'll be very lucky to get anything from this line of enquiry.'

'I'm afraid I agree,' murmured Summerby. 'Still, look at it this way. It's the ideal case for an officer with a young baby. No long hours, no running around. Use the time wisely, Jon. We'll give it another week and I'll have to look at moving you to something else.'

'OK, Sir.' Jon got up, wondering if he'd die of frustration before then.

He headed down the corridor and opened the doors to the station's main incident room. Around a dozen officers were busy on the phones, civilian assistants were typing up reports and the allocator was giving out a load of actions to a group of plain-clothes detectives.

Jon glanced hungrily at the whiteboards, eyes moving over the grainy CCTV stills of the balaclava-clad gang. Dotting the board were photos of the burnt-out getaway cars from each robbery.

From the corner of his eye, he saw McCloughlin staring at him from his inner office, hands on hips. What are you doing on my territory? his posture demanded.

Fuck you, Jon thought, savouring the prospect of the phone call his former boss was about to receive from Summerby. He looked around and spotted one of his civilian assistants at her desk nearby. A glamorous-looking woman in her forties, she was elbow deep in piles of witness statements. 'Hi there, Pam, how's it going?'

'It's Pat,' she coughed, and Jon cursed his inability to remember names. 'Not too bad. We've got a lot of typing to do.'

He noticed the note of impatience in her voice. Obviously my trivial demands are inconveniencing you, he reflected. 'Looks like it,' Jon replied, keeping his voice friendly as he removed the list of car registrations from his book. 'When you get the chance, can you start calling these owners?'

She gave a heavy sigh. 'Yes. But I don't know when, it's very busy in here.'

Jon lowered his voice. 'Don't worry, you're about to be allotted some time for it. I'll make a start on these ones.' He removed the top three sheets from the list and left her to it.

He spent the rest of the morning working his way through the numbers, frequently getting answer machines at people's homes. Many were recorded by women – wives or partners. Jon left terse messages, asking the man to call him as soon as possible and not giving a reason why.

Pat walked into his side room just before lunch with a piece of paper in her hand. 'DI Spicer, I think I've got something for you.'

'Go ahead,' he replied, motioning at the spare seat opposite.

'Well, DCI McCloughlin instructed us to spend the morning on your calls.' She gave him a look that spoke volumes about McCloughlin's manner when he gave the command. 'Anyway, this man's answers were most odd.'

'How do you mean?' Jon asked, placing his elbows on the table.

'Well, I started off in the usual way. Said I was with the Greater Manchester Police and explained we were investigating an assault that took place in the car park at Silburn Grove last Thursday night. Well, he immediately asked how I had his phone number.'

'And?'

'I told him a car with a registration very similar to his was seen leaving the scene. He became very flustered and asked me to repeat when and where the incident took place, but I could tell he was just playing for time. When I asked if he drove an estate car he started complaining about his right to privacy and then hung up.'

For the first time in days, Jon felt the blood quickening in his veins. 'How old did he sound to you?'

'Not young. Hard to say, forty or over?'

'Really?' The answer caught Jon by surprise. The person who dialled 999 had described the attacker as a lad, not someone over forty. Perhaps we've tracked down the victim of the incident, he thought, taking the sheet of paper from her. A large star had been drawn next to a name near the bottom of the page,

DEREK PETERSON,
5 BURMAN STREET,
CLAYTON.

'That's great, Pat, cheers.'

'Shall we carry on calling? DCI McCloughlin said we were allocated to you for the morning.'

'No, it's nearly lunch anyway. I'll give you a shout if I need any more help.'

She walked off and he turned to his computer. After logging

into the PNC, he typed Derek Peterson's name and address into the search field. The man's record came up an instant later. Date of birth 1956. That made him forty-seven years old. Jon's eyes scanned downwards. A fine for gross indecency in 1993. Ten years ago he'd been arrested for exposing himself in the trees near to a children's playground. Jon felt his lip twitch with disgust. After that he'd been placed on the sex offender's list. The incident had also cost him his job in a care home for youngsters. Jon found himself immediately jumping to the conclusion that the man was a paedophile. Within a year of his conviction he'd informed the police of his move to Burman Street, but no further breaches of the law since then. As a result, his name had dropped off the register five years later. Jon then accessed VISOR, Manchester's Violent Sex Offender's Register. Nothing on that.

Feeling the muscles in his shoulders tensing up, he snatched the phone and started stabbing in the man's number. Half way through he stopped. OK, he thought, the man might be a seedy pervert, but he's also the victim of a vicious assault.

He put the phone down and breathed deeply. This wasn't the right attitude. He needed to suppress his own opinions and question the person in a professional and sympathetic manner if he hoped for any cooperation. How would Rick handle this? He'd go and see him face to face, that's what he'd do. He'd sit down and approach it gently. Right, decided Jon, picking up his jacket and heading for the door.

Four

The drive to Clayton took Jon half an hour. Derek Peterson lived near the end of a drab and anonymous row of houses. Lads slouched at the corner, watching one of their group as he raced up and down the road on a miniature motorbike. Jon could see the area teetering on the edge of depression. Most of the tiny front gardens were unkempt, long grass engulfed a broken fridge in one. A few houses were boarded up. Residents were beginning to abandon the area and others were unwilling to move in.

He parked outside number five, worrying as he always did about some scrote damaging his car as soon as his back was turned.

There was a Volvo estate on Peterson's drive and its registration matched the numbers and letters reported by the anonymous caller. Jon looked at the front of the house. Most of the curtains were drawn and the view into the living room was blocked by a sheet of dirty yellow netting. What's the betting the inside of the house will be dim and musty, he told himself, getting his warrant card out and ringing on the bell. The netting to his right twitched, but by the time he'd turned his head the material had dropped back into place. It hung motionless as though it hadn't shifted in years.

Jon gave the door three loud raps with his knuckles. I'm not going anywhere, the harsh sounds announced, and moments later he heard movement behind the door. The lock rattled and the door opened up a crack to reveal a face that sagged with grey skin. The eye that wasn't partially shut by swelling switched nervously from Jon to the lads on the street corner beyond. 'Yeah?'

Jon sensed discretion was the best option, so he kept his ID close to his chest and his voice low. 'Derek Peterson? I'm DI Spicer from Greater Manchester Police. Could I come in for a quick word?'

The door didn't move. 'What's it about?'

'I think you know, Sir. You received a call from one of my colleagues about an incident in the car park on Silburn Grove.'

The man sighed and the door opened a bit further to reveal an ugly lump on the man's forehead. It was capped by a fresh scab. He peered towards the street. 'Have you come in a patrol car?'

'No, Sir, that's mine parked directly in front of your house.'

Peterson looked slightly relieved and Jon guessed he didn't want the neighbourhood knowing about this little visit. 'It won't get nicked there will it?' he said, trying to establish some rapport.

The man gave a snort as if to say, depends on your luck.

Jon gestured with his hand. 'Maybe it's best we chatted inside?'

The door swung open and Jon stepped into the hall. As he suspected, the air was heavy with stale odours. Fried food and dirty carpets. Peterson walked into the front room and, without offering Jon a seat, slumped into an old armchair.

The telly was on, day time drivel that was barely different from the crap filling the evening schedule. Peterson looked like an apathetic sponge, soaking the lot up anyway.

Jon switched it off, not prepared to compete with the idiot box for the man's reluctant attention. The light in the room seemed weak and Jon wondered if it was on a dimmer switch only turned half way up, but when he saw the silhouettes of dead flies piled in the dirty lampshade he knew the interview was destined to take place in the gloom.

'Derek,' said Jon, sitting down and taking out a notebook and pen. 'Those are nasty injuries you've got there. Have you had them checked out?'

The man didn't respond and in the silence the whine of the miniature motorbike outside reached a crescendo as the machine sped past.

Jon shrugged. 'What happened in that car park last Thursday? We received a call from someone saying a serious assault was taking place.'

Peterson was still looking at the dead screen. 'Nothing much.'

'Nothing much? Someone's had a go at you. It looks like they meant business.'

Peterson draped a wrist over the armrest. 'Someone jumped out on me. He was carrying some sort of weapon. I don't know what.'

'The man who rang us said it was an iron bar.'

Peterson glanced across at Jon, obviously unsettled by the amount he appeared to know. 'Yeah, it could have been.'

'And he struck you across the face and head with it? From your injuries that could well be GBH. Have you visited a hospital?'

He shook his head.

'Could I ask why not? Regardless of what you were doing in that car park, you're the victim of a serious offence. You have every right to seek help, be it medical or from the police.'

'It's not that bad. Besides, what would you lot do?' The question had an accusatory ring to it and Jon sensed Derek Peterson didn't regard the police as a force to protect him.

'We need to find the man who did this, Derek. If he's responsible for the other attacks that have taken place, he needs to be stopped before someone gets killed.'

Peterson flipped his hand over and turned the palm upward in a tired attempt at exasperation. 'I don't need the attention, OK? You'll have seen my record.'

He looked at Jon for affirmation and received a single nod.

'The animals round here, if they found out about me, they'd drive me from my home. Paint on my front door, bricks through the windows. It happened before and where were you lot then?'

Jon thought of the change of address on the man's record. He wanted to take a deep breath, but didn't like the idea of drawing the fetid air any further into his lungs than was necessary. 'Derek, whatever happened as a result of your previous charge I can only apologise for. But we need your help now.'

'Forget it,' Derek said, reaching for the remote, then looking irritated when he realised the TV was turned off at the set itself.

'Is there nothing you can give me by way of a description?

You needn't involve yourself any more than that. How old was your attacker? Was he taller than you?'

Peterson turned the remote over in his hand. Coming to a decision, he hauled himself up slightly in his seat. 'Mid-twenties. Bit taller than me. Heavily built.'

'So, six foot or over?'

'Not quite as tall as you.'

Jon was six-foot-four. 'About six-one or two then?'

Peterson gave a nod.

'And you said he was heavily built. Like he did weights? Body builder size?'

'Like you I'd say. Do you do weights, officer? Make yourself big for when you need to apply a bit of force?'

Jon let the comment pass. 'What about his hair?'

'Cropped short, again like yours.'

Jon's pen paused and he wondered if Peterson was just stringing him along. 'What was he wearing, Sir?'

'Oh, I don't know. One of those hooded tops. Red, I think.'

'How do you know it was hooded?'

'Because it was over his head of course.'

Got you, Jon thought, going back to his notes. 'But you just said he had cropped hair. How could you tell that if the hood was up?'

Peterson looked flustered. 'It slipped down when we were struggling.'

'You struggled with him? I thought he just struck you a couple of times and ran off. What happened if you struggled with him?'

Peterson's eyes moved back to the telly. Breaking eye contact. Getting ready to tell a lie.

'I got a hand up and pulled his hood back. I think that rattled him and he ran off then.'

'So you saw his face?'

'Er, glimpsed it I suppose.'

Jon kept looking at him, pen poised above the note pad.

'Average looking. White. Nothing in particular stands out.'

'Thin in the face or round? Prominent nose? Big eyes? Small eyes? Far apart or close together?'

Peterson waved his hand impatiently. 'I didn't see. It all happened so quickly.'

'How quickly? He struck you, what, twice? You struggled and he ran off.'

'Yeah, it was all over in seconds.'

'But, Sir, I have the recording of whoever called us that night. They had time to get to their car, call nine-nine-nine and then be put through to an operator. I was able to hear screaming in the background. The call lasted a good twenty seconds.'

Peterson sat forward and rubbed at his neck with the end of the remote. It wasn't a natural movement and Jon knew he was feigning confusion. 'I don't know, I was being attacked for fuck's sake. Maybe I was yelling, who knows?'

'I'm confused by the blood as well. A trail of it led away from the shed towards a small stream. Was that yours?'

'I suppose so.' Jon saw an idea occur to him. 'Yes, that's right. I chased him. He ran off, splashed through the water. Maybe I was yelling as I chased him.'

'Could I take a sample of your DNA? It only involves a mouth swab, then we can compare it to samples recovered from the scene.'

Peterson looked very uncomfortable. 'Do I have to?'

'No, Sir, it would be an entirely voluntary gesture on your behalf to assist us with our enquiries.'

He shook his head. 'I don't trust all that stuff. It's too like big brother.'

Despite his distaste for the man sitting opposite him, Jon was inclined to agree. DNA matches only proved blood or bodily fluids belonged to someone. They didn't conclusively prove that person was at the scene of a crime. People being sent down for crimes they insisted they didn't commit was nothing new, but when that person's guilt rested on the opportune discovery of DNA, Jon couldn't help feeling uncomfortable – he knew the potential for a stitch-up was immense. 'OK, Sir,' he said, backing off. 'Very last thing. The man who called. You were with him I take it?'

Peterson rolled his eyes at the ceiling.

'Is that a yes?'

'Yes.'

'Can you tell me anything about him?'

Peterson looked at Jon. 'Apart from the fact there was a bald patch on the top of his head, all I can say is that he gave a mediocre blow job.'

You win, Jon thought. That's enough for me. He stood up, took out a card and handed it to Peterson. 'Don't hesitate to call me if anything useful comes back to you. And I'd get a doctor to look at those injuries.'

Peterson looked Jon's card over. 'Yeah, will do.' Leaning to the side, he slid the card into his back pocket.

Jon drove back towards Longsight, turning the interview over in his head. Peterson was lying, that much was obvious. But why? He could understand the man's reluctance to get involved. Local press, or any press for that matter, loved a crime that had some sordid sex thrown in, as Peterson had already discovered to his cost.

But why the deceit over his attacker's description? Jon couldn't help feeling that it was more than a random attack. After all, it didn't appear that the other man had been assaulted. Was the assailant only after Peterson?

He pulled into a lay-by and reached for his mobile, scrolling through the numbers until he reached Rick Saville's name. 'Rick, it's Jon Spicer here. How are you?'

'Jon! Good to hear from you. I'm not bad. Yourself?'

'Yeah, I'm OK.'

'How about Alice and the baby?'

'Yeah, they're good too. We still haven't got used to getting up for the night feeds. Don't suppose anybody does. Listen, how stacked out are you at the moment?'

Rick gave a sigh, then lowered his voice. 'Not at all. This rotation I'm on is just about finished, thank God.'

'What was it, complaints or something?'

'Yup. And I've got a few complaints of my own. It was pure shite.'

Jon grinned. 'Well, I might have something a bit more interesting for you. It's about this case I'm on.'

'What is it?'

Jon glanced at the debris littering the grass verge. Empty crisp packets, a plastic carton, a trainer with no laces. Messy bastards. 'This guy was attacked in a car park near Middleton.'

'Yeah, I saw a report in Saturday's paper.'

'There's a witness to the attack out there somewhere. I need to track him down.'

'Are you liaising with Stonewall and True Vision?'

'True what?' He reached into the glove compartment, trying to find a pen.

'True Vision. It's a web site we run for reporting hate crime.'

'We? Some sort of a group you belong to?'

'Yeah, it's called the police force.'

'No shit? We've got a web site for reporting this kind of stuff? No one told me. What was the other name you mentioned?'

'Stone . . . look, shall I just meet you at Longsight station?'

'Yeah, nice one. When can you get over there?'

'About half an hour?'

Derek Peterson waited until the copper had shut the front door behind him, then he stood up and went over to the window. The movement made his head wound start throbbing all over again, and as he watched the policeman through the dirty netting, he pressed the fingers of one hand against his temple in a futile attempt to dull the pain.

Meddling bastard police. He couldn't believe the guy in the car park had supplied them with his car registration. Typical of his luck. The officer was now walking towards his car parked out on the road, examining it as he did so. Peterson hoped the bunch of ferals on the street corner had at least put a side window through and emptied the contents of the glove compartment, but the copper seemed satisfied no damage had been done. His type probably left the glove compartment open to show would-be thieves there was nothing of value inside. Following their own sensible advice on crime prevention, living boring, stilted lives. Everything done according to the rules. Well, it was an approach that held precious little interest for him.

How could it, given that his sexual preferences made him a criminal in the eyes of the law.

The car pulled away and Peterson turned from the window. The room was dull and silent without the light and sound from the telly. He switched it back on and lowered himself into his chair, but soon his thoughts returned to the night of the attack. That little git with the crowbar. How the hell had he tracked him down? And what was his name? He couldn't remember, there had been so many like him over the years – sallow complexion, smattering of acne, pathetic attempt at stubble. Hardly the bronzed and beautiful boys of his dreams. Still, you took what you could get, even if it was some skinny-arsed little weasel so defeated by life he had given up trying to control what happened to him.

That's what confused him. In his time working at the care home, he'd been careful to pick out the ones he sensed would keep their mouths shut. The ones with a numbness in their eyes, who no longer questioned what authority dictated. Often, when he got them on their own, the ease of their submission surprised him. He came to realise that these were the lads who had been through it all before. Uncles, older brothers, babysitters' boyfriends – someone else had broken them in, making everything so much easier for him.

But this one had obviously decided to fight back, even if it was after a delay of several years. Peterson stared at the floor, weighing up the situation he was now in. He'd taught the lad a lesson all right. After disarming his attacker, he'd used a restraining hold he'd learned at the care home to bend the lad over. Of course he was wearing a shell suit, so yanking his trousers down had been easy. Then, as he worked him with the metal bar, he'd explained once again all about the need for not getting any stupid ideas. By the time he'd finished, the lad was a sobbing mess, humiliated and broken once again. He would never talk, shame would see to that.

But the other man in the car park was a different matter. How much had the bumbling idiot seen? Peterson thought he'd fled as soon as the lad had appeared with the iron bar, but perhaps he'd watched for a bit before running to his car and ringing the bloody police. Had the name of the care home come out? He'd certainly not mentioned it and, as far as he could remember, the lad hadn't either. As long as the witness didn't come forward, all the police had was his car registration, and that was it. Even if they somehow traced the lad, what could happen? There was no way he could prove anything about what had gone on all those years ago.

Peterson jabbed the off button on the remote and flung the control on to the sofa. He'd never got his blow job the other night and he was pent-up with frustration. Listlessly, he climbed the stairs and turned the computer on in his bedroom. From his favourites list, he logged on to the appropriate site and went into the forum room to see if there was any local action being arranged for later on.

Some general stuff about the police being at Silburn Grove car park. From the postings, it sounded like they were talking about the copper who'd just been sitting in his front room. Nosey big bastard. Peterson scanned the comments, stopping at a suggestion to use a nearby car park instead. Someone said he'd be going there tonight and another had immediately replied that he'd be there too.

Peterson added his own comment then logged onto streetmap.co.uk to find out exactly where Daisy Nook Country Park was.

Five

Jon had just sat down with a cup of coffee when Rick walked through the door, eyes sweeping the room before settling at Jon's raised hand. As he started to cross the room Jon took in his trendy suit and fashionably messed-up hair. There was a take-out cup from some flashy coffee bar in his hand. 'Still drinking that frothy shit with chocolate powder on the top?'

Rick smiled. 'Still taking yours black like some sort of frigging cowboy?'

Jon stood, and as they shook hands, the other officers in the room turned back to their computers.

'You're not looking that knackered,' Rick said, sliding over a chair.

'Really?' Jon answered, aware that the purple smudges below his eyes seemed to have taken on the permanence of tattoos.

'All right, I lied. You look shit. Happy though, but still shit.'

'Cheers.' Jon tested his coffee and it nearly took the skin off his upper lip. 'Jesus! That machine must heat the water with a nuclear reactor or something.'

Rick crossed his legs and took a sip from his own cup. 'Wouldn't drink that stuff if they paid me. So you've got a witness to the attack?'

Jon nodded. 'Here, you can listen to him.'

He took a tape recorder out of the bottom drawer of his desk. A cassette with a recording of the 999 call was already in.

Rick listened to it, eyes focused on the opposite wall. 'Sounds nasty. Are you checking registrations that correspond to the attacker's?'

'Were. It wasn't the attacker who drove off, it was the victim.'

'You traced him?'

'This morning. He lives in Clayton. Thing is, he's bullshitting me about whoever jumped him. I think they knew each other. If I could trace the caller it would be a massive help.'

Rick put his cup down. 'So you haven't contacted Stonewall or True Vision?'

Jon opened his palms. 'Never heard of them. I put an A board up in the car park appealing for information, approached a few cars one evening. Nothing.'

Rick raised an eyebrow. 'You hung out in the car park? I bet that was interesting.'

Jon looked at the floor. 'You could say that. To be honest, the whole business of loitering in car parks is lost on me.' He glanced up. 'Apart from asking to get beaten up, why do they do it?'

Rick sighed. 'They're not asking to get beaten up. Would you say that if it was a young lad and his girlfriend shagging in their car?'

'I doubt it.'

'So it's OK for heterosexual couples to have a bit of fun in a deserted car park, but not gay males?'

Jon leaned back. 'All right, don't get arsey. But you've got to admit people are more likely to take offence to a couple of men doing it. Besides, they're not travelling there as couples, they're travelling there alone, looking for casual sex. Why do they do it?'

Rick shrugged. 'The thrill of it I suppose. It's not my cup of tea, in case you're wondering.'

Jon gave a quick shake of his head. No, but I wonder what is?

'Besides, haven't you and Alice ever been tempted to indulge in a bit of outdoor action?'

A memory of one Sunday afternoon on a remote hill in the Lake District flashed into Jon's head and he couldn't help smile. 'Maybe, but I do know her for Christ's sake.'

'But not knowing the other person is what it's all about for some people. Especially if they haven't come out. Anonymity would be vital for them.' He shot a glance at the computer.

'What?' Jon asked, knowing something had just occurred to his friend.

'There's quite a community for this. It's all linked up to the dogging thing that's been in the papers.'

'Dogging? I thought that was men watching other couples have sex in their cars?'

'It was originally, but it's more part of the swinging scene nowadays. All sorts are at it. Log on and I'll show you.'

Jon typed in his password and moved his chair to one side, allowing Rick access to his computer. He went on to the internet, then typed 'Swinger's Haven' into the search field.

A home page came up with a paragraph of writing in the middle. To the side was a panel of boxes. Jon leaned forwards to read them.

Real Wife Swaps. Swingers Café. Chat Room. Forum. Dogging Sites. Personal Pages. Sexual Health. Terminology. Contact Us.

'Who runs this site?' Jon asked, reaching for his coffee.

'God knows. I heard about it a while ago. I've never actually visited though.' He clicked on 'Dogging Sites' and an inner screen came up with a map of Britain inside.

'Here we go,' murmured Rick, clicking on the Manchester area. A new screen appeared listing locations in the area. Rick scrolled down the screen, stopping at a panel titled 'Middleton'.

Jon scanned the text. 'The car park at the bottom of Silburn Grove is good for dogging action most evenings after nine. Especially popular with gay men.' He shook his head as Rick went back to the home page and clicked on 'Forum'. He then selected 'North West'.

General discussion, news and chat for swingers and doggers in the North West. Please don't post anything here about specific meet ups, use the chat room for that.

Rick clicked on the link and a grid format page came up with an entry in each left hand box.

Are you a newbie needing help?

Photos from Mark and Jo's Munch Party

In a quandary and need advice?

My new boobies!

Rick started moving down to the lower entries before Jon had even read the first. 'Hold up. I don't understand all this.'

Rick glanced at him. 'It's just a standard internet forum. You've never used one before?'

'No.'

'OK look, the discussion topic is here.' Rick pointed to the uppermost left hand box. ' "Are you a newbie needing help?" ' He ran his finger over the adjacent boxes. 'The author was TopCat, there've been 9,532 viewings and 376 replies. Last one was posted today at three-o-four p.m. by Fair Maid.'

Jon looked at his watch. 'That was six minutes ago.'

Rick nodded. 'People are logged on all the time. See?' He pointed to a line of text at the base of the screen. 'In total there are seventy-two users online, twenty-nine visible, eleven hidden and thirty-two guests.'

'And these are all people in the north west?'

'Not necessarily. But if you've entered this region's chat room, you're probably local. We are one of thirty-two guests. If we want to add a topic, we'll have to register with the site and become a member.'

'Add a topic?'

Rick sighed. 'This cyberspace stuff confusing you, Jon? Think of it like the notice board in your rugby club. Only this is a club for people who like to have sex in car parks. We can pin up a piece of paper asking if anyone's got information about what happened in Silburn Grove.'

Jon bounced the heel of his palm off his forehead. 'Sorry mate, I'll try and get with it.'

'Right, it's your computer, so you should register.'

Jon's eyes shifted uneasily to the other officers in the room. 'I don't want my bloody details on there!' he hissed.

Rick's eyes were on the screen and a smile was breaking out on his face. 'I think you may feature already. Look at that entry. Policeman at Silburn Grove. It was posted last Friday at nine forty-eight p.m.'

'Shit. What does it say?'

'Let's see,' Rick clicked on the box to open up a fresh page.

Beware. In the light of the assault in the car park on Silburn Grove yesterday, the police have taken quite an interest. I drove there just now, only to have this copper approach my car asking for info. While he's there I suggest using the car park at Daisy Nook, it's a lot more secluded anyway. PubDog.

I saw him too! Big bastard with a crew cut? I was getting my hopes up until he flashed his badge!!! Tall'n'Hairy.

I know what you mean. I was hoping he was about to give me a flash of something else. PubDog.

The car park at Daisy Nook it is then. I'll be there 2nite at 10, if anyone wants some action. SXi.

See you there, Angel-from-heaven.

Likewise. Mr P.

Jon knew his face was bright red. At least the one with his cock out hadn't posted anything up. He took a hesitant sip of coffee, waiting for his blush to subside.

Failing miserably to suppress the grin on his face, Rick said, 'Looks like you made quite an impression.'

'Ha fucking ha,' Jon replied, still unable to look directly at his colleague.

'Word travels fast on the internet.'

'Too right. There wasn't a single car turning up there by Saturday night. Now I bloody well know why.'

Rick clicked back a screen. 'There may have only been four replies, but eighty-two people have viewed that topic. I reckon we should add an appeal for help.'

Jon shifted in his seat. 'Can you do it? I feel like a right pillock having sat there scaring everyone off. Maybe you could say you're a colleague on the case.'

Rick's fingers hovered over the mouse. 'OK. Let's do it then.'

He clicked on register, accepted the site's agreement terms and went through to an on screen form. 'We need a username. How about Big Jon?'

Jon shook his head. 'No way. Let's go for Slick Rick.'

His colleague grinned. 'Maybe we'd better keep it straight.' He typed in DS Saville. After entering a password and his email address, Rick completed the rest of the form, then clicked on submit.

A screen popped up telling him confirmation had been sent to his email address. Rick closed down the screen, logged into his email account, clicked on the confirmation number waiting there, following the link back to the web site and entered the number in. 'OK, we're a new member. What do you want to say?'

At five-thirty on the dot Jon turned his computer off and headed for the door. As he crossed the room he could feel a few of the other detectives watching him enviously. None looked like they were getting home early.

He was nearly at the door when he heard a voice behind him. 'That officer in earlier. Was he going on about gay sex?'

Jon turned around. The detective who'd spoken was leaning back in his chair, gut straining against the buttons of his shirt. Several other men were looking over with smirks on their faces.

'What if he was?' Jon answered.

'What is he then? Some sort of shirt lifter himself?' He glanced at his mates, finding approval in their eyes.

Jon felt a surge of anger. The bunch of cowardly pricks had suddenly found the courage to start on Rick. He stepped closer to the officer. 'Why, you've got a problem with that, you fat fuck?'

He kept eye contact until the other man looked away. 'No, I didn't think so.' He walked out of the room.

A short while later he pushed his front door open. A delicious aroma greeted him as he stepped inside. Voices in the front room. Alice's and his mother's. Punch looked tentatively round the corner then gave a snort of delight and bounded towards him. Jon crouched down and reached both hands round his dog's head to rub behind its ears. Then he straightened up and walked into the front room. Alice was on the sofa with Holly at her breast, folds of a baggy purple jumper half covering the feeding baby.

He looked across to his mum who was perched on the edge of an armchair. 'I've been waiting to cuddle her for twenty minutes. Even you never fed this long.'

He smiled at the sight of her. She measured five-foot-two at the most and people always had trouble accepting that she had produced someone of Jon's size. Despite being in her mid-sixties, she was sprightly and trim with bright eyes and surprisingly smooth skin. Only her hair belied her years; the white strands that had started appearing a few years ago were now gathering in number, creating a silver sheen over the russet tones below.

'Mary's brought us round a lamb casserole,' Alice said, looking up with a tired expression.

'Oh, it's nothing.' His mum waved a hand, eyes still on Holly. 'Is she finished yet?'

Alice directed her gaze at the opposite wall for a second. 'I think so.'

How the hell can you know? Jon thought, baffled by the mysteries of motherhood.

Mary immediately sprang out of her seat and almost yanked Holly off Alice's breast. 'Look at you, you gorgeous little thing,' she cooed, expertly flipping the baby forwards and burping her with miraculous speed. She then positioned Holly on her shoulder. 'Don't they smell so lovely at this age?' she murmured, planting a kiss on the back of Holly's neck between each word.

Jon felt pressure against his legs and looked down to see Punch eyeing him hopefully.

'Will you take that silly dog of yours out? He's been pacing around like a prisoner,' Alice said.

Jon glanced down at his wife. Silly dog of yours? A few weeks ago, he was our big baby. 'OK, I'll pop out with him now if that's all right.'

'Yeah.' Alice's eyes didn't go anywhere near the animal.

Jon looked out the window. The day was fading fast. It didn't seem like yesterday when it was light until ten o'clock at night. 'What's Dad up to?' he asked, loosening his tie.

Mary gave a theatrical scowl. 'There was some rugby match on the box. Who are they, Salford Red Socks or something?'

Jon grinned. He was certain his mum purposely got the name of the rugby club wrong – after all, her husband had played for them in the days before everything turned professional.

It amused him how the sport was a source of constant ribbing between him and his father. His dad had played Rugby League, a version of the game made popular by the men who'd laboured in the region's mines, mills and docks.

But Jon had won a place at the local grammar school and ended up playing the game's other code – Rugby Union. More popular down south, the version was associated with England's posh schools. His dad would never let him forget it, continually making jokes about the southern softies who only played Union because they couldn't take the knocks that went with League. Jon often suspected the reasons why he played with such determined ferocity on the rugby pitch was to disprove his father's jibes. It took until his mid-twenties before he realised that had probably been his dad's plan all along.

He got changed into his running gear and popped his head back into the front room. 'Mum, you staying for some food?'

'No, your father will be expecting his. I'll get off in a minute.'

'Let him cook his own.'

She gave him a look. 'Your father couldn't boil a bloody egg.'

He could if you ever let him in your kitchen, Jon thought, giving her a kiss goodbye.

A few minutes later he reached the playing fields of Heaton school where he let the dog off the lead, watching as he raced off into the dusk, following the scent of something. Probably rabbits that had colonised the edge of the golf course.

Jon stuck to the perimeter of the playing fields, using the light from the streetlamps that had just flickered into life. As he made his way round he was aware of the occasional ragged form flittering in the air above his head. Bats. They swooped and darted in pursuit of the flying insects attracted by the streetlights' glow.

When Jon reached the edge of the golf course Punch reappeared out of the gloom ahead, tongue hanging from his mouth. They completed their normal run and were home half an hour later.

After he'd showered and eaten, Jon sat next to Alice on the sofa. The telly was on low but both of them seemed to spend more time gazing at Holly as she lay on the brightly coloured floor mat. Jon found it amazing how such a tiny thing could exert such a powerful pull on their eyes. Gravity itself had shifted and the centre of the universe was now in the middle of their front room.

'I can't believe what's happening over there.'

Jon looked at his wife, realising that something on the telly had attracted her attention. He glanced at the screen where a government minister of some description was denouncing the barbaric acts being committed by terrorists in Iraq.

'They're decapitating hostages. Why?'

Jon tipped his head back against the sofa and sighed. How to explain the motivation behind an act like that?

'What sort of people are they?'

He rubbed at his temples, not wanting to get into it. 'I'm not making excuses, but not every Iraqi believes they're being liberated, Alice. Those terrorists are freedom fighters in many Iraqis' minds. We've invaded their country don't forget.'

Alice shifted to look at him. 'That's what I don't understand. They said the Iraqis would welcome our troops by throwing flowers into the path of their tanks. They said we'd win their hearts and minds through our civilised approach. What's civilised about those shock and awe tactics? Firing thousands of missiles into a crowded city in just two nights.'

He could hear the tension rising in her voice as she went on.

'There was a photo, Jon. An Iraqi boy being carried into a hospital by his dad. The top of his head was missing. It was just a baby for Christ's sake.' She waved a hand at the TV. 'If we're killing their babies how will that make them feel?'

Grainy footage of men with faces covered behind red-checked scarves now filled the screen.

'They're going to execute another hostage tomorrow if our troops don't withdraw. How can human beings be so cruel to each other?'

Seeing the tears in her eyes, Jon reached for the remote and switched channels. 'Ali, don't watch if it upsets you so much.'

'What, and pretend it's not happening? That's not any sort of answer.'

'I didn't mean that. Just, I don't know. Try not to dwell on it, that's all.'

She wiped the tears away. 'I suppose you're right. It's just so bloody tragic.'

Jon leaned his forehead against her temple. 'You're tired, babe. Why don't you get some sleep? I'll do the next feed.'

'You sure?' She glanced at Holly who was still fast asleep. 'It'll probably be around midnight.'

'Yeah, no problem. I'll see you later.'

Alice slid off the sofa and crawled over to the baby, then lowered her head and kissed her forehead. She stood up and stepped towards the door.

'Where's mine?' asked Jon, looking up at her expectantly. 'There was a time when you'd never go to bed without kissing me first.'

'Oh, sorry. Forgot about you,' she replied, bending forward.

As their lips touched, he thought how he, too, had slipped down in the pecking order of her affection. As she straightened up his eyes skimmed over her. The sleepless nights were beginning to show on her face. Nothing too dramatic, more just a subtle loss of her previous healthy glow. It seemed to have affected her hair too, drying it out and robbing it of its lustre. 'Hey, have you booked that appointment at Melvyn's salon?'

Alice's hand went to her fringe and she brushed it back from her eyes. 'Why, do I look like I've been out scaring crows?'

He smiled. 'Course not. It would be nice, that's all. Besides, you haven't seen that lot since Holly was born.'

'I don't know. I still feel all fat.'

He watched as her hand now went to her stomach, fingers probing through the baggy jumper at the fold of flesh pregnancy had left her with. 'Come off it Ali, you look fine. That little bit of weight will soon disappear, especially with breastfeeding. I think you should book an appointment. My treat don't forget.'

'What about Holly?'

'Take her with you. Jesus, they'll love it.'

Her smile wasn't natural. 'OK, I'll think about it.'

Once she'd gone Punch crept into the room, cautiously skirting the baby and settling down in the corner where he could look at Jon, who flicked through the channels, stopping when he saw *An American Werewolf in London* starting on Channel Five.

'Hey Punch, this is a class film,' he said, crossing his legs.

He watched the opening credits. Shot after shot of bleak and forbidding moors, their upper slopes shrouded in low cloud. His mind went to what had recently happened on Saddleworth Moor and the film took on a new poignancy.

The two young American backpackers clambered from the rear of the sheep truck and made their way into the isolated village, experiencing a frosty reception from the flat cap-wearing locals in the pub called The Slaughtered Lamb.

'Typical bloody Yorkshiremen,' muttered Jon, wondering exactly where the film had been shot.

Unwelcome in the village, the Americans headed back out across the moor. When the bloodcurdling howl pierced the darkness, Punch's ears pricked up and he looked around.

'It's only the telly, boy,' Jon chuckled, realising his eyelids were beginning to feel heavy.

The beast attacked seconds later, tearing one tourist to shreds and slashing the cheek of the other before the locals gunned it down. The survivor then awoke in a London hospital, but it wasn't long before he started dreaming of forests and racing through the trees in pursuit of deer.

As Jon continued to watch he could feel sleep creeping up on him also. He sat upright, determined not to nod off before Jenny Agutter's shower scene with Van Morrison singing that it was a marvellous night for a moon dance in the background.

Moments later the scent of pine began filling the air around him and he looked up at the dense canopy of branches above his own head. Dots of sunlight shone down, speckling the carpet of pine needles at his feet. He had a rucksack on his back and was walking fast, a sense of urgency spurring him on. Each footstep created a soft crackle in the silent wood. He wondered why he was hurrying when a branch snapped somewhere off to his side.

'Oh no,' he groaned, breaking into a jog, guessing what the dream would lead to.

He weaved between the tree trunks, rough bark catching on his clothes as a sickening fear rose in his throat. A keening cry suddenly cut through the forest. It was a desolate and terrible sound, the noise a creature makes when it needs food.

The terror that now flooded him was clammy and cold. It was a terror that came from the knowledge that what hunted him could not be reasoned with. It possessed no compassion because it was not human. It was a primeval force, merciless in its savagery.

Jon blundered onwards, now able to hear his pursuer as it raced through the trees behind. As hard as he tried, Jon couldn't break into a sprint. His legs were heavy and sluggish, despite the adrenaline coursing through him. The creature was closing in, its call getting louder and more insistent.

Desperately Jon tried to drag himself out of the dream, his sweaty back tingling with the anticipation of the claws that he knew were about to puncture his flesh. In the nick of time his eyes snapped open and he found himself staring at the television. The film had ended but the shrill noise still filled the room. He looked down and saw Holly wriggling on her mat, face red and mouth open. Punch was lying next to her, gently licking the top of her head, trying to offer some comfort.

Disoriented, Jon slowly stood. 'It's OK,' he said to both of them. He bent down and picked Holly up before stumbling into the kitchen to get a bottle.

Six

It was late by the time Peterson got to the car park at Daisy Nook. To his annoyance, he'd fallen asleep in front of the box, waking up well past midnight, an erection jutting out from his jeans. Time to get that sorted he decided, reaching for his car keys.

As his headlights illuminated the parking area, Peterson frowned. It was tiny, or perhaps intimate was a better word. He glanced at the dashboard clock. Shit, the only ones likely to be out this late on a weekday night were people like him – the desperate, who didn't need to bother getting up the next day for work. And the sad fact was, all too often those ones weren't that bothered about personal hygiene either. What had the guy on the forum said? Ten o'clock onwards, Peterson thought.

He swung his car round and reversed into a corner, headlights facing outwards so he could signal any arrivals. Turning his lights off, he left the engine idling and reclined his seat slightly, leaning the back of his skull against the headrest. Darkness was all around, thick and heavy, pressing in on the windows. He liked the dark, the way it aroused people's more basic desires. How many acts that would cause outrage if performed during the day, safely took place under the cover of night?

With his eyes half shut and a hand massaging his groin, he watched for the telltale sign of any approaching headlights. The minutes ticked slowly by. From somewhere nearby an owl hooted, the call both forlorn and inquisitive. Is there anybody else out there, it seemed to say.

Peterson was beginning to wonder the same thing. He lowered a window to let in some air. A single light twinkled far across the fields and a sheep bleated. What if I'm in the wrong car park, he suddenly wondered. There could be another one on the other side of the park. I didn't think to check the map properly. A sudden image of a busy car park flashed across his mind, men clambering from one vehicle to another, perhaps a young chicken who would come over to Peterson's car . . .

With the thought that he was missing out tormenting him, Peterson turned off his engine and opened the door. The interior light came on and he squinted at the sudden brightness. After climbing out and shutting the door behind him, he tried to examine the tarmac itself, looking for signs of recent activity. Wedged-up tissues, discarded condoms, empty bottles of poppers.

But the light inside his car had messed up his ability to see. The darkness swam with unnatural reds and oranges, blinking reviving a burning comet-shaped ball from where he'd glanced at the bulb itself.

Car keys dangling from his fingers, he slowly made his way across to the other side. Something was on the ground. He crouched down and patted the tarmac, fingers making contact with an empty packet of cigarettes. Looking up, he could see that the thick undergrowth separating the car park from the fields beyond was now only a few feet away. Bulky white forms seemed to float there. Sheep, slowly making their way from the field's edge. There was a strange smell in the air, sharp and musty. Cheap aftershave? He heard a sound close by and slowly stood. Was it a cough? His night vision was beginning to return, the swirls of colour fading to reveal his surroundings in a monochromatic grey.

He sensed more than saw something near the tree. 'Hello?' Peterson said, heart quickening with the thrill of someone else being there. 'There's no reason to be afraid.'

He peered at the area below the branches, trying to detect forms in the dark shadows lurking there. Then he stepped closer, holding a hand out. 'Please, I think we're looking for the same thing. There's no need to be shy.'

Was that the shape of something crouching at the base of the trunk? Something denser, blacker than the shadows around it? Peterson leaned forwards. That smell again. Not aftershave. More the tang of something unwashed.

With a sudden snarl, an inky mass shot upwards and outwards. Frozen to the spot, Peterson felt his eyes instinctively widen, allowing a fraction more light on to his retina. Pointed ears, a muzzle, something swinging towards his face. The impact caught him on the side of the neck, raking downwards across his throat. He wasn't aware of stepping backwards, or even falling, but now he was on his back, the black form moving in a blur above him as his torso rocked with fresh blows. Feebly, he lifted a hand to defend himself. His fingers made contact with thick, coarse fur before his hand was knocked away. Now there was liquid flying around, landing on his face, getting in his eyes. Rain? No, the droplets were shooting upwards, out of him. When he tried to shout only a bubbling rasp escaped.

Then the thing was gone. Coldness took its place, emanating down in waves from the star filled sky above. He tried to breathe in, immediately choking as a thick warmth flooded into his lungs. He tried to cough the liquid back out, unaware that most of the muscles in his neck now lay in tatters on the ground about his head.

SEVEN

The coffee machine squeezed a final dribble out into Jon's cup and he turned round to head for his office.

Halfway to the door he realised he'd forgotten to stop in the car park for a cigarette. He came to a halt, one hand sliding the packet of ten Silk Cut out of his coat. But then his eyes strayed to his office door.

He'd been turning over in his mind the development with Derek Peterson since waking up and now he was itching to get to his computer. Sod the cigarette, he decided. I should chuck the things in the bloody bin, he thought, but instead he pushed the packet back into his pocket. Just in case the morning turned sour.

A few of the fraud team were already in and he gave a general wave in their direction, not waiting for any response. As his computer booted up he reflected on the case again. Since Derek Peterson was the victim, the attacker was still out there. If only he could trace the person who had called 999 a lot more of what actually took place in the car park would be revealed.

Jon typed Peterson's details into the computer then reached for the coffee cup, blowing air across the surface of the liquid as he scanned the man's record.

Gross indecency in 1993. Lost his job at the Silverdale facility for young offenders. He'd been placed on the sex offenders' register after that and it looked like his employment record had taken a turn for the worse. In fact, Jon wondered, thinking about the state of the man's house, he probably hadn't worked since.

He looked at the personal details section. Prior to enrolling as a mature student at Salford Polytechnic in 1988, Peterson had worked as a finance officer for the council. The course he'd signed up for lasted one year. Health and Social Welfare. Jon

49

shook his head. About five hours a week and an automatic pass for anyone who turned up for over half the lectures. That had obviously been enough to get him a job as a care assistant at the young offenders' facility. Classic behaviour of a paedophile; secreting himself into a position of trust that brought him into contact with youngsters.

He leaned back, allowing his mind to construct a possible scenario for the incident. Peterson worked in the care home from 1989 to his arrest in 1993. Four years with vulnerable teenagers. Peterson appeared to have been singled out by his attacker. Could there be some sort of a connection to the period Peterson spent at the Silverdale facility?

Jon made a mental note to pay the place a visit. He took a tentative sip of coffee. Still too bloody hot. What about Peterson himself? He didn't like the fact a policeman had come knocking on his door. No surprise in that neighbourhood. Jon contemplated turning up in a patrol car with a uniform. Would a bit of pressure make the bastard cooperate or would it make him clam up even more?

His phone went. 'DI Spicer.'

'Jon, it's Sergeant Innes in the radio control room.'

'Morning, Graham. What can I do you for?'

'You're currently logged on to the record of one Derek Peterson.'

Jon's eyes went to his computer screen. Anyone else accessing a person's police record was alerted to the fact if another officer was also logged on. 'I am.'

'Is he of especial interest to you?'

'He is.' He leant forward. This is going to be interesting.

'Then you might like to know that his body's just been discovered in a car park by a lake at Daisy Nook Country Park.'

Bloody hell. The place mentioned on that dogging web site. 'Where's that?'

'Just off junction twenty-two of the M60. Out near Oldham.'

Jon pictured the geography of Manchester. Oldham was on the north-east edge of the city, not far from where Peterson was attacked the other night. 'OK, what's the score?'

'A fisherman found his body at first light. Little more than an hour ago.'

'And is the scene secure?'

'Yes. Uniforms have taped it off and I've called out the major incident wagon.'

'Who else have you let know?'

'No one. I was thinking of putting a call in to McCloughlin. His syndicate is down for the next runner.'

'Don't.' Jon realised the word had come out with a little too much force. 'Peterson is central to a case I'm on. I'll let DCI Summerby know and see how he wants to play it.'

'Your shout, but I need to allocate it a FWIN and put it on the system.'

'Of course,' Jon replied, hanging up. Once the crime had been given a Force Wide Incident Number and entered on to the computer it wouldn't be long before his superiors spotted it. He needed to contact Summerby to make sure no one else was given the case. He picked up the phone and punched in his senior officer's number. Engaged.

He'd go up there himself. After hurrying across the office, he bounded up the stairs and knocked on Summerby's door.

'Come in.'

Summerby was just replacing the phone, his eyes on the computer screen. 'Ah, Jon, what brings you up here so bright and early?'

'Morning, boss. I was just talking to the radio control room. There's been a major development with my case.'

Summerby motioned to a chair, one eye still on his computer screen. 'Sit down.'

Jon perched on the edge of the seat. 'Yesterday I questioned the man who was attacked in the car park at Silburn Grove on Thursday night. When I asked for a description of his attacker he fed me a pack of lies. He'd also failed to seek medical help for the injuries he'd sustained. He was hiding something and I believe it was the fact that he knew his attacker.'

'Interesting.' Summerby finally dragged his eyes from the screen. 'So what's your next move?'

'Well, Sir, it's already been decided for me. His body was

discovered in a car park by Daisy Nook Country Park this morning.'

Summerby's eyes slid back to his screen. 'Derek Peterson? This was the man you interviewed yesterday? Details have just gone on to the computer.'

'I gathered they were about to. That's why I came up to see you. Before word starts getting out ... ' An image of McCloughlin was in his mind and he chose his words more carefully. 'You know the politics something like this can create.'

Summerby's eyebrow was raised. 'Indeed I do. You're wanting this one for yourself, I take it?'

Jon nodded.

'It's Category A. Members of the public at risk, Major Incident Room facilities, dedicated SIO and high level of media interest anticipated.'

'High level of media interest?'

'You obviously haven't actually read the incident details.'

'No,' Jon replied, wondering what was causing the dubious expression on Summerby's face.

'The man's throat was ripped out. He also suffered extensive lacerations to his face and chest.'

Jon had to gulp before any words would come out. 'Same as the woman up on Saddleworth Moor?'

'Seems so. When the press learn of this, it's going to be madness.' He reached for his A to Z of Manchester and turned to the index. 'Daisy Nook Country Park, here we are.' Summerby flicked to the overall map of the city and turned the book around for Jon to see. The park was on pages eighty-six and eighty-seven, near the edge of the grid of squares that covered the city and its outlying areas. A couple of inches to the right and the grid ended to be replaced by an expanse of green. Saddleworth Moor. 'There can't be five miles between the two killings.'

Jon studied the map. Jesus, could some sort of wild animal really be stalking the outskirts of Manchester?

'DI Spicer, are you sure you want involvement in this? It's going to be in the glare of the media. I don't need to mention the hours you'll have to put in.'

To keep his hands from fluttering with excitement, Jon placed them between his knees. He'd have to forget nine to five on this one. It would be evenings, late nights, weekends. The works. He thought about how Alice would cope with Holly on her own. But what else could he do? They both knew his job wasn't governed by normal hours and this case had suddenly got too good. 'It'll be fine sir. Both mums lives near by, they're more than happy to help out.'

Summerby nodded. 'Well, if you're sure, I'm happy for you to take it on. Obviously we'll have to make arrangements with the divisional bobbies handling the investigation on Saddleworth Moor, but I'm sure they'll understand this is now a case for the Major Incident Team. I'll let the necessary people know. You get over there. Here, I'll print you a copy of the report.' He clicked his mouse and the printer began to whirr on the corner of his desk. 'You know what the bit of water's called that this car park is next to?'

'No.'

Summerby had a wry smile on his face. 'Crime Lake.'

'You're serious?'

'Afraid so. Earned that name when a body was dumped in it. Couple of hundred years ago, mind you.'

Shit, the papers were going to have a field day.

Eight

Once Jon had fought through the traffic to get on to the M60, he flicked a switch on the dashboard of his unmarked car. Flashing lights and a siren came on behind the vehicle's radiator grill. The cars in front jerked out of his way. This is more like it, Jon thought, not dropping below eighty until junction twenty-two appeared.

Racing on to the slip road, he forced his way across a busy roundabout then switched the siren off as he entered a residential area, vehicle lurching over a succession of speed bumps. After a quick glance at the open A to Z on the seat beside him he took a right turn and emerged at the junction for Coal Pit Lane, unkempt farm land directly in front. Beyond the fields was a hill, topped by a row of electricity pylons. Jon's eyes moved past the ugly structures to what rose up in the far distance: the muted browns of the moors.

He turned right, following the roughly surfaced road as it ran alongside fields dotted with sheep. He looked at the animals. Is there really some sort of a beast preying on you? For a second he could believe it – if any animal had the word victim stamped all over it, it was sheep.

Soon he spotted a small sign for Crime Lake and seconds later he was easing up by a tiny car park, lowering his window and holding up his identification as he did so. The uniformed officer standing in front of the police tape at the car park's entrance pointed him towards an Italian restaurant just down the road. The building stood on its own, a large expanse of tarmac to its side. 'Plenty of room in there, boss.'

He pulled up behind the major incident wagon. A couple of officers in white scene-of-crime suits were unloading equipment from the rear of the vehicle. Excellent, Jon thought, forensic recovery should be good. As he climbed out of his car he checked the sky. Grey and impassive, but no immediate sign of rain. Even better as far as collecting evidence was concerned.

A sergeant was talking to an old boy with a rucksack and narrow holdall at his feet. The fisherman who found the body. Jon went over, warrant card out. 'DI Spicer. How are you, Sir?'

The elderly man turned towards him. When he spoke there was a fleck of spit on his lower lip. 'Norman Bell.' He smiled briefly. 'I've had better starts to a morning's fishing, that's for sure.'

Good on you, thought Jon. Still got your sense of humour. He glanced at the man's rucksack. 'Got a flask in there?'

The man nodded.

'Why not pour yourself a brew while I bother you with a few questions?'

The man squatted down and began opening the side pocket of the rucksack. Jon looked at the sergeant. 'Everything under control?'

'Yes, Sir. The boys have taped off the car park. I thought we'd set up the rendezvous point here. Pathologist and crime scene manager are on their way.'

'Good stuff. How long have you been here?'

'About twenty minutes.'

'OK. If any reporters show up later on, I want them referred on to me. No one is to say a thing, all right?'

'Sir.'

Jon nodded as the fisherman straightened up, a steaming cup now in his hands. 'There's a spare one if you want a drink.'

Jon shook his head. 'When did you get here, Mr Bell?'

'Seven-thirty. I'm secretary of the local fishing club. I get here before the other members arrive, and tidy the car park.' A look of disgust crossed his face. 'You know, from what gets left here from the night before. Someone's got to do it.'

Jon thought of Peterson being there. That bloody figured. 'And was there anyone else here when you arrived?'

'Not a soul. We get a few dog walkers using the area, but none were around this morning.'

The sergeant turned to Jon. 'Mr Bell didn't take a good look at the body, Sir. He saw the legs and blood, then immediately called nine-nine-nine.'

'I knew he was a goner straight away. I drove an ambulance for almost thirty years. Something about the way they lie.'

'You did the right thing not touching the body, Mr Bell. There's an amazing amount forensics can pick up nowadays if no one has contaminated the scene.'

'Oh aye, I've seen it on the telly.'

'Well, Sir, I'll leave you with the sergeant here, he'll make arrangements for you to give a statement.' He turned to the officer. 'Who's checked the body?'

The sergeant nodded towards a young officer sitting in a patrol car. His face looked white as a sheet. 'PC Evans. He's feeling a bit queasy.'

Jon's eyes went to the restaurant. 'Check with the people who live above this place. They may have heard something.'

Jon walked back round to the car park entrance, immediately noticing Peterson's dark blue Volvo parked to one side. After signing in with the officer he stepped towards the inner ring of tape. The car park was big enough for a dozen or so cars at the most. At the far end, under the overhanging branches of a tree, a white tent was already up, concealing the body and protecting vital evidence from the elements.

Jon looked over his shoulder. 'Who's the Crime Scene Manager?'

The officer consulted his clipboard. 'Richard Matthews.'

No Nikki Kingston then. Jon felt disappointment tinged with relief. He reflected on their last encounter. It was at the height of the race to catch the Butcher of Belle Vue. He'd been in the pub, a couple of drinks the worse for wear when she'd showed up with a vital piece of evidence.

He wasn't quite sure how it happened. A grateful hug from him maybe, but they'd ended up kissing for a few seconds before he summoned the will to break it off. Still tempted, aren't you though, he thought, deciding it was best to steer well clear of her.

He looked around. The car park was circled by trees and he could hear the drone of traffic from the nearby ring road. No point in crossing the inner tape until he'd got the OK from Richard Matthews. Instead, he followed the tape round the edge of the tarmac to a small gate that led to a gravel pathway. A graffiti-covered sign said, *Crime Lake. No motorbikes.* His eyes flicked over the collection of signatures scrawled on the sign's edge. Didn't anyone have normal names any more? Half of these seemed to be in a foreign language.

Between the dying leaves still on the trees he could see the pale shine of water. Crime Lake. He lifted the striped ribbon and stepped through the gate, noticing that several paths branched off between the trees. Bloody great. It was going to be a nightmare trying to decide where to end the crime scene.

He took the path that led down to the dreary-looking expanse of muddy water and past another couple of signs that read, *No fishing from the tow path.*

The lake soon narrowed into a canal, and as he followed it along, a row of four eager geese paddled over. Jon held his palms out. No bread I'm afraid. He looked at the sullen sky. Winter's on its way, you lot are best getting the hell out of this country.

After a few minutes he reached a junction in the canal. He took the right hand fork and crossed an overflow, water trickling off through the undergrowth to run down the slope into the valley below. After a couple of stone steps the canal seemed to dry up and he found himself on an aqueduct. Blocks of stone that must each have weighed tons made up the ramparts and, looking over their edge, he saw that the construction spanned a river a good thirty feet below – evidence of the incredible effort spent on creating Manchester's industrial past. The banks of the river were wild and overgrown, the ground leading off into thickly wooded slopes. Plenty of cover for a killer, man or beast.

He retraced his steps to the junction where he spotted an information board beside a tree. The plastic cover was pock-marked with cigarette burns, making it hard to read the writing below.

Medlock Valley. Daisy Nook History Trail.

His eyes went to a small red square. *You are here.* A paragraph of writing told him that the aqueduct was built in the 1790s and used to carry a branch of the Hollinwood canal. Not any more, thought Jon. Heavy industry had died out in these parts decades ago.

He examined the blue band that marked the route of the river Medlock. Where did that flow from, Jon wondered, looking up the valley and settling his gaze on those brooding moors once again. He reached for the zipper of his jacket as a sudden chill went through him. Above the hill's curving outline, scraps of grey cloud were streaming across the sky. Shit, rain was on its way. He turned for the car park.

Back at the crime scene a couple more people in white suits were putting on gloves in preparation for entering the inner circle of tape. One he immediately recognised as Doctor Collyer, the home office pathologist.

Jon hurried over. 'Morning.'

The pathologist looked up, owl-like eyes accentuated by the white hood of the crime scene suit. 'Good morning, Detective.'

A look passed between them that spoke of horrors mutually shared. The last time they'd met, they were standing over the remains of the Butcher of Belle Vue's third victim. Jon let his expression reflect the pathologist's. I remember, mate. How could I ever forget?

'Richard Matthews, good to meet you.'

Jon turned and saw the crime scene manager looking at him, eyebrows raised in anticipation of a response. He was a slightly overweight man of about forty.

'DI Jon Spicer, likewise.'

No one shook hands. It didn't really go with wearing latex gloves.

'Mind giving me a shout once it's OK to step inside?' Jon said to both of them

'Of course,' Matthews replied, beckoning to the video recorder chap who was approaching them from the car park's entrance. Jon glanced at him. A young man with a shaved head and a ring through his right nostril.

The three men walked across a series of footplates and entered the white tent. Jon had just climbed into a crime scene suit when Matthews poked his head out, face a shade more pale than when he went in. 'Whenever you're ready.'

Jon immediately padded across the footplates, stooping slightly as he stepped inside the tent. He sniffed the air. Blood. A smell that now set him on edge whenever he passed the open door of a butcher's shop.

The home office pathologist was looking at him, alarm showing in his usually impassive eyes. 'I've never seen anything like this before. Keep to the footplates, there's a lot of debris around his head.'

The video recorder stepped to one side. Oh shit, here we go, Jon thought. Breakfast, don't you dare come back up.

Derek Peterson was on his back, one arm pointing to the side, the other bent in on itself so the fingers were tucked under his armpit. For a moment it looked like he was frozen in some sort of bizarre dance move. Most of the left hand side of his face was hanging off, one eyeball sliced open, blood-smeared jelly bulging out. His throat was in a similar state, great furrows of flesh ripped out to expose the bony cartilage of what Jon assumed was his windpipe. He saw that the debris referred to by the pathologist was shreds of flesh.

'If he didn't die of shock, he'd have bled to death in a matter of seconds.' The pathologist pointed at Peterson's mutilated throat. 'I don't know what type of weapon could do this. Not only has it severed the exterior and interior jugular veins, it's gone through his carotid artery, taking out the surrounding muscles at the same time. And look at this.' He crouched down to extend a finger closer to the corpse's upper chest. 'See the lacerations to the cricoid cartilage?'

'His windpipe?' The bile was churning in Jon's stomach.

'Yes. I'd say the weapon was multi-pronged and fashioned from a very resilient material, metal being the obvious choice. Whoever wielded it was a very powerful man.'

Was no one going to say what seemed totally obvious? Jon gave a nervous laugh. 'I feel like I'm in a scene from *American Werewolf in London*.'

'I'm sorry?' the pathologist replied, but Jon caught the look of agreement on the video lad's face.

Sure enough, the younger man eagerly chipped in. 'You know, the scene on the moor when the American gets ripped to bits? The doctor in London was going on about the attacker having the strength of a madman.'

Christ, another aspiring horror film director, Jon thought.

'I'm sorry, I'm not familiar with the film,' said the pathologist, standing up. 'Surely you're not suggesting a werewolf did this?'

Jon held up his hands. 'God no, not at all. But these injuries and the ferocity of the attack . . . Could it have been some sort of wild animal, like they think killed the woman up on Saddleworth Moor? I mean, you're talking about a multi-pronged weapon. Surely that's another name for a claw?'

The pathologist crossed his arms, taking his time before he spoke. 'I'm afraid we're straying on to territory that is outside my expertise. Cause of death was from loss of blood, as a result of multiple lacerations to the throat. If you want a time of death, I'd say late last night. Once I get him back to the mortuary I'll provide a far more considered report.'

OK, no need to get so bloody touchy.

The video recorder coughed. 'The attack up on Saddleworth Moor. I saw the crime scene footage. It got, you know, e-mailed round.' The pathologist glared at him and Jon guessed some sort of morgue protocol had been broken. The video recorder stumbled awkwardly on. 'The injuries are startlingly similar.' He pressed his fingertips into his cheek. 'Where she was swiped, you could clearly see where the claws went in. A row of four.'

Jon glanced down at the tarmac, looking for footprints or other evidence of an animal. On the ground in the far corner of the tent was a set of car keys, a number marker already placed next to them. He looked questioningly at the crime scene manager.

'I presume they're the victim's. The key fob is for a Volvo.'

'Yes,' chipped in the video recorder. 'Probably flung from his hand during the attack.'

'Mind if I bag them up? We'll be needing to get into his house.'

Richard Matthews sucked in his cheeks. 'I'll get them dusted for prints, then you can be my guest.'

From outside the tent Jon heard the low rumble of thunder.

He glanced back at Peterson's bloody remains. 'What about that hand tucked under his armpit. Have you examined it yet?'

The pathologist shook his head. 'We called you in as soon as possible.'

'Could we take a quick look?'

The video recorder held up the camera as the pathologist pulled Peterson's hand out. The fingers were clamped together in a rigid grip. As the first droplets of rain begin to hit the tent roof Jon could clearly see several long black hairs caught between the dead man's fingers.

Nine

As he waited for Summerby to answer his phone, the rain drummed down on the roof of Jon's car. Memories stirred of childhood camping holidays spent near Southport, the hours huddled in a cramped tent, praying for the incessant patter of rain to cease. He grinned, recalling how his younger sister, Ellie, would quietly colour in her books while he fought over war comics with his younger brother Dave.

Our kid, Dave. Jesus, what a nightmare. What was he up to now, Jon wondered. If anyone deserved to be labelled the black sheep of the family, it was his younger brother. Despite all his dad's efforts, and later his own, they couldn't persuade him to get involved in sport. Didn't matter if it was rugby, football or even lacrosse if he fancied it – anything to divert his energy away from getting into trouble the whole time.

He shook his head. Complete waste. He knew his brother was far more intelligent than him, could have gone to university any day. But by his late teens he'd started to dabble in drugs and soon developed a nasty little liking for speed. Their dad had kicked him round the house the first time he was arrested for stealing cars. The second time he stopped speaking to him, and when he offended again he booted him out of the family home altogether. Dave had his bags already packed to move out anyway, claiming he was off to live in a squat.

Jon looked at the fingers of his left hand as they rested on the steering wheel, focusing on the nicks and scars that formed a cicatrix over his knuckles. If he hadn't channelled his aggression – which seemed to be a genetic trait of his family – into rugby, there was a good chance he'd have gone the same way. He knew of his dad's reputation when he worked on the docks and drank in the pubs around Salford, but neither of them had gone off the rails like Dave.

'Come on, pick up,' Jon whispered, mobile phone pressed to his ear.

The line suddenly clicked. 'DCI Summerby speaking.'

'Boss, it's Jon Spicer here, I'm out at Daisy Nook Country Park.'

'What's it looking like, Jon? You sound like there's an army marching past.'

Jon nodded. 'Just a touch of Manchester rain. It's looking grim, boss, very grim. The guy's throat has been ripped to shreds. Much more damage and you could have seen through to his spine.'

'Thanks for that. I'm trying to eat a piece of toast here.'

'Sorry, Sir, but I need you to understand the savagery of the attack. It's, well, I can only describe it as inhuman.' Silence at the other end of the line. 'Sir, are you still there?' Jon asked, wondering if he'd lost his signal.

'Yes, I can hear you. You're suggesting an animal killed him?'

'Well, it's certainly a strong possibility, Sir. There were hairs caught under his nails. Big black buggers. I gather there were similar ones found at the murder scene on Saddleworth Moor.'

'Anything else? Paw prints in the vicinity for instance?'

'We've got a tent over the body and the crime scene manager is here, so everything's pegged down, but a search of the surrounding woods won't reveal much. The rain has seen to that. I've called the coroner and he's given the green light for an autopsy. We'll get the body over to the MRI as soon as possible.'

'OK, that's all good. But if it is some sort of wild animal responsible for these attacks we're not, strictly speaking, talking about a murder investigation here.'

Jon picked at the steering wheel. 'Perhaps we should be talking to experts in other areas? People with experience in hunting and tracking for instance. I gather someone connected to Buxton Zoo is already giving advice. What do you think?'

'We can consider that at a later stage. But until we can conclusively prove otherwise, we should assume it's murder.'

'Fine with me, boss. I'd like to see the officer in charge of the Saddleworth Moor inquiry at the Mossley Brow nick. If a person's doing this, he had a major grudge against the farmer's wife and Derek Peterson. Find out what that is and we're a heck of a lot closer to finding the killer. Peterson worked with young offenders; maybe it'll turn out that victim number one did too.'

'OK, I'll ring ahead to the station at Mossley Brow and let them know you're on your way. See you back here later.'

Jon turned to his A to Z. The police station at Mossley Brow was on page eighty-nine, the last one covered by the map. After that was the green expanse of the Peak District National Park. The most direct way to the station was along a road that twisted through the fields he'd seen from Coal Pit Lane before eventually emerging at Mossley Brow itself.

Jon was just putting his car in gear when there was a knock on his window.

In the shadow cast by a large umbrella stood a figure. The raindrops clustered on the glass prevented Jon from making out if it was male or female. He pressed a button and his window lowered.

'Detective Inspector Spicer? Carmel Todd, *Manchester Evening Chronicle*.'

She was well spoken, no trace of Mancunian accent in her voice. Cheshire set, perhaps? Jon took in her long blonde hair and minimalist designer glasses. She was attractive, but not in the delicate and pretty sense of the pampered individuals who swanned around the city in their little sports cars. Attractive as in strong, straight features and a little make-up.

'The officer at the car park entrance said you were in charge.'

Jesus Christ, how did you get here so fast, Jon thought, giving a slight nod, inviting her to carry on. He could sense her assessing him, weighing up his cropped hair, scar over his eyebrow and lump where his nose had been broken. Am I a grunt or do I just look like one? What will you go for, charming or pushy? I know you'll be desperate to get something out ahead of the nationals.

She leaned forwards and a gap opened up at the top of her white blouse. It took all his effort to keep his eyes on her face.

'I gather there's a body in there with extensive mutilations.'

Jon rubbed his fingers across his chin. 'You gather? How have you gathered?'

Her lips tightened in response, expression saying my business, not yours.

He breathed in. 'The body of a middle-aged man was discovered at first light this morning. Until his family has been contacted and a formal identification made, I can't comment further.'

Her eyes had lost their sparkle. Just a business-like determination remained as she scrabbled for more information before the window went back up. 'This place is well known as a meeting spot for gay men. Is there some sort of a connection?'

Jon returned the tight-lipped expression. My business, not yours.

'Is it true his injuries bear a remarkable similarity to those of the woman found up on Saddleworth Moor?'

The window stopped and Jon looked through the three inch gap at her blue eyes. Who the fuck fed her that?

'I'll be issuing another statement later today.' The crack closed and he pulled out of the restaurant car park. With windscreen wipers moving steadily back and forth, he followed the rough road across the swathe of fields. Bedraggled groups of sheep stood about, some grazing, others just standing with heads bowed as they waited for the rain to pass. Soon the potholes got worse and, as the road narrowed to little more than a single lane track, he began to regret his decision to go cross country. At one point the dry-stone wall on his left had collapsed and, steering round the pile of stones, he wondered how often cars actually passed this way.

After almost fifteen minutes, houses started to appear on either side of the road and he emerged at the junction in Mossley Brow. The sloping roads and steep terraces of houses gave the town a crooked feel. Jon soon found the police station, an austere building constructed from the same rough blocks of dark grey stone that had been used for the neighbouring buildings.

He parked in a space at the front, crossed the puddle-strewn car park and went up the glistening stone steps. One of the blue double doors of the station entrance was slightly ajar and he stepped into a foyer whose walls were lined with numerous posters and notices.

A woman behind the counter smiled pleasantly at him. Jon thought of the battle-hardened stares of the staff at his station in Longsight. Not too many robbing scallies, violent drunks and scowling prostitutes around here then. He returned her smile then held out his warrant card. 'DI Spicer. Hopefully the officer running the Rose Sutton case is expecting me.'

Her face flinched slightly at the mention of Rose's name. 'Oh, right, I'll just make a call.'

She swivelled in her seat, dialled a number, and relayed the message in hushed tones before turning back to face him. 'Inspector Clegg will be with you shortly.'

'Thanks.' Jon put his hands in his pockets and turned to study the walls around him.

A poster about rural crime and how best to guard against burglary in isolated properties.

A notice about the need to record the chassis numbers of all agricultural vehicles, even those not registered for use on the public highways.

What would it be next? Posters on sheep rustling? He heard the lock click on the door at the side of the reception desk. 'DI Spicer, through here.'

Jon turned round. An officer with brown curly hair and slightly red cheeks was standing there. Probably late forties, Jon thought, and easily my height. His eyes dropped momentarily to the man's outstretched arm as it held the door open. Fingers like sausages, rolled up sleeves and a forearm that resembled a large leg of ham. The bloke was big and not through pumping iron in any gym.

Jon walked over. 'Good to meet you. I'm called Jon.'

Their hands connected and Jon's fingers were crushed momentarily in the other man's grip. He looked into his eyes, wondering if it was a deliberate ploy. Some sort of signal to the city copper about how things were done around here.

'Inspector Adam Clegg, Sir. Would you like a brew before we get started?'

'Sounds good.'

Clegg led the way to a small kitchen and took two mugs from a cupboard. 'Tea or coffee?'

'Black coffee, cheers.'

The other officer tipped a heaped spoonful into each cup, then filled both from a stainless steel urn on the side. Jon looked at the object and was reminded of the kitchen at Cheadle Ironsides rugby club before they got the wall-mounted water heater installed. It had been several years before. 'Don't see many of those nowadays.'

Clegg paused, a bottle of milk in his hand. It was a glass pint, not a plastic litre carton. 'What's that?'

Jon's eyes wavered between the bottle and the urn. Take your pick, he thought. 'The urn.'

'Oh that. Well, it serves our needs well enough. Terrible news about this morning.'

Jon nodded. 'I don't think lacerations describe his injuries. His throat was pretty much ripped out.'

Inspector Clegg crossed his massive arms. 'Sounds like Rose. Her throat had been opened right up too.'

Jon noted his use of the woman's Christian name. 'And you think she was attacked by an animal?'

Clegg raised one shoulder and let it fall. 'The hairs caught under her nails belonged to a panther. I understand some were recovered on the victim this morning too.'

'Yup. They've gone for analysis.'

'Well, if it is a person doing this, they don't deserve to be classed as human. Ripping apart man and beast without distinction. The rear legs of the ewe found by Rose's body had been almost stripped to the bone. Are we saying a person did that? Ate the meat raw up on that godforsaken moor?'

Jon looked away from the man's stare. Feelings were obviously running high on this one. 'I heard you've been talking to the guy who runs the black panther enclosure at Buxton Zoo.'

'Jeremy Hobson? Yes, he's here right now as a matter of fact. An expert in the behaviour of big cats. He's giving advice on how the bloody hell we're going to trap this thing.'

'But if it killed this morning's victim, it's come down off the moors. Stand in the car park by Crime Lake and you can hear traffic on the city's ring road zooming past.'

'From what Mr Hobson tells me, a panther's hunting range can cover many miles.'

'And this Hobson bloke, you're happy letting him know all the details of the investigation?'

'Yes. He understands everything is strictly confidential,' Clegg replied, carrying on down the corridor.

'So are you local to here?' Jon asked.

'I am. Born just down the road, schooled in the village.'

'Been in the job long?'

'Fourteen years.'

That means you joined at around thirty, Jon thought. 'So what did you do for a living before this?'

'My family owned a cattle farm. We gave up when milk prices got too ridiculous. The bloody supermarkets are killing off small scale farming in this country.'

Jon thought about the glass bottle of milk. Purchased locally and probably produced the same way.

'So you weren't tempted to turn your hand to farming sheep up on the hills?'

Clegg let out a guffaw. 'Now that is a bloody hard life. Besides, the price for lamb is even worse than for milk.'

They'd reached a closed door at the end of the corridor and Clegg paused, one hand on the brass door knob. 'I'll apologise now. This isn't the biggest room to work in. We were using it just for storage.'

'Why not somewhere bigger?' Jon asked.

'We wanted somewhere away from where we all work on a day-to-day basis. Somewhere private. These photographs aren't the nicest things you'll see.'

In the dank undergrowth, the golf ball seemed to glow with an unnatural brightness. The creature lowered its head and sniffed the dimpled surface. High above, the tail end of the rain cloud moved slowly towards the distant hills, pushed by a breeze that, at ground level, was laced with the scent of humans.

It stayed on its stomach, invisible among the plants that flourished beneath the tree. Drips fell steadily from the branches, some shattering on dying leaves of bracken, others absorbed instantly by the thick black hair covering the creature's back.

Out on the fairway a pair of multi-coloured umbrellas tilted, then collapsed to reveal the two golfers who had been sheltering beneath the taut nylon canopies. The men spoke, words indistinct. One then gestured towards the ancient looking oak that overhung the green, his hand see-sawing in uncertainty. The other glanced upwards, appraised the sky, then nodded. Umbrellas were slotted into golf bags and they began striding forward.

The creature watched them approach. Then, with a final sniff of the golf ball, it seemed to flow backwards, merging silently with the shadowy slope that led down to the river.

Ten

The door opened on a small room that still smelled of old cardboard. A couple of notice boards had been wheeled in, one covered by a sheet. Jon scanned the other. Photos of dead sheep covered it. The limp corpses were stretched out on a variety of terrains – blood-stained grass, patches of forest floor, moss-covered banks. Clumps of fleece were dotted round the bodies. His eyes lingered on the animals. Intestines hanging out, milky eyes staring upwards, rumps partially missing.

In the middle of the room was a desk that took up almost all the available floor space. Sitting at its side was a man with a thick shock of ginger hair. As Jon stepped into the room he was struck by the pale blue eyes looking up at him.

'DI Spicer, from the Major Incident Team in Manchester.'

'Jeremy Hobson. I run the panther enclosure at Buxton Zoo.'

He half stood to shake hands, revealing a pale green pair of canvas trousers below the darker green of his woollen jumper. Jon spotted the zoo's logo on its breast.

Spread out across the table was an ordnance survey map. Jon recognised it immediately as Explorer OL1, the Peak District's dark peak area. He used the reverse of the same map for Sunday rambles around Edale. The map had been marked with a smattering of red crosses with dates beside them. Jon saw they stretched from the edge of Mossley Brow, across to Holmbridge and then south right down to Ringinglow.

'Sheep-kill locations farmers have reported to me in the last few years,' Hobson explained with a tilt of his head towards the notice board. 'The photos are mine. I've made it a bit of a hobby trying to track this fellow.'

'This fellow?'

Hobson looked at him as if he was a particularly slow school boy. 'The panther.'

Bloody hell, Jon thought. I wish everyone wouldn't take it for granted there's one out there. 'Ever actually seen it?'

'Not once.'

'What about tracks or hair or – what do you call it – droppings?'

'You mean spoor. No, I haven't found definitive proof yet.'

Jon's eyes went to the black cross by the edge of Holme. 'That where Mrs Sutton was found?'

'Correct.'

Jon looked at the left-hand edge of the map. It ended at Mossley Brow. He tapped the air six inches to the side of the thick paper. 'A man was discovered around here this morning. He was in a car park at the edge of some fields.' Hobson didn't seem surprised. You already know, Jon thought. Clegg has told you.

'What sort of fields? Ones used for grazing sheep?'

'Yeah, I saw sheep in them.'

Hobson began clicking his tongue as he studied the map. 'There are swathes of field to the north and south of us. That land could comfortably allow the animal access to the fields you mentioned.'

Jon pointed to a pair of red lines running past Mossley Brow. 'That's the A635 and A670. You're saying, if there is a creature, it crossed both roads looking for food?'

'It's familiar with the presence of man. I imagine it's observed cars crossing the moors at night. As long as the roads were quiet, it could have done.'

'But why should an animal that's happily been hunting sheep in some of England's wildest terrain leave it for inhabited areas and roads?'

Hobson pursed his lips. 'I really don't know. What if it's no longer hunting sheep?'

There was silence in the room as Jon digested the implications of the comment. 'Had Mrs Sutton been, you know . . . fed on?'

Clegg closed the door. 'See for yourself. We keep this board

71

covered up because the woman's nephew is a constable here.' He yanked the sheet off, revealing the set of photographs below.

Jon was immediately struck by how similar the woman looked to the slaughtered sheep on the neighbouring board. Like so many of them, she was lying on a patch of wiry grass, clothing around her neck shredded to tatters. Like them, her limbs were slack and outstretched. Like them her wounds gaped open, red tissue below the skin no different to that of the sheep. A sense of alarm filled him. He'd seen countless bodies in the surroundings of Manchester. On pavements, in doorways, hallways, beds and baths. He'd seen the damage inflicted by guns, knives, baseball bats, bricks, machetes and razors. But this was different. This was someone who'd been savagely torn open, someone whose rain-soaked body had then lain on a dark moor, not touched by a streetlight, car light or any electric light at all. Only the moon had illuminated what took place that night.

His eyes focused on her wounds. 'Is any of her missing?'

'Some,' Clegg replied. 'Mainly from her throat. But there had been a lot of wildlife activity by the time Mr Sutton found her.'

I'm not sure if I want to hear this, Jon thought. 'Meaning?'

'Mr Sutton was initially attracted to the body's location by the squabbling of crows. We also recovered a feather that has been identified by a park ranger as that of a Peregrine falcon. We think the bird of prey found her at first light, then was chased off the, er, kill, by the crows.'

This sounded more and more like a bloody wildlife documentary. Something David Attenborough would narrate from the plains of Africa. 'So we don't know who or what was responsible for removing her flesh.'

'True,' Hobson answered. 'But if it was the panther, its fear of humans has been overcome. Was there any evidence of flesh having been removed from this morning's victim?'

'He's being taken for a post mortem as we speak. I'll let you know.' He waved a hand towards the images of partially consumed sheep. 'He didn't look like that though. The guy's throat was ripped out, that appeared to be all.' Jon watched as a glance bounced between Clegg and Hobson. 'What? How is that significant?'

Hobson placed his forearms on the table, lacing his fingers together. 'To answer your question, I'll need to describe the hunting techniques of the panther.'

This guy was itching to give a lecture. 'Go ahead, I'm all ears.'

'OK. You're aware black panthers and leopards are the same species, *panthera pardus?*'

Jon shook his head. 'But leopards are covered in spots.'

'Black panthers are actually melanistic leopards. That is to say, they have very dark coats in the same way as albino leopards have very white coats. The spots are just harder to see. Black panthers in their natural habitat are extremely rare, doing best hunting in the dense forests of Asia. The reason we've had several sightings of them in this country is because their exotic colouring makes them very attractive to lovers of unusual pets. It's highly likely that, in the past, individuals escaped from private collectors. Many also believe that when the 1976 Dangerous Wild Animals act made it illegal to keep them as pets, numerous animals were released into the wild.'

Sensing that the other man was only just getting started, Jon pulled a chair out and sat down. 'Any ever gone missing from your zoo?'

Hobson smiled. 'Never. The fence to their enclosure measures thirty feet high and extends below the ground by another ten feet.'

'Go on.'

'A few basic facts. Leopards live for up to fifteen years and measure over two and half metres from nose to tip of tail. They're big, powerful animals.'

'So what do they prey on in the wild?'

'Gazelles, antelope, impala, monkeys, baboons, even young wildebeest. They'll also prey on snakes and peacocks if they're hungry enough. Of course, when their hunting territory overlaps with grazing land, they'll take sheep and goats too. The variety of their diet is due to the fact that leopards are highly adaptable, able to survive in almost any habitat that affords them cover. That includes savannah, forests, jungles and cold mountainous areas.'

Jon glanced at the map with its scattering of crosses. 'And how big is an individual leopard's territory?'

Hobson pulled up the sleeves of his jumper and placed his forearms on the table. Jon couldn't help noticing they were covered in white hairs. 'Anything up to forty square kilometres. They're solitary animals and very shy by nature. This reclusiveness and their camouflage make them notoriously difficult to spot, as many disappointed customers on safari tours will tell you.'

Jon sat back, liking the sound of this less and less.

'Now, as regards hunting, they employ two techniques. First is the ambush, usually employed where cover is dense. The leopard will position itself overlooking an area used by its prey – cover could be ground foliage, rocks or the lowermost branches of a tree. When an animal comes within striking distance, the leopard pounces. If it is in a tree, it will almost always drop to the ground before attacking, though in some cases they've been observed launching themselves directly on to the back of their target. This method of attack is unique among the big cats as a result of a leopard's exceptional climbing ability.'

Jon recalled a scene from some distant documentary. 'Don't they then drag their prey back up into the tree?'

'Yes. Leopards can lift carcasses three times their own body weight up to a height of six metres if necessary. I once saw one in a Kenyan national park hefting a young giraffe up a trunk, remarkable sight. However, they'd have no need to do that in Britain since we have no predators big enough to drive them away from their kill.

'The second hunting technique is common to all cats, including domestic ones. It's called the stalk, run, pounce approach. The leopard will creep up on its prey, belly close to the ground, ears pointing forward. This phase of attack will usually be initiated using the cover of vegetation. Once within striking range the leopard transfers its weight on to its powerful hind legs and sprints towards the animal.'

He contracted his freckled fingers into hooks and pressed their tips against the map. 'From there it will use its claws to move up to the animal's head and bite through the base of the skull or, in some cases, latch on to the throat and suffocate the animal by crushing its windpipe.'

Hobson sat back and Jon couldn't help thinking that the man was enjoying himself. He glanced again at Rose Sutton's photos. 'Was she killed in that manner?'

'No.'

'Was the sheep?'

Hobson stood and pointed to a photo of the sheep's carcass. It lay on its side, eyes missing, mouth bloody, hind quarters eaten away, scraps of intestine littering the surrounding grass. 'I'm not sure. The crows had been ripping at the dead ewe. More so than Mrs Sutton. It's hard to say which wounds were caused by which animal.'

Jon looked at Clegg. 'Where is the sheep's carcass? We should get a pathologist to conduct a proper examination.'

His colleague glanced at the ceiling, as if having trouble trying to recall the information. 'Er, it was disposed of, I think.'

Jon sat up. 'You think? What the hell does that mean?'

Clegg's eyes dropped. 'Mr Sutton burnt it.'

Christ Almighty, Jon thought. 'That sheep was a vital part of the crime scene.'

'Well, the SOCO was satisfied there was no need to store it.'

Jon shook his head. Whoever the SOCO was, he should be sent back to training college. And Clegg should have known better too. This whole investigation was a shambles.

Hobson sat down. 'My take on events is this. The panther had made its kill and then Mrs Sutton turned up as it was attempting to feed.'

'Maybe she even tried to shoo it away, Rose was a plucky woman,' Clegg added.

'Her throat injuries arose from the panther swiping at her to protect its kill,' Hobson concluded.

Jon shut his eyes. If it was a panther, this wouldn't be a case for the police much longer. And then it would be back to Summerby for the next mind-numbing case. He searched for ways to refute the theory. 'The man discovered this morning. He was no farmer protecting his sheep.'

'No,' Hobson agreed. 'But he was in a car park that bordered a field of sheep. Was there some sort of a hedge between this car park and the field?'

Jon thought for a second. 'Yes. A tree and a bramble patch.'

'A tree?' Hobson's white eyebrows were raised.

Jon nodded.

'It should be checked for claw marks. Many of the attacks I've documented on livestock in this area take place close to woodland, scrub or dry stone walls. The panther uses this cover to stalk the sheep which, all too often, tuck themselves into these same spots for a bit of protection from the elements. Rose Sutton was found by an outcrop of rock.'

Shit. It was beginning to sound more and more like a horror film. Jon held up a finger. 'But our man this morning had driven to the car park. Surely you're not trying to claim a vehicle pulling up with its headlights on wouldn't scare the animal off?'

Hobson shrugged. 'Do we know how long it was between him parking there and being attacked?'

'No.'

'What if he'd been sitting there a while?'

Knowing Peterson, he would have sat there half the night for the possibility of sex. 'OK, so our man could have been loitering there for a bit. Perhaps he needs a piss. He gets out of his vehicle, wanders too close to the undergrowth and bang, something attacks him. I still reckon any panther in the vicinity would have just run away.'

Hobson uncrossed his arms. 'As I mentioned earlier, perhaps this animal has conquered its fear of humans. If it has, we've got a major problem on our hands trying to catch it.'

Jon looked at him. 'How so?'

'Leopards are wickedly intelligent. Many who have studied them have commented that if lions shared the stealth and cunning of leopards, humans would have died in their thousands over the centuries. Have you ever heard of the Man-Eating Leopard of Rudraprayag?'

Here we go again, Jon thought. You're bloody relishing this.

'Over an eight-year period from nineteen eighteen to nineteen twenty-six a single leopard killed one hundred and twenty-six villagers in Nepal. The animal grew more and more bold, even climbing through windows and taking victims from their beds. A bounty of one thousand pounds – a small fortune in those days – attracted hunters from all over. None could get near the beast. Eventually a man called Jim Corbett was called in. Corbett was born in north India and had been a hunter all his life. Even he began to believe the animal had a sixth sense when it came to outwitting its pursuers. One time Corbett waited three weeks in a tower that overlooked a bridge the leopard was known to cross. The day after he gave up on that location, the animal crossed the bridge and claimed more villagers on the other side.'

Once again Hobson sat back, a satisfied look on his face. Jon waited for him to carry on before realising the man had finished speaking. For fuck's sake. 'So what happened in the end?'

Hobson flicked a hand. 'Oh, he got it eventually. But by then the animal was old and decrepit. My point is, catching the beast will be incredibly hard. Traps, poisoned carcasses, marksmen in hides – a leopard will sense them all a mile off.'

Jon tapped his fingers on the table. Hobson's unquestioning assumption that a leopard was responsible for the attacks rankled him. 'Inspector Clegg, is there any chance of speaking to Mr Sutton? There are still many more traditional angles of investigation to cover before we assume this is the work of some phantom beast.' He shot a glance at Hobson. So you can stop drooling over your bloody maps. Hobson's eyelids flickered momentarily and a red spot appeared on each cheek. Good, Jon thought. I hope that stung.

Clegg moved towards the door. 'We can try him from the phone in my office.'

Jon nodded to Hobson. 'Thanks for your talk. It was very illuminating.'

'No problem,' Hobson replied, pale blue eyes dropping to the table as he reached for a pen.

Once they were further down the corridor Jon said quietly, 'What's the score with that Hobson?'

Clegg glanced over his shoulder at Jon. 'He's an acknowledged authority on the behaviour of big cats. At the moment he's trying to plot the animal's territorial movements by time and place of attack.'

'I don't like him. He's got some sort of agenda.'

Clegg paused in the doorway to his office. 'He's been nothing less than helpful, Sir.' Jon registered the unnecessary emphasis on the word sir. 'All his time and effort is given voluntarily.'

Exactly, thought Jon. There's something in it for him. 'The media is already reporting that a black panther carried out the attack on Saddleworth Moor. If they start writing that the animal has killed again, what do you think will happen to visitor numbers to the panther enclosure at his zoo?'

Clegg's jaw set a fraction tighter. 'If you don't mind me saying, that seems a very cynical approach to take.'

You haven't worked the cases I have, Jon thought. 'Maybe. But I want Hobson's access to this investigation limited strictly to his area of expertise. Which means not leaving him unsupervised in an office where there are documents and reports about the investigation. Now, you said back there Mrs Sutton was a plucky woman. You knew her?'

'Yes, she was a good friend of my elder sister. Use to help out on our farm when we were younger.'

Jon groaned inwardly. The guy's got a personal stake in this. 'Are you happy being involved on the case?'

'More than happy. I requested it, in fact.'

Jon could see Clegg's jaw was firmly set again. I won't argue the toss – at least, not yet. 'What sort of a person was she then?'

'Salt of the earth, to use a cliché. She went to school here in the village, then got a qualification in child care.'

Jon's eyes locked on the other man's 'Child care? You mean she went into further education?'

'Yes, that's right.'

'Where did she study?'

'At the local sixth form college.'

'When?'

'Must have been back in the late sixties. Why?'

'This morning's victim completed a course in Health and Social Welfare at Salford Polytechnic in nineteen eighty-eight. I was hoping they might have been students on the same course. Did she work in any city centre facility for young people?'

'No. She worked as a nursery nurse just round the corner until she married Ken Sutton.'

'When was that?'

'The late eighties. I remember because my sister was a bridesmaid.'

'And then she moved to Sutton's sheep farm?'

'That's right, across on the Holme side of the moor.'

Jon mulled over the information. 'The victim this morning was a forty-seven-year-old named Derek Peterson. He lived in Clayton and worked in a care home for young offenders until convicted for gross indecency in ninety-three. He was attacked in a car park used as a meeting spot for gay men last Thursday. Anything I've just said could link him to Rose Sutton?'

Clegg was slowly shaking his head. 'I don't think so.'

Jon sighed. 'What about the crime scene itself? Did forensics recover anything?'

'Forensics? We took a pathologist up there and he had a good look around.'

'What about the Scene Of Crime Officer?' Jon said incredulously.

'Oh yes, he poked around after he'd filmed the body.'

'I assume before poking around, he taped the scene off?'

Clegg's eyebrows lowered. 'No point. What would he seal off? A few miles of open moor? The body had lain there all night, during which time there'd been a major storm. She may as well have been hosed down before we got there.'

'Jesus,' Jon cursed under his breath.

'Don't treat us like bumpkins, Sir.'

Jon looked at the other man, seeing his cheeks were flushed red.

'I saw the expression on your face as you were looking at the posters in reception. We might lack the sophisticated training and ample resources you lot enjoy in the Major Incident Team, but we did all we could at the time. The pathologist was happy, as was the coroner.'

Jon held up a hand. 'I'm not questioning your ability, Adam. But I would have expected this SOCO to have conducted a thorough search. I'd appreciate a look at the reports later on.'

Clegg still looked a bit cross. 'I think it might put things into perspective if you see for yourself where she was found.'

'Fine by me,' said Jon. 'Let's go over there now. Give the farmer a call, I'd like to speak with him too.'

Clegg sat down, opened a file and dialled the number written on the inside page. After waiting for a good minute he hung up. 'No one at home.'

'Has he got a mobile?'

'No. There's no reception at the farmhouse and the signal is extremely patchy on the moors.' He looked at his watch. 'Best we drive over there and see if we can catch him when he comes down for lunch.'

Jon realised his own stomach was uncomfortably empty. 'Is there somewhere I can grab a sandwich before we head over?'

ELEVEN

Trevor Kerrigan picked up the keys to his Mitsubishi Shogun. As he walked towards his front door the colours in the elaborate stained glass window at its centre were glowing and he felt a sense of personal satisfaction – as if the weather had brightened solely because he had willed it.

He turned his head and called out to the corridor behind him. 'Off to hit a few at the club, see you later, duck.'

'OK, see you later, love,' a female voice answered from the depths of the house.

Kerrigan opened the door and paused at the top of his steps. He liked to imagine how he must appear to the traffic passing on the main road in front of his house. Though he wasn't a tall man, he believed there was an air of authority about him. The kind that successful businessmen like him gave off. He adjusted the gold sovereign ring on his left hand, rotating it slowly back and forth. Up until a couple of years ago he'd sported several other rings too, but the infuriating craze for bling had forced their removal. There was no way he was looking like those ridiculous darkies, shouting their stupid hip-hop and grabbing their crutches like fucking apes. He surveyed the road for a moment longer, then looked down at the marble lions flanking him. 'Hello there lads.'

The lions gazed across the narrow garden with its manicured strip of lawn and collection of Greek style urns. As Kerrigan followed the path across the front of his house, he raised the fob on the collection of keys and pressed a button. The door to his double garage rose slowly, revealing the powerful-looking vehicle inside. He walked round it to the rear of the building where a high density foam sculpture of a male head and torso was mounted on a spring-loaded pole that, in turn, was connected to a barrel-sized base unit filled with water.

Kerrigan paused, breathed in, then slowly raised his head. 'You talkin' to me?' he murmured through barely parted lips. 'You are?' He stepped up to the figure, bowing his forehead so it came to within millimetres of the face. 'You fucking talkin' to me?' As if released from a catch, his head bobbed forward, connecting with the figure's nose, rocking it backwards. In the same movement, he bent his knees, dropped a left shoulder and brought a fist up toward the stomach area of the bag. Not wanting to risk his gold ring, he pulled the punch, conveying the sense of impact with a comic-book 'Kapow!' The torso quivered on its pole and Kerrigan gave it a mocking grin. 'Not so tough now, are you?'

Practising his technique of intimidation was a routine he liked to maintain before going anywhere. In his line of work it was best to stay sharp when dealing with employees or clients.

He released the central locking on his car, opened the boot, then hauled his bag of golf clubs off the shelves built into the side of the garage and placed them in the vehicle. Settling into the driver's seat of the Shogun, he watched the steady flow of cars passing by. He knew that living right next to a busy main road leading into Manchester city centre was unnecessary for someone with his income. He also knew that his house was out of keeping with those on either side. But since he'd bought the semi adjoining his and knocked through, his home had suddenly become a six-bedroom detached. After that, some carefully chosen embellishments had served to further distinguish him from his neighbours, setting him apart and letting everyone know – in no uncertain terms – that he was a man of standing.

He liked to give this message out to the scum who surrounded him. After all, they generated his income and it was important they knew who was boss. Pointing his key fob at the road, he pressed another button and the wrought iron gates began to open. Kerrigan started up the engine, but didn't move the vehicle forward. He couldn't suffer the indignity of having to wait for a gap in the traffic before being able to pull out of his own driveway. Instead he waited for the traffic lights thirty metres down the road to change to red. Only once they had, forcing the stream of cars to slow down, did he put his vehicle in gear and move down the driveway. An approaching car, having to stop anyway, flashed him and Kerrigan was able to drive out on to the road without a problem.

The route to Brookvale Golf Course took him through the drab terraced streets of Droylsden, but the green of the fairways came into view within ten minutes of setting off from his house. He pulled into the club's entrance, the suspension on his Shogun barely registering the speed bumps as he cruised along the short drive to the car park. He got out of his vehicle and was walking round to the boot, when his mobile phone rang. He glanced at the screen. Milner. What did that idiot want?

Holding a hand up in greeting to a couple of men making their way to the clubhouse, he turned round and got back in his car, not wanting any other member to hear his conversation.

'John. What's up?' he snapped.

'Ah, hello, Trevor. You OK, boss?'

'Fine. What is it?'

'Erm, I'm at a house on Ackroyd Street.'

Immediately Kerrigan commenced a mental scan. He prided himself on his ability to recall the details of every late payer from memory. 'Skinny woman with shit teeth and a little kid. How much is she behind?'

'This week or all together?'

'This week, for starters.'

'Thirty-two quid just to cover the interest.'

Kerrigan started calculating. Allowing for the rates of interest he charged, she probably owed in excess of three hundred quid. Not a massive amount in itself, but when added to dozens and dozens of other amounts like it, it soon funded his leisurely lifestyle and two holidays in Barbados each year. He also knew that letting one late payer get away with it sent out completely the wrong signal. 'Are her curtains open?'

'Yeah.'

'So what's inside?'

Movement at the other end of the line. Kerrigan could picture Milner stepping across the patch of grass, in all probability having to pick his way past mangled toys, discarded nappies and dog shit.

'There's a TV on.'

'Widescreen?'

'Yup.'

'DVD underneath it?'

'Think so.'

'What else? Sofas, armchairs? Kids' toys?'

'No sofa. The kid is on the floor playing on a video game.'

'So she can afford Sony fucking Playstations can she?'

'Hang on, she's seen me looking in. She's coming across to the window.' The other man started speaking away from the phone. 'Come on love, you're well overdue. You know the score. Listen, if you . . . ' His voice came back on the line. 'No use, she's drawn the curtains. Said she's not opening the door to anyone.'

'You already tried telling her you were a registered bailiff?'

'Yeah, when I arrived. She was half out the door with the kid and a shopping bag on her arm. Stepped back inside, saying she knows her rights and I'm not coming in.'

Bollocks, Kerrigan thought. She must have been to the Citizen's Advice Bureau for help. 'She was going shopping, so she's got cash in there. Keep knocking. On her door and her windows. Make it loud. Let the neighbours hear. If she was going shopping, she needs food, especially for the kid. She'll open the door eventually.'

'How long do you want me to keep trying, boss?'

Kerrigan rolled his eyes. Did he have to hold every fuckwit's hand in this life? 'As long as you want to pick up your bonus this month, that's how long. You think I got to sit here at my golf club because I gave up every time some stupid bitch blew her giro on gin and then tried to close her curtains on me? Now don't bother me again until you've got the cash!'

He slammed the phone down on the passenger seat. Breathing deeply, he flicked the radio on, wanting to distract himself from the pond life he had to deal with. There was some sort of news flash going on. A woman was reporting that another body had been found with extensive injuries to the throat and upper chest.

Police refused to confirm or deny a connection with the woman found up on Saddleworth Moor. Kerrigan gave a low whistle. Now there was something to talk about in the members' bar.

TWELVE

Outside the rain had stopped and the cloud layer had started to break up, allowing a few shafts of sunlight through.

A light breeze was blowing as they walked to a café further down the small high street. Jon was surprised at how much less everything cost compared to the chains of sandwich shops that had slowly taken over the centre of Manchester.

'Can we eat on the way?' Jon asked when Adam gestured to the stools lined up along a narrow formica counter. 'I don't want to miss him.'

'Fair enough,' the other man replied, picking up his roll and opening the door.

At the car park Adam thought for a moment. 'I've got to visit my sister in Holme later. It might be easier if we go in separate cars.'

'No problem,' Jon answered, unlocking his. 'You lead the way.'

'OK. I'm parked round at the rear; back in two ticks. We'll take the Tintwistle road, it's the most direct way to Sutton's farm.'

Jon had managed to bolt down half his barm before Adam reappeared in a four-wheel drive Nissan that was bright with police markings. He waved at Jon then pulled out of the car park. As they headed south along the main road Jon was aware of the greyish-brown hills rising up in the distance on his left. In the foreground buildings, lampposts and trees glided past, but the moors beyond didn't seem to move. The land had a brooding stillness about it that hinted at how long it had existed, all but unchanged, over the centuries.

By the time the road led into Tintwistle, Jon had noted several Land Rover Defenders passing them by, their wheel arches caked with mud, some with cages on the back for livestock or sheep dogs. As they passed a pub called The Shepherd's Rest, he noticed a road sign informing him that the A6024 was open.

The valley began to steepen and fir trees closed in on both sides, dimming the interior of the car. Then the road rose more sharply and suddenly they emerged from the trees. On his left the edge of the moor loomed over him, rising up so dramatically that almost all his view of the sky on that side of the car vanished. He looked at the long grass on its plunging slopes, broken by clumps of bracken, swathes of purple heather and gnarled branches of gorse. Behind the bushes he glimpsed the occasional white fleece of a sheep.

At the turning for the A6024 the road rose more steeply still. Dropping into a lower gear, Jon noticed the landscape was dominated by a coarse brownish grass, not a single tree in sight. Apart from scar-like grooves cut by small streams, the only break in the monotony of the moor was the drystone walls. He looked again at the undulating contours of the land. Jesus, it resembled the bunched muscles of an enormous animal, ready to rise up at any moment and shake itself free of the tiresome little constructions of rock built across its back. This, Jon realised, was a place that merely tolerated man: in no way had it been tamed by his presence.

They finally reached the summit of the moor. Towering above him was a radio mast, struts of wire leading off at diagonal angles down to the ground. Glancing in his rear view mirror he saw the plains of Cheshire and Lancashire framed there for an instant. As he crossed the plateau he was aware of the strength of the wind as it buffeted his car. Before long the road started its descent and a sign announced *13% gradient. Use low gear!*

The road curled round, giving a bird's-eye view of sheep-dotted fields, dense patches of woodland and darkly glistening reservoirs. Nestled at the head of the valley was the village of Holme. He'd stopped there for lunch with Alice once. As in many of the places on this side of the moors, the local people had been weavers before the industrial revolution swept their cottage industry into the cold and imposing mills. He remembered the tea-room pamphlet informing him that this region was where the Luddites smashed the shearing frames that threatened their way of life.

They hadn't descended far when Clegg's vehicle began to indicate left; it then slowed at the entrance to a narrow lane. A boulder was carved with the words *Far Gethen Farm*.

Jon followed Clegg on to a rough road that twisted down towards a cluster of stone buildings just visible in the distance. After a couple of minutes the road turned sharply to the left, entering a courtyard made up of a ramshackle assortment of barns with a large farmhouse at the end. Heavy slabs of moss-covered stone made up its roof and small windows were set far back into the thick walls, giving the house a beady-eyed appearance.

The courtyard was littered with dirty straw and oily puddles. Jon opened his car door. The smell of manure mixed with sharper chemical notes hit him. A chorus of bleats was coming from the barn to his side. Looking for a relatively clean patch of ground, Jon placed his feet on the bumpy surface. Immediately he noticed a row of dead rats neatly lined up by a mound of broken tiles. A cat with half-closed eyes observed him from the top of the pile. My work, its expression said. By the tiles was a row of white plastic containers. Jon peered at the labels. Twenty-five litres of formaldehyde liquid. That's the sharp tang in the air then, Jon thought, as memories of the first autopsies he'd witnessed made an unwelcome return.

As Adam picked his way across to the front door of the farmhouse, Jon continued to look around. By a red McConnel tractor with an aluminium trailer attached to the back was a line of sharpened stake posts and rolls of wire. He made his way over to where he could hear the sheep bleating. The corner barns were open ended, both containing pens that were crammed with animals, many with long straggly tails matted with excrement.

Turning back to the courtyard, he spotted a quad bike through the open doors of the barn opposite. Adam was trudging over. 'He's not in, but I imagine he can't be far away.'

Jon turned to watch a chicken as it raked the barn floor before expertly pecking out seeds from the strands of straw at its feet.

The sound of an engine grew louder before a Land Rover bounced into view at the other side of the fields bordering the farm.

'This'll be him,' said Adam.

Seconds later the vehicle pulled up before them. The silver-haired driver assessed them for a moment before muttering something to the man in the passenger seat. Then he pushed open the door of the battered jeep. A Border Collie that was caked in mud immediately jumped down, eyes flashing at the two strangers. Jon crouched down and held out a hand.

'Here boy, come here.' The animal looked at him warily before slinking off towards the farmhouse, body close to the ground. Not your friendly household pet then, Jon thought, straightening up as the driver approached them with a stiff-legged walk. He was wearing what appeared to be a pair of waterproof dungarees, the legs merging into rubber boots just below his knees. The garment was totally covered in grime.

Christ, the bloke must be over seventy, Jon realised. I've seen younger men driving to the shops in electric buggies, and this old boy is still out working the fields.

'Ken, this is DI Spicer. He's from the Major Investigation Team in Manchester,' Adam announced.

'Is he?' the man replied, eyes on Jon.

Even though his answer was abrupt, Jon heard the clipped tones of a Yorkshire accent. He stepped forward with his hand held out. 'Pleased to meet you.'

The farmer regarded his hand for a moment before grasping it briefly. His skin felt like dry leather and, given his age, Jon was surprised by the strength of his grip.

'I'm sorry about your wife, Mr Sutton.'

The comment elicited a curt nod.

Jon coughed in order to put a space between his condolences and his next comment. 'I understand the attack occurred after you lost a number of sheep.'

'I have. And I assume your job is to try and solve the problem.'

In the background Jon saw the younger man climb out of the vehicle. He had sandy-coloured hair and wore combat fatigues and army boots. Under his arm was a rifle-shaped carry case and in each hand a heavy-duty walkie-talkie. Jon watched as he walked silently across the courtyard to disappear into the farmhouse. Obviously Sutton and his friends had their own ideas about how to solve the problem. His eyes shifted back to the old man. 'I'm here to add what I can to the investigation.'

The farmer grunted at his politician's response.

Let's move the conversation away from this, Jon thought. 'So, how long have you owned the farm?'

'Been in the family for generations.'

'What breeds of sheep do you have?'

'Just Swales.'

Swaledales. The only breed of hill sheep he'd ever heard of. 'The ones in that barn look like they're ready for shearing.'

Sutton's eyes went to the animals. 'Only if I want a field of stiffs once winter sets in.'

You idiot, thought Jon, realising the sheep would need all the protection they could get out on the moors. Sutton moved past him, entering the nearest barn and then climbing into the pen. The animals shied away from him, jostling with each other to get into the opposite corner. Keeping his legs wide, he stepped across the layer of straw, arms held out. He allowed four animals to squeeze past, then, as the fifth tried to get round, his hand shot out to grab the animal by the back of the neck.

He dragged it into the centre of the pen and lifted a leg over its back. Gripping the animal's shoulders between his knees, he yanked its head back and inserted his fingers into its mouth. Jon was shocked at how roughly the man treated the animal. But then it dawned on him that, to the farmer, it was merely an investment that he aimed to profit from. He thought of the collection of fluffy sheep that dangled from the mobile above Holly's cot. Reality suddenly seemed a lot harsher.

'So why have you rounded this lot up?' Jon asked.

'I've fetched them down for tupping.'

At last, a bit of information in return, Jon coaxed the conversation on. 'That's when you put a ram in with them?'

'Yes. Though I need to check their teeth, worm them and prepare their feet first.'

'What does that involve?'

'Dipping their hooves in formaldehyde solution to stop foot rot, clipping them if they're overgrown. Some of this lot need burling as well.'

'Burling?'

'Trimming the tops of their tails, so the tup takes to them a bit easier.'

'And once they're all pregnant, what do you do with them?'

'Turn this lot out into the lower fields. They're a bit lean. I need to get them on better grass. Then, come the spring, they'll lamb.'

Satisfied the animal was OK, he released it from between his knees. It moved unsteadily forward and he slapped it hard across its rump to get it out of his way. The animal staggered under the force of the blow before running back to join the rest of the flock.

'Do you bring all your sheep off the moors for winter?'

Sutton shook his head. 'We leave some out on top, I take bales up for them, but these breeding ewes need a bit of looking after.'

'What about the lot in the next barn?' Jon looked over to the pen across the courtyard.

'Them? Misfits they are. I've pulled them in so they can go for slaughter.' He climbed back out. 'Are you here to learn about hill farming?'

'No.' Jon saw his attempt at breaking the ice had amounted to nothing. 'I'd like to talk to you about your wife, Rose.'

The man's eyelids gave the slightest flutter, but stopped short of a blink. 'I've given a statement. Have you not read it?'

'I have a few questions of my own. You won't be aware of this, but we found another body this morning. The man had very similar injuries to those of your wife.' Now he had the farmer's attention. 'I'd like to see where you found her if possible.'

'Who was he? This man you found this morning,' Sutton asked quietly.

'We can't release a name yet, his family haven't been informed.'

'Where was he found?'

'Around five miles from here, towards the city. In a car park by the edge of a lake.'

Sutton's eyes lifted to Jon. 'How old was he?'

'Mid-forties.'

'Mid-forties?'

Jon studied the other man. 'Should his age be of any concern to you?'

'What?' Sutton's eyes refocused, brittle exterior closing back over. 'It's not.'

'It seemed to cause you some concern.'

'No. It's a shock, that's all. To hear someone else has died.'

'It is,' Jon replied. 'So, the place where you found her ... '

Sutton crossed his arms. 'I'm not going back up there now. It's my lunch. Adam, you can take him if you want.' He nodded towards the quad bike. 'Keys are on the hook. I'll be around here when you get back.' Without waiting for an answer he set off across the courtyard, glancing about his feet. 'Chip!' he barked aggressively. 'If that bloody dog is in the upper field again ... Chip!'

The animal materialised from beneath the tractor, jinking round a stray chicken before submissively approaching Sutton, ears pressed close to its head. 'Get in there,' Sutton growled, jabbing his finger at a kennel. The dog slithered inside.

The cat jumped down from the mound of tiles, ignoring the chicken to trot alongside the farmer with its head held high. Sutton opened the front door of the farm and first the cat, then the man were swallowed by the darkness within.

Jon stood staring at the farmhouse. He had the distinct impression that attitudes to death were a lot different here. Sutton seemed to accept it readily as part of life, but only in the order he sanctioned.

The cat was free to kill the rats, but not the chickens. Under Sutton's supervision, the dog could harry and torment the sheep, but not chase the cat. The sheep were a mere commodity, to be protected and fed until their time for slaughter. And Sutton was master of them all. Jon thought about how the sheep dog had deferred to him and how the cat had ingratiated itself. Even the sheep seemed to sense that the farmer was boss.

But now things were different. A new element had been introduced that upset the established order. It had been killing his sheep, costing him money. It didn't take much to see that Sutton regarded it as a lot more than a threat to his income – it was a challenge to his rank and, with the death of his wife, a personal enemy. He guessed the farmer didn't want the creature merely trapped or tranquillised: he wanted it dead.

Jon turned to his colleague. 'Well, that's us told. Do you know the way?'

Adam nodded. 'Better change our shoes.'

But I haven't got any others, Jon thought, watching Adam as he opened his vehicle and got out a pair of green wellies. His eyes turned to the fresh black mud sticking to the farmer's Land Rover. Bollocks, I'm going to get covered.

'Haven't you brought anything else for your feet?' Adam asked, now pulling out a thick ski jacket.

'No,' Jon replied, opening his boot and taking out a thin waterproof coat.

'Sure you'll be warm enough in that?' Adam observed him dubiously as he put it on.

How the hell should I know? thought Jon, glancing at the sky.

'There's a fair wind up there, that's all. Shall we see if Ken can lend you anything?'

'No, don't worry,' Jon didn't want to add to the farmer's perception of him as a clueless city boy. 'We're not going to be long, are we?'

Adam shrugged, then walked over to the barn housing the quad bike. He took the keys from the hook and started the machine up. 'Climb on,' he said, jabbing a thumb at the pillion seat behind him.

Jon looked around for a crash helmet, saw none, then climbed gingerly on to the rear seat.

'Keep a good hold of my jacket,' Adam instructed as the vehicle jerked forward, nearly throwing Jon off the back.

Adam steered the bike up a rough stone track that led along

the side of the farmhouse then came to a halt at a gate. Jon jumped off to open it and Adam drove into the field beyond. After swinging it shut and hooking the loop of chain around the gate post, Jon climbed back on the bike and they set off across the thick grass, sheep scattering before them.

At the far side, a low building with a series of railings in front of it was nestled against the drystone wall that meandered along the foot of the slopes. Immediately behind it the muted tones of the moor began. Jon was struck by the abruptness of the change. It seemed like the moor was pressing down from above, only held back by the barrier of stone which, at any moment, would collapse, allowing the wild land to engulf the cultivated field below.

He leaned forwards and raised his voice over the bike's engine. 'What's that building over there?'

Adam turned in the direction of Jon's outstretched finger. 'Sheep sheds. There's a trough built into the courtyard for dipping them. The workers drive the animals between the railings where they queue up for their bath.'

Jon nodded, eyes now on the moor itself. 'That's some change. The green of the grass and the brown of the moor.'

'The field's been seeded and treated with fertiliser. You can't touch the moor. ESA – environmentally sensitive area,' Adam shouted back.

They soon stopped at another gate by the side of the sheds. Once through it Adam announced, 'Hold tight, it gets a lot bumpier from now on.'

Ken Sutton stood by his kitchen window, head slightly bowed. Once the sound of the quad bike's engine had completely died away he turned to the young man. He was sitting in the wooden chair at the side of the Aga, hands hovering just above it.

'Still not used to the chill, Andrew?'

'Chill? It's bloody freezing,' he replied, guttural accent placing an emphasis on the word bloody.

Sutton shrugged. 'No more than usual for this time of year.'

'Yeah?' Andrew replied, his blond hair catching the light.

'Well, it's in the high eighties back home. That's the usual temperature for this time of year in South Africa.'

Sutton had stepped over to the kitchen table where two large pieces of paper were spread out. One was a map of all the farmland he owned, the other was a more detailed rendition of the area surrounding the farm house itself. 'So what are your thoughts?'

Andrew looked over his shoulder, unwilling to take his hands away from the heat source beneath them. 'I can set up motion sensors across that top field. Start them on a level with the farmhouse, then position them in an arc going outwards to those buildings, the ones near that wall—'

'The sheep dipping sheds,' Sutton cut in.

'Right, them. Then they can follow a line back across the field to the track. I'll hook them up to a unit you can keep here in the farmhouse. That way nothing can come down off the moor without us knowing about it. You'll have to clear that field of sheep though, otherwise the sensors will be going off every five minutes.'

'If that's what it takes.' Sutton's eyes were on the pieces of paper before him. 'And what about defences for the farmhouse?'

Reluctantly, Andrew moved away from the Aga. He reached into the pocket of his camouflage jacket and brought out a plastic bag full of dark brown strips of meat. 'Biltong?'

Sutton regarded the contents suspiciously. 'What did you say that stuff is made out of again?'

Andrew gave a brief smile. 'Dried impala with a few spices.'

Sutton shook his head. 'I'll do without.'

The younger man took out a thin length of rigid meat and bit off the top third, exposing clean white teeth as he did so. 'You got the stakes and fencing like I asked?'

'Yes, six-feet posts and medium stock fencing. It was all dropped off earlier today.'

'Barbed wire?'

'There are plenty of rolls in the barns.'

'Good. So we plug these gaps.' Using the piece of meat as a pointer, Andrew indicated the open-sided barns before tapping the entrance to the courtyard itself. 'And we put up a gate here.

Barbed wire at the top. Basically, we'll turn your farmhouse into a kraal.'

'That will be enough?'

The younger man popped the remaining meat into his mouth. 'If the Masai keep out lions, leopards and hyenas with a barrier of thorny branches, six-foot high metal fencing with barbed wire should do for you.'

Sutton looked uneasily at the layout of the farm buildings. 'What about security lights?'

'I'm no electrician, but they can't do any harm if someone can put them up. Have them so they point outwards into the fields.'

'What about the barn doors? Shouldn't we nail them shut?'

'Only if this animal has learned how to open a latch.' Sutton fixed him with a stone cold stare and the smile fell from the younger man's lips. 'Sorry, mate, just a joke. We can nail them up if you want. Tell you what might be better though.'

Sutton waited in silence for him to carry on.

'Bring the sheep from the top field into the courtyard each night. If they start bleating, we'll know something's out there.'

Sutton nodded in agreement. 'Yes, I like that idea. OK, best you make yourself scarce. I don't want you around when those two come down off the tops.'

'Fine. Any problem if I have a bath?'

'No, you do that.'

Andrew picked up his rifle case then turned back to Sutton. 'I've been meaning to say. Have you got a CD player in the house? I brought a few discs over with me, a bit of music would be nice with my bath.'

'Discs?'

The younger man grinned. 'You know, round silver things?'

Sutton looked back, face impassive.

Andrew's expression fell. 'Jesus, you really don't know what I'm talking about.'

'I've no use for stuff like that.'

Andrew raised a hand, palm upwards. 'No CD player, no DVD player. A black and white telly and a few dusty videos. Tomorrow you'd better tell me where the nearest town is. I can't play cards with you every night.'

Sutton shrugged. 'There's a pub in the village. It shows football some nights.'

'Football,' Andrew sighed. 'Any women drink there?'

'One or two. But mind yourself, the local lads won't like an outsider muscling in.'

'We'll see,' he replied with a grin, wandering out of the kitchen and up the dark stairs.

Sutton folded the maps up and placed them in the kitchen table's drawer. Looking around the room, he spotted the younger man's combat boots by the back door. After hiding them in a cupboard, he went over to the sink and filled the kettle.

Clegg gunned the engine and they began bouncing up a narrow track that soon thinned to little more than a sheep trail. As they climbed up, the wind steadily increased in strength. Soon the few twists of gnarled gorse that eked a stunted existence were left behind. Coarse grass that shifted and swayed in the wind like the pelt of an animal was all that surrounded them.

Frequently the bike's wheels skidded for purchase on the boggy ground. By the time they reached the high ground the wind was a continuous roar of air that made Jon's eyes stream and his ears ache.

They made their way across the relatively flat land at the top, Clegg frequently having to steer the bike round little ponds of black water. Jon peered about. Apart from the radio mast and a distant fence that he guessed marked the edge of Sutton's land, there was absolutely nothing to signal the existence of man. They reached the crest of a small hillock and Adam brought the bike to a halt. On the other side the land dropped away in a series of parallel grooves, as if a giant claw had raked its surface. Racing away below them were a dozen or so sheep. Suddenly they cut to the side, running single file along an invisible path before disappearing from sight.

Further down the slope a collection of boulders fringed with gorse bushes and clumps of heather broke through the surface of the land. Adam switched the engine off and almost shouted, 'She was found down there.'

This bloody wind is going right through me, Jon thought, wiping a tear from the corner of his eye. He looked at the ground beneath the tyres. The grass was thin, exposing the dark soil beneath. Peat. He climbed off the vehicle and liquid oozed beneath his feet. Looking into a nearby pool he saw that the water itself was quite clear; it was the soil at the bottom which made it appear black. Apart from a few lichens that looked prehistoric in their simplicity, the water was utterly devoid of life.

Adam was already trudging away and he started to follow. Immediately his foot sank into a rut in the turf and he felt ice-cold water flood into his shoes. Fucking great. Keeping to the thicker clumps of grass, Jon hopped his way down the slope, relieved that the wind's strength lessened with each step. By the time he reached the boulders the bottoms of his trousers were completely soaked, but only a strong breeze remained.

Keeping away from the stream of water flowing down the middle of the shallow ravine, he could now see the grit-stone rocks were shaped in a rough semi-circle, the ones in the middle a good four feet high. The soil at their base was riddled with hoof prints and Jon spotted tufts of white in the small growths of heather. The shivering fragments of fleece contrasted with the purple flowers that clung to the tops of the plant. A small glimpse of beauty in such a desolate place.

'As you can see, sheep use this as a spot to shelter in. She'd parked the quad bike where I've left it and clambered down here on foot. Hobson reckons the panther was lying in wait for a sheep on top of these rocks. Maybe Rose heard it bleating with distress and knew it was being attacked. Anyway, her body was lying right here.' Clegg pointed to a spot where the rocks on one side of the miniature amphitheatre ended.

Jon took a deep breath and looked around. I hate to admit this, he thought, but if a panther exists, it's a perfect spot to ambush a sheep 'And there were no paw prints found in the peat?' he asked, crouching down to examine the ground.

'With the storm that night, there weren't prints of any kind.'

Jon rubbed the back of his neck. The attack had taken place

too long ago, there was nothing for him here. 'Shall we head back before my bollocks freeze off?'

'Right you are.'

After making their way back up the slope, they climbed on to the quad bike. Jon tapped his colleague on the shoulder. 'I was just wondering. How near are we to where Brady and Hindley buried those children?'

Adam Clegg's shoulders visibly slumped. 'I was wondering when you'd ask.'

He started up the bike and drove across a couple of ridges before pulling up next to a cairn on the highest crest. 'This is the top of Black Hill, which is, strictly speaking, part of Wessenden Head Moor.'

'How big is the moorland?'

'I don't know, thousands of acres if you include Marsden Moor as well.' He pointed west. 'Saddleworth Moor is over there. That's where they found three of them. The body of the lad is still buried out here somewhere, God bless his soul.'

As Jon looked out across the silent land he knew it wasn't the wind that was causing the hairs on the back of his neck to rise. Wild and bleak as it was, the place had a strange kind of allure, there was no denying it. With a shudder he turned his head to stare down at the relatively flat land stretched out far below. The density of buildings slowly increased until a cluster of tower blocks, chimneys and cranes were visible in the distance. Manchester. Beyond it the air grew grey and hazy.

'Rain moving in off the Irish Sea,' Clegg announced. 'It'll be here in another half hour or so.'

Jon stared at the floating veil, thinking about the water saturating the ground beneath them and how it drained into the little streams that, over thousands of years, had carved narrow ravines in the slopes.

Looking again at the plains below he remembered a geography lesson from school. Something about the number of rivers that ran through Manchester on their way to the coast. Unsure why he thought it important, he leaned forwards. 'All these streams that run off the moors . . . '

'Cloughs is what they're called.'

'Cloughs then. They eventually turn into rivers, right?'

'Of course. The Etherow, Goyt, Tame and Medlock. They all rise on these moors. Apart from the Medlock, they converge at Stockport to form the Mersey. That's why the area below is known as the Mersey basin.'

'Where does the Medlock lead?'

'Right into the centre of Manchester. I think it eventually merges with the Manchester Ship Canal at Salford.'

A collection of black shreds suddenly scored the mottled greyness above them. Jon looked up at the crows as they traversed the sky in an unnaturally straight line. Instead of trying to fight the current of air, the birds were passively allowing themselves to be swept along, heads angled at the men below. Then, with an invisible adjustment of their wings, they plummeted as one, disappearing beyond the contours of the moor. Jon wondered if they were the same birds found feeding on Mrs Sutton's corpse. Pushing the thought away, he tried to focus on what Adam had just told him. The information seemed significant somehow, but the constant buffeting of the wind was giving him a headache and when Clegg turned the handlebars to begin the bumpy ride back to Far Gethen farm, he didn't complain.

Thirteen

They slowed to a stop in front of the barn and Jon climbed off the quad bike. While Adam drove it slowly back inside, he examined his feet. Smeared black earth clung to the sides of his shoes and fragments of gorse were caught in the soaking laces.

'OK,' said Adam, hanging the keys back on the hook. 'You'd like a word with Ken?'

They walked across the courtyard to the front door of the farmhouse. Adam knocked loudly on the heavy wooden door then opened it. The kitchen was pretty much as Jon had expected – flagstone floor, chunky wooden table and an ancient Aga with tea towels and oven gloves draped over its front rail.

A Welsh dresser stood opposite Jon and he noticed the pair of walkie-talkies standing upright in a base unit, battery lights glowing as they recharged. The shelves above were lined with plates painted with images of foxhunts. Hounds raced across landscapes, horses vaulted hedges and, in one, a stag was being brought down in the shallows of a river, eyes wide with terror.

'In here.' Ken's voice came from further inside the house.

Seeing Adam removing his boots, Jon crouched down and took his shoes off, realising his socks were totally saturated. They crossed the kitchen and Jon glanced back to see a trail of glistening footprints behind him.

The doorway led straight into a large living room, where an enormous fire crackled away in the hearth. Apart from the weak light filtering through the windows, the flames provided the room's only illumination.

Sutton was sitting in an armchair before the fire, dark lines etched into his weary face. A mug was balanced in one hand, curls of steam rising above the rim. 'There's tea in the pot.'

'Jon? You want a cup?' asked Adam.

'Please. Chuck in a couple of sugars too,' Jon replied, glancing up at the animal heads lining the walls. There must have been a dozen foxes, a few badgers and several varieties of deer, some with antlers, others without.

Adam went back into the kitchen and Jon turned to Sutton who was staring impassively at the fire. Wondering where the younger man with the rifle was, Jon pointed to the armchair opposite. 'Mind if I sit down?'

Ken grunted and Jon took it as a yes. Taking out his notebook and pen, he eased himself into the seat, trying to keep his sodden socks from view by tucking his feet under the chair. Waves of heat began pushing against his face and he hoped the warmth would soon work its way down to his frozen shins and ankles.

'So you've seen the moor,' Sutton stated, eyes still on the flames.

'Yes. It's certainly an unforgiving place. I'm sorry you had to find your wife up there.'

'Oh, she didn't mind it. The place has a strange kind of beauty.'

Maybe if you're hiking over it occasionally, Jon thought. But that's bloody it. 'Your wife, Mr Sutton. Aside from helping you out on the farm, what else did she do with her time?'

Sutton turned his head towards him. The rims of his eyes were red and emotion played at the corners of his mouth before he spoke. 'She did more than help out. She ran this bloody place.'

Jon's pen remained at the top of a blank page. 'With your help?'

'I do what I can, which is less and less these days.'

'What about children?'

Sutton shook his head. 'We married late. Maybe that's why we were never blessed.'

'So who helps out now?'

Sutton tilted his head to the window. 'There're lads on neighbouring farms. People pitch in for lambing. We look out for each other.'

Jon couldn't see him running the farm for much longer. He wondered if the old man would stay in the farmhouse once he was forced to sell off the land. 'The man who was in your jeep. Is he from a neighbouring farm?'

Adam reappeared with the tea, handed a cup to Jon and sat down on the sofa.

Sutton nodded. 'A neighbour, yes.'

'So your wife. How would you describe your marriage? Did it have its ups and downs?'

'Of course. Doesn't yours?'

Jon imagined Alice's reaction when he mentioned he was working on another murder investigation. It's about to, he thought. 'Did you argue much?'

Sutton gave a sigh that combined exhaustion and frustration. 'Listen, lad, I don't know what your job involves and I don't think you know mine. But let me tell you, running a farm like this is hard. You have to work as a team to keep on top. There's no packing up at the end of the day to catch the train home. So we'd argue sometimes, but we were a bloody good team, Rose and me. A bloody good team.'

Jon spotted a glistening in the man's eyes as he turned back to the dancing flames. 'Did she have any outside interests? Friends or social groups for instance?'

'She knew everyone in the area. We'd go for drinks some nights in the village.'

'I'm sure you've been asked this, but what about people she'd fallen out with?'

'Rose? She was friends with everyone.' There was a defensive note in his voice. 'Adam, you tell him. Friends with everyone she was.'

Jon glanced at his colleague who gave a silent nod. 'Adam mentioned she worked in a nursery before you married. Did she stay in contact with her former workmates?'

'She'd see them every now and again, I suppose.'

'At their houses or just crossing paths in the village?'

'I don't know. Both. If there was a birthday or something. She'd go for the odd meal with friends and old colleagues. They're one and the same, I suppose.'

'These sheep you've been losing – could Rose have had an argument with any dog owners crossing your land?'

Sutton held up a finger. 'It's no dog that's been killing our sheep. I can save you time by telling you that for certain.'

The anger bubbling in his throat encouraged Jon to pursue the subject. 'Can you be certain of that?'

'When a dog worries sheep, it tries to snap at their legs. If it latches onto a limb it might rip the flesh by shaking its head from side to side.'

Jon's mind went to the image of the terrified stag on the plate in the kitchen. The cluster of dogs hanging off it.

'Creates a certain type of wound,' Sutton continued. 'Messy. It doesn't jump on to a sheep's back and then bite through the top of their spine. And it doesn't then eat half the animal either.'

'Have you had problems with dogs worrying your sheep then?'

'A few.'

'The most recent?'

'Early last spring. An idiot couple with an Alsatian. Two ewes miscarried.'

'You spoke to these people?'

'Oh, I was for more than speaking to them.' He pointed to a metal cabinet in the corner. 'If Rose hadn't stopped me, I'd have shot that bloody dog.'

'So what happened?'

'They paid for the lambs.'

'Did you get involved in this?' asked Jon, turning to Adam.

'No, I didn't. How did they pay you Ken?'

'Cash of course. Rose spoke to them. I was too angry for words.'

'Did you get their names or anything?'

'No.'

'Were they local?' Jon asked.

'Of course not. Day trippers they were. From a city I should think.'

We'll never trace them, Jon thought. 'Have you ever had to shoot a dog, Ken?'

'Once. About eight year ago.'

Jon saw Ken's eyes connect briefly with Adam's once again. These two are sharing a lot of information I don't know about.

Adam coughed. 'Ken had to shoot a Collie. It was all properly documented, the report will be at the station.'

'And the dog's owners? Who were they?' Jon asked.

Adam shrugged. 'I don't know.'

Jesus Christ, Jon thought. 'Well, we'd better dig that file out. I take it the owners weren't too happy?'

'No they weren't.' Sutton smirked and Jon saw cruelty in the twist of his lips. 'I gave them a sack to carry the animal's body in. Saved the boot of their car from getting covered with blood.'

Jon glanced at the gun cabinet. 'So what sort of weapons are in there?'

Sutton placed his mug on the hearth. 'I own a Browning twelve-bore shotgun and a Ruger point twenty-two rifle.'

'License for the shotgun and firearms certificate for the rifle?'

Sutton looked at him as if he was stupid. 'Of course. Shall I fetch them from the kitchen?'

Adam gave another cough. 'Ken's just put in an application at the station for a Remington two four three-calibre hunting rifle.'

More information emerging only when it has to, Jon thought. 'Two rifles? What's wrong with just the one?' he asked Sutton.

'I use the twenty-two for vermin control. Rats and the odd fox, mainly. But I've been having problems with a few deer lately. They can cause a lot of damage, so I need something with more range and power.'

'And this Remington will give you that?'

'It will,' Sutton replied.

Jon sat back. 'The man you were with earlier. Was he carrying the twenty-two rifle?'

'No, that was his own weapon.'

Jon didn't like the fact that several guns were being kept on the farm. 'Is it licensed?'

'Of course. And, as the land owner, I've granted him full permission to discharge it anywhere in the areas designated by my firearms certificate.'

'Which are?'

'The area immediately surrounding the farm and the upper moor land.'

Jon tapped the pen against the top of his notebook. The heat from the fire was now getting uncomfortable and he swivelled his knees away from the flames. 'I presume this hunting rifle you're applying for would also be big enough to bring down a panther if you happened to spot one?'

Sutton breathed in slowly through his nose, as if considering the possibility for the first time. 'I suppose it would.'

You're a crap actor, thought Jon. 'You seem certain a panther is killing your sheep, Mr Sutton, despite any actual evidence.'

Jon watched as he passed a hand over his lips. 'Something's killing them. Something that doesn't belong in this country.'

Strange, Jon thought. That sounded like a touch of nervousness. 'And you believe the same creature killed your wife?'

Sutton sat up in his seat. 'What else did, man? Tell me, what else did?'

Jon kept his expression neutral. 'I aim to find out.'

Looking disgusted, Sutton turned away and muttered, 'Well, you won't do that warming your socks in front of my fire.'

Jon looked down to see curls of steam rising from his wet feet. Shit, I must look like a right fool. He shifted in his seat again. 'The nature of the bite marks on your dead sheep. Did you observe those yourself or were they pointed out to you by a third party?'

'You mean Hobson? He showed them to me, yes.'

'Has he been to your farm much?'

'Every time we find a dead sheep, even if it's just a scattering of bones.'

'You'd take him to the remains each time?'

'Rose would usually. She was fascinated by the whole thing.'

Another bloody link Adam forgot to mention, thought Jon. 'So Hobson and your wife were quite well acquainted?'

Sutton stared at him. 'What are you suggesting by that?'

'Nothing,' Jon replied. 'I'm trying to ascertain who knew your wife, that's all.'

Sutton glanced at the clock on the wall. 'Is that it? It will be dark soon. I've got to burl those ewes.'

'One last thing. Does the name Derek Peterson mean anything to you?' Jon watched the man's face carefully, but spotted nothing as Sutton replied that it didn't. He closed his notebook and they all stood. 'Thanks very much for your time.'

Sutton flexed his knees a couple of times before walking stiffly towards the door. In the kitchen he started climbing into his waterproof trousers as Jon reluctantly slid his now warm feet back into his cold and soaking shoes. Adam put on his boots and opened the door. Cold air rushed in and Jon saw the light was beginning to fade.

'What do you want to do next?' Adam asked as they walked towards their vehicles.

Jon's eyes strayed to the sheep watching them from the corner of the pen, their muzzles seeming to smoulder in the rapidly chilling air. 'Have a word with you, but not here,' Jon murmured. 'Let's stop at the top of the lane.'

'OK,' Adam replied cautiously.

They waved goodbye to Sutton who briefly held a hand up in return as he strode over to the barn. What a life, Jon thought, watching him in his rear-view mirror as he drove away.

At the end of the track to Sutton's farm Jon pulled over and got out. Adam came to a halt and Jon got into the jeep. 'You didn't tell me Hobson knew Rose Sutton.'

Adam raised his eyebrows. 'It slipped my mind. To be honest, I thought you knew.'

'How the hell would I?'

'That's a good question, now I think about it. Sorry.'

Did it slip your mind deliberately or are you just slow? Jon wondered. 'I thought Sutton's behaviour was odd.'

'How do you mean?' Adam started adjusting the fan vent on the dashboard.

'When I mentioned the possibility of a panther just now, it really unsettled him. He almost seemed scared I thought.'

'Scared? Wary, maybe. It killed his wife after all.'

Jon shot him a glance.

'I mean, he believes a panther killed his wife,' Adam hastily corrected himself.

'I'm not sure. He looked like he was sweating it a bit. You're happy with his alibi? What was it, some sheep market up in the Lake District?'

'Yes, he was staying at a hotel in Keswick.'

'Statistically we're always best off looking at immediate family in murder cases.'

Clegg shook his head. 'He can't have done it. There are plenty of witnesses who saw him stagger off to his room at gone two in the morning. Totally pissed apparently, and his bar bill backs that up. Next day he was down for breakfast at seven sharp. To get from Keswick to here and back again in under five hours is practically impossible.'

'Practically, but not totally.'

'No, but then he'd have had to get Rose up on to the moor, kill her, tidy himself up and set off back to Keswick. Not possible in the time he had.'

'What about the other guy? The one with the rifle. Do you know him?'

Adam shook his head again. 'I only saw him from behind as he was walking towards the farm house.'

'Sutton said he was a neighbour.'

'Not from any farm I'm familiar with.'

'There are too many people roaming around with hunting rifles. It's an accident waiting to happen, especially with everyone so on edge. Can you find out who that bloke is and if he has a license for that gun?'

'Will do.'

'And keep back approval for Sutton's application for that Remington hunting rifle.'

'It's already been signed off.'

Jon's eyes narrowed. 'It's obvious he doesn't want that rifle for culling any deer.' Adam shrugged again and Jon's suspicions moved up a notch. 'I'd like to speak with Rose's friends as well. Someone is hiding something. I know Sutton said they were a good team, but there's more to a marriage than that. Maybe she was having an affair. There was a bit of an age gap between them, and no kids either. When I mentioned another person being killed this morning, he was concerned to know the person's age. Perhaps there's something in that.'

He watched as Adam continued to fiddle with the fins of the heating vent.

What's on your mind? Jon wondered, sensing undisclosed information in the silence. 'Adam, if you've got anything to say about this that is relevant to the investigation, now is the time.'

Keeping his eyes averted, the other man shook his head.

This is your last chance, mate, Jon thought. 'You're sure?'

Their eyes met. 'Yes, absolutely.'

Bollocks, thought Jon, you're lying. His immediate reaction was to cut him from any further involvement in the investigation. Then he remembered the saying about keeping your friends close and your enemies closer. What was Clegg? Deciding it would be better to keep an eye on him, he said, 'And can you find the file on that dog he shot? I'd like the owners traced, interviewed and eliminated. In an ideal world, I'd like the same for the owners of that Alsatian, though God knows how we'll ever find them.'

'So what's the next step in the investigation?'

Jon could tell the other man was worried that his role in the case was about to evaporate. 'I need to get back to my nick and report to the boss. We'll be setting up an incident room at Longsight for Peterson's death, but I'd like to keep your room at Mossley Brow open too. Can you continue acting as my point of contact here?'

Adam looked relieved. 'With pleasure.'

'It's going to be necessary to start moving the files, photographs and records on Rose Sutton over to Longsight. I'll get an indexer to start putting everything we have on her into HOLMES.'

Adam looked disappointed.

'We have to work these cases side by side,' Jon explained. 'It's the only way to uncover whatever links Peterson to Mrs Sutton.'

'I know,' Adam replied, looking out the window towards the road as it dropped down into the tiny village of Holme. 'I need to drop by at my sister's. Which way are you driving back?'

Jon ducked his head so he could see the summit of the moors through the windscreen. 'That's the quickest way isn't it?'

Adam nodded. 'Yup. Best you set off now while there's still some light left.'

'What, beware the moon and all that?' Jon grinned.

The serious look remained on Adam's face. 'It's just a long walk down if you get a puncture. Reception from your mobile comes and goes up there, remember?'

'Fair enough. I'll be in contact soon.' Jon climbed out, got back into his own car and set off up the steep road. On reaching the level ground at the top, he could see the sun was now just a faint smudge of órange on the western horizon. There wasn't a single other car in sight and suddenly he felt very small as he crossed the empty terrain. After a few minutes he reached the other side of the plateau and was surprised to feel relief at the sight of the pooled lights of Manchester twinkling away below.

His mobile phone started beeping away in his pocket. Jon realised he'd had no signal for the past three hours and he quickly fished it out of his jacket. The voicemail symbol was flashing so he pressed the button that connected him to his messages.

Summerby's voice immediately came on the line. 'Jon, you might want to get back here at some stage. Apparently you promised a press conference this afternoon and we now have a shoal of reporters circling in reception. The press liaison officer would be pulling his hair out – if he had any.'

Fourteen

Adam Clegg watched Jon Spicer's rear lights grow faint as the vehicle laboured away up the hill. His finger continued to pick nervously at the slats on the air conditioning vent as a succession of thoughts ran through his head. Spicer knew he was being evasive – the way the atmosphere had just tightened between them was unmistakable. Clegg leaned his head to the side, weighing up how the obvious loss of trust may have damaged their working relationship. Not too badly it appeared, since he was still on the investigation.

He let out a sigh of relief, his breath fogging the side window like ice spreading across water. At least he could continue to exert some control on what the glare of the investigation revealed, subtly guiding its light from the areas he needed to remain in shadow.

Putting the car back into gear, he turned left and followed the steep road as it plunged down into the tiny village of Holme. The narrow rows of dark stone houses clung to the sloping side streets, many of which were still cobbled. Parked vehicles rested unevenly on their suspensions, as if an earthquake had been frozen in the act of buckling the road. Clegg followed the twisting high street, his eyes gliding over a pub called The Old Tup, a couple of tea rooms clearing up for the night, a closed butcher's and newsagent's, then finally the brightly lit interior of the small tourist office. He spotted his sister standing alone as usual behind the counter. From her expressionless stare, he wondered if dusk had made it impossible for her to see through the windows on to the street beyond.

He pulled into the half deserted Co-op car park, listening to the sound of a babbling brook as he walked to the rear of the tourist office. A bell jangled briefly on opening the back door and the smell of freshly printed paper filled his nostrils. On racks and shelves beside him were neat stacks of photocopied sheets – areas of local interest, walks in the surrounding countryside, summaries of the village's history – including accounts of the great flood of 1936 that washed many of the original weavers' cottages away down the valley.

He emerged from the rear of the premises into the front room where, alongside the ordnance survey maps and glossy National Park guide books were pencils, rulers, rubbers and other small items, all bearing a ram's horn emblem and the words, *Holme of the weavers' art.*

'Adam, I wondered if that was your jeep going past just now.' His older sister's blue eyes twinkled as she smiled, her hands going to the back of her head to adjust the band keeping her frizzy brown hair in its ponytail. 'What brings you over the hill?'

Adam gave a half smile, unable to keep the worry from his eyes. 'We need to have a chat, Edith. Are you closing up soon?'

She glanced at the door, concern now making her eyebrows tilt. 'I doubt we'll get anyone coming in now. What's happened?'

Adam moved across the room and positioned himself in the corner by the till, out of sight from the street. The familiar reassurance he felt in the company of his older sister flooded him and he started speaking quickly, keen to unload all his anxieties on to her. 'There's been some developments in the investigation into Rose's death. Someone else was killed this morning and now there's an officer from the Major Incident Team in Manchester sniffing around. He's linking both deaths and moving the investigation to the city, proper incident room, team of officers on outside enquiries. They'll be going into Rose's life . . . '

His sister held up a finger and the rush of words died in his throat. She took the set of keys lying by the side of the till, walked over to the front door, locked it and flipped the sign over to *Closed.*

'Now,' she said, a firm note in her voice. 'Start again and take it slowly this time. 'What do you mean someone else has been killed?'

'Some bloke from Manchester. A car park queer.'

She shook her head in question.

'You know, one of them who hangs around in public places looking for other men. Toilets and that.' His mouth was turned downwards in disgust.

'And he was killed. Why are they linking it to Rose?'

'His injuries. They were the same,' he replied, gesturing towards his neck.

His sister's hand went to her throat and she pinched the neck of her blouse closed. 'Oh my God.' Her eyes drifted to the side, then turned back to her brother. 'Who was this man?'

'He was called Derek Peterson.' Adam let the name hang. Not seeing anything register on her face, he continued. 'He was in his forties, lived in Clayton on the edge of the city. Worked in a care home for young offenders, but got convicted for gross indecency. There's no way Rose knew him, is there?'

Slowly, Edith turned her head from side to side. 'I don't think so. Surely the investigation will soon discover that?'

'You don't understand the way this is going to work, Edie. They'll delve into every aspect of Rose's life, rake through it all. The officer who turned up today is already talking about re-interviewing all Rose's family, friends and acquaintances. Not just the friendly chats I've carried out. They'll be knocking on your door, no doubt about it.'

'Wanting to know what?'

'Any secrets she might have had. Searching for motive. Reasons why someone might have killed her.'

'Someone? What happened to the beast that's been taking Sutton's sheep?'

'He's refusing to accept that. Says it has to be treated as murder.'

'He? Who is this damned he?'

'He's a Detective Inspector called Jon Spicer.'

'What's he like?'

Adam inserted the tip of a knuckle between his teeth and began to gently nip at it as he contemplated an answer.

'Stop it,' Edith snapped, slapping his hand down. 'How many times have I told you not to do that?'

He looked at her with the hurt eyes of a chastised schoolboy. 'He's no fool Edie. God knows what courses he's been on, but this is the sort of case he's been trained for. He already knows I haven't been totally straight with him.'

Edith crossed her arms. 'You stupid fool, Adam Clegg.'

'I think Ken has his suspicions too,' Adam added miserably.

'Why?'

'You know what Ken's like, man of few words. But when Spicer told him about the man who was killed last night, he suddenly seemed interested. Wanted to know the victim's age and description. Spicer picked up on it too, even asked me later if Rose could have been seeing another man.'

Edith rolled her eyes. 'Why I ever let you two involve me in your stupidity,' she hissed. 'You'll have to tell this Spicer person the truth then, won't you?'

Adam let out a bitter laugh. 'And have Ken Sutton find out I was having an affair with his wife?'

'Why would he find out?'

'Gossip, it always leaks out sooner or later.'

'So what do you propose? Keep playing it your way and risk ruining your entire career? And what about me? You're asking me to lie to a police officer too. I could go to prison for that couldn't I? Impeding a murder investigation. I let you two meet in my house for God's sake. What if someone saw something?'

'Edie, she always walked there remember? I'd leave by the front, she'd leave by the back and go across the fields to the village where her car was parked. No one ever saw a thing.' He knew his sister couldn't argue – if anyone saw anything, word would have got out by now.

'You still haven't told me what you think we should do.'

'Just tell them who Rose was friendly with. Make out the marriage was fine. Don't give them any cause to suspect anything.'

'I don't know, Adam. This is all sliding out of control.'

'Edith! You can't tell them the truth about me and Rose. If Sutton finds out . . . God knows what he's capable of.'

She looked back at him, her expression giving nothing away.

'Edie, come on. Apart from a heart of ice, the guy's got

several guns. I remembered something today as a result of a question Spicer asked. You know that time a few years back when Ken killed the dog worrying his sheep? His first barrel only peppered the animal's back legs. Sutton then admitted he walked up to it and emptied the other barrel point blank into its head. He then tied it to the bumper of his Land Rover and dragged it across the field to the owners. The couple were totally distraught, insisted he was grinning as he did it.'

She stayed silent for a while before reluctantly nodding. 'So I cover up for you. What then?'

'When they can't find anything on her, they'll focus the investigation on where it should be.'

'You mean catching the beast?'

He glanced at the now black windows, towards the darkness beyond. 'Exactly. Catching that bloody thing out there.'

Fifteen

Jon slowed down as he passed the main entrance to Longsight police station. Holy shit, there was a TV crew there. As he tried to spot anything that would indicate whether it was from a local or national station, he saw an arm pointing in his direction. That blonde from the car park at Crime Lake. The photographer with her started turning, a camera going up to his face.

Jon accelerated round the corner, relieved to pull into the staff entrance at the side of the building. Not pausing at his office, he made his way straight up to Summerby's room. Gavin Edwards, the Press Liaison Officer, was inside. He was five foot-six at most and Jon couldn't decide what caused the guy most angst – his lack of height or his rapidly disappearing hair. He'd come from a London newsroom where they evidently thought each day was an episode of *24*. If things weren't tense enough, Edwards would manufacture it so they were. Nervously, he peered down at the throng of people on the pavement below.

'Ah, Jon, here at last,' Summerby said with a theatrical flick of his eyes towards Edwards.

As if on cue, the other man whirled round. 'This is the big one, Jon. Once it goes out on the wire we can expect interest from across the world.'

That's DI Spicer to twats like you, Jon thought. 'Yeah, sorry for the delay. I was visiting a farm, didn't realise there was no signal there.'

'On the moor where Mrs Sutton was found?' Edwards asked, eyes shining.

Jon could see the connections coming together in the man's head. 'That's right. And yes, the injuries from both victims match and no, I don't believe we have a savage beast out there slaughtering people.'

'But surely . . . ' Edwards began.

Jon cut him off. 'Boss, what were the results from the PM?'

Summerby drummed his fingers on the armrest of his chair, making a sound like a horse galloping. 'He's typing up as we speak, but he said all his findings concur with his analysis at the scene. Time of death sometime between midnight and four in the morning. Oh, and from the angle of the lacerations on both sides of his face and neck, he believes the attacker was carrying a multi-pronged weapon in each hand.'

An image of a beast standing up on its hind legs and lashing out with both its front paws flashed in Jon's head. 'Did we track down a next of kin?'

'Yes, the body was cleaned up and an ID was made by his brother half an hour ago. Confirmed as one Derek Peterson.'

Jon sat down. 'This wild animal theory is going to be a major problem. There's a supposed expert in big cat behaviour helping out at Mossley Brow nick. He's taking it for granted a panther killed Rose Sutton and Derek Peterson. If the press link the two incidents together, interest levels are going to go through the roof. I'd prefer to play down the Peterson killing.' He heard Edwards snort. 'We've got a couple of sensitive leads on Derek Peterson. They link into the gay scene and if the press go steaming in we could lose them.'

'So what do you propose?' Summerby asked.

'Is Peterson's brother still here?'

'Yes, there's a counsellor with him.'

'If we can make sure he's kept away from the press, I can issue a statement that just covers the basics without giving away Peterson's identity.'

'They won't be satisfied with that. You'll have to toss them something,' Edwards butted in.

Jon didn't bother looking at him. 'Maybe if I hint at an imminent development and ask them for a bit of restraint.'

'What sort of imminent development?' Edwards again.

You flying out of this fucking window, Jon thought, finally turning his eyes to the press officer. 'I'll let you know when I think of it,' he replied, praying something would come of Rick's appeal on Swinger's Haven.

Edwards looked incredulous. 'Stories this juicy don't crop up every day. Their editors down in the big smoke will be screaming for something.'

The big smoke, Jon sneered to himself. If you're so in awe of London, why don't you piss off back down there. 'I'm not releasing some half-baked observations that risk blowing this panther thing out of all proportion. We can buy more time if we say the victim hasn't been formally identified. At least that way we can delay conjecture about the two deaths being linked. What do you think, boss?'

'We can get away with saying the next of kin hasn't been located, but only for a while. Just don't forget it's a two-way thing with the press, Jon. They can help as well as hinder.'

'Agreed.' Jon stood up. 'I'll get it over with then.' As he headed back down the stairs he could hear Edwards hurrying to catch him.

'I've set things up in meeting room two. Want me to show them in?'

'OK.' Jon watched the other man as he rushed off towards reception. Jon ducked into the toilets and looked at himself in the mirror. Shit, I look knackered. He massaged the skin below his eyes in the vain hope of removing the dark smudges seemingly ingrained there. Summerby was right, this investigation was going to be conducted under a very bright spotlight. The fluorescent strips glared down at him and he knew how a rabbit must feel. 'Come on, Spicer, you'll be fine,' he murmured, straightening his tie. Remembering the media awareness course he'd recently completed, he reached for a hand towel to wipe the dampness from his forehead, knowing it would look like a layer of grease on the TV screen.

As he walked into the room all noise quickly died away. Edwards had been busy. At the end of the room a collection of screens bearing the logo for Greater Manchester Police had been erected. A lectern stood waiting for him, microphones for several radio stations already clipped to it. Jon walked to the front of the room and tapped them with a finger. 'Can we have these mikes and all tape recorders off, please? Those too,' he said, looking into the video camera lenses that were trained on him.

Satisfied his instructions had been followed, he surveyed the room, trying to impose an air of authority. 'Right, before my official comments, a quick word.' Hands paused on writing pads. 'I know you all, quite literally, scent blood on this one; however, I'm appealing for some leeway here. We'll keep you up to date on everything, but until certain avenues have been followed up we need the details of this morning's killing minimised. I'll explain why as soon as possible. Can I expect your cooperation with this?'

Sideways glances were exchanged.

'Why? Is today's victim special?' an older guy at the back asked.

'It appears he was frequenting places used by homosexual men for casual sex. If this becomes a focal point of your reports we risk losing potential witnesses.'

'And this car park at Crime Lake is one such place?'

'Yes.'

'Surely that will be common knowledge?'

'Only to those on the scene, not to the general public. It will help us if things stay that way. You know how this works – any appeal for witnesses will draw a blank if you're all splashing the fact it's a dogging site. Some restraint then, ladies and gents?'

More glances were exchanged and a ripple of reluctant nods slowly spread across the room. Seizing the opportunity, Jon nodded to a cameraman. 'OK – to proceed with my statement.' He heard a slight crackle as the mikes came back on. Put your hands behind your back, he thought, knowing the stance imparted a more measured appearance. Keeping his head still and eyes trained on a point just above the reporters staring at him, he announced, 'My name is DI Spicer and I work for Greater Manchester Police's Major Incident Team. At seven forty-five this morning, the body of a middle-aged Caucasian man was discovered in a car park by Daisy Nook Country Park. From injuries found on the body, the death is being treated as suspicious at this stage. Until a post mortem has been carried out and a formal identification made, I cannot comment further. Any witnesses are urged to contact the incident room at Longsight police station.'

He took a step to the side, suddenly wishing the exit wasn't at the other end of the room as a clamour of disappointed voices rang out.

'Is it true the victim's torso was severely lacerated?'

'Does this carry the hallmarks of an attack by a wild animal?'

'Are you linking this to the killing of Mrs Sutton up on Saddleworth Moor?'

Bollocks, thought Jon. He turned to them once again. Holding up both hands, he said, 'As you can understand, I cannot comment further until the victim's family have been informed. However, at this stage we're not linking the death of Mrs Sutton with this morning's incident.'

There was a pause as over a dozen reporters mentally dissected this. None looked convinced.

'OK everyone,' Gavin Edwards said, taking the stage. 'I'll be issuing a press release within the next half hour. Updates will also be available on the voice bank; for those reporters not from Manchester the telephone number will be on my press release.'

Jon made it to the door and started hurrying away down the corridor. A woman's voice called out behind him. 'So there'll be no need to visit the moors where Mrs Sutton died?'

Jon recognised the voice. That bloody woman from the *Manchester Evening Chronicle*. Carmel something. He tried to wave the question away. 'That's correct.'

'So why do you have peat and bits of heather on the bottoms of your trousers and shoes? Surely you've been up to Saddleworth Moor already?'

He looked down. Fuck, he'd forgotten his shoes were filthy. He reached for the handle of the nearest door. To his relief it opened on an empty meeting room. 'In here.'

She hurried inside, failing to hide the pleased look on her face. Shutting the door, he turned to her. She was almost a foot smaller than him, but she didn't flinch at his most menacing stare.

'DI Spicer, the Red Tops are sending teams up from London. The *Mail*'s already here, desperate to find out where today's victim lived so they can start door to doors on his street. Now I know he had injuries to his face and neck, and you've just pretty much confirmed to me that you've been up on to Saddleworth Moor. My news editor expects me to deliver first on this one. It's my patch. I have the local contacts. If a Red Top beats me to the story, my job's on the line. Why shouldn't I go with this information?'

'How did you find out about his injuries?'

She shook her head. 'I'm sorry.'

Jon scrutinised her and she kept looking right back. She's got balls, he thought, his respect for her growing. 'If you print those details, I'll see you're barred from every news conference I ever hold.'

He saw her stance soften slightly and he knew she'd picked up on the hollow ring in his voice. 'DI Spicer, if I lose my job, you wouldn't need to bar me from future conferences. What am I supposed to do?'

Jon let his shoulders relax a little too. 'You tell me.'

'How about a deal?'

'Go on.'

'I keep back what I know, you give me an exclusive interview with the family of this morning's victim.'

'I said in my briefing, we haven't identified him yet.'

She gave him a look and Jon knew she didn't believe his lie. He weighed up the offer, knowing he was in a corner. 'OK, you're on.' He reached for the door.

'Hang on,' she said. 'When do I get it?'

'At a time to be determined by me.'

'Tomorrow.'

He stopped. 'You what?'

'Tomorrow.'

Christ, she was hard. 'The guy's just had to take a long look at what was left of his brother. He's with a counsellor as we speak.'

Her eyes gleamed. 'That bad, was it?'

'That bad. You're not talking to him tomorrow. He's been instructed not to deal with anyone from the press and I intend to post an officer at his house to make sure of it. When the time's right you get your interview, OK?'

She held up a finger. 'But it's got to be morning. Lunch time at the latest, so we have it for the morning edition the next day.'

'Fine.' Jon opened the door, feeling that he'd just been fleeced. She pressed a card into his hand and marched off down the corridor.

'Well, I've seen better dealings with the press,' Edwards sighed, up in Summerby's office.

Jon could feel that his face was still flushed from the encounter. He looked at Edwards, thinking, you don't even know about the exclusive interview I've just promised. 'OK, I underestimated how desperate they were for information. Promising to keep them in the loop has worked for me before.'

'With the local press, yes. This lot aren't so easy to deal with,' Edwards said.

I realise that now, Jon thought. 'What do you reckon they'll be saying tomorrow morning?'

Edwards crossed his legs and tipped his head back, drawing out the moment. 'Hard to say. You tried to palm them off and they won't like that. Depends on the editor in charge of each paper, but it's best we assume the worst. The Monster slays another, that sort of thing. Maybe even, Panther slays, police delays.'

Jon fired a glance at him, looking for any visible signs he was being sarcastic, but Edwards kept a straight face and Jon turned to Summerby who was looking far from amused. 'OK. So it's a case of damage limitation. Jon, there's no point hoping this panther theory is going away. It could even divert attention away from Peterson's car park liaisons if the press are marching around up on the moors. Maybe we mention this Hobson fellow, say he's advising us on the possibility of it being an ABC, to use the correct terminology.' He gave a quick cough at Jon's inquisitive glance. 'Alien Big Cat. I've been on the web, there's certainly a load of stuff about the things.'

Jon looked down at his knuckles. 'I'm reluctant to involve the man. He seems to be taking a strange delight in events, and I wouldn't mind betting he'll be raising the admission price at his zoo pretty damn soon.'

'Be that as it may, we can't stop the press taking the most sensational approach possible. And assuming a person carried out the attacks, it could help us if he thinks we think it was a panther.'

'Or it may encourage him to strike again,' Jon stated. 'He's obviously staging things to make it appear that way. We may feed his desire to repeat the performance.'

Summerby shrugged. 'Anyway, we can't control the headlines. So, next steps?'

Jon was about to answer when there was a knock at the door. Hearing it open, he looked over his shoulder. No, he thought. This is all I fucking need.

McCloughlin stepped into the room. 'Gentlemen.' His eyes cut straight past Jon to Summerby. 'I gather we have quite an incident on our hands.'

Summerby nodded. 'DI Spicer attended the crime scene this morning and has met with the officer in charge of the Sutton investigation out at Mossley Brow. He was just about to outline the next steps he was going to take.'

McCloughlin was pacing up and down the side of the room, head lowered and tongue running across his lips. Jon thought of a hyena circling the kill. 'So, DI Spicer. What are you going to do next?'

Jon sat upright and directed his answer at Summerby. 'Sir, the contents of all the bins have been seized and the collection of refuse from the area around Crime Lake has been suspended. Officers are searching the edge of the field for any sign of the weapon. A crime scene manager is overseeing a fingertip search of the car park and he'll be reporting back with any finds tomorrow morning. After this meeting, I'll initiate proceedings to obtain Peterson's bank, credit card and telephone details, and I've posted a uniform at the door of his house. First thing tomorrow we'll go in, search the premises and complete an inventory. We'll also talk to neighbours and friends to map out his last twenty-four hours.'

'Yeah, yeah,' McCloughlin said. 'So you've covered off the standard first actions for a major incident. What about other stuff?'

Reluctantly, Jon turned to his former SIO. 'What other stuff?'

McCloughlin stopped in his tracks. 'Reacting to the particular circumstances of this case. The body was found by a frigging lake. Have you arranged for it to be dredged? What about divers? If you've just slashed somebody up, a dirty great lake would be a pretty inviting place to throw your weapon.'

Shit, he's right, Jon thought, noticing Edwards nodding away in the periphery of his vision. 'I'll extend the perimeters of the crime scene to include the lake.'

'And the moor,' McCloughlin continued. 'What sort of a search have you arranged for up there?'

'It's already been searched. I'm getting the report tomorrow, but a crime scene manager attended and the site was signed off. To be honest, there's not a lot there apart from an outcrop of rocks. Any evidence was washed away long ago.'

'It's a moor right? Thick grass? Clumps of peat?' McCloughlin demanded.

Jon nodded. You're lining me up again, you bastard.

'Disturbances to the soil? Signs of digging? What about a sweep of the area with metal detectors? You've just killed someone in what's effectively a bloody great field. How about just burying the weapon rather than risk carrying it back to the road. And talking of roads, how did the attacker get there? How did he leave the site of the murder? He would have been drenched in the victim's blood. I doubt he caught a sodding bus home.'

Holding McCloughlin's stare, Jon unclenched his teeth with a conscious effort. 'I'll look into it.'

Summerby cleared his throat. 'Thank you for those pointers. Now, if you could allow me to discuss the way forward with my officer?'

McCloughlin broke eye contact with Jon and turned to Summerby. 'Come on, Edward, we can't afford any screw-ups on this.'

Jon saw the fingers being waved dismissively in his direction. You're so close to having those broken, he thought.

Summerby continued looking at McCloughlin and said nothing. A second passed before McCloughlin moved towards the door. 'I'll leave you to it then.'

Gavin Edwards also got to his feet. 'I've got some stuff to clear too.'

Once the door had shut behind him, Summerby looked at Jon. 'Still happy taking this on?'

Anger boiled in his chest as he thought of McCloughlin's attempt to have him dismissed. He had to prove the bastard wrong. 'Of course, Sir. If I can count on your support when he tries to scupper me again.'

Summerby gave a grim smile. 'To let you know a secret, I've never liked that abrasive prick. I'll keep him off your back, don't you worry.'

It was almost eight-thirty before he got a chance to call Alice.

'Jon! You were on the local news. Your mum was here when you were on. My family rang to let us know as well. How come you were giving a statement? I don't understand.'

Reacting to the shrill note edging into her voice, Jon made his own words sound calm. 'Babe, things have blown up a bit in my face here. The case I'm on might be linked to the death of that woman up on Saddleworth Moor.'

'What? You're involved on that? The report said there were similarities between both deaths. What did they mean?'

Hating himself for bullshitting his own wife, he said, 'Alice, it's just reporters jumping to conclusions. Listen, I've got some more stuff to sort out. I'll be a while longer. How's my little girl?'

'She's OK. When will you be home? I'm really tired.'

'Has mum gone?'

'Yeah, an hour or so ago.'

Jon glanced at his desk. There was enough preparation work to keep him there half the night. 'I'll be back to do her bottle. Elevenish?'

'Oh.'

'Shall I pick up anything on the way home?'

'Yes, we need more nappy sacks. Why have you got more stuff to sort out? You're not in charge of the case are you?'

Just tell her you are, a voice said. Jon shut his eyes and shied

125

away from the admission. 'Not really. It's just that I attended the crime scene, so it was me who gave the statement.'

Silence on the other end of the phone.

'Alice?'

Nothing.

'Alice, are you there?'

'They can't dump that on you. Not now.'

'It's all right, babe. There'll be a whole team on it, not just me.' He thought about the size of the workload hurtling his way. 'It won't be that bad.'

'Really?'

'Of course.'

'Well, I'll see you later then.'

Jon replaced the phone and lowered his head. You spineless prick, he cursed himself. Sooner or later, that lie is going to cost you. He spun in his seat, fished the cigarettes out of his coat pocket and headed for the car park.

The match was still flaring in his cupped hands as he touched the tip of the cigarette against it. Angrily sucking the smoke back, he immediately regretted his eagerness as phosphorous-laced fumes ripped at the back of his throat.

'Fuck!' He flicked the still burning match away and watched as it fell like a miniature comet towards the black tarmac.

When he pulled up at the twenty-four hour garage on the A6, his dashboard clock read 10.27 p.m. Knowing the doors would be locked, he marched across to the attendant's booth where an elderly man was fumbling for change, bent over by a cough that seemed to bubble up from the bottom of his lungs.

Tapping ash from a lit cigarette, the attendant reached to the side and the intercom came to life. 'Sounds like you need some fags to go with that cough.'

'Aye, that's what I'm here for.'

The two men burst out laughing, though whether at each other, themselves or death itself, Jon wasn't sure.

'Forty Berkleys mate.' The old man slid a tenner through the gap under the window.

He listened to the old man's wheezes as he shuffled away.

Please don't let me end up like him, he thought, aware of the packet of ten in his own pocket.

The speaker crackled again. 'Yes boss?'

Jon placed his hands on the counter, his car keys clinking against the metal surface as he did so. 'Do you have any packs of nappy sacks?'

'Nappy sacks? Yeah. Anything else?'

His eyes went to the rack of confectionary by the till. 'Some Extra Strong Mints too.'

The man walked out from behind the counter, fetched the items and came back, a puzzled look now on his face. 'Was it you I saw on the telly earlier? Giving that statement about the bloke who was found this morning?'

'You must have a good eye for faces,' Jon answered, slipping a fiver under the window. To his annoyance, the man didn't pick it up.

'So what's the score then? The newswoman said you lot aren't denying there's a link to the woman who got ripped apart up on Saddleworth. That means there is one, right?'

Here we go, thought Jon. Like I'm about to reveal anything to you. He nodded at the items in the man's hands. 'Listen, I'm in a bit of a rush here. Can you just give us them and do my change?'

As if Jon's terse reply contained a secret nugget of information, the man touched a finger to the side of his nose. 'Message taken, boss. Message taken.'

He was home five minutes later, the remains of an Extra Strong Mint wedged in the corner of his mouth. Except for a low murmur from the TV, the house was silent and calm. He hung his jacket on the banister and looked into the front room. Alice was in a pair of pale blue towelling pyjamas, fast asleep on the sofa with Holly stretched across her lap. He glanced about for Punch. Strange, no dog. He walked down the short corridor into the kitchen. Empty. As he started making up Holly's bottle, a thought suddenly occurred. Oh no, the stupid mutt. He knows he's not allowed upstairs. Jon stood on the bottom step. 'Punch? Punch, are you there?' he whispered, trying not to wake Alice.

He heard his wife stir. 'Jon. Is that you?'

'Hi babe,' he replied in a soft voice, stepping through the door and crouching down in front of the sofa. 'You OK?'

Alice struggled up on to an elbow, eyes bleary with sleep. 'What time is it?'

'Just after ten-thirty. She's not been squawking yet?'

'No.' She rubbed at her left eye. 'You've been smoking.'

Jon leaned back on his haunches. 'I had a sneaky one as a wind-me-down.'

She sat up straight now. 'Jon, what are you doing letting yourself start again?'

'I know. I'll pack it in again soon. It's just work at the moment is getting to me.'

'What about Holly? There are statistics that link passive smoking to cot death. You should be thinking about her.'

Fucking hell, that's a bit extreme, thought Jon. 'Ali, it was over two hours ago.'

'But I can still smell it.'

'Yeah, but . . . ' he gave up. The conversation was irrational. 'Where's Punch?'

'In the yard.'

'The yard? What's he doing out there?'

'Jon, I'm really sorry to say this. Just after you rang I caught it licking Holly's face. Like it does to a bone before it starts chewing it. I just don't feel safe with that animal in the house with our baby.'

Jon shook his head. Am I hearing this right? 'Say again.'

'I don't feel safe with him in the house.'

'What, you thought Punch was about to bite Holly? Ali, the dog's being protective, he would never hurt her.'

'I've seen it looking at her. It doesn't like her. It's jealous. We can't risk it.'

Jon looked down at their baby. This was just paranoid. Alice wasn't like this. What the hell was going on? 'You've locked him outside? It's raining out there.'

'The shed's open. I put his basket and food bowl in it.'

Jon bit his lip, stood up and walked to the back door. He opened it and looked out. Punch was curled on the concrete in the corner. His coat was glistening under the streetlight and Jon could see shivers running down his back. He wanted to shout into the house that she was totally out of order. 'Punch, come here, boy!'

His dog got uncertainly to its feet, the stump of its tail beginning to wag. Jon gestured into the kitchen. 'Come on!'

Punch trotted over and climbed the steps, droplets of rain beaded on the fur above his eyes.

'You stupid thing, what are you doing there?' Jon reached for a tea towel and began rubbing him down.

'Jon, he's not staying in this house.'

He glanced over his shoulder and saw Alice in the kitchen doorway, Holly cradled in her arms. 'Ali, I'll keep the kitchen door shut and we can talk about it in the morning. He can't sleep out in that shed.'

'And Holly? You value the dog above our daughter?'

Jon's hands paused. What sort of a question was that? Carefully, he formulated an answer before opening his mouth. 'It's not a case of who I value more, Ali, this is crazy. What's really the matter?'

'Fine!' He'd never heard so much venom in her voice. Punch shrank away beneath his fingers and Holly started to cry. 'Have it your way. You can sleep down here with your precious dog!'

She slammed the kitchen door shut and he heard her stamping up the stairs. He looked at Punch's sad brown eyes. 'What the fuck was that about?'

Faintly at first, Holly's crying was picking up in strength. He noticed the half made-up bottle by the sink. 'Stay there boy.' He quickly washed his hands, mixed powder with the water, then warmed it in the microwave. Closing the kitchen door behind him, he climbed the stairs. 'Ali? I've got her bottle. Do you want me to feed her?'

'Did you wash your hands?'

'Yes.'

'Give it to me.'

He stepped into the dark nursery. Alice raised her eyes only enough to look at the bottle in his outstretched hand, but he could see she was crying. 'Are you all right, babe?'

She turned away. 'Oh, forget it. I'll give her breast milk.'

Sixteen

The movement Alice created getting out of bed awoke him. Holly was whimpering in the nursery. The sliver of window visible at the edge of the curtain was pitch black and he looked at the bedside clock. Five twenty-six. He'd tried to sleep on the sofa until about one-thirty with no success. Finally he'd crept up the stairs and slipped into bed beside her, relieved she didn't wake up. The need for more sleep actually made him feel nauseous, but his mind was already accelerating away, multiple considerations clamouring for attention.

How long could he hold off letting the press know Derek Peterson's identity?

Was there a connection between Hobson and Mrs Sutton?

What the hell had got into Alice?

Ten minutes later she came back and got into bed without a word.

'Alice, can we talk?'

She nestled down under the duvet with her back to him. 'What about?'

What about? How about your terrible mood? 'You seem a bit stressed out. Are you feeling OK?'

The mattress moved slightly as she shrugged.

He reached a hand out and ran a forefinger along the back of her neck. 'Who'd have thought such a little thing could knacker us out this much?'

Abruptly she sat up, and in the half light, he could just make out her crossed arms as she looked down at him. 'Am I being over sensitive?'

Just a bit, he thought. 'I don't know. Over-tired maybe.'

She moved a hand towards her eyes, pushed a strand of hair he couldn't see away. 'I do feel emotional. Sorry if I snapped at you earlier.'

Relief. At least she acknowledges she's acting strangely. He remembered the salon. 'Did you ring Melvyn about that haircut?'

She sighed. 'No. I haven't had time. Maybe in a few weeks, once Holly's in more of a routine.'

'You should pop in anyway, just for a chat. Catch up on what's going on, remind yourself of what a laugh you had working in that place.'

'I don't know. I'm hardly looking my best at the moment.'

'So? That's what beauty salons are for. Book a manicure and makeover too. I said I'm paying.'

Her hand dropped down to his head. Fingertips began massaging at his skull, tingles spread along his neck. 'I can't stop the tears sometimes. There's so much to do. Sometimes just the thought of ironing makes me tired.'

'Don't worry about it,' he replied, hooking a forearm across her thighs and squeezing. 'You've been through a massive change. I mean, you've given birth, Alice. Jesus. It's a huge thing.'

'What if I can't cope?'

'Ali, it's not just your responsibility. I'm here.' He thought about how early he needed to be in at the station. Before eight preferably.

'I still feel really uneasy about having that dog in the house.'

That dog? Not long ago it was Punch. 'You feel that he's some sort of a danger to Holly?'

'I know he is. You know they say dogs have the same intelligence as a young child? They advise you not to leave a baby alone in a room with a young brother or sister.'

Those bloody magazines you read, he thought. 'Why?'

'Jealousy. They realise the baby is taking attention away from them. Depriving them of love. It causes resentment . . . babies are always getting injured by their siblings.'

First I've heard about it. Dreading what she was about to say, Jon asked, 'What are you suggesting then?'

'Can't he go to your mum and dad's?'

You know he bloody can't, Jon thought. 'My mum will never have a dog. It might mess up her perfect house.'

Her fingers were now working at the back of his neck, causing him to feel drowsy. 'Well, there's rescue centres. Places like that.'

Jon propped himself up on one elbow. 'You are joking?'

Her hand withdrew and she re-crossed her arms. 'No.'

From her tentative tone, he realised there'd been too much aggression in his voice. 'Ali, I'm not dumping Punch in some abandoned dog's home because he licked Holly's head.'

No answer. The silence stretched out until he swung his legs over the edge of the bed and stood up. 'I'm going for a shower.'

The sky was still pitch black as Jon swung his car into the police station car park. He looked at the dashboard clock. Twelve minutes to seven. Oh well, he thought, at least I'm in early. He came to a halt and looked over his shoulder. The back seats were folded down and Punch lay on a rug, a forlorn look on his face.

'All right boy? Bet this feels a little weird.' He got out of the car and opened the hatchback door. Punch sat up as Jon reached for a bottle of water and filled his dog's bowl. Then he unfolded the neck of a sack of dog biscuits and sprinkled a few on some flattened-out newspaper. 'OK boy. I'm going inside for a bit.' He pointed at the station building. 'In there. You stay here. You'll be OK. I'll be back soon.' He glanced at his watch. 'In about two hours.' Punch's stare didn't waver. 'OK, maybe two and a . . . ' He stopped talking. What am I doing? The dog doesn't speak bloody English, for Christ's sake. And it certainly can't tell the time. He closed the boot then went back to the driver's door. After lowering the window a couple of inches, he found a piece of paper and scrawled on it, 'If the dog's barking, let me know. DI Spicer, extension two-seven-four.'

After placing it on the dashboard and giving Punch a guilty wave, he hurried away to his office. The corridors were quiet, just the sound of a radio playing somewhere, a night shift officer singing tonelessly along. Jon opened the doors to the incident room. His incident room. Dark tables and desks, lifeless computer screens. Not for long, he thought, running the heel of his palm over the wall switches and listening to the chorus of buzzes as the strip lights flickered to life.

A feeling of exhaustion suddenly cascaded over him and he stepped back into the corridor, letting the door swing shut. What the hell am I doing? I shouldn't be here. Alice is stressed out. She needs me at home and here I am, heading up a bloody double murder investigation. He thrust his hands into his coat pockets and looked up at the ceiling, not knowing what to do. His fingers brushed against the packet of cigarettes and he took them out. Good thinking. Coffee and a smoke, that'll clear my head. Once his cup was full, he set off to a different side door, not wanting to smoke a cigarette in full view of his dog.

He exhaled, the vapour in his breath combining with the smoke to create an impressive cloud. As it churned slowly away from him, a pair of headlights cut through it, adding to the dramatic effect. The car came to a halt and he spotted the bald head of Gavin Edwards through the windscreen. Bloody great.

'DI Spicer. Didn't know you smoked,' the press officer announced as he climbed out.

'Just the odd one. More a social thing really.' He glanced to his side, painfully aware that he was alone. 'You're in early.'

Edwards puffed out his cheeks, the shape of his face reminding Jon of a potato. Holding his briefcase before him as if to protect his groin he said, 'It's this case Jon. It's preying on my mind.'

You and me both, Jon thought, grinding the cigarette out and accepting that his opportunity for quiet contemplation was over. 'What's bothering you?'

'Withholding Peterson's ID. That, and not coming clean about the possible connection to Mrs Sutton's murder. I'm afraid that by withholding information we'll have given the papers opportunity to speculate freely. They'll be creating the stories they know will have maximum impact.'

Jon had to nod. The bloke was probably right.

'And let's face it. A wild animal on the loose in Britain is good enough. But when it starts eating people . . . it's any reporter's wet dream.'

Jon leaned forward, invading the other man's personal space. 'There's nothing to prove it's the work of an animal.'

Edwards held up a placatory hand. 'I know. But there's nothing to disprove it either. And I'm worried the papers will exploit the space we created. I think we should call another press conference as soon as practical.' Three beeps came from his jacket and he fished a mobile phone out and started reading the text message.

Jon tipped the dregs of his coffee down a nearby drain, glad of the chance to consider his options.

'Events have overtaken us,' Edwards announced with a grim look. 'That was a contact I have at the *Manchester Evening Chronicle*. They've tracked down Peterson's address. There's a photographer on his way to the house now.'

Fucking hell, Jon thought. I haven't even been there yet. 'How have they found that out?'

'Who knows? They could have run a check on his car registration. It was parked by the body, wasn't it?'

'That would have taken the cooperation of someone with access to the DVLA's database.'

Edwards shrugged. 'Or maybe a neighbour rang them to say there was police activity at the house.'

Jon wasn't accepting that. His mind switched back to the possibility someone at the station was tipping the press off. After all, didn't that reporter from the *Chronicle* appear at Crime Lake with miraculous speed? 'OK. So we now have no option but to issue another press release. How early can we do it?'

'The earlier, the better. The *Chronicle* will be working on its lunchtime edition now. The nationals will be blocking in their lead stories. You release more details and they'll snap them up.'

'Can you do it? I need to get a team over to Peterson's house as fast as possible.'

Edwards ran a hand over his bald head in a gesture of unnecessary drama. 'Sure. I can do it. But we need to work out what I'm going to say.'

Jon looked at his watch. Five past seven. He stepped towards the doors. 'Come on then, let's get started.'

By half past seven they'd worked out the main points of the release. They'd give Derek Peterson's name out, along with his street. Information received since Jon's statement had revealed possible links to Mrs Sutton's death. These were now being investigated and the police at Mossley Brow were assisting in this. A post mortem was also being carried out to compare and contrast the nature of each victim's injuries. Finally, an expert in the behaviour of big cats was being thoroughly briefed on all new developments though, Edwards was to stress, this was just one of several avenues being investigated at this stage.

'Is that enough?' Jon asked, eyes on the hastily scrawled sheet of paper.

Edwards' mouth was partly open and he bounced the end of a biro between his teeth. Click. Click. Click. 'Until we see this morning's papers, I don't know. They'll be asking what the nature of the injuries were.'

'Tell them it was something sharp. Possibly a short-bladed knife.'

'They'll want to know if we have any suspects – human that is. Have we?'

Jon shook his head. 'The only thing I've got at this stage is a bloody request for witnesses posted up on a dogging website.' He clocked Edwards' look. 'Exactly. That's why I need to get over to Peterson's.'

The door opened as the first members of the Outside Enquiry Team reported for duty. One held a bundle of newspapers. He held them up so Edwards could see. 'Reception said these are for you. That's one hell of a front page on the *Chronicle*.'

Edwards got up from his seat, took the papers and returned to Jon's desk, cradling the bundle like an archaeologist with a precious find. 'Oh.'

Jon stood up to see what sort of a headline could have provoked such a reaction.

WANTED DEAD OR ALIVE!

The page was almost completely covered by a shot of the moors. Superimposed over the top was a close up of a black panther, mouth wide open and fangs exposed. Jon could almost hear the ferocious snarl leaping from the page. Sweet Jesus, he thought, eyes dropping to the subhead below the image:

£50,000 offered for the Monster of the Moor.

He began to read the paragraph of text at the base of the page.

> *This morning Manchester faces a deadly threat. There is an enemy stalking us that attacks without warning, without compassion. It seems likely the animal has struck twice now, each time savagely ripping its victim apart. With the help of a prominent local businessman, the* Manchester Evening Chronicle *will put a stop to this evil. We're offering a £50,000 cash reward for anyone who captures the Monster of the Moor, dead or alive. Further reports on pages 2, 3, 4 and 5.*

You bitch, Jon thought, an image of Carmel in his mind. Cancelling her exclusive hardly seemed an effective sanction now. He jabbed a finger at the front page. 'This is going to fuck everything up.'

Edwards slid the paper off the top, revealing the first of the national tabloids.

Beast terrorises Manchester.

He flipped through a succession of similar messages, stopping at the first broadsheet.

Copy cat killer?

'Nice headline,' Gavin murmured, examining a panel of photos that included a panther, mountain lion, jaguar and lynx. 'Well, they didn't mess about,' he quietly announced.

Jon placed the heels of his hands on the table, lowered his head and took a couple of deep breaths. I'm so out of my depth, he thought. What the hell do we do now? Gradually he noticed the room had gone quiet. He looked up to see all eyes upon him. It's your call, he realised. Just stick to protocol, it's all you can do at this stage.

'Right everyone. Let's sit down in five minutes. I just need to make a call.'

Before the officers turned away he caught the sceptical expressions on almost all of their faces. Edwards looked like he'd just developed a sudden case of toothache.

'I still say we stick to our original statement,' Jon whispered, painfully aware of the uncertainty in his voice. 'It's all conjecture and media bullshit. Surely our job is to bring a bit of restraint and rationality to all this?'

Edwards nodded. 'You're right.'

'Then add in something about us taking a very serious view of people carrying firearms on public land. Mention a custodial sentence, the last thing we need are a load of would-be Rambos roaming about with loaded shotguns.'

'Will do.'

Jon picked up a phone and dialled Summerby's number. As the line buzzed Jon stared down at his shoes. What the hell have I got myself into? I should never have asked to take this thing on, I haven't got nearly enough experience. I'll just have to tell him the case has come at the wrong time. I need to be at home, sorting things out with Alice.

The phone continued to ring. Come on, please pick up . . . After waiting another five rings he reluctantly replaced the receiver and glanced around. All six of the Outside Enquiry Team were now in, as were the essential members of the incident room. OK, he told himself, treat it like the talk before a rugby match. Fill them in on what we're going to do, get their enthusiasm bubbling, then get them out there. You can have a word with Summerby later on.

Taking a file from his desk, he moved to the centre of the room. 'OET? Gather round please. First things first: despite this morning's papers, we're treating this as a murder case. I don't want to hear any whispers about some fucking Monster of the Moor, all right?'

A few uncertain nods.

'Listen, if the powers that be decide it is a panther doing the killing, the role of the Major Incident Team ends and the involvement of the RSPCA or some other outfit begins. Now I'm assuming you're all keen to work this case?'

Everyone stared back, heads now eagerly bobbing.

'Good, because I don't want any one who's not a hundred per cent.' He looked down at his file, needing to break eye contact. You fucking fraud, he thought. 'The MO for Derek Peterson is identical to that for Rose Sutton, so we're assuming the same person or persons were responsible for both deaths. Now I'm going to need five officers to help me go through Peterson's property. You may have heard he was into a bit of car park action with other men.' He opened the file and handed out copies of Peterson's police record. 'As you can see, he was done for gross indecency back in ninety-three, an offence that cost him his job as a care worker at the Silverdale facility for young offenders.'

'That place,' an officer with curly black hair sighed knowingly.

'Sorry, what was that Detective . . . ' Jon waited for the officer to identify himself.

'DC Murray, boss. Hugh Murray. It's like a bloody hotel. More facilities than most kids enjoy.'

'You've been there?'

'A few times. I used to work on the Child Protection Unit.'

'Good. After we've been through Peterson's house you can get over there and dig out all the information you can on the man. My hunch is that he was attacked by someone who knew him. There was a witness to the early part of the assault . . . '

'At Crime Lake?' A female officer with a carefully arranged mess of collar-length brown hair asked.

Jon shook his head, aware he'd got ahead of himself. 'Sorry, no. Peterson was first attacked in a car park at Silburn Grove, Middleton, last Thursday. His assailant was described as a young lad by the person who rang nine-nine-nine. I suspect Peterson could have encountered his attacker during his time as a care worker.'

'Encountered as in what sense?' asked DC Murray.

'Possibly an abusive sense, given his record. While you're at the facility we'll go through Peterson's place looking for any evidence relating to his time at the Silverdale or any link to Rose Sutton.'

Starting at the left-hand edge of the group, he counted off the five officers. After getting each one to introduce themselves, he said, 'You lot with me. Now, Detective . . . ?'

'DC Adlon. Joseph Adlon.'

'I'd like you to coordinate the uniforms in a door-to-door of

Peterson's street.' He turned to the woman who'd asked the earlier question.

'DC Gardiner, I need you to liaise with Inspector Clegg. He's the officer in charge of the Sutton enquiry over at Mossley Brow. After we've finished in Peterson's place I need you to bring back the list of all Rose Sutton's family and friends interviewed so far and start moving all her case files over too. OK with that?'

'No problem.'

Jon closed the file and stood. 'Let's meet in the car park in ten.'

Seventeen

Jon walked quickly over to his desk and called home. Alice answered just as he was about to give up. 'Hi Ali, it's me.'

'Jon, you don't normally ring from work.'

The comment took him by surprise. Wasn't it obvious things weren't exactly normal? 'No. I wanted to check you were OK.'

'Why? Shouldn't I be?'

Actually, no. You were in a foul mood last night. And you've kicked our dog out of the house, remember? 'Well, you know . . . you were upset.'

'Oh that,' she said breezily. 'My hormones again. They go up and down like a bloody yo-yo at the moment.'

Unable to see her face, Jon tried to focus on the intonations in her voice. It sounded like the Alice he knew and loved. But was it an act or had her dark mood really passed? 'So what you said about stuff. Punch for instance . . . '

'Oh Jon. I know it's not easy, but we can't have him in the house. Sorry.'

Still she sounded so normal. Like they were debating whether to ditch a cheap piece of furniture. 'Ali, I can't leave him at some kennel for strays. We need to talk about this properly.'

'Jon, Holly's crying. I have to go.'

'OK, I'll try and call later.'

'Fine. Speak to you in a bit.'

The line went dead and Jon found himself staring at the mouthpiece of the receiver as if he could find a clue to his wife's behaviour in the arrangement of holes there. He dialled his mum and dad's number.

'Hello?'

Dad. Why did he always sound vaguely surprised at the

phone's ability to transmit voices into his ear. 'Morning, Dad. You all right?'

'Yes.'

Jon waited for him to elaborate. Nothing. Christ, the man was awful at speaking on the phone. 'Did you see Salford playing the other day? That Aussie they've brought in looks like he'll be useful.'

'He does. You want your mum?'

Jon gave in. 'Yeah, go on then.'

'Mary! It's Jon. He wants a word.'

A bang as the phone was put down on the wooden sideboard. Jon could see his Dad wandering back into the front room where his paper and cup of coffee awaited.

'Hello, Jon. Everything all right?'

'Yeah—'

'Have you seen the morning news? That case you're on is talk of the town.'

Jon shut his eyes. 'I know. Listen, can you pop round ours later? Alice was a bit upset last night.'

'Upset?'

'Over-tired I think. She's probably going a bit stir crazy in the house with just her and the baby. She could do with some company.'

'She should get some fresh air. Take Punch out for a walk.'

'She won't be doing that. She kicked Punch out.'

'Kicked Punch out?'

'She doesn't want him in the house anymore.'

'Why on earth has she decided that?'

'She thinks he's a danger to Holly.'

'Danger to Holly?'

'I know. She reckons Punch is jealous of her.'

'Well, now you mention it, I've heard that before too. Dogs are pack animals, very sensitive to where they lie in order of importance.'

Jesus, not you too, Jon thought. 'Mum, we're talking about Punch. He's a total softie.'

'True, but you can never really tell what an animal is thinking.'

'Mum, it's not like Alice to be so harsh.'

'She's protecting her baby, Jon. Maternal instinct.'

'She's acting strange more like. Emotional.'

'Has she rung Amanda?'

Amanda. Alice's mum, who had just gone on holiday with her latest boy friend. 'She's in the Canary Islands for the next fortnight, remember?'

'Oh yes. I'll give Alice a call. See if she wants to go out for a coffee or lunch.'

Jon felt the tension in him abate slightly. 'Thanks, Mum, that would be a great help.'

'Where's the dog then?'

'In the back of my car. I didn't know what to do with him. I don't suppose he could stay at yours?'

'Ours? I don't know.'

'Just for a day or two.'

The silence spoke volumes as she searched for a valid reason to say no. He cut in, not wanting to hear what she came up with. 'Don't worry. I'll see if someone else can take him in.'

'Well, if you're sure. I don't want to be awkward . . . '

His mobile started to ring. 'OK. I've got to go. Speak to you later.' He hung up without waiting for a reply, angered by what he perceived as selfishness on her part.

As soon as he saw Carmel's name on the screen, he took the call. 'You lot ever tell the fucking truth? You can forget—'

'Jon, it wasn't my story. Look at the names on the front page. The news editor coordinated the whole thing. Him and a rich businessman mate who's offering the reward.'

'And who is that?'

'I don't know. Honestly. They've got me on background stuff. You'll find my piece on Alien Big Cat sightings on page three. You realise they've got Peterson's address?'

'Yeah. Nothing to do with you either?' he said, marching towards the side exit.

'Listen. I just wanted you to know that I kept my word.'

'And I don't believe you. The interview's off.' He hung up, taking a small amount of pleasure in cutting her down. The other officers were in the car park waiting for him. 'Right,' he barked. 'Let's get over to Peterson's. By the way, it fucking stinks in his house.' Setting off towards his vehicle, he called over his shoulder. 'I can take one other.'

He opened up his car and Punch scrabbled excitedly to his feet. Jon leaned forward, extending a hand over the seat so his dog could nuzzle eagerly at his palm. 'Hello boy,' he smiled, spirits lifted by the animal's uncomplicated affection.

The other door opened and an officer peered in. 'Sniffer dog, boss?'

'No. My mutt, Punch. He won't bite.' He glanced at his colleague's questioning expression. 'Don't ask.'

The uniform standing at the front door looked concerned when their convoy of unmarked police cars pulled up. His face quickly showed relief when he realised they were fellow officers – a bit of company at last.

Telling Punch to stay put, Jon led the search team up the pathway, keeping his face averted from the press photographer standing on the pavement. Flashing his ID at the officer, he took out Peterson's set of keys, selected the one for the front door and opened it. The same stale smell greeted him. No wonder he had to leave his house to find a shag.

He led the team into the front room, noting that no one was hurrying to take a seat. 'OK. We're looking for documents, letters, anything relating to his time at the Silverdale facility, or his little car park hobby. Keep an eye out for anything linking him to Rose Sutton.' He pointed to two officers. 'Hugh and Paul, start upstairs. Susan, you and me will search in here. Alan and Mark, check the kitchen.'

Pulling on latex gloves, the officers moved off. Jon looked round the room. A unit stood at one end of it, shelves full of books, videos and magazines. By the television was a cabinet topped by an inch-thick layer of letters and junk mail. 'You take the shelves Susan. I'll start over here.'

There must have been several months' worth of post accumulated there, much of it unopened. He searched for signs of the sender, flipping envelopes over and scanning numerous logos and addresses.

Centurion Double Glazing. Capital One credit cards. United Utilities. Scottish Power. BT. The Telegraph Wine Club. Jon frowned, surprised Peterson was interested in wines.

Next was an open letter from the Benefits Agency. Along with details of his disability allowance was a reminder that the lease on his current vehicle was coming to an end. The letter asked that he choose a vehicle from the accompanying list. Jon slid out the piece of paper. Volvos, Toyotas, Renaults. All new. Jesus, he thought of the crappy old Ford he and Alice couldn't afford to replace.

Continuing through the pile, he found an envelope that appeared suspiciously anonymous. A PO Box number in Basingstoke was the only indication of where it had come from.

Knowing that no one could prove who opened it, he took out a penknife and ran the blade under the flap. Inside was a receipt from a mail order chemist. An order of Cialis soft tabs, whatever they were. Jon scanned the panel at the bottom of the document. 'Try our other premium quality drugs for enhancing male sexual performance!'

He replaced the sheet and carried on with his search, aware that he'd found no personal correspondence yet.

'Some interesting choices of home entertainment here, boss.'

He glanced at Susan who was crouching in front of the shelf unit. From the way she was holding the DVD case by just a forefinger and thumb, he suspected she hadn't found *The Sound of Music.*

'Go on then, as if I can't guess.'

'*Chicken Run.*'

'Not the animated film about those cute hens?'

'No. Though there seems to be quite a few cocks in it.'

Jon gave a snort. 'Just be glad you're not going through his bedroom.'

'Yeah, I owe you a drink for sparing me that.'

A voice sounded from upstairs. 'Boss? We've got some interesting stuff here on his computer.'

Jon rolled his eyes at Susan then called out, 'Used the internet for keeping up with world news did he?'

'That'll be a no. Come and see.'

Before climbing the stairs Jon looked down the corridor towards the kitchen. 'How's it going in there, lads?'

'Could make a fortune from recycling his empty cans of Asda strong lager,' came the reply.

At the top of the stairs Jon headed for the doorway with the flickering blue light. The two officers were in front of the computer screen. 'I went into the history file, last site he'd been on was a right pervy one.'

'Called Swinger's Haven by any chance?'

The officer looked surprised. 'Yeah. Are you behind the appeal for witnesses posted there?'

'I am.'

'Well, there's been no replies to your posting, but I think he'd visited the forum bit just before. Appears he was checking for meets in the local area.'

Jon leaned forward to read the screen, relieved they hadn't scrolled down to the comments about himself.

'This one here, it says "Likewise. Mr P." I think that's from him.'

'How come?'

He pointed to the scrap of paper sellotaped to the side of the monitor. 'SH. Username – Mr P, password – 5Burman. That's this address isn't it? 5 Burman Street. SH stands for Swinger's Haven because when I typed that username and password in, it gave me access.'

'Nice one, Paul. OK, unplug it and bag the whole thing up. The IT boys can go through everything properly.'

Jon glanced round the room, eyes lingering for a moment on the double bed. It was covered by a crumpled duvet and he could see a large grease mark on the pillow where Peterson's head had rested.

His mobile phone started to ring, Rick's name showing up on the screen. 'Rick, how's things?'

'Good. Can you talk?'

'Yup, fire away.'

'We've had a hit with the request on Swinger's Haven.'

'Yeah?' Jon paused, looking over his shoulder at the computer screen. 'We're on it at the moment. Doesn't seem to be any replies that I can see.'

'A guy just called me. We gave my telephone number, remember?'

Jon felt a trickle of excitement run down his neck. 'What did he say?'

'He heard the radio reports and thinks the person found yesterday is the same person he was with a few nights ago at Silburn Grove car park.'

'With? What did he mean by that?'

'You really want me to elaborate?'

'No thanks. Can he come to the nick?'

'No, he's not prepared to meet there.'

'Where then?'

'Next to the library is a nursery play area. You know it?'

'By those arches?'

'Yeah, there's some benches that face back at those arches.'

'What time?'

'In an hour.'

'Right, I'll meet you there.'

Eighteen

Jon just had time to call into a coffee shop by the library and grab a cup to take away. He followed the circular exterior of the library round to its main entrance, where the usual smattering of students were hanging around on the front steps.

To his right, a tram tooted its horn, then pulled away from the platform with an electric whine. Jon looked at the bronze tableau of women advancing forward in what appeared to be a disintegrating blanket. As usual, he wondered what the hell the statue was all about. On the benches just past it he could see Rick, also sipping from a paper cup.

Jon walked over in the shadow cast by the gothic town hall buildings that loomed over St Peter's square. 'Morning Rick. Little cold for an outside meeting, isn't it?'

Rick looked up with a smile and a shrug. 'Maybe he'll be happy to go somewhere warmer.'

Jon sat down and crossed his ankles. Visible in the windows between the arches was a day nursery. A set of toddlers sat entranced around a staff member as she read a story. Jon's mind went to his own baby, still months away from being able to sit up, let alone be read to. He wondered how Alice was and started to reach for his phone.

'Check out this guy. I think it could be him,' Rick said quietly.

Jon's fingers curled back round his coffee cup and glanced to his right. A man with a pudding-bowl haircut was tentatively making his way along the arches. He was about forty years old, five-foot-seven or eight tall, wide hips giving him a womanly shape. Gripped in front of him was a newspaper, held as if to fend off any unwelcome approach. His eyes settled for a moment on Rick and Jon, skittered nervously past them, then slowly returned.

'It's him,' Rick murmured, getting to his feet. 'Adrian? It's Rick. We spoke earlier this morning.'

'Ah.'

He didn't move, but gripped the paper even more tightly across his stomach. Jon spotted a wedding ring on his finger.

Rick gestured to his side. 'This is my senior officer, DI Jon Spicer. He's leading the investigation.'

Jon stood, but decided not to offer his hand. The bloke looked like he would be terrified by any physical contact. Instead he pointed towards the library. 'There's a coffee shop round the corner. Can we get you a drink?'

The man was silent for several moments. Finally he replied. 'There's a café in the library itself.' His voice squeaked with nerves.

'Whatever you prefer,' Rick answered.

They walked in awkward silence until they reached the library's entrance.

'I think I'd prefer it in here,' he said, making eye contact with Rick for a split second.

Jon and Rick dropped their cups into a bin. They filed through the library's swing gate, crossed the foyer and went down the wide stone steps into the basement café where a woman was bustling around behind the counter.

'What would you like?' Jon asked.

The man glanced at his watch. 'Erm. A tea. Thank you.'

'Rick, another frothy coffee?' He let one eyebrow arch up and Rick gave him a polite smile.

'Yes, thank you, Jon.'

As the woman served their drinks, Jon looked down at Adrian. 'Do you work in the city centre?'

He glanced about, checking that no one was within hearing distance. 'Yes. I work for the council, in the town hall offices.'

Jon made himself look interested. 'That must be a great building to work in. Architecturally I mean.'

Adrian frowned. 'It's a little cramped. Not designed for all the computers we can't seem to survive without nowadays.'

Jon smiled. 'Yeah, same can be said for most police stations.' He nodded at the corner table. 'Over there?'

Once they'd sat down, Jon took out his notebook and pen. 'Now Adrian, everything you tell us is in the strictest confidence. Are you clear about that?'

'That's a promise is it? I have your promise? I can't let anyone know that I . . . that I was there, in the car park.'

'You have my word,' Jon assured him, hoping the case wouldn't develop in such a way that a court appearance would be necessary. 'So can you tell us exactly what happened?'

Adrian coughed nervously, then interlinked his fingers. 'I arrived at the car park at about ten o'clock. No one was there so I walked over to the brick shed at the end to wait.'

As he spoke his face slowly changed from a light red to a deep purple. You poor bastard, Jon thought. This is excruciating for you, isn't it?

'Why leave your car?' Rick gently prodded.

'I don't like staying in it.' He glanced up. From his imploring look, Jon could tell he didn't want to explain why.

'Sorry Adrian,' Jon said. 'We need to be clear on why. The attack took place by that shed. It could be important.'

Adrian made an attempt to clear his throat. 'I'm not . . . not the only one who uses the car.'

Right, Jon thought. Can't have other men's spunk on the wife's seat. 'So you were waiting by the shed?'

'Yes, there're trees behind it. It's quite a private area. The car turned up about ten minutes later. A dark blue Volvo, I gave part of its registration to the emergency operator when I called.' Seeing Jon's look of acknowledgement, Adrian paused. 'Is it the car? The car of the person found yesterday morning?'

'We think so, yes.' He got the photo of Derek Peterson out. 'Was this the man who arrived in the Volvo?'

Adrian nodded. 'Now he's dead?'

Jon gave a single nod.

'And he was called Peterson?'

'He was.'

For a few moments Adrian's lips moved as he tried to form a word. Then he gave up and just stared at the table.

Jon met Rick's gaze, then turned his eyes towards Adrian and gave a little nod. Your turn.

'Adrian. The Volvo had just arrived . . . ' Rick prompted.

Head still bowed, Adrian continued. 'Yes. He parked about ten metres away from my car. I stepped out from the side of the shed, waited for him – Peterson – to see me, then I moved back into the shadows. A few seconds later I heard his footsteps. He came round the corner and stood before me.' Adrian's head sagged lower as if weighed down by shame. 'We had just got started when . . . '

'Sorry Adrian.' Jon kept his eyes on his notebook, avoiding eye contact. 'I take it you were . . . the height of your head was at . . . '

'I was kneeling, yes. Then I heard movement in the undergrowth behind us. Twigs snapping, then a shoe crunching on gravel. I hadn't time to look up before there was this . . . this kind of stifled cry. So full of rage it was.'

'From the attacker?' Jon asked.

'I think so. Then came the sound of something striking Peterson. He staggered back against the wall of the shed and I rolled on to the ground and covered my head with my arms, waiting to get hit. But the noises continued above me. I looked up and saw it was a young man. They were chest to chest, grappling with the weapon. Blood was dripping down Peterson's face. The younger man was hissing bastard, bastard, bastard and Peterson's whole posture changed.'

'How do you mean?' Jon sat forward.

'Well, at first he was just as surprised as me. But then he recognised the guy who'd hit him.'

'How do you know he recognised him?' Jon cut in.

'He just did. You'll see when I carry on. Peterson kind of squared up to him, did something to break the younger man's grip on the metal bar. By now I was on my feet, I moved around them and was going towards my car. It looked like Peterson was going to disarm him and I thought we could both make a run for it, but Peterson didn't escape when he had the chance.'

Adrian raised a hand to the bridge of his nose and pinched it.

'Peterson got hold of the young guy's wrist and twisted it up and behind his back. It must have really hurt because the lad let go of the bar with his other hand and started to gasp.' Adrian's eyes were now squeezed shut. 'He kept twisting the lad's arm up, forcing him to bend forward. Then . . . then he pulled the lad's tracksuit bottoms down. I actually said to him, what are you doing? He told me to piss off. He had the bar ready and I backed off, away from it all. It was then the lad started to scream.'

Jon lifted one hand from the table. 'Hang on, I think I've lost you here. It was the lad screaming, not Peterson?'

'Yes. The lad. I'm sure Peterson knew him. That's why he did it, he was punishing him, I'm sure.' He turned towards the wall and shook his head.

'Sorry Adrian, you're saying Peterson assaulted his attacker?'

Adrian ran a hand down the side of his face. 'He'd bent him over. He used that metal bar on him, I know he did.'

'You mean he inserted it into the lad's anus?'

'I didn't actually see, but the screams. What else was he doing?'

Jon turned the information over in his head. Christ, Adrian was probably right. 'So you went back to your car and rang nine-nine-nine?'

'Yes, the screaming went on and on. Then Peterson reappeared. By now the blood was completely covering his face and sweatshirt. He had this look on his face. Sort of shocked but also triumphant. He swapped the bar to his other hand, opened the car . . . '

'He was still carrying the weapon?'

'Yes, he shoved it under the driver's seat. At that point I rang off and got the hell out of there.'

'Did Peterson follow you out?'

'He did.'

Jon sat back. Jesus, that put a whole new angle on the incident. No wonder Peterson didn't want to report it. 'Adrian. I really appreciate you coming forward with this information. How are you doing for time?'

Adrian glanced at his watch. 'I should be going.' He stood up, then noticed his untouched tea. 'Sorry, I completely forgot about it.'

Jon waved a hand in dismissal. 'Not a problem. Adrian, at some point, we'll need to take a formal statement. When's the best time to contact you?'

'Will it be used to identify me?'

'No, absolutely not. Should we call you at your office?'

'Yes. My office.'

Rick straightened up. 'I've got your work number, Adrian.'

Jon stood up and held out his hand. It was gripped momentarily in a sweaty palm, then Adrian hurried off between the tables. Jon moved round to the empty seat, stretched his legs out and reached across the table for his coffee. As he did so, he ran over Adrian's version of events. Jesus, Peterson was a sick fuck. To actually shove an iron bar up some poor bloke's arse. He looked up. 'Why assault someone like that?'

'I think Adrian was right. Punishment surely,' Rick replied.

Jon took another sip. The answer was lacking somehow. Punishment beatings involved smashed kneecaps or shattered faces. This was more like rape. 'It wasn't just punishment. I think it was sexual humiliation. The lad had the audacity to attack him, Peterson was showing him who was boss. And to me that suggests, at some point, Peterson was in a position of authority over the lad.'

'You mean this Silverdale facility? The lad was in there when Peterson was on the staff?'

'That's my guess. Peterson was into young boys. The DVDs in his house are proof of that. I think this lad was abused by Peterson. He was trying to settle scores. Only it all goes horribly wrong, and Peterson bitches him again.'

'So the next time he catches Peterson up in Daisy Nook Country Park he comes armed with something a lot more serious.'

'Looks like it. What I can't figure out is what Rose Sutton did to piss him off so badly. Don't forget, she was slashed to ribbons before the iron bar attack on Peterson. And why was he fucking around with an iron bar at all? Why not just go for Peterson with the same weapon he used on Rose Sutton? It was pretty effective first time after all.'

'Maybe he ditched that one and had to get hold of another.'

'Or go back and retrieve the first one.'

Rick shrugged. 'I guess we'll find out when we nail him. I tell you one thing. He'll have had some serious injuries from the bar. Internal ones.'

Jon pulled out his mobile. Seeing there was no signal, he drained his coffee and led the way up the stairs. Once outside under the library's portico he looked out at the needles of rain slicing through the air. As he waited for the crime scene manager to answer his phone he watched a magpie as it hopped along the edge of the tram platform, totally unperturbed by the passengers waiting there. Its head dipped to the side and it dropped from view on to the rails, reappearing a couple of seconds later. Then, emitting a sharp clacking sound, it flew to the top of a black metal pole and alighted on the CCTV camera mounted there, long tail raising and lowering as it balanced itself in the light breeze. Weren't those things rare once, Jon wondered, trying to remember a childhood rhyme about good luck if you spotted more than one. Now they were common as pigeons.

'Richard Matthews here.'

'Richard, DI Spicer. Are you still at Crime Lake?'

'Yes.'

'Can I ask a favour?'

'Go ahead.'

'Has Peterson's Volvo been towed yet?'

'No, a flat-bed truck is on its way.'

'Just check for me and see if the driver's door is open.'

'OK. I'm in the caravan at the moment. Two seconds while I put some gloves on.' Jon listened to the movement at the other end of the line. 'Right, I'm by his vehicle. I'm trying the door. Yes, it's open.'

'Good. Now, take a look under the driver's seat. Anything there?'

'There is. It looks like a crow bar.'

'OK, careful to avoid touching the ends of it, can you lift it out and tell me what you see?'

'I've got it. Yes, there's something here. Appears to be blood, possibly faecal matter too.'

Jon closed his eyes, imagining the years of misery the lad must have endured. Was it any wonder he ended up so desperate for revenge? 'I'll need you to take swabs and test for DNA. We need a result as soon as.'

'It's top of my list.'

'Cheers, Richard.'

Jon hung up and looked at Rick. 'If the lad was in the Silverdale facility, he's a young offender. If he's a young offender, he's got a record.'

'And if he's got a record, his DNA is on the national database,' Rick finished the sentence.

Jon held up a hand and they slapped palms together. 'Don't you just love it when a plan comes together?'

Rick gave him a cheesy grin. 'I'd better get back to Chester House.'

'You still working on that complaints thing you mentioned?'

Rick threw a glance upwards. 'Just finishing it, thank God.'

'So what's next?'

'I'm starting a stint with the Drugs Squad next week.'

'Fancy joining this investigation in the meantime? I could do with the help.'

Rick looked him in the eyes. 'Some mad bastard ripping people's throats out? To be honest mate, I thought you'd never ask.'

Jon smiled. 'Nice one. Why don't you get it cleared with your boss then come over to the incident room. I'll bring you up to speed.'

Rick glanced at his watch. 'He's in a meeting until lunch. Why don't I come over now and just clear it with him later?'

'Fair enough.'

As they reached Jon's car Rick ducked his head for a better view through the rear window. 'What's Punch doing in there?'

'Spot of bother with Alice. She's decided he's a danger to Holly. Won't have him in the house.' As he opened the door Punch's face lit up with delight. 'Hello there stupid, you OK?'

The dog stared back tongue protruding from the side of its mouth as they got in.

'He didn't try to bite her, did he?' Rick asked, clipping in his seatbelt.

Jon started the engine and reversed the car out of its space. 'No.'

'Scratched her?'

Jon shook his head.

'Am I missing something here?'

'Not really.' Suddenly he had the urge to describe out loud the bizarre turn of events. Perhaps it would make everything clearer in his head. 'She saw him lick Holly on the head. And because he licks his bones before chewing them, she concluded he was getting ready to do the same to Holly. To be honest, she's not been herself since the birth. She gets wound up very easily, worries about things too much.'

'Wound up about what?'

'I don't know. Stuff that's out of her control. Iraq, for instance. She was crying the other night because she reckons our forces are killing their babies. She goes on and on about it.'

'Any other things like that?'

Jon glanced suspiciously at him, sensing something behind the question. 'Things like what?'

'Morbid thoughts. About death, people being injured. That sort of stuff.'

Jon dug his fingernails into the leather of the steering wheel. 'She worries about Holly being OK. She gets up to check she's still breathing during the night. Reckons the baby monitor might not be working.'

Rick remained silent for a few seconds. 'What about in the mornings? Is she getting up all right?'

'Rick, we've got a three-month-old baby. She's frigging knackered.'

'Yeah, but you're getting up aren't you?'

'What's your point here?'

'I've got an older sister. She's got two kids. Both times she suffered from post-natal depression. Feeling that she couldn't cope, that she was failing as a mother, lethargy, dark thoughts. Fretting about her baby. She wouldn't leave any windows open in case a fox got into the house and carried it off.'

Jon looked at him. 'A fox?' Even as he heard the incredulous note in his voice, he knew Alice's fears about Punch were just as groundless. 'You reckon she's depressed then?'

'I'm no doctor, mate, but it sounds very similar.'

Jon felt a sense of dread. My God, he thought. 'I should have spotted it myself.'

'No. It's quite subtle at first. She obviously hasn't seen it either.'

'So what happened to your sister? Did the kids go into care?'

'What?' Rick smiled. 'Course not. Her GP prescribed anti-depressants. They took a few weeks to kick in, but she's fine now.'

He was taken aback by Rick's almost flippant tone. 'But addicted to pills for the rest of her life?'

'For fuck's sake, Jon, it's not like that nowadays. They take them for about six months, then gradually get weaned off them. It's no big deal. You make it sound like her brain was turned to mush. It's not *One Flew Over The Cuckoo's Nest*. Medicines have come a long way since then.'

Jon pinched his lower lip between a finger and thumb. 'So I need to get her to a doctor's.'

'I think you should discuss it with her first. You know, a few gentle nudges about how she's feeling. Perhaps float a visit just as a possibility.'

'Yeah, you're right. I don't suppose you could take Punch for a day or two?'

'Jon, I live in a flat. Not a chance.'

'Yeah, thought so,' Jon replied, eyes on his dog's reflection in the rear-view mirror.

Nineteen

Ken Sutton stood looking up into the oak tree in the field above his farm. Andrew was perched on a bough, drilling a block of wood into its upper side. Once the screw was properly in he hitched the electric screwdriver on to his tool belt and looked down. 'Next.'

Ken held up the last square of wood. Keeping his grip on the bough with one hand, Andrew reached down with his other and was just able to take it. He placed the block over a cross he'd scored in the bark earlier on, positioned another screw then drilled it through and into the branch itself. Once he'd done the same with three other screws he sat back and looked around him. Four other blocks of wood were held firmly in place on the tops of neighbouring branches. 'This takes me back to building tree houses when I was younger. First plank then.'

Ken crouched down and hooked his fingers under the end of the six-foot length of timber at his feet. Standing it upright, he raised it to within reach of Andrew's hands. The weight on his fingers disappeared as the plank vanished up into the branches.

Andrew laid it between two boughs, wedging the outer edge against two blocks of wood. The screwdriver was lifted from his tool belt and the plank soon fixed in place. One by one, Ken passed up the other planks and soon Andrew had created a small platform between the tree's lower branches.

Crouching on it, he took a spirit level from his belt and placed it on the wooden surface. 'Not bad for a rush job. Right, next is the carpet. You're certain this hasn't been near any chemicals recently?'

'Only if you count sheep piss. It's been in the end barn for months.'

'Sheep piss is good.'

Ken heaved the roll of dusty carpet up on to its end. Crouching down again, he gripped the lower part in a bear hug and straightened his legs. The top of the roll was now about four feet above his head. Andrew lay over the edge of the platform, grasped it in both hands and began pulling upwards. Bits of straw, dried earth and wood lice began dropping out of the bottom end into Ken's hair.

Andrew dragged it over the edge and unrolled it across the platform, a variety of startled centipedes and spiders fleeing for the edges. 'Perfect. This'll keep the draught off my arse.'

Ken was bent over, running a hand through his hair to dislodge the debris caught in it. 'Just the camouflage, then.' He turned to a mound of netting that lay in the long grass. After scooping it up, he flung it upwards with both arms. Andrew's outstretched fingers caught a corner and he yanked it on to the platform like a fisherman pulling in his catch.

'What's the view up there like then?' Ken asked, looking across the field.

Andrew peered out from between the bare branches. 'It's fine.' He lifted an imaginary rifle and pointed to a patch of grass about thirty metres away. 'We tether up one of your old ewes there and bang, it's game over.'

Ken crossed his arms and scanned the bottom edge of the moor. Nothing moved in the brown landscape.

'Come on, you bastard,' he murmured to himself.

Twenty

Jon spent the rest of the morning coordinating the other strands of the investigation, including the dredging of Crime Lake.

DC Susan Gardiner arrived back just before lunch with the first boxes from Mossley Brow. After logging them in, she placed them in the corner by Jon's desk.

'Did you get the list of people interviewed so far?' he asked.

She nodded. 'That one on the right. In the orange folder.'

'How did Clegg seem to you?'

'Agitated to see all the files go. He wanted to know how things were progressing.'

I bet he was, thought Jon. He lifted out the orange folder and opened the cover. Inside was a pile of statements, accompanied by Personal Descriptive Forms of each person questioned. Jon scanned over details including age, weight, colour of hair. His eyes automatically went to the box indicating whether the person had consented to a DNA swab. Most had. The first few names meant nothing to him. Then his fingers stopped flicking through the sheets. Edith Clegg. Adam's sister and Rose Sutton's bridesmaid. Jon thought about Adam's evasiveness. Questioning Edith about Rose might also reveal a bit about Adam. It seemed a good place to start. 'Fancy a drive out to Holme?'

Rick looked up from the adjacent desk. 'Why not?'

The tourist office in Holme only had one hiker in it. Jon and Rick stood outside until the woman behind the counter had served him, then they crossed the street and went in.

'Edith Clegg?' Jon asked politely.

'Yes,' she replied, her smile suddenly becoming fixed in place as he produced his warrant card. 'DI Spicer and DS Rick Saville, Greater Manchester Police. Could we have a word?'

Her eyes dropped to the till, then lifted slowly back up again. 'Is it about Rose?'

'That's right,' Jon replied, looking meaningfully around the empty room. 'We can call back later if now isn't convenient.'

'No, that's fine. How can I help?'

'You were very close to Rose, I understand?'

'That's correct. I have given a statement you know.'

'I do. It's just that I have a few questions of my own, if that's all right.'

She nodded and as Jon got out his book he noticed that the smile still clinging to her lips didn't match the cautious look in her eyes. 'How long had you known Rose?'

'We grew up together – in Mossley Brow on the other side of the moor.'

'Nice place to live. What brought you over here?'

'When we sold the family farm I needed somewhere else. Property was slightly cheaper here and it's nice and quiet.'

'How about Rose? Why did she move?'

'She got married.'

'I gather Rose's parents have both passed away.'

'Yes. Her father died when we were all at school. Her mum lasted until about twenty years ago. She developed MS. Rose nursed her for many years.'

'She seemed to have had a very caring side to her, what with her job in the nursery.'

A genuine smile now appeared on Edith's face. 'Yes, she had such a kind nature.'

'It seems a bit odd that she never chose to have children of her own.'

Edith's face clouded. 'She married late, I suppose.'

'Yes.' Jon went to some notes he'd jotted down back at Longsight. 'Married to Ken Sutton in nineteen eighty-eight. Thirty-nine is a bit old, even for nowadays.'

'Well, as I said, she took care of her mother for all those years.'

'Yes you did. And how long had she known Ken Sutton before marrying him? Did he sweep her off her feet in a whirlwind romance?'

The attempt at making her smile again didn't work. 'She'd met Ken. You know, crossed paths over the years. But they didn't start seeing each other until after Elsie – that was her mother – finally died.'

'So things did move quite fast between them.'

'Yes. I was quite surprised. But she was almost forty by then. I think she was afraid of ending up alone.'

Jon looked for a wedding ring on Edith's hand and didn't see one. 'You think she rushed into the marriage then? He was, by my reckoning, fifty-four when they tied the knot.'

'Rushed into it?'

She was stalling for time and Jon sensed that he'd hit upon something.

'You know the saying,' he continued. 'Marry in haste, repent at leisure. Was she happy with Ken?'

She squared off a stack of leaflets on the counter between them. 'I'd say they were content enough. They weren't like young teenagers, all giddy and starry eyed. Too old for that.'

'Yes, but every relationship needs a bit of romance. Was Ken very affectionate towards her?' Jon thought of the man's frosty exterior and couldn't imagine it.

'I suppose so, in his own way.'

'Really? When I spoke to him, he emphasised the effective-ness of their teamwork round the farm. There wasn't a lot of grieving for a lost lover.'

She looked directly at Jon. 'Who knows what goes on behind closed doors? Apparently happy marriages suddenly break up, hopeless ones stand the test of time.'

'You knew Rose. You were her bridesmaid, one of her best friends. Surely she confided in you.'

Edith shook her head. 'As I say, they appeared content enough.'

'How would you describe Rose's relations with other men?'

Her eyes opened wider for just a fraction of a second. 'How do you mean?'

'Did she have many male friends?'

'Not really. The farm is a full-time job, not much time for

socialising with people, male or female. The odd visit to the Shepherd's Rest, but that's hardly private.'

Jon soaked up the sudden rush of information – he hadn't got round to asking where she might meet her friends, male or female. 'I don't know, there must be plenty of quiet spots in the countryside nearby if you were looking for somewhere more private.'

Now she adjusted a pot of pens. 'I really couldn't say.'

Don't worry, Jon thought, you're telling me enough as it is. 'Tell me about Jeremy Hobson. Didn't the two of them spend a lot of time together up on the moors?'

'Jeremy Hobson? The man from Buxton Zoo?' There was a note of disbelief in her voice.

'You think it impossible they could have been having an affair?'

She opened her mouth to reply, but stopped. 'That's not a question I can answer without implying she was having an affair with someone.'

'Was she?'

'I don't know! We didn't sit around discussing that sort of thing.'

Satisfied there was a can of worms waiting to be opened, Jon changed tack. 'Does the name Derek Peterson mean anything to you?'

'No.'

'He was the man discovered yesterday morning. There are some similarities to Rose's death.'

'Oh.'

'You're not interested in what those similarities are?'

She nodded at the radio. 'There was something on the news. They – you – aren't denying their injuries were similar.'

'Peterson trained as a care worker. Could he have met Rose at any sort of conference or training event?'

'I don't know. Rose didn't travel much outside the area. She did her nursery care course at the local school – the sixth form college nowadays. Was he from around here?'

No, Jon thought. And Rose was ten years older than Peterson. 'OK, thanks for your time, Miss Clegg. If we need to ask you anything more, is it possible to call again during office hours?'

'Unless it's the weekend. It can get quite busy then.'

Jon thanked her again then crossed back to the door, Rick just behind. Once outside he rubbed his hands together. It was only just after three o'clock but the sun had already dropped below the jagged ridge that loomed over the village. Only the tops of chimneys on the houses set higher up on the opposite side of the valley were still bathed in light. At street level the gloom and cold were gathering in strength. He set off at a brisk pace towards their car. 'So, was Hobson slipping it to Rose Sutton? Someone definitely was.'

'Could have been Edith Clegg,' Rick said provocatively. 'I didn't notice any wedding ring on her finger.'

Jon glanced to his side. 'Could have been. I think a few more questions in these parts will turn something up.'

At the car Jon looked through the misty windows. 'Poor mutt. Fancy a walk round the car park while he stretches his legs?'

'No problem,' Rick replied.

Punch jumped out a little stiffly, had a good stretch, then trotted off, nose to the ground. Jon and Rick began a slow stroll along the car park's perimeter.

'What if an animal is doing this?' Rick stated in a neutral voice.

Jon breathed in, his eyes on the miniature ravine to his right, the sound of running water audible from the thick shadows at the bottom. 'It could have been if only one person was killed. But two? I don't believe it.'

'But how many sightings of mystery black cats are made in this country each year? How often are the remains of sheep and deer discovered? Jesus, in my mum and dad's village a pony was attacked. Great big claw marks down its flanks. I remember the photo on the front page of the local rag.'

'And how many panthers have been photographed, not to mention caught?'

'I've seen photos. And there are loads of credible witnesses.'

'And I've seen plenty of photos of the Loch Ness monster, UFOs and Bigfoot. Don't believe in any of them though.'

'There are more things in heaven and earth than are dreamt of in your philosophy.'

'You what?'

Rick smiled. 'Hamlet. What about the article in the Police Journal last year? How many coppers were on that golfing day? Ten, twelve? They all witnessed a large puma-like cat cross the fairway not fifty metres in front of them. I don't know in what kind of numbers, but these things are out there.'

'Yeah, I remember the piece too. But whatever they glimpsed, it didn't race up the fairway and start ripping chunks out of them, did it? The animal, and it was probably a big dog, raced off into the woods at the side of the golf course.'

By now they were standing at the corner of the supermarket. In the glow of the exterior lights Punch was exploring the deserted loading area by the side of the building, poking his snout into piles of empty boxes. A rat shot out from under an industrial-sized bin, heading straight towards them. Both men jumped back and it switched direction, streaking across the tarmac for the safety of the nearby stream.

'Punch! See it off!' Jon waved in the direction of the fleeing rodent. 'There, there!'

His dog tensed, then started looking up at the sides of the building.

'Not squirrels, a rat. There!' Jon pointed in its direction again, but it had disappeared over the wall. 'Stupid dog.'

Punch was still excitedly examining the gutters, stumpy tail wagging back and forth as Jon's mobile started to ring. He examined the outer screen and looked at Rick. 'It's the CSM from Crime Lake.' He flicked the phone open. 'Richard, how's things?'

'Fine, thanks. I have a result from that iron bar. It matches a Danny Gordon. I'd fax his record over, only I'd run out of paper if I did.'

Jon grinned. 'What's he been up to?'

'Shoplifting, burglary, joyriding, drunk and disorderly, ABH. He started young, been in and out of homes since a teenager, then juvenile detention facilities and finally graduated to Strangeways itself.'

'Music to my ears,' Jon said. Knowing the answer already, he then asked, 'Is the Silverdale one of the places we've had the pleasure of putting him up in?'

'Yes. Two stints there. One in nineteen ninety-five, then another in ninety-seven.'

'Is there an address for him?'

'Last court appearance he was NFA.'

No fixed address. Minor setback, Jon thought. Scrotes like him rarely stray far from their usual areas. 'Cheers for doing that so quickly Richard.' He hung up and looked at Rick, triumph dancing in his eyes. 'Forget black bloody panthers. The youth Peterson assaulted with that iron bar is called Danny Gordon. He was inside the Silverdale same time Peterson was on the staff there. It was a revenge attack, I'm certain.'

'And Rose Sutton?'

Jon shrugged. 'We'll uncover her connection to Danny Gordon soon enough.' He rang DC Murray's number. 'Hugh, you at the Silverdale facility yet?'

'Yes, boss, I'm with the director right now.'

'We need the records on a Danny Gordon. He did a couple of stints there. One in nineteen ninety-five, another in ninety-seven. Understood?'

'Boss.'

Twenty-One

Jeremy Hobson put on a pair of latex gloves then opened the fridge marked *Not for human use*. All the shelves had been removed to make room for a large plastic crate. Hobson picked it up and placed it on a cutting board next to a metal sink.

He peeled back greaseproof paper to reveal a pile of dead chickens, their claws poked out at awkward angles, necks and feathers bent to the side. After extricating the uppermost bird, he dropped its partially plucked carcass on to the cutting board. As he reached for a serrated knife sticking to the magnetic strip above the sink he looked into the adjoining office.

A young man was standing in front of a TV monitor, flicking between the views from various cameras mounted within the panther enclosure. 'Martin, isn't it?' Hobson asked.

The youth didn't look round. ''S right.'

'I asked you to put those carrots in the water vole runs. Could you do it please?'

'Yeah.'

Shaking his head, Hobson pierced the bird's stomach, then drew the blade up to its breast. Placing the knife to the side, he reached in and tugged out the animal's entrails before dropping them into the washing up bowl in the sink. Then he removed a cleaver from the collection of butcher's implements and brought it down on the bird's neck. After sweeping the decapitated head into the washing up bowl, he rotated the bird, then brought the cleaver down again, chopping it in half. He repeated the procedure with the next bird, then looked down. Lined up on the concrete floor were three stainless steel buckets. He dropped the four chicken halves in to the first bucket.

After dividing up the remaining birds and placing them in the other buckets he reached for a pot of powder on the windowsill.

The label said *Vionate, vitamin mineral supplement.* He dusted the contents of each bucket in a layer of yellowish powder.

Next he lifted up the bowl of innards and stepped over to a large bin in the corner. On the wall above a laminated notice read, *All bones and waste meat must be double bagged in heavy duty bin liners.*

He tipped the bowl up and the chickens' innards slid with a wet plop into the bin. After peeling off his gloves, he dropped them into the bin too then replaced the lid.

'Right,' he said under his breath, surveying the row of buckets. 'Mweru and Mara first.' As he bent down to pick up two buckets, the young man spoke from the office.

'Can I help feed the panthers?'

Hobson straightened back up. 'Feeding the panthers is a privilege that is earned. Seeing as you haven't done anything I've asked of you, no, you can't. In fact, you haven't even earned the right to watch it on the CCTV. Now, if you don't start doing some work you can go back to the Silverdale. There's plenty of others there who'd jump at the chance of a work placement like this.'

Twenty-Two

By the time Jon and Rick got back to Longsight, most of the Outside Enquiry Team were waiting for them. Summerby was also there, looking isolated and uncomfortable in a seat by Jon's desk.

'Sir,' Jon shrugged off his jacket. 'This is DS Rick Saville. We worked together earlier this year. I've brought him in because he's in between rotations at Chester House.'

Summerby shook Rick's hand. 'Accelerated promotion scheme?'

'Yes sir.'

'What did you graduate in?'

'History and Law. Exeter University.'

Jon saw Summerby beam. Here we go, time for a bit of university banter. He busied himself with a file, irked by the fact he could never join in such talks.

'My eldest son went there. Veterinary science.'

'Couldn't lure him into the job then?'

'No, he prefers working with animals,' Summerby replied.

Jon's chin went up. 'He could have got a posting in Salford.'

Summerby gave a light hearted tut. 'So, what developments have we got?'

Jon turned to his In tray. As requested, Danny Gordon's record was there. It ran to several sheets. Jon's hand paused before picking it up. Was now the time to express his doubts over heading the investigation? But with the discovery of Danny Gordon's DNA, things had really started moving. His fingers hovered in mid-air. If I get into tracking Danny Gordon, I know the thrill of the hunt will be impossible to resist. But then again, how long can it take to find him? There's a limit to the number of stones he can hide under.

'Oh, by the way,' Summerby's voice was little more than a whisper. 'I had a meeting this lunchtime with the Chief. He's following the media coverage on this and was anxious to know what progress was being made. I fended off McCloughlin's concerns.'

Jon looked up. 'McCloughlin was in the meeting?'

'Yes, it was a status meeting on current workloads for the Major Incident Team. McCloughlin was loud and clear about having spare capacity now he's wrapped up the post office raids.'

Jon felt a flash of irritation. The bastard wasn't getting a crumb. He picked up the print-out. A photo of a sallow-faced male was at the top, shaved head tilted back, mouth hanging slightly open in a poor attempt at a sneer. 'Seems King Asbo here was the mystery assailant of Derek Peterson. One Danny Gordon, born nineteenth of March nineteen eighty-one. Cautions for shoplifting from eighty-eight. Moved on to burglary and joyriding, did time in juve centres, including the Silverdale. Finally made it to his natural abode – eighteen months in Strangeways in ninety-eight for possession of heroin, another two years in two thousand for the same thing, in and out since then.'

'How have you placed him as Derek Peterson's assailant?'

'The witness to the attack finally came forward and described what happened. Initially Gordon came at Peterson without warning, wielding an iron bar. Peterson managed to disarm him, then proceeded to sexually assault Gordon with the weapon.'

'I beg your pardon?'

Jon nodded. 'You heard right. The witness saw Peterson put the weapon under his car seat before fleeing the scene. The CSM recovered it, swabbed it and found Gordon's DNA.'

Summerby regarded his fingernails for a few moments. 'The things people do. So, you're thinking Gordon caught up with Peterson again in the car park at Crime Lake?'

'Only this time he didn't take any chances with his choice of weapon,' Rick added.

'Why was he after Peterson in the first place?'

'Gordon was in the Silverdale facility at the same time Peterson worked there,' answered Jon. 'From videos we recovered from his house, Peterson had a liking for younger men. And a record for gross indecency. My guess is he was abusing the kids at the care home while he had access to them.'

'And his motivation for killing Rose Sutton?'

Jon felt his lips tighten. 'I don't know. But it's just a matter of time before we find the link to both victims, I'm sure.'

'When are we bringing this Danny Gordon character in?'

Jon dropped the print out on his desk. 'He's NFA. I'll contact his probation officer and put the word out, try the hostels, usual stuff.'

Summerby nodded. 'Anything interesting in Peterson's house?'

'Apart from the video collection, his computer. He was using a web site called Swinger's Haven to arrange his evening liaisons. Signing himself in as Mr P. There seem to be regular users of the site in this area. If Danny Gordon knew who Mr P was, he'd also know when and where Peterson was going to be on the nights he went out looking for sex.'

'Good work.' Summerby stood. 'I'll leave you to it.'

Boosted by his senior officer's approval, Jon turned to the room. 'Listen up everyone. We have a prime suspect.' He'd just brought the team up to speed when DC Murray walked in with a folder.

'You wanted to know about Danny Gordon?' he announced with a grin.

Jon waved him forwards. 'We're all ears, mate.'

Murray headed to the central meeting table and opened the folder. 'Danny Gordon's file from the Silverdale. Why we're kept so busy.'

John listened as the officer described how Gordon had absconded repeatedly from the facility, usually to be found sniffing glue or shoplifting in the city centre. He also had a history of violent outbursts, frequently attacking staff members and fellow offenders.

'We need to find him. Any pointers from the facility?' Jon asked.

'According to the director, if anyone will know, it's this lot,' Murray replied, producing a photograph of a group of lads crouching around a football on the unnatural green of an

Astroturf pitch. 'They formed a five-a-side team, were top of the league the staff organised. The director made a few phone calls and got the whereabouts of the rest.'

He held a finger to the person at the right hand edge of the shot. 'Michael Close. Lives in Aberdeen and works on the rigs in the North Sea. He's our second least promising bet. Did his stint at the Silverdale and has kept his nose clean ever since.'

'Who's the least promising one?' Rick asked.

'Him,' Murray replied, pointing to the next youth. 'Kevin Russell. Died last year when the stolen BMW he was travelling in left the M60 somewhat prematurely with the junction for the M56. No loss to his queen and country. The next one in is our man, Danny Gordon. Crap at football apparently. The guy at his side is James Field. Car thief. Scored all their goals and completed a course in . . . wait for it, car mechanics, while at the facility. Now works in a garage near Ashbury. Last up is Lee Welch, has another four years to go in Strangeways for holding up a jeweller's in the city centre.'

Jon bent over to examine the photograph more closely. Five fairly ordinary looking teenage lads. Danny Gordon was smaller and thinner than Jon imagined him from his mug shot. He was in the middle, looking somehow vulnerable, one hand resting on the football, no smile on his face. Jon wondered exactly what Peterson had done to him. Michael Close was lanky with a mop of brown hair and a friendly expression. He moved to the last two members of the team who were still alive.

Lee Welch had narrowed his eyes to mean slits and was succeeding quite well in looking like a proper thief. Only stick-thin legs betrayed the intimidating look he was trying to achieve. Next to him was James Field. The name had a slightly posh ring to it, Jon thought, staring at the youth. Jon had played in enough rugby teams to know with a glance that the lad was a natural athlete. Fifteen or sixteen, but with a fully adult physique. He was clearly of mixed race, one parent either African or Caribbean.

Jon looked at his watch. Five-twenty. Most offices would be shutting. 'Right, I want each of these people interviewed face to face. It's too late now, but two of you can get started on the drive up to Aberdeen. Any takers?'

The eyes of every single team member slid towards the floor.

'That's a surprise. Well, using my right as boss, I'm giving it to you two, Ashford and Rhea. I'll phone ahead for you.' He turned to a relieved looking DC Murray. 'You're obviously on a roll. Lee Welch is yours to interview. Rick and I will visit James Field's place of work first thing in the morning. Gardiner, you get over to the young offenders' probation offices by the law courts. Find out who was in charge of Danny Gordon and see what he knows. Paul, start asking questions at the soup kitchens and hostels. He may be using them.'

Just before seven Jon got the opportunity to slip outside into the car park. Punch was asleep on the blanket and Jon's heart sank when he realised how long the dog had been stuck in the car. Waking him with a gentle tap on the window, Jon opened the boot. 'Coming for a walk?'

Punch scrabbled to get a firm footing on the loose blanket, then jumped down on to the asphalt. Clicking a lead on to his collar, Jon set off out of the car park, crossed the main road and headed along the other side towards Crowcroft Park.

The noisy rush of commuters driving home meant there was little point in trying to phone Alice until he was in the park itself. He let Punch off the lead, took a seat on a battered bench then got his phone out. How to play it?

'It's me,' he announced cautiously.

'Hi.'

The single word gave nothing away. 'How's things back home?'

'All right thanks.'

Now he detected the flatness in her voice. 'Was Holly good for you today?'

'Not so bad. We both got some sleep after lunch.'

'Good. There's still more to do here, but I shouldn't be that much longer . . . ' He let the sentence trail off, testing the water.

She sighed. 'So I'll just do tea on my own?'

'Probably best. I'll grab something here.' He watched as

Punch circled round on the grass in front of him, before squatting down and curling off a spindly turd. 'Great,' Jon groaned, realising he'd come out without any plastic bags.

'What's great?' Alice asked.

'Punch has just crapped on the grass,' he replied, patting his pockets and finding a latex glove.

'Oh.'

This is as good a time as any, he thought. 'How do you feel if Punch—'

'I've said. We can't have the dog in our house. It's too risky.'

Anger flared. 'My mum can't look after him.'

Nothing from his wife, just a faint squawking in the background.

'Ali, did you hear?'

'Holly's starting up.' Her voice sounded leaden. 'Probably needs changing.'

Nice, he thought. Making your priorities clear then. He pressed the red button, unsure if she'd hung up on him first. How could she be such a fucking cow? Surely being depressed didn't excuse that? Well, if she expected him to hurry back to help out, she was in for a long wait. He had plenty to do earning the money needed for the mountain of nappies, baby milk, clothes and other stuff she so happily took for granted.

He snapped the glove on, reached down and gingerly hooked his fingers under the warm sausage Punch had left, all the while picturing Alice wiping Holly's dirty bottom back home. The lump hit the bottom of the bin with a quiet thud and Jon's phone started ringing again. Hope reared up. Maybe she was ringing to apologise. He removed the glove and looked at the screen. Senior's name glowed there, the ex-Marine who coached at the rugby club. 'Senior, how's it going?'

'You training tonight or what, Slicer?'

Short and to the point as usual, Jon thought. 'No mate. I'm stuck in a big case.'

'Yeah, I saw your ugly mug on my telly. Did your mother never teach you how to knot a tie?'

That's rich, Jon thought with a smile, picturing the moth-eaten jumper, tracksuit trousers and slip-on shoes Senior favoured in the club bar. 'Saturday's looking out too, sorry.'

'Bloody useless you are, Slicer. What's more important? Getting out and playing a match with the boys or getting your face on the bloody telly? You'll be wearing fucking make-up next. Not that it'll do you any good, I've seen better looking arses on the monkeys down at the zoo.'

Jon heard him start to chuckle at his own joke and he couldn't help but grin. He was about to reply when he heard an anxious barking in the background. Senior's Labrador, Bess. She'd been badly affected when the household's other dog, an Alsatian called Arthur, had died a couple of months ago. He glanced towards Punch as a thought suddenly occurred. 'Senior, could Bess do with some company?'

'The dog could do with bloody tranquillisers.'

'I need somewhere for Punch to stay.'

'What's wrong with your own house?'

'Problems with the missus.'

There was a pause and Jon knew the implications of his answer were sinking in. 'You'd better bring him round, then. Not that you'd remember, but training finishes about eight-thirty. Any time after that.'

Jon pulled up outside Senior's house just before ten. The lights were on downstairs and in the corner of the front garden was the usual pile of tackling bags and training bollards. It always amazed Jon how the things were never stolen – but every kid on the nearby estate knew not to aggravate the Sullivans. If Senior didn't find you, one of his two equally stocky sons would.

Jon opened the boot of his car. 'Come on boy, got a new place for you to stay. Just for a bit.'

He could see Punch had sensed the fake cheer in his voice. The dog didn't move. 'Come on, you can kip next to Bess tonight. You remember Bess? You play around with her on the touchline.'

Punch sat up and looked at the house.

'That's it. Come on.' He patted his hand against his thigh.

Warily, Punch jumped down. Jon scooped up the dog bowl

and biscuits, folded up the blanket and carried it all up to Senior's front door. It was opened by Judith, Senior's wife. A neatly dressed woman in her late fifties, she ruled the Sullivan household with a rod of iron. The fact that Senior, who used a non-stop stream of profanities in the rugby club, didn't dare swear in his own house was testimony to that.

'Come in, Jon,' she said, drying her hands on a flowery apron. 'He's in the telly room.'

Jon stepped inside, Punch sticking close to his heels.

'Have you eaten? There's some cheese and biscuits out.'

'No, I'm fine thanks,' said Jon, placing Punch's things on the mat.

'What about you?' she addressed Punch, whose stump of a tail finally began to wag. 'Have you had your supper?'

Jon thought guiltily about the chip shop saveloy he'd tossed to him earlier. 'That would be great, Judith. I'll bring some tins round tomorrow.'

'No need,' she replied, still looking at Punch. 'We've got crates of the stuff. Come on then, Bess is in the kitchen.'

Jon watched as she led Punch away. Bess appeared in the kitchen doorway and the two dogs touched noses, then squeezed past to sniff each other's rear end. Feeling a lot happier, Jon pushed the door open on his right.

Senior was in his armchair, slippers on in place of his shoes, stumpy legs stretched out before him.

'All right, Senior?' Jon asked, placing his mobile phone on the coffee table before slumping on to the sofa.

'Yes,' Senior replied, reaching for the remote and killing the TV's volume. His bull neck swivelled round and he looked at Jon. 'Getting the overtime in then? Hoping for that promotion?'

Jon slid his fingers along the armrest. 'Hoping to get a good night's sleep.'

'What about this case? You're not seriously after some wild animal, are you?'

Jon shook his head. 'We've got someone in mind, don't worry.'

Seeing that was all the information he was going to get, Senior harumphed. 'So, Punch needs a crash pad then?'

Jon sighed. 'It would be a massive favour, believe me.'

Senior glanced to the door. 'She hasn't kicked your sorry arse out too?' he said, deciding it was safe to swear.

'Not yet.'

'Any reason for all this?'

From his tone, Jon knew that Senior meant was there any rational reason, something that a male brain could understand. How to answer? Somehow he didn't think Senior would have much time for words like hormones or depression. 'She's been feeling down recently. Tired out as much as anything.'

'What, too tired to walk the dog?'

'No, the dog thing's different. She thinks that Punch could be, well, sort of a threat, you know? To Holly.'

'Come again?'

Judith stepped into the room with two cups of tea.

'Cheers,' Jon said, sitting up to take one. He cleared his throat before continuing. 'Punch was licking Holly on the head. Alice was, I mean is, afraid the dog's jealous. Basically, she's worried Punch might bite the baby.'

Judith and Senior touched glances.

'Our kids used to ride around on our Boxer dog's back. Remember Bruno, Judith? Lovely breed Boxers, no threat at all.'

Judith crossed her arms. 'That's hardly a help to Jon and Alice is it? How are you both finding it with the baby?'

'Well, hard work. But we knew it would be. Alice is feeling pretty exhausted to be honest.'

'Is she sleeping all right? It's not easy being a mother.'

Jon thought about her raising her two boys. Junior and Rob. They both played for Ironsides and were enough of a handful on the pitch. 'You're right,' he answered, feeling himself opening up. 'She's not herself. A colleague with some experience of this mentioned post-natal depression.'

'Oh, you poor loves,' Judith said, a concerned expression on her face. 'You must make sure she has plenty of company, people to do things for her. Can I help out? Maybe do the shopping or clean the house?'

Jon smiled. 'That's really kind, but looking after Punch is help enough. Both our mums are around; at least Alice's will be back from holiday soon.'

'Well, you just say. I'll cook you some meals, that's always a help.' She left the room, apparently to start straightaway.

Senior waited for a second before leaning over to Jon. 'What's she depressed about?' he asked suspiciously.

Jon sipped at his tea. 'Nothing in particular. She feels anxious all the time. Now I look back, I can see how odd she's been. She was going on about Iraq the other night. Worrying about the fact civilians are being killed.'

'Jesus Christ,' Senior stated ominously.

Jon gave him a questioning glance but Senior shook his head. 'Come on Senior, what?'

The other man glanced at the door again. Keeping his voice low, he said, 'There's going to be some shit hitting the fan soon.'

'What do you mean?'

'I was at a regimental dinner the other day. There was a lot of chat about what's going on over there. Stuff that won't do your missus any good when it makes the news.'

'Go on.'

'They've been getting a bit too rough with a lot of prisoners.'

'Too rough?'

Senior hunched a shoulder. 'It goes on during any conflict. The problem is those bloody things.' He directed his gaze to Jon's mobile phone. 'They've been photographing it, and now images are leaking out.'

'From where?'

'The big prison in Baghdad. The one the Yanks took over from Saddam Hussain. Abu Ghraib. They're really laying into the prisoners they've got locked up in there. More than just scaring them with guard dogs.'

'Doing what then?'

'One photo had this hooded guy balancing on a stool. Wires hanging off him.'

'A prisoner?'

'Someone they'd pulled in. A terrorist probably. There was more. A few had died during interrogation. Wrapped up in cling film, probably suffocated.'

Jon stared at him in disbelief.

'Don't look so shocked, it's a war, Slicer. You can't pussyfoot around.'

'No, but aren't there conventions for this sort of thing?'

Senior raised his eyebrows. 'Like the enemy'd stick to? They're sawing people's heads off, remember?'

'Those gung-ho Yanks are a bloody liability.'

Senior fixed him with a cold stare. 'I gathered there are photos from Basra too. Our boys aren't blameless either. Anyway, don't tell me you've never got carried away with some little thief you've nicked.'

Jon pictured the times when he'd lost control. There'd been quite a few, but never amounting to more than a few bruises on the suspect. A broken tooth on one occasion. But then he thought of the politicians selling the reason for the invasion with smoothly delivered words. 'Yeah, but our whole approach over there is promising a change from Saddam, introduce peace, freedom, democracy. We're meant to be the good guys.'

Senior gave a dismissive wave. 'Slicer, I might be a bone-headed ex-Marine, but you don't really think I believe that's why we're over there?'

'No, but that's the official line the politicians spout. How does that square with torturing suspects?'

Again Senior shrugged. 'Give me a war where this stuff doesn't go on. The only difference with this one is the souvenir snaps they've been stupid enough to send to their mates back home. It'll reach the press soon, mark my words.'

Jon's eyes strayed to the clock display on his mobile. Ten-twenty. 'I've got to go. Holly will be wanting her bottle.'

He had reached the doorway when Senior said his name. He looked back into the room. The other man was sitting in his armchair, one finger raised to his lips. Jon returned the gesture with a nod.

Ten minutes later he unlocked his front door, eyes automatically moving to the end of the corridor in anticipation of Punch bounding delightedly towards him. All there was were a few dead leaves lying on the carpet. Their dry, lifeless forms made him feel uneasy and he found himself picking them up and tossing them out the door.

The house was quiet. He leaned into the front room. Empty. Kitchen lights were off. Hanging his jacket on the banister, he climbed the stairs. Little sucking sounds from the nursery. He looked in, just able to make Holly out in her cot, her eyes open and a dummy moving back and forth between her lips.

Just in time, he thought. He hurried down the stairs and flicked the kitchen light on. Alice's dinner stuff was all still out, plate lying on top of other dirty washing up in the sink. Opening the fridge, he saw she hadn't prepared a bottle. Shit. He touched the kettle, relieved it was only faintly warm. The water was about right for Holly's bottle. After washing his hands, he mixed up four ounces then climbed back up the stairs.

Once she was safely on his lap, he removed her dummy, instantly replacing it with the bottle's teat before she could start crying. She began sucking away and Jon was able to relax. The curtains weren't quite drawn and through the gap he was able to see a black cat sitting on their yard wall. It appeared to be sunning itself in the orange glow from the streetlamp above. After a minute the animal stood up and stretched. Then it looked into his yard before dropping silently down on to the concrete. Watching it, Jon wondered how a panther might compare. Was it five, ten, fifteen, times larger? What did a panther weigh? Six stone? Maybe more? And was that how it moved, cautious yet graceful? He craned his head to watch as the cat began to explore. It approached the patch of wall to the side of their back gate, sniffed, then turned round and sprayed the stone with urine. One day, Jon thought. Punch is missing for one day and already the bloody cats are claiming the yard as their own.

Holly's head slumped back, milk glistening on her chin. The bottle was almost empty so he returned it to the windowsill, burped her, then placed her gently back in the cot.

In the darkness of their bedroom he could see Alice's form curled beneath their duvet. Her breathing was slow and deep. She probably hadn't even woken when he unlocked the front door. Well, so much for talking things through with her tonight.

First thing in the morning, he told himself, as a wave of exhaustion crashed over him. Shedding his clothes as quickly as possible, he slipped beneath the covers and closed his eyes.

Twenty-Three

The bells in the tower were ringing furiously, but the noise they produced was high pitched and tinny. One hand resting on the rough stone of the parapet, Jon turned his eyes from the minaret that towered above him and looked out across the desert plain. Through the heat haze, far away on the horizon, a dark shadow wavered, expanding out and then contracting back in on itself. Jon squinted, trying to make out if it was approaching or retreating. Sheets of rain drifting down? Its black edges were growing more defined, and he realised with a sense of dread that it was advancing across the sands with incredible speed. What was it? One moment it seemed like the billowing sail of a ship, then it changed to something more like liquid, silently flowing forwards like an ocean bed creature. A dust storm? But there was no wind to propel it forward.

In the foreground was a train of camels. The animals were running, long legs seeming to intertwine for a moment before stretching apart again. They were crying out in distress, but the sound that came from their mouths – just audible above the infuriating bells – was the grating whinny of horses. Suddenly he had a sense of the sheer scale of the thing as blackness swept around the animals' legs before swallowing them up completely.

Now the stone beneath his palm started to tremble and shake. He began to moan, knowing only seconds remained before the fortress was engulfed. Finally his eyes snapped open, the bells morphing into the electronic ring of his mobile. Alice's hand was on his shoulder, roughly shaking him.

'I've got it,' he said, sitting up in the darkness.

'It's in your trousers.'

He blinked, realising his hand was scrabbling about on the bedside table. Trousers. She's right. A moment later the phone was in his hand. The screen's clock read five fifty-three. 'Jon . . . DI Spicer here.'

'Sir, it's Sergeant Morris, radio room at Longsight.'

A burst of adrenalin brought him fully awake. 'What's up?'

'Sorry to ring so early. We've received a call from Inspector Clegg, Mossley Brow. Ken Sutton just turned up at the station there. He's got the body of a panther in his trailer outside.'

By the time Jon got to Mossley Brow the sky was beginning to lighten. Parked in front of the station was the red McConnel tractor Jon remembered from Sutton's farm. A crowd of people was gathered round the aluminium trailer attached to the rear, several police officers amongst them.

Jon parked on the opposite side of the road and hurried towards the excited babble of voices. A person with a camera was on the station steps, directing proceedings.

'OK, please step to the side those of you at the front,' he shouted, sweeping one arm outwards as if parting a curtain. A young man with blond hair began to straighten up in the trailer, obviously struggling with something heavy. That other bloke from Sutton's farm, Jon thought, as a chorus of cheers rang out and the photographer's flash started going off.

He was about to move round to the back of the tractor when he spotted Carmel Todd chatting animatedly to a colleague. How did she get here so fast? He scanned for other familiar faces, soon spotting Ken Sutton at the edge of the crowd, his face totally expressionless.

Avoiding Carmel, Jon walked round to the front of the tractor, knowing what he was about to see. The young man had his arms hooked under the front legs of a large black cat. Its head lolled forward, a long drool of blood hanging from its partly open jaw. The man was grinning triumphantly at the camera as more flashes went off.

Jon spotted Clegg by the station doors. The man's eyes were fixed on the spectacle, a huge smile on his face. 'What the hell is going on?' Jon demanded.

Clegg's eyes met his and his smile faltered. 'They've caught it, boss, it's over.' He nodded at the trailer. 'The blond guy bagged it in the field above Sutton's farm. He was waiting in a hide he'd built in a tree.'

Jon looked down the steps. 'Why do I appear to be the last person to be told about this?'

Clegg's eyes swept over the crowd of excited locals. 'Word travels fast. I called your station at Longsight.'

Yeah, and who else, Jon thought, glancing at the reporter from the *Manchester Evening Chronicle*. 'And the journalists? Who tipped them off?'

'The guy in the trailer. He rang in for his reward.'

'And did you find out exactly who he is?'

'A relative of Sutton's apparently. I'm not sure of his name.'

'You were meant to be checking on his identity and firearms certificate.'

Clegg looked awkward. 'It was on my list, I just hadn't quite got round to it.'

Useless prick, Jon thought, turning towards the crowd. The photographer had cocked his camera so its lens pointed up at the orange sky. With his other arm he started to gesture again. 'Can you get it so its head is hanging over the side of the trailer? Yes, that's it, perfect. Just lift it up a shade.'

Blood started streaming over the metallic surface and the photographer focused in on it. Slowly he moved down the steps, finally crouching below the animal's head and shooting upwards for a more dramatic angle. Onlookers vied to get in at the edges of the shot, young lads holding their thumbs up. Jon was reminded of a photo of a lynching in America's deep south. The same cruel triumph shone in everyone's eyes.

The photographer stood up and looked at Carmel. 'I've got plenty.'

With an anxious glance at the cars pulling up on the main road, she walked over to the trailer. 'Andrew, we need to get a move on. We'll go in my car.'

As Andrew jumped down, Jon could see people with cameras climbing out of the cars. Rival journalists.

Carmel waved at Ken Sutton. 'Your tarpaulin. Can you pull it back over the animal?'

He nodded, and started to approach the trailer. Jon went

down the steps and gripped the young man's upper arm. 'You shot that animal?'

'Yeah!' he beamed.

'Then I'd like to ask you a few questions.'

Carmel's arm shot out and her fingers curled round Andrew's other arm. 'He promised me an interview, it's a condition if he's claiming the reward money.' She glanced at the swarm of approaching reporters, then back at Jon. 'Can we discuss this somewhere more private?'

Jon gave the young man a little grin. 'Now you know what it feels like to be the quarry.'

'Eh?' he said, looking confused.

'Let's go to the station,' Jon replied, leading him up the stairs. 'Inspector Clegg, please secure the body of that animal. I don't want anyone to touch it.'

Now inside reception, Jon nodded at the woman behind the counter. 'Coming through please.'

She pressed the buzzer and they had just stepped through into the corridor beyond when the first reporter burst through the front doors. 'Excuse me! Excuse me! *Daily Mail*, could I speak with you please?'

Jon watched Carmel click the inner door shut, the middle finger of her right hand raised at the man on the other side of the glass. Jon couldn't help smirking with amusement. She turned round, professional front now restored. 'DI Spicer. That lead article wasn't my doing.'

Jon folded his arms. 'I don't remember inviting you through this door.'

Carmel looked dismayed. 'Please. You can't kick me back out there.' She glanced over her shoulder at the throng of faces pressed against the glass.

Jon turned on his heel. 'Come on.' He marched down the corridor towards Clegg's office. The kitchen was on his left and he veered inside. Thank Christ for caffeine. Grabbing three mugs, he said, 'Tea or coffee?'

Andrew spoke first. 'Tea please.'

Once the drinks were made, Jon led them into Clegg's office

and pointed to a couple of chairs. He perched on the edge of a desk. 'You're giving her an interview?'

The young man nodded. 'Shit yeah. Fifty grand, I'll do the thing naked if she wants.'

Carmel gave a girly laugh that rang as totally fake to Jon. 'We could discuss that, I suppose.' She reached for a notebook and pen.

Jon held up a forefinger. 'No you don't.'

She registered his expression and slid the notebook back in her handbag. He turned his attention to the younger man. 'What's your name?'

'Andrew Du Toit, Sir.'

The accent was unmistakable. 'South African?'

He nodded, still smiling.

'What are you doing in the UK?'

His expression grew more serious, but his eyes radiated confidence. 'Staying on my uncle's farm.'

Jon remembered the farmer claiming that the younger man in the Land Rover was a neighbour. How many other lies was the old boy telling? 'Ken Sutton is your uncle?'

'Yes, my mum is his sister.'

'How long has she lived in South Africa?'

'She emigrated in the early sixties.'

'And you were born there?'

'Yup, nineteenth of July, nineteen eighty-one. It's all on my passport.'

'When did Ken Sutton contact you?'

'He called just after his wife's death. I've worked on game reserves around the Kruger since I was fifteen.'

'In what capacity?'

'Guide, tracker, all sorts.'

'Hunter?'

'Yeah, sometimes animals need to be culled.'

'I saw you at Sutton's farm the other day. Have you got a licence for the rifle you were carrying?'

He nodded, reaching into his jacket. Jon saw the blood smeared down its front. 'Licence and permission from customs to bring it into the country.'

Jon scanned the pieces of paper. They looked genuine enough, though he'd check later. 'May I keep these for the time being?'

'Sure.'

Jon relaxed a bit, more confident of the man's cooperation. 'What happened last night then?'

'At Ken's farm?'

'Yes.'

'I built a hide in the oak tree in the field above his farm, it borders the moor itself. Then I tethered a sheep a short distance away. I set up a spotlight, then waited for nature to take its course.'

'The sheep was attacked then?'

'Oh yeah. The cat approached the stake-out at about ten past four. The sheep started bleating like hell, so I knew it was out there. As soon as I heard it strike, I hit the light. She was on the sheep's back.' He clicked his fingers twice. 'Two shots, first hit its rear leg, second was a headshot. Bullet went straight through and ended up in the sheep. Two dead animals.'

'And it's a panther?'

He nodded. 'To be honest, I didn't think it would be that easy. Leopard is one of the most difficult animals to hunt. But that old girl? She's well past her prime.'

'You can tell its age?'

'I can tell she wasn't young. Overweight, a couple of teeth missing, eyes going rheumy. They suffer the same stuff we do in old age. Take a look at her kidneys when you open her up. They're one of the first things to go in big cats.'

'Was it capable of killing a human?'

He nodded without hesitation. 'She may have been old, but that doesn't pose a problem for hunting humans. We're easy prey. Compared to an impala and most other animals, our sight, hearing and sense of smell are non-existent. We can't run very fast and without a weapon, we have no real means of defence. Check what's in her stomach. Big cats' digestive systems are quite slow because, in the wild, they can go several days between feeds.'

Jon considered the advice, realising the dead cat could be a valuable source of forensic evidence. The memory of Derek Peterson's shredded neck made an unwelcome return. 'What about its claws? Could there be debris trapped there?'

'You mean like under human nails?'

'I suppose so.'

'I doubt it. Any kind of cat – big or small – is meticulously clean. Always washing and grooming. Plus their saliva is packed with powerful enzymes that break down scraps of food. Prevents the likelihood of infection.'

Jon wished he'd let Carmel take notes. He could have photocopied them. 'What do you propose doing now?'

Andrew shrugged. 'Not sure. I had planned to go straight home if I shot it. But I'm getting more used to your weather. Ken could do with a hand on the farm as well. Plus a couple of guys in the local pub asked if I wanted to run out for Glossop rugby club.'

'You play?'

'Yeah, fly half. You?'

'Flanker.'

'Ah right. You guys reckon you're gonna win the world cup this year?'

Jon knew he should resist the temptation of slipping into informality. He smiled, happy to fail for the moment. 'I think we could do it.'

Andrew tilted a hand. 'You're in with a shout if you protect Wilkinson. He kicks anything.'

Jon spotted Carmel's eyes glazing over and he stood up. 'I'll send an officer in to take a full statement. And could I request that you don't leave the area without letting Inspector Clegg know first? This is an ongoing murder enquiry.'

'Can I take him to our offices in Manchester?' Carmel asked.

Jon directed his answer at Andrew. 'Yes. Don't say a word until she's given you a signed contract, understand?'

Carmel widened her eyes, as if surprised by his insinuation. 'When can we expect another statement, DI Spicer?'

Jon held a hand to his ear, thumb and little finger extended. 'Contact the press office.'

He headed for the back door of the station, crossing the car park to where Sutton's trailer was parked. Clegg and a couple of other officers were standing by it. Jon went over and lifted up the tarpaulin. The coppery smell of blood hit him. He looked at the panther for a few seconds, taking in the massive paws and imagining the size of the claws sheathed inside them. Even stretched out in death with blood matting its coat, the animal was magnificent. It must have measured six feet in length and he couldn't guess how much it weighed. The same as an adult human, easily. With a twinge of sadness, he let the cover fall back. His eyes settled on the semi-congealed drips of blood on the trailer's side. 'We'll need a DNA test to confirm it matches the hairs recovered from both victims. And we'll need an autopsy. See if there's any human tissue floating around in her stomach.'

Twenty-Four

'DCI Summerby.'

'Morning, boss, it's DI Spicer.'

'Jon, where are you?'

'At Mossley Brow nick. I assume you've heard?'

'Yes, is this for real?'

'Afraid so. I've seen the carcass myself. A bloody great panther.'

'Ye gods!'

'I'm arranging for an analysis of its stomach contents and we're getting a DNA profile too. See if there's a match to the hairs found on Peterson and Sutton.'

'You think there will be?'

Jon hooked a finger into the telephone cord and stretched the coils taut. The panther was a major development but, in his view, nothing more than a distraction. Danny Gordon still needed to be caught. 'Not really.' He twisted his finger free and the length of plastic sprang back into shape.

'How so?'

'I questioned the guy who shot it. South African called Du Toit, nephew of Ken Sutton. He's worked on game reserves all his life and he reckons the animal was a geriatric. I'm still very much of the opinion Danny Gordon is our killer.'

'It would make things a damn sight simpler if it turns out to have been that cat.'

'True, but I'm not convinced.'

'What's the progress with finding Gordon?'

'He's of no fixed abode, but we'll get scent of him soon. If not we could consider naming him in an appeal for information.'

'Talking of which,' Summerby replied, 'we need to get a

statement out about this panther straight away, the phones are going mad here.'

Jon nodded. 'I'll get on to Gavin Edwards.'

'Fine, I'll relay your news to the incident room. Will you be heading back soon yourself?'

'I'll be there in an hour.'

Jon was about to call the press office when his finger hesitated over the buttons. He called home instead, a slight sense of unease mounting with each unanswered ring. Bollocks, he cursed as the answer phone clicked in. She's probably upstairs feeding. 'Ali, it's me. Sorry to miss you this morning. Give us a call on my mobile.' He replayed the message in his head. Too unemotional. 'I love you, babe,' he quickly added, before hanging up.

The incident room at Longsight was subdued and Jon sensed the news about the panther had sucked the urgency away. Why bust a gut until it was confirmed the cat wasn't a man-eater? Time to dispel that notion, he decided, clapping his hands together.

'Right! Let's have some fucking action.' He started firing questions about. 'What's going on with the door-to-doors? Have Rhea and Ashford got to Aberdeen yet? Is DC Murray at Strangeways? What's the news from the team dredging Crime Lake? Any responses to our appeal for witnesses? Sergeant Biggs, a progress report on the interviews taking place around Mossley Brow.'

As activity broke out across the room, he dropped the evidence bag with the sample of panther blood on his desk. Rick caught his eye from his desk alongside. 'You look halfway through an exercise in sleep deprivation.'

Jon took in his colleague's immaculately styled hair and crisp pale blue shirt. He managed a quick smile. 'Probably because I am.'

'What's in the evidence bag?'

'Panther blood. We need to get it tested.' He picked up the phone, noticing the file at the top of his in-tray. It was a report from Richard Matthews, the CSM for the car park where Peterson was found. He replaced the handset. 'Shit, he's already finished up?' The report listed various findings from the spot, confirming that the dredging of the lake and fingertip search of the surrounding fields had failed to find the murder weapon. 'I was hoping he'd run this test for me.'

He sat down, his mind going over who else could ensure that the blood sample would be treated as a genuine priority over samples from other investigations that also would have been filed as urgent. Nikki Kingston. She'd never failed him before. Then again, that was before she'd made a pass that he'd turned down. He dialled her number. 'Nikki, it's Jon Spicer.'

'DI Spicer, what a pleasure.'

He heard the note of reservation in her voice. 'How's it going? You keeping busy?'

'It's not too manic at the moment.'

Great, he thought. Deciding it was too early to come out with his request, he continued with the small talk. 'Where are you?'

'At the scene of a rape in Openshaw. The carpet in the front room where it happened is infested with fleas and I've just been crawling about swabbing for semen. Some people live like bloody animals. Anyway, I'm sure that's not why you're ringing. A favour, is it?'

'Well, yeah. A DNA test on a sample of panther blood.'

'Really?' Enthusiasm now flooded her voice. 'Of course, you're on that case, there was stuff on the news. What was the creature like? Big as a tiger?'

'Not far off. You wouldn't like to have met it in a dark alley, put it that way. Beautiful animal. Shame it got shot really.'

'I'd love to see it up close.'

'Well, I'm trying to arrange an autopsy for it. We're storing it in the morgue at the MRI until a vet with the necessary experience can be found. I'll see if you can pop in.'

'So you need to see if its blood matches the samples of hair recovered from the victims?'

'You got it,' he replied, always impressed with her sharpness. 'How easy will that be?'

'Should be straightforward, as long as the hairs contained sufficient DNA for a profile.'

'They did,' Jon replied, recalling the report. The hairs themselves had been scored into wafer thin slices, mounted on glass slides and analysed under a microscope. Characteristics on the cuticle, cortex and medulla had led to their being identified as those of a panther. But, crucially, a DNA profile had also been obtained from the keratin proteins that forms the hairs themselves.

'Listen, I've got a kit in my car outside. It's not acceptable to use as evidence in court, but it'll do until the lab can give you an official result. How's that?'

'I'll get it biked over.' After taking her address, he replaced the receiver and looked up, the smile still on his face. Rick was staring at him accusingly. 'That was the Nikki you said you'd be steering clear of?'

'It's only a DNA test.'

'How's Alice?'

If the question was designed to bring him back down to earth, it worked. 'I haven't had time to speak with her. I'll try calling her again.' He looked for Rick's reaction and got a silent stare. 'Don't look at me like that. When am I meant to find time?'

'How about now?'

'I could if you'd stop frigging well nagging me like an old woman. Anyway, we need to get over to James Field's place of work, remember?'

'Jon, it's your wife's health we're talking about here.'

Rick was right, and he shouldn't let the fact she'd been a complete bitch about Punch interfere with his judgement. But the seed of resentment was there. 'I'll try her, OK?' He dialled home. Still no answer. 'How about we drop in later today? You haven't seen her for a few weeks. It would be useful to know what you reckon.'

Rick stood up. 'No problem.'

They drove towards Piccadilly station, followed the road to the Apollo then turned left at the roundabout leading to Temperance Street. The road was narrow, lying in the shadow of a series of arches that carried the train line connecting Manchester to Sheffield.

Jon regarded the countless red bricks that formed the huge spans, marvelling at the effort involved in their construction.

The number of men who'd laboured to create the world's first industrial city always fascinated him – almost twenty thousand navvies were needed to dig the Manchester Ship Canal alone. Some of those were his relatives from Ireland who went on to settle in the city.

The space below each arch had been utilised by a series of garages. Cars in various states of repair clogged the street and what little pavement there was.

'Best we park here or we'll get boxed in,' Jon said, pulling over. They climbed out and approached the first garage. A flaking sign said, *Taylors Autos*. Jon looked at the cannibalised remains of vehicles piled up around the entrance. 'I wonder if every re-spray done on this street is for legitimate purposes?'

Rick chuckled. 'I'm sure everything is declared to the taxman.'

A man emerged through the doors built into the second archway, an engine part with wires that dangled like innards gripped in his hand.

Jon stepped forward. 'A and L Repairs. Which one, mate?'

The person lobbed the part on to a stack of similar objects, his eyes moving over Jon before he nodded to his left. 'Fourth along.'

'Cheers.'

They continued up the street. The tarmac could have done with a resurface decades ago, there were craters dotted around, most filled with puddles of oily water. Jon watched the colours shimmering on their surfaces as he passed. The double doors of A and L Repairs were closed, but a smaller door cut into the left-hand side was ajar. From inside came a crackling sound accompanied by erratic flashes of blue light. Jon squinted into the gloom beyond, then pushed the door fully open.

The shaft of daylight fell on a figure who was hunched over a vehicle, welding torch poised in his hand. The pointed flame flickering from its end caught Jon's eye, its hiss reminding him of a snake's tongue. The man turned his head and lifted up his visor; a big black beard hung over an oil-stained Manchester City shirt. Jon guessed he was about fifty.

'Is James Field around?' Jon asked.

He tilted his head. 'At the back.' Not waiting for a reply, he lowered his visor and adjusted the torch's nozzle so the flame contracted into an intense blue spike. He brought it against the bodywork and sparks sprayed out. Jon stepped inside, the air was heavy and metallic, a smell that took him back to school and metalwork lessons. Welding a toasting fork his parents never used.

The concrete floor was awash with silvery shreds and scraps of wire. He edged round the side of the vehicle, careful to keep his eyes away from the brilliant flame. Two more cars were parked behind it and beyond them was the rear part of the garage. A strip light hung from the high vault of bricks above, though it was only partly successful at illuminating the area below it. Jon could see a work bench littered with tools. A small reading lamp was positioned at its edge and sitting in a battered old office chair next to it was a young man. His feet were propped up on a tool box and his gaze was directed down at a book.

'James Field?'

No response.

Jon moved closer, holding a hand out at waist level and waving it near the person's face. 'James Field?'

He looked up, one hand tugging out his earphones. 'Yeah?'

Jon took out his warrant card. 'DI Spicer and DS Saville, Greater Manchester Police. Got a minute?'

'Yeah.'

To Jon's surprise, he didn't seem at all bothered about two policemen suddenly rousing him from his break. 'It's about Danny Gordon.'

'Danny Boy? What's he done now?' The accent was unmistakably Mancunian.

A low rumbling gathered in strength, turning into something like thunder as a train passed overhead. James Field stood up, threw his book into a locker and swung the dented door shut. The noise of the train receded.

'Can we talk outside?' Jon asked. 'It would be a lot easier.'

Field nodded and Rick led the way back to the entrance. Out on the street Jon could see Field was in his early twenties. His head was shaved and he was wearing a pair of filthy overalls, the straps looping over solid shoulders. Jon took out his notebook. 'When did you last see Danny Gordon?'

Field thought for a moment. 'I don't know. A while.'

'As in weeks, months or years?'

'Oh years. Five, easily. What's he done?'

'We just need to speak to him. You two were mates at the Silverdale?'

The whites of his eyes showed as he looked up at the dirty sky. 'The Silverdale? Yeah. That's where I met him. We were friends, but that's a long time back.'

'Did you keep in contact afterwards?'

'A bit to begin with, but he started robbing again. I wanted to learn a trade, started doing mechanics.'

Jon was impressed that the young man had resisted the easy option back into crime; it took a lot of determination to do what he'd done. Not wanting to appear patronising, he just nodded. 'Any ideas where he hangs around nowadays?'

Field puffed out his cheeks and let the air escape from between his lips. 'Squats.'

At the mention of the word an image of his younger brother flashed in Jon's head. The few times Jon had seen him since he'd left home, Dave had told him he was living in squats round the city.

'Any particular squat?'

'They change all the time, don't they? A place in Ancoats, but I'm going back years. They knocked it down recently to build more executive flats.'

'Can you tell me about a staff member at the Silverdale? Derek Peterson.'

The name prompted a humourless smile. 'Mr P.'

Jon connected with Rick's glance. Peterson's name on Swinger's Haven.

Field shook his head. 'He still at that place?'

Hardly, Jon thought, picturing his corpse in the MRI's morgue. 'Why did you call him Mr P?'

By bracing his shoulders back, Field pushed himself clear of the wall. He nudged at a lump of plastic with the toe of his trainers. 'We always said the p was for piss-head.'

Jon remembered the mention of cans in Peterson's kitchen. 'Did he drink on duty in the Silverdale?'

Field continued toying with the lump of plastic. 'Yeah. He had his little cliques, invite them into his office when he was on night shift, offer them booze.'

'What little cliques? Kids in the facility?'

Field nodded. 'He always steered clear of me. He liked the sickly-looking quiet ones.'

'What do you mean liked?'

'They'd get booze, smokes. He'd bring them magazines. Wank mags, anything. It was a power thing. You were either one of his favourites or you weren't.'

Jon contemplated how the man must have manipulated the youngsters. It didn't take much to guess how he called his favours in. 'Was Danny Gordon one of his favourites?'

'I suppose.'

'Peterson would get him drunk?'

'Yeah.'

'How was he after these drinking sessions?'

'How was he?'

'Happy, sad, chatty, subdued?'

'Subdued. He had a hangover.'

Jon rolled his pen between his fingers. 'Did he ever say what happened during these drinking sessions?'

'Not really, it was all part of the clique thing. They liked being secretive, it was a way of gloating at us lot who weren't included.'

'But you were mates with Danny Gordon. Didn't he let on anything to you?'

'Nah, we didn't talk about it. I didn't want to give him the satisfaction of blanking me.'

'Do you remember the names of the other kids in these cliques?'

Field frowned. 'One was called Sawyer, little weaselly guy. Another called Dealey or something. He didn't stay at the Silver very long. There were a couple of others. Not sure of their names.'

Jon jotted the two surnames down. They'd need to trace

every person in the facility from when Peterson was an employee. He closed his notebook and looked around. 'How long have you worked here?'

'Since doing my qualifications. Two years or so.'

'So you've got your own place?'

'Yeah, Ryder Brow. Three stops on the train.'

'You work in a garage and you don't drive?'

'Not on what I earn.'

It was a shame. The guy was obviously bright enough to have fought his way through the pitfalls of a care home upbringing. He deserved better than this. Jon watched as Field flicked the piece of plastic up. He knocked it slightly higher with his other foot, then volleyed it across the narrow street. It clattered off the wall and bounced behind a pile of hubcaps.

'Still play football? I gather you were top scorer for that team at the Silverdale.'

He smiled. 'That was just kids' stuff. Half of them couldn't run the length of the pitch.'

Jon took in his stocky build. 'You should have played rugby.'

Field laughed. 'I liked the look of it. Jonah Lomu. There's no prissy diving in rugby, is there?'

Jon's eyes lit up at the comment. Cheadle Ironsides were always on the lookout for new players, and this guy looked like he could be really useful. 'I see you more as a Jason Robinson type. Plays for Sale Sharks?'

'Yeah, I know. Billy Whizz they call him.'

Jon nodded. It occurred to him that the first team captain, Ian Reynolds, ran a big garage in Stockport. He was always moaning about how hard it was to find reliable mechanics. 'Why don't you give it a go? I play for a club near here. Cheadle Ironsides. Training is Tuesday and Thursday nights at seven o'clock.'

Field looked unconvinced. 'How'd I get there?'

'Someone'll give you a lift. The lads live all around this area.' He took out one of his cards. 'Give me a ring. About Danny Gordon if you hear anything, or about the rugby.'

Reluctantly, Field took the card. As they walked away Jon looked over his shoulder. 'You've heard of Reynolds' Garage in Stockport? The guy who owns it plays for the club. He needs decent mechanics too. I'll introduce you to him, I bet he pays better than this place.'

An uncertain smile was now on Field's lips. He looked at Jon's card properly this time. 'Cheers.'

They'd taken a few more steps before Rick said, 'I can't believe you're using a murder investigation to recruit players for your rugby club.'

Jon shrugged. 'That's how it works, mate.' He fell silent, thinking about how the course of his younger brother's life might have been different if he'd only got into sport and off the streets.

As they got to the car Jon glanced at his watch. Eleven-thirty. No one from the Outside Enquiry Team would be reporting back until after lunch. 'Fancy dropping by ours then?'

Rick looked across the roof of the car at him. 'I don't want it to look like we're checking up on her.'

'It won't. I'll say we were just passing by. She'll be fine.'

After reversing out of the narrow street Jon drove back to the roundabout. As they went past the turn-off for the A57, Jon saw Rick gazing up the road towards Belle Vue, The Butcher's dumping ground earlier that year. 'Good to be working with you again.'

'Say again?' said Rick, turning his head, a haunted look on his face.

'It's good to be working with you again,' Jon repeated.

Rick smiled. 'Cheers. Never a dull moment with your cases. Even if I end up needing sleeping pills.'

'Only way for it to be,' Jon answered, now heading down the A6. They continued past Longsight police station, leaving the main road a few minutes later and cutting across a couple of residential streets before pulling up outside Jon's house. He looked at the front door, wondering what sort of a greeting awaited them. God, I hope she's all right.

His key turned in the lock and the door opened to the sound of Holly crying. 'It's me, babe, Rick's here. We're just popping in to see the baby.'

Behind him Rick gave a tentative call. 'Hi Alice.'

Jon could hear her getting up in the front room. He stepped

through the door. Damp baby clothes were draped in a line along the radiator; Holly was lying in a vest on the change mat in the centre of the room. By her side was an open nappy sack with a dirty nappy in, a pack of wipes next to it. Alice had just got off the sofa and was running her fingers through her hair. She was still in her dressing gown and alarm showed in her eyes. 'Rick,' she called back. 'I'm not even dressed yet, look at me.'

Rick appeared in the doorway. 'Hey Alice, do I care? It's great to see you.'

Alice managed a smile but she was obviously flustered. 'Would you like a coffee?'

'I'll make them,' Rick offered.

'Nonsense, you sit down.'

Alice stepped towards the door and Jon could see she was going to take Holly with her.

'Well, at least let me have a cuddle.' Rick's arms were outstretched.

'Oh, you really want a crying baby?'

Rick grinned. 'Doesn't bother me.'

Alice delayed for an instant before holding Holly out. Totally relaxed, Rick took her and began a gentle rocking. Holly's sobs died away.

'A natural,' Alice said, crouching down to grab the nappy sack. 'Right, drinks.' She left the room and Jon raised his eyebrows and looked at Rick. His partner nodded towards the kitchen.

Jon walked down the short corridor. Alice was filling the kettle. 'Sorry I missed you this morning, Ali. It was better to sneak out and leave you a note.'

'You could have called to say you were bringing Rick round. You never drop by during the day. The house is a total mess.'

Jon opened his palms. 'Ali, we've got a young baby. The house is meant to look like a bomb's hit it.' She fired him an irritated glance. 'Not that it does. There's just a bit of healthy untidiness. Besides, Rick doesn't mind.'

'I saw a report on the news. They've caught that animal?'

'Yeah, this guy from South Africa shot a panther.' He didn't want to get into the details of the case. 'Have you got much planned today?'

Alice was peering into a cupboard. 'We've got no coffee. Ask Rick if he wants tea.'

Jon bent his head back and called down the corridor. 'Rick. Do you fancy tea, mate?'

'Whatever's easiest.'

Alice made three cups then plucked a hair band off the windowsill and began to tie her hair back. Jon watched sunlight catching in the blonde strands. There was something sensual about the sight and he was reminded of lazy Sunday mornings – waking to find daylight peeping round the curtains, slowly making love then falling back asleep. Jesus, that now seemed part of another life entirely.

In the front room Rick had sat down on the sofa. Holly was cradled in the crook of his elbow, eyes shut and one arm hanging limply down. Alice set his mug on the table, then took a seat herself, drawing her long legs up under her.

'So,' Rick said. 'You've got yourself one beautiful baby.'

Alice's lips relaxed enough to allow a brief smile. 'Thanks.'

'How's she sleeping at nights?'

Alice kept her eyes resolutely on Holly. 'OK. She's awake every three hours I suppose.'

Rick gave a low whistle. 'I can't imagine it. I know my sister found it tough.'

He paused to allow her a response. Alice completely missed the cue, Jon noted, not even asking what the baby's name was or how it was doing now. Instead she crossed her arms and drew in a breath. 'You just have to get on with it, don't you?'

Jon was watching Rick. Go on, he thought. Mention your sister going to see the doctor. Rick caught his eye and opened his mouth.

Alice spoke first. 'It's good news about that panther isn't it?'

Jon sensed the diversion on his wife's part. She'd never normally mention his work inside their home.

'A lot of people must be very relieved,' she continued. 'People were starting to keep their kids in once it got dark.' Her eyes moved back to Holly.

Rick nodded. 'Does the health visitor always manage to turn up at an awkward moment? My sister thought her one had some sensor that told when anyone was about to bath their baby.'

Alice shook her head. 'She doesn't visit any more. I said there was no need. I can take her to the local clinic when she's due to be weighed.'

'What's it like there?'

'I don't know, I haven't been yet.'

Rick looked surprised. 'You should pop in. My sister found it a great way of meeting other mums. There's information about all sorts of groups and meetings too.'

The silence was broken by Jon's phone beeping. Alice and Rick turned to him as he checked the screen. A text message from Nikki Kingston. He slid the phone back into his pocket.

'Work?' Alice asked.

He nodded.

She turned to Rick. 'Well, I don't want you getting in trouble by being here.'

Jon saw Rick's face redden at the politely phrased dismissal. He tried to reach for his drink.

'Here,' Alice took Holly back and started straightening her vest.

Rick gulped back his tea. 'Well, good to see you, Alice. We'll have to get Jon to baby-sit so we can go out. How about the cinema?'

She glanced up. 'Maybe in a while. I couldn't leave Holly for that long yet.'

'Course. When you're ready.'

Shocked by his wife's rudeness, Jon stood. 'Right, we'd better be going. I'll ring you. Hopefully it won't be a late one tonight.'

'OK,' she said. The word was full of casual cheer but she didn't meet either of their eyes.

As they walked to the car, Jon clicked on the message. 'Fucking hell.'

'What?'

'The hairs found on Rose Sutton and Derek Peterson? They weren't from the panther shot this morning.'

Rick's mouth fell open. 'That means there's another one out there.'

'Who fucking knows. We need to get back to the station though.' As he started the engine he looked at Rick. 'She isn't right, is she?'

'No. My sister wouldn't admit it, not for months. You need to have a talk with her. I think she knows something's up.'

Jon's eyes were checking the rear view mirror as he pulled out. 'Yeah mate, and when the hell am I supposed to find the time to do that?'

Twenty-Five

Summerby was waiting for him back in the incident room. After updating his senior officer, Jon called everyone round the centre table. 'OK, let's see where everyone's at. First bit of news I have is that the DNA of the panther killed this morning does not, I repeat not, match the DNA from the panther hairs recovered from Peterson and Sutton.'

He watched as the information sank in. DC Gardiner was the first to speak. 'So not only is there a second animal out there, it's the one forensically linked to our victims.'

Everyone looked at Jon for his response. He gestured towards Gardiner. 'Forensically linked is the correct choice of words. That's all the link is. It doesn't conclusively prove a panther killed Peterson and Sutton.'

Murray gave a tentative cough. 'The PM on both victims talks about their injuries being caused by the same type of weapon. A multi-pronged implement. Now we have an actual panther carcass. It's indisputable this animal was living up on the moors. Doesn't that massively increase the possibility there's a second animal out there too?'

'Theoretically, yes. But I'll say again, this is a murder investigation. And we have a prime suspect called Danny Gordon.' He saw the door to the incident room open. McCloughlin stepped through, moving silently along the wall and taking up a position at the edge of Jon's vision.

'Don't mind me.'

Jon tried to resume where he'd left off, but his mind was suddenly blank.

Summerby uncrossed his arms. 'Any word from Aberdeen yet?'

The office manager spoke up. 'They rang in half an hour ago.'

Looking down at a piece of paper, he continued. 'Michael Close is on a week's climbing holiday on the Isle of Skye. Up in the Cuillins apparently and not contactable by phone.'

'Hang on,' Jon said. 'The local nick were meant to check he was available for questioning.'

The other man was still looking down at the message. 'A mix up of dates. He's due back day after tomorrow. Rhea and Ashford are wondering what to do.'

Jon looked away. A day to drive back down, only to then turn round and head straight back up. Shit. Two of his Outside Enquiry Team out of action. 'Tell them to book into a hotel and see if you can send anything up there for them to do. Even if it's just typing up reports for entering into HOLMES. Right, what about Lee Welch?'

Murray opened his notebook. 'Reckons he bumped into Gordon a maximum of four times since their days in the Silver, as he called it. He wasn't the most willing of people I've interviewed, but he claimed they had nothing more than casual chats.'

'Did he have anything to say about Peterson?'

'Not a lot. Said he kept contact with the screws to a minimum.'

Jon wanted to laugh at Welch's choice of words. His whole life had been a rehearsal for his inevitable progression to adult prison.

'Gordon's probation officer?'

'Yes, boss,' Gardiner replied. 'He signed Gordon off last year and hasn't had cause to see him again since. When he had him on his books Gordon was living in a squat in Openshaw. We called at the address, it's still being used as a doss house today. There were a few in there. They hadn't seen Gordon for a few days, said he sometimes hung around with a black guy called Jammer. Medium height, dreadlocks.'

'How's the name spelt?'

Gardiner's shoulder rose and fell. 'They weren't sure. He was just known as Jammer.'

'Anything on the PNC?'

'Nope.'

'OK, what else?'

DC Collins spoke up. 'I had this Jammer person mentioned to me too. I dropped by at the soup kitchen that parks up behind the Piccadilly Tandoori.'

Jon knew the restaurant, a crooked white building that stood marooned on a patch of waste ground opposite the station. He'd fallen in there once after a drinking session round town. Never again. Behind it was a smattering of benches and clusters of bushes. Not near any shops, it had been colonised by a collection of drunks who could be found there at most times of the day, lolling around in various states of oblivion. 'What did the piss-heads have to say?'

'No one had seen him for a few days either. Someone thought Jammer had got hold of some cash, so they'd be getting off their heads at his place.'

'Which is?'

'They didn't know.'

Jon felt no more than a pang of irritation. The net was closing round Gordon. He'd circulate his photo to the entire police force. It shouldn't take long before they hauled him in.

'What about computers?'

Jon turned to Rick. 'What's that?'

'Any sign of a computer in that squat?' Rick asked Gardiner.

'Computers? They didn't even have electricity.'

'If he was tracking Peterson's movements through Swinger's Haven, he needed access to a computer. Perhaps we should start asking round the internet cafes and local libraries.'

Jon nodded to the allocator. 'Get that actioned. And everyone add this Jammer character to your list. We need him traced and interviewed. Next, Rose Sutton's associates. How's that going?'

Gardiner consulted her notes again. 'Thrived on the farm life. Content and cheerful. Seemed like a lovely marriage.' She looked up. 'More comments like that. She appeared to have found herself a happy role in life.'

Bollocks, thought Jon. 'Never be taken in by public personas. There must have been a downside, there's always at least one.' Images of his despondent wife, crying baby and abandoned dog vied for position in his head.

'One person mentioned seeing her crossing some fields to a car park near Holme once or twice. The lady said there was a guilty look about her. The only other thing that seemed worth noting was the issue of losing sheep to the mystery panther. But even then, she viewed it very pragmatically. She would report anything to Hobson, reckoning he was the only person capable of catching it.'

Hobson's name again. It was cropping up too much. 'Ken Sutton suspected his wife of something. The officer at Mossley Brow, Adam Clegg, was holding back on me too. I want to know if Jeremy Hobson and Rose Sutton were having an affair. Let's check him out properly. Is he married? Where does he live? He's an authority on big cats. Where did he study? Now, switching back to Peterson, I don't suppose the door-to-door provided much?'

Adlon shook his head. 'He was regarded as a bit of a recluse. Would nod hello and that was it. Never had any visitors.'

Thought as much, Jon thought. 'OK, you and Paul can have Hobson. Dig around a bit, but keep it discreet. DS Saville and myself talked to James Field. He hadn't seen Gordon in years, but he did provide us with enough information to suspect Peterson was using his capacity as a supervisor in the care home to abuse Gordon and a number of other boys. I have some surnames here. Once Gordon's in custody we'll need to trace these people. As far as I'm aware, none ever made a formal complaint against Peterson, but I bet a few drank a toast to the man's death. Right, let's get going.'

Everyone rose to their feet and from the corner of his eyes, Jon saw McCloughlin head towards the door. He turned to Summerby. 'What was he doing here?'

Summerby smiled regretfully. 'He asked the Chief if he could keep tabs on this, seeing as he hasn't got a major workload at the moment.'

Jon fought the temptation to punch the wall. 'What was your response? I thought you were keeping him off my back?'

'I am, but I can't bar him from meetings. I said things were progressing well, but we need something, Jon. What are your feelings on how soon it'll come?'

Jon sat back. On top of everything else, he thought, I don't need this shit. He wanted to reveal everything happening back home, get some time off, holiday, compassionate leave, anything. So what if the case was looking like a career maker? As Rick had implied, there were more important things in life than the job. But McCloughlin's lurking presence had his hackles up. Another twenty-four hours, he decided. If they hadn't achieved a breakthrough by then, he'd throw in the towel and sod the consequences for his career. 'We're close, I'm certain. I'll put out an alert for Gordon. In fact, what about naming him in a press appeal?'

'Good idea, get on to Gavin Edwards. I'll be upstairs.'

It was just after ten o'clock when he got home. As he unlocked the front door he could see shifts in the glow visible at the edge of the front room curtains. The telly was on. She was still up.

'It's me.' He closed the door behind him, finding himself automatically looking to the end of the corridor again for Punch.

'Hi.'

It was a statement, not a greeting. No warmth in the word at all. Jon pulled in a breath and entered the front room. Seeing that Holly was asleep on her mat, he turned to the sofa. The remote was in her hand and the telly abruptly died. Even though she looked tired, anger shone in her eyes. 'How dare you bring Rick round like that?'

Jon felt his stomach sink. 'Say again?'

'You know. Turning up like that without warning.'

He glanced around. The room was still a mess, another full nappy sack now on the carpet. 'Ali, it's not about how clean the house is. He was more interested in seeing Holly.'

'Oh, that was the reason for the visit then?'

'Yeah, and to see you of course.'

'To see me.'

Jon let his set of keys swing from his middle finger, their movement marking out the silence. I'm too tired for this, he thought, just wanting to sit down and put the telly back on. 'He's concerned for you. The same as I am.'

'What have you been saying?'

Checking Holly was still asleep, Jon perched on the edge of the armchair. 'Ali, Rick's sister has had a couple of kids. She found it really tough going after each baby was born.'

'You've been comparing notes. Discussing me.'

'No, not at all.'

She crossed her arms and drew her knees further up under her. Noting the defensiveness of her posture, Jon continued. 'All I did was mention how knackering it can be.' The urge to sit back in his seat was strong, but he knew he had to keep focused.

'Go on then, what did you say about me?'

Jon sighed. 'Ali, this isn't some sort of conspiracy. He mentioned that his sister found it hard in the first few weeks. She didn't feel able to cope. She became very tearful, just like you said you are sometimes.'

Her shoulders dropped. 'You're saying I'm a failure as a mother.'

'No! Jesus, Ali, stop putting words in my mouth. Rick's sister went to the doctor and it turned out she was depressed.'

'Oh great, so I need happy pills to prop me up. I am not depressed.'

'You're hardly yourself, Ali. What about Punch? You haven't even asked where he is.'

'Will you get it into your thick head that Punch is not part of our family. It's a dog. An animal. It's got more in common with the panther out there than us.'

Jon felt his eyes sting at the harshness of her words. 'That's proof you're not yourself.'

'Punch feels his position in the house is threatened by Holly. No one can predict what it might do to her.'

Jon shook his head. 'That dog would never hurt anyone. It would lay down its life defending us, Holly included.'

'You might be prepared to risk it, I'm not. I'm not going to let anything hurt my baby.'

'So you don't give a shit where Punch is?'

'I was wondering,' she said, avoiding his eyes.

For a second Jon was tempted to say he'd had the animal put down. Just to see what reaction the comment might prompt. 'Senior is looking after him.'

Silence fell. Try again, Jon thought. 'Ali, do you not agree you're tired out?'

'I'd be a lot less tired if I had a husband who got home at a normal time.'

Oh no, Jon thought. You're not turning this on me.

'How many hours have you spent at home recently?'

Jon closed his eyes. Shit. She's got me here. 'Ali, I can't help my job.'

'You can't help trying to take on the world. Why did you let yourself get dragged into this panther business?'

'I didn't let . . . ' The lie died on his lips. He hadn't just held his hand up for the case, he'd grabbed it with both arms, despite his senior officer's concerns. 'It was just how things developed, I didn't know what it was about to become.'

'You had a choice, Jon, you must have. But you chose to take it on. Look at me and tell me that I'm wrong.'

He dragged his eyes up to her face. 'Ali, I wish it was that simple. There are protocols to be followed, expectations . . . ' The deceit was poisoning him. My own fucking wife, he thought. If I can't be straight with her, what have I got left?

Her chin was jutting forward as she waited for his answer.

'OK,' he held up a hand. 'I'll see Summerby tomorrow and get moved off the case. Is that what you want?'

'I want you here a bit more. Why can't you just have a less important role on it?'

'Fine. I'll ask for one. And my job prospects will probably be damaged forever.'

'But do you want to be here, Jon? I'm not sure that you do.'

Jesus Christ, this was supposed to be about you, he thought. Yes, I want to be here. No, I don't want to sacrifice my career. When did life turn into such a bloody tightrope walk? 'Ali, in an ideal world, we'd be rich and living in the sun. But we're not. So I've got to work. Luckily, I do love my job. But I love you and Holly and Punch too.'

He flicked his eyes up and saw her blink at the dog's name. Good, he thought. Just so you know we're not finished on that subject either.

'So I'm trying to balance things as best I can. Sorry if it's not perfect.' He saw an opportunity to move the spotlight back on her. 'Are you sure having me around is going to improve things for you?' He noticed her arms gripping her sides more tightly. 'You seem so stressed out recently.'

'I do feel sad.'

Thank God, she's admitting something is wrong.

'It's all so totally tragic.'

Jon cocked his head to the side. 'What is?'

'Iraq.'

Oh sweet Jesus, not that again.

She reached over the arm of the sofa and picked up several sheets of A4. 'I've been on some web sites. There's so much stuff you don't hear about on the telly. Did you realise no one has any idea how many civilians have been killed since we invaded? The British and American forces are making no attempt to keep count, by their own admission.' She tapped the print-outs. 'According to these people, its thousands upon thousands. Children, babies, blown to bits. Christ Jon, they're just collateral damage. If we went there to free these people, why don't we have the decency to keep count of how many we kill as part of that process?'

The papers were shaking as she put them down to angrily wipe a tear away, her eyes now fixed on Holly.

This is exactly what I mean, thought Jon. And you can't even see it. Morbidly dwelling on death and destruction half a world away. 'Ali, why are you letting yourself get so worked up? We can't stop what's happening. Why don't you just leave it?'

'Turn a blind eye? Push it to the side because it's not happening here? I will not!' Holly's arms and legs flinched at her raised voice. Her eyes fluttered open and her lips began to move. 'Think about it, Jon. What would you do if someone destroyed your family? Me and Holly. Murdered.'

Jon knelt down to scoop his daughter up. 'She's hungry. I'll get her bottle.'

He walked from the room but she followed him to the kitchen. 'You wouldn't rest until you'd tracked them down, I know you wouldn't.'

I wouldn't rest until I'd stamped the last breath out of their blood-soaked faces, Jon thought.

'This war has only just started. People will want revenge for all the death we've unleashed over there. It will be revisited on us, I know it will.'

Jon turned round, Holly now crying in his arms. 'For fuck's sake, Ali, stop it will you? Can't you see you're upsetting her?'

Alice's eyes suddenly focused on their baby, and the fire burning within them vanished as tears welled up. 'Oh my poor darling. I'm sorry, I'm so sorry.' She laid a palm on the baby's head, then trailed her fingers over the soft sheen of hair.

The gesture contained such sorrow Jon used the excuse of opening the microwave to move Holly away from his wife's touch. 'I'll take care of this feed. Why don't you go to bed?'

Alice stood there a moment longer, the mournful look still on her face. Then she seemed to crumple. 'Yes, you're right.' She turned and walked from the room as if already in the grip of sleep.

Jon watched her go with a sense of foreboding. What's happening to my wife? The microwave pinged and he took the bottle out, quickly tested its temperature, then placed the teat in Holly's mouth. Leaning against the kitchen cupboards, his eyelids lowered. He had the sensation of falling backwards, or was it just the waves of tiredness pressing down? He opened his eyes and watched as Holly eagerly drained the bottle.

Ten minutes later she was safely tucked up in her cot and he was back in the kitchen, making a cup of black coffee. In the front room he turned the computer on and accessed the internet. He went to the history file to see which sites his wife had been looking at. BodyWatch. Troops Out. Al Jazeera. Something by Robert Fisk. An essay by John Pilger from the *New Statesman's* web site. God, she was wallowing in it.

He moved the cursor to the search field, typed in Post Natal Depression and hit enter.

Top of the search was something from the Royal College of Psychiatrists. He clicked on it and read the heading on the document that appeared.

What does it feel like to have PND?

He scanned the subheadings below.

Depressed. Irritable. Tired. Sleepless. Unable to cope. Anxious.

Chin propped on his hand, he read the paragraph that followed.

You may find that you are afraid to be alone with your baby. You may worry that he or she might scream, or choke, or be harmed in some way. You worry that you might lose him or her through infection, mishandling, faulty development or cot death.

He thought about how Alice had taken to checking Holly in the night, afraid she couldn't hear her breathing. The irrational fear of Punch began to make perfect sense. Scrolling down the document, his eyes were snared by another subheading.

Do women with PND harm their babies?

He had to take a sip of coffee before reading on, eyes slowing at the second to last line. *Rarely, she may feel so suicidal that she decides to take her baby's life and her own.*

Alice's last words before going to bed sprang into Jon's head. But it wasn't what she said that caused the apprehension he felt; it was the melancholy way she had caressed Holly's skull before walking from the room. No, she wasn't that bad. She needed to see a doctor and tomorrow he'd try and broach the subject again. But she hadn't lost the plot so completely that she'd . . . he didn't dare even think the words.

By the time he closed down the computer, his coffee was stone cold in his mug. The kitchen sink was half full of old washing-up water and he tipped the dregs in, watching the dark cloud of denser liquid billowing out across the bottom, enveloping a teaspoon that lay there.

He remembered his dream, the blackness engulfing the desert fortress, camels whinnying like horses, church bells ringing from minarets. Why minarets? He shook his head. This bloody business in Iraq is getting to me too.

Twenty-Six

Trevor Kerrigan opened his eyes and smiled. The bedroom curtains were closed, the faint glow of dawn just strong enough to pick out the floral pattern printed on them. Last night's weather forecast had indicated that conditions would be perfect for his early morning round of golf.

It was part of his weekly routine to rise in the semi darkness on a Friday and be on the course well before anyone else. There was something deeply satisfying about being the first person on a pristine fairway, the cropped grass shimmering with dew-covered spiders' webs, the top layer of sand in the smoothly raked bunkers still damp.

He slipped out from under the duvet, leaving his wife fast asleep on the other side of the mattress. Pausing at the end of the bed, he turned an ear towards the window and listened. That was another good thing about these early starts. Hardly any bloody traffic on the roads.

The wheels of his Shogun crunched to a stop in the empty car park. A glance towards the clubhouse revealed grilles over the windows and shutters over the doors. Not even the groundsmen had turned up yet. As he hauled his golf bag out of the boot he looked up at the gradually lightening sky. There was some low cloud on the horizon stained a faint pink by the yet-to-appear sun. Above that the heavens were blank, as if wiped fresh and clean for the coming day. Somewhere in the depths of the golf course a pheasant sounded its klaxon call, the sound reverberating in the silence.

After placing his ball on the tee, he selected a driver, then looked down the deserted fairway. Pockets of mist clung in the dip created by the River Medlock as it meandered its way along the side of the course. Barely visible in the mist, about two hundred yards away was the green. The shadow to its left was a dense grouping of gorse bushes and he knew two kidney-shaped bunkers lay in wait to its right. A good drive would get him to within chipping distance of the green.

Lazily he swung at the air to the side of his ball, using the movement to gauge his muscles and joints. A bit of stiffness in the left shoulder. He reached his arm up over his head, bringing it round like a swimmer doing backstroke. A few more repetitions and he was satisfied it was loose enough. He stepped up to the ball, fingers and toes rippling, buttocks clenching and unclenching as he made infinitesimal adjustments to his posture. First shot of the day, he thought. And if I cock it up, it could throw me out for the rest of my round.

The club connected with a pleasing crack and he completed the swing before looking up, knowing it was a good one. The ball was almost invisible against the grey sky before it suddenly reappeared below the horizon and bounced to within metres of the gorse bushes.

'Nice one, Trevor,' he murmured, sliding the driver back into the bag. Now for the next pleasure – walking down the unblemished fairway.

As he strode over the grass he breathed in the chill morning air. Another few weeks and it'll be too cold for this, he thought. His mind turned to Milner. He'd turned up with some cash, but not the full amount. She would settle up a bit more the following week, he'd asserted. Trevor analysed the conversation. He knew the signs. Milner suddenly becoming an advocate for the woman, making excuses for her, buying her more time. It all pointed to the probability she was settling her debt by spreading her legs for him. He considered going round and demanding some of that payment for himself – God knows he'd been happy enough to accept favours like that plenty of times in the past.

He couldn't help grinning at some of the memories. Best time was when he got into the property game, buying up dingy bedsits and then renting them out to the dross who could afford nothing else. Always rent to women, was his motto. Preferably abandoned and damaged ones, those struggling to cope with what life had dealt them. There were plenty of rent days when tenants would literally get on their knees and beg. He found it the ideal position for them to bargain from. Most seemed to accept what he suggested as an unavoidable part of life. One or two would try and refuse. But, truth be told, their defiance only excited him. He liked a verbal tussle and there was only one time when events had escalated to brute force.

The business with Milner, however, was a different matter. There was no way he could allow an employee to get away with it. After all, it wasn't just the client getting shafted. It was him, too. And Trevor Kerrigan took it from no man.

He paused to glance over his shoulder. A line of dark footprints stretched all the way back to the start of the fairway. He nodded, pleased to have been the first to mark the virgin grass. His eyes turned to the green ahead. There was the white dot of his ball, just short of the green. He leaned his head to the side. What was that by the edge of the bushes? Something red. He continued on his way, his eyes fixed on the scrap of colour. As he got closer he could see the object was made from material. Flimsy material. A pair of knickers? Maybe some couple had been using the golf course for a spot of open air shagging. Yes, they were knickers all right. He could now make out their lacey edges. Within metres of the bushes he heard a sound – high pitched, girlish. Surely not. They couldn't still be at it, he thought, not in this temperature. But a branch was moving. Shaking slightly. Rhythmically. Oh yes. He hoped she'd be on top. Then he could get a good look at her before bawling them out.

He crept quietly up to the bushes but the dense clusters of spikes stopped him from seeing between the short branches. With a leering smile ready on his face, he stepped round. Confusion made his expression falter. Something black, crouching low. But rearing upwards towards him fast. Very fast. Teeth. Great snarling teeth. And a sharp, sour smell. He just had time to ball his fingers into a fist when a blow caught him under the chin, snapping his head backwards and exposing his throat. The second swipe tore his windpipe out.

Twenty-Seven

'That's your bloody phone.'

Jon's eyelids felt glued shut. He moved away from Alice's elbow as it jabbed him in the ribs. Now sitting on the edge of the bed, he grabbed his mobile.

'Spicer here.'

'Morning, Sir, it's Sergeant Innes at Longsight.'

Jon managed to grunt in reply.

'Sorry for the early call.'

'What time is it?'

'Just after seven.'

He'd been asleep for what? Six hours. He felt like he needed sixty more. 'What's up?'

'A body has just been found on the Brookvale golf course. Severe lacerations to the face, neck and upper chest.'

Jon was on his feet and reaching for his trousers. 'I'm on my way.'

The sun was just clearing the trees by the time Jon arrived at the entrance to the golf course. The brightness would be short lived. Despite the weather forecast, a slab of grey cloud was moving across the sky and Jon thought it would be raining by lunch. His tyres made a drumming noise as he drove over the cattle grid and on to the gravel drive beyond. It rose up and, looking to his left, he saw the brown of the moors in the distance. To his right the chimneys, towers and cranes of Manchester were just visible.

As he pulled into the car park at the side of the clubhouse, he noted a green van, two police cars and a monstrous four-wheel drive already parked there. A sign to the side was headed by the words, *Club rules*. He read the first one. *No trainers or shirts without collars allowed*. Thinking how much he hated the petty rules and sad hierarchies of these places, he deliberately parked in the slot reserved for the President.

At the tee-off for the first hole three lines of footprints led across the still damp grass. They ended at a patch of sunlight that was creeping up the fairway, pushing back the shadows cast by the pine trees behind them.

'Who's been down there so far?' Jon asked, after introducing himself to the uniforms.

'The groundsman and the constable who first responded to the nine-nine-nine call.'

Jon's eyes went to the distant bushes. A bag of golf clubs and two arms, flung backwards, were just visible. He looked over his shoulder at the jeep. 'That his car?'

'Yes. Registered to a Trevor Kerrigan of The Beeches, Droylsden Road.'

'Have you run his details?'

'No need, Sir. Kerrigan's well known in this area.'

'Why?'

'He's a loan shark. Loads of reports linking him to intimidation of people owing him money. He's almost been collared for assault on several occasions, but either the victims won't testify or one of his thug employees owns up.'

'So no shortage of people bearing a grudge.' He looked back at the fairway. The crime scene manager was still fifteen minutes away. He didn't want to wait that long. 'I'm going to take a look.'

As he ducked under the blue and white ribbon of police tape stretching across the top of the car park, the sergeant said, 'Sir, is this another one?'

'Another what?' Jon waited, forcing the officer to say it.

'Another victim of a wild animal. Because if it is, the panther that was shot out on Saddleworth Moor can't have been the killer, can it?'

Jon took a step back towards the other man, his stomach pressing against the striped ribbon. 'Sergeant, we've got enough shit with what the press are stirring up. I will not have anyone referring to attacks by wild animals, is that understood?'

'Sir.'

Jon marched down the centre of the fairway, rolling his tongue round the inside of his mouth as he did so. Shit, I forgot to brush my teeth. He patted his jacket pockets searching for mints. Bollocks, forgot those too. He felt slightly unsteady as if he was walking on a layer of foam. Christ, I'm tired, he thought, glad to step into the sunlight and feel its faint warmth on the back of his neck.

When he'd left Alice she was sitting up in bed, Holly feeding at her breast. But his wife's head was hanging forward and he couldn't even tell if her eyes were open as he said that he'd be back soon. He checked his watch. Seven forty-eight. Give it until eight, then he'd ring his mum and see if she could go round and stay with Alice until he got back. Which would be when, he asked himself. Lunchtime, no later. I'll get things rolling here then phone Summerby and request that he take over the case.

He circled the far side of the green, glancing into a pair of bunkers as he passed them. A set of tiny footprints ran across the far one. A stoat or squirrel he thought, wondering if any tracks might remain where the body lay. With each step, more of the corpse came into view. Arms stretched out either side of a balding head that was peppered with droplets of blood. The guy was spread-eagled, cropped grass stained a dark crimson beneath his upper half.

Jon continued round until he could see the entire body. Where the throat should have been was just a gaping great hole, glistening flaps of flesh hanging down. Twenty, even ten minutes ago, that wound would have still been bleeding, Jon thought. He scrutinised the dense grouping of gorse, the rims of his eyes feeling red and itchy. One bush had grown outwards, giving the clump a rough L shape. The attacker had obviously been concealed behind it, waiting for Kerrigan to approach. Was it a random attack or had it been planned? If it was premeditated, as Jon suspected, how did the killer know Kerrigan would be here, alone, at this precise time?

Jon's eyes moved slowly over the scene before him, desperately searching for any clue that may have been left behind. The bushes had grown into each other, forming an impenetrable barrier. There was no way the attacker could have retreated through them into the rough at the edge of the fairway. Which meant he'd have walked over the edge of the green. Shit, half an hour ago, this area would still have been in shadow; the attacker's footprints standing out in the damp grass. As Jon stared, he wondered whether four feet or only two would have made the trail.

'Get a grip,' he whispered, snuffing the thought out before it could take hold, but as he backed away from the scene he couldn't help glancing between the trees behind him. He set off towards the car park, pulling his mobile out as he did so.

'Mum, it's me. Sorry to call so early.'

'That's OK, love. What is it?'

'Mum, can you go over to ours and stay with Alice? She's not so good. I don't want her on her own and I won't be back for a bit.'

'The baby blues is it?'

'Baby blues? I think it's a bit more serious than that.'

'Is she expecting me?'

'No.'

'Is it right that I just turn up? On your doorstep unannounced?'

It's never bothered you before, he thought. 'Course. She won't mind. She should rest, Mum. She needs a bit of fussing over.'

'And when will you be home, then?'

The implication of the question was clear. This is your job, not mine. 'As soon as I can. Late morning, hopefully.'

'OK, but I can't stay too long. I have to be at Our Lady of the Angels for mass at noon.'

Jon closed his eyes for an instant. The interminable hours you forced us to spend in that bloody church when we were kids. He remembered the little games he, Dave and Ellie would play to try and pass the time: searching the hymnbooks for lines they could couple with rude words, kicking the padded cushions away as they all had to kneel for prayers. 'I'll be back, don't worry.'

'Right, I'll get dressed then.'

As he got back to the car park a familiar red Mercedes was

reversing into the corner. Collyer, the home office pathologist. Sure enough, the man unfolded his long limbs from the vehicle and walked round to his boot.

'Prompt as usual,' Jon said, feet crunching over the gravel.

The pathologist turned his head. 'No flies on my corpses,' he replied.

Jon smiled, not able to quite manage a laugh. 'It's like the other one I'm afraid. Not pretty.'

'I didn't expect it to be,' he replied, climbing into a white body suit. He removed a large briefcase from the boot. 'Lead the way.'

Jon retraced his footsteps back down the fairway, coming to a halt at the edge of the green and extending a hand. 'It's all yours. I suspect the attack was launched from the cover of those bushes, so I've kept well away from that area.'

'Fine.' The pathologist pulled on white overshoes, a facemask and hair net. He then approached the body. After slowly circling it, he opened his briefcase and knelt down by the head for a closer look. He removed a thermometer and inserted the end into the wound. After that he examined the hands, taking more time over the man's right fingers. Next he retrieved the thermometer, checked it, then returned it to its case. Finally he took out another pair of overshoes and walked over to Jon. 'A couple of things you should see.'

Jon slipped them on, then followed the pathologist back across the green.

'Judging from the temperature inside the throat wound, the victim's been dead for an hour at the most. This attack was more ferocious than the last. He's really gone to town this time. Look at the flayed edges of the wounds. That suggests multiple strikes with the pronged weapon I described. He hasn't just torn the throat open, he's pretty much removed it. See here? That's the clavicle showing through.'

'Collar bone to me?' Jon asked, feeling the bile churning at the back of his throat.

'Collar bone to you. He's even damaged that. Look, can you see those four nicks in the bone? That's where the prongs made contact.'

Jon crouched down and leaned in close. The pathologist was right. Four chips to the bone, identical spaces in between. 'Can you look at those nicks under a microscope to see if any traces of the weapon have been left in the bone?'

'Yes, that's a good idea. Now, the reason why this attack was more savage could be this.' He moved down to Kerrigan's right hand. 'You see the sovereign ring? It's been dented and there's a black hair caught in the rim.'

'He punched his attacker?' Jon bent forwards. 'That hair. It looks horribly similar to the ones recovered from Sutton and Peterson.'

'But there's more. Look closely at the ring and you'll see some other matter caught there. I'd hazard a guess that's some of your attacker's epidermis.'

'Skin? We can test for DNA?'

'Correct.'

Jon slapped a fist into his palm. 'Brilliant. Can I leave you to it? I need to get over to the victim's house.'

'OK. I'll speak to you soon.'

'And can you make that DNA test a top priority?' Jon called over his shoulder, halfway across the green.

Up above him the cloud had closed in on the sun, snuffing out its welcome glow.

It was mid-morning before he got a chance to make it to Summerby's office. He was about to knock on the door when his mobile rang. 'Hi Mum, everything all right?'

'She's not here. I'm outside your house, but no one's in.'

Alarm bells rang in his head. 'Have you brought your key?'

'Yes.'

'Then open the door, she's probably asleep.'

'OK, I'll call you back.'

He stood in the corridor, nervously jiggling the phone in his cupped hand. Probably nipped out to the shops. Yeah, we needed some coffee. Or maybe in the back yard. It had just started to drizzle, she was probably getting the washing in before it got wet.

His phone went again and he'd answered it before the end of the first ring. 'Hi.'

'She's not here.' Faint irritation was in her voice.

He wanted to demand that she search the whole house, but he knew it would sound melodramatic. 'Not upstairs then?'

'The buggy's gone, she must be out.'

'Hang on then, I'll try her mobile.' He hung up and speed dialled Alice's number. Her recorded voice asked him to leave her a message. 'Ali, it's me. Call me when you pick this up. OK, speak to you soon.'

He rang his mum back. 'It's on answer phone. Can you stick around and call me as soon as she turns up?'

'But I'm expected at—'

'Mum, I'm sure your church will survive if you miss just one bloody service. Alice isn't very well.'

'All right,' she finally replied. 'I'll do a spot of vacuuming.'

'Thanks, Mum.'

He knocked on Summerby's door and went in. Gavin Edwards was there by the window, eyes directed to the sky as if he could gauge the coming media storm by the greyness of the clouds outside.

'So,' his senior officer announced, hands crossed on the desk before him. 'Same hallmarks as the other two?'

'More than that,' Jon sat down, the taste of a hastily gulped can of Red Bull still in his mouth. His heart rate was slightly up and he could feel the press of blood behind his eyes. 'The pathologist found a hair on the victim's right hand. I'm getting used to recognising panther hairs and it looked identical to the ones from Sutton and Peterson.'

'Hairs caught under the victim's nails again? Isn't that a bit too convenient?' Summerby demanded.

'Not under the nails, sir. It was snagged in the rim of a sovereign ring he was wearing. There was also what appeared to be a scrape of skin caught there. It could be that Kerrigan struck back at his attacker and took off some of his skin in the process.'

'What is he, an ex-boxer or something?' Gavin Edwards asked from the corner.

'He was known to be violent. I think we can assume he knew how to throw a retaliatory punch.'

'So who was he?' Summerby asked, eyes on the notes in Jon's lap.

'Trevor Kerrigan, lived in a house called The Beeches on Droylsden Road.'

'The Beeches? That sounds a bit grand, isn't it just terraced houses along there?'

'He was the area's biggest loan shark. Nasty piece of work according to the local officers. Got a record that stretches back over thirty years. Early stuff on tax evasion and fraud. He rented bed-sits. Seems he packed that in during the recession of the eighties to focus solely on money lending. Plenty to suggest he uses intimidation and low level violence to collect what's owed him, but nothing has ever resulted in a conviction.'

'A man with many enemies,' Summerby leaned back. 'You think that Danny Gordon will feature on his list of debtors?'

'That's my guess.'

'Still no sign of him?'

'Unfortunately not.' He turned to Edwards. 'You issued his name and description?'

'Yes, the release went out yesterday evening. Too late for the first editions to major on it, but local radio have picked it up. No calls through to the incident room then?'

'A few,' Jon replied. 'Just vague sightings in the city centre. Nothing solid as yet. I gather there's already been quite a reaction to this latest killing.'

Summerby laughed. 'A reaction? People are getting bloody hysterical. We've got sightings of panthers being called in from all over the place. People won't walk in parks. The council has had to issue an appeal for calm. I've never experienced anything like it.' He picked up his phone. 'Let's meet again at four.'

Taking the cue, Gavin made for the door. Jon stayed in his seat. 'Sir, could I have a word?'

Summerby met his eyes, then glanced at the press officer who was hovering at the door. 'That's all Gavin, thanks.'

The door closed and Summerby replaced the phone. 'What's up, Jon?'

Jon took a breath in. 'I'm not sure I can continue being SIO on this case.'

'I beg your pardon?'

'It's my wife, Sir. Things have gone a bit downhill at home.' He found himself flicking the fingers of his hand, as if warding off an irritating insect. Christ, Jon, this is Alice you're talking about. 'Since having the baby she's got more and more stressed. That and being tired. She's not coping too well.'

'You mean she's depressed?'

He couldn't bring himself to agree. Somehow it felt like he was betraying her. 'Not depressed, but she needs support. I'm never there for her.'

He watched Summerby thinking it over. 'When this case kicked off, I asked you whether it was a good idea for you to take it on. You assured me that it was. As I remember, you mentioned there was plenty of help from members of your family and hers.'

Jon recalled his blithe assurance. What a prick you were, he told himself. 'I did, yes. But the case isn't what it first appeared.'

'Few cases are. Now we're in the thick of it and you want to walk away? I've got the Chief breathing down my neck, DI Spicer.'

You also don't want to jeopardise the holiday you've no doubt booked the day after you retire, Jon thought. 'Sir, you also reserved the right that, if things got out of hand, you'd step in to take command.' Admitting defeat was not something Jon ever permitted himself to do. He searched for the words. 'I feel that point has been reached.'

'Do you realise how I've fought your corner with McCloughlin? This will make me look a complete fool.'

Jon felt himself shrivelling in the chair. He tried to sit up. 'What can I say? Alice isn't well. She's . . . ' What? He thought. On some motorway flyover contemplating jumping off? Is Holly in her arms? He squeezed his eyes shut. 'She's struggling.'

'Has she seen a GP?'

'No.'

'Maybe that should be your first priority. It would help put things in perspective. Perhaps it's just a case of some medication.'

Jon sighed. 'I can't head this thing up. It's too big. I'll work as part of the team no problem, but I don't know how to run the whole show.'

Summerby rolled a pen back and forth with the tip of one finger. 'Fine. You'll need to take me through your policy book. I want to know about all of your decisions so far, the reasoning behind them, what is being currently actioned. I'm assuming you've got everyone trying to locate Danny Gordon?'

'Not everyone, no. I've got people looking into Jeremy Hobson's past, others asking questions out at Mossley Brow.'

'Sod that. Who are those officers kicking their heels up in Aberdeen?'

'Rhea and Ashford.'

'Fly them back down here if necessary. I'll see the Chief about getting some more men on the case.'

Halfway down the stairs Jon paused on a landing and rang his mum again.

'No, she's not back yet. Jon, you sound very uptight.'

'Things are really busy here, that's all. Don't forget to call me—'

'I know, I know. Now can I get on with this cleaning?'

He felt as though everything he cared about was under threat. Scrolling down through his phone book, he called Senior's number. 'It's Jon. Everything OK, mate? Punch not being too much bother?'

'The dog's fine. They've been tearing round the park like a couple of nutters.'

'Great. I'll try and pop round later.'

He carried on down the stairs, aware that the can of Red Bull had added a coating of fur to his teeth. 'Toothbrush,' he muttered, hurrying past the incident room to the car park. Minutes later he was pulling up on the garage forecourt. Inside he headed for the toiletries section. Seven quid for a toothbrush and toothpaste? Cursing the fact he was being ripped off, he placed the items on the counter.

'I bet you're living in that police station, aren't you?'

He looked up, realising it was the same attendant from the

other night. 'Not far wrong.' He removed a ten–pound note from his wallet.

'Or do you prefer not to be travelling the roads at night? Safer to stay in the cop shop?'

Jon put the money on the counter, sensing a wild theory on how to solve the case coming his way.

'I wouldn't worry. The Medlock flows into town a good mile north of here.'

Jon looked at the attendant. 'Say again?'

The man gave a knowing wink. 'The Medlock. I've been looking at the city centre map too.' He opened a large format A to Z and pointed to the page. 'The beast is following the river, right? It killed the woman first, now it's crept down off the moors and killed that guy by Crime Lake. Now it's got another on the Brookvale golf course. Look, the Medlock runs off the moor and passes through both spots. The animal is probably heading towards the city centre as we speak. Am I right, or am I right?'

Jon managed a tight-lipped smile. That was the half-formed thought that had occurred to him on the moor, as he was sitting on the back of Sutton's quad bike looking down towards Manchester. What had Adam Clegg called it? The Mersey basin. And the Medlock flowed right into the heart of the city before emptying into the Manchester Ship Canal. Jesus Christ, it'll be mayhem if people start believing that.

'Good imagination, mate.'

The man laughed. 'That's what my teachers said at school. Didn't get me far though, did it?'

Jon drove round the corner then immediately parked up. He took his own A to Z of Manchester from the glove box and turned to the overall map at the front. There was Saddleworth Moor, a near blank expanse just beyond the right-hand edge of the map's grid. He looked at the square nearest to it, then turned to that page and studied the main features there. Saddleworth Moor golf course. Moorgate Quarry, Ladcastle Quarry (disused). He turned to the page before. An empty area called High Moor dominated it. A patch of blue caught his eye. Lower Strinesdale

Reservoir. And there, above it, was the thinnest of black lines. The River Medlock.

The area below was covered by page seventy-four. More details filled that page and he had to scan a swarm of words before finally finding the ones he was looking for. The Medlock. Still just a black line, it emerged by Sun Hill, disappeared again, then popped up further down the page at Lees Cemetery. It had widened considerably by the time it meandered past Oldham Golf Course. He turned to page seventy-three. Now it was marked as a blue line, making it easier to pick out as it trailed off the corner to continue on page eighty-seven. He saw the words Daisy Nook Country Park and Crime Lake. He remembered looking down at the river from the bridge, noting how the overgrown banks would have provided cover for an attacker. The river branched away, passing beneath the M60 ring road and on to page eighty-five. Brookvale Golf Course. Shit, the thing ran right past where Kerrigan's body had shown up. Jon looked down the page. Now it was just above Droylsden. Next was page ninety-seven. There it was again, meandering innocently through an area that was crowded with residential streets and industrial properties. At Philips Park it disappeared, emerging to the left of Beswick in a Public Open Area. Now he was on the red grid of enlarged squares that detailed the city centre itself. Familiar names sprang out at him. The Town Hall and Library. Piccadilly Gardens. The Arndale Shopping Centre. Bridgewater Hall. Granada TV Centre.

The river ran right through the heart of Manchester. Could an animal seriously be following it into the centre of the city? And if it was, what sort of panic would that create?

He drove straight back to the station and, A to Z in hand, bounded up the stairs to Summerby's office. 'Sir, I know this sounds strange but . . . ' he stopped. There on the other side of his senior officer's desk sat McCloughlin.

They locked eyes for an instant before McCloughlin turned back round.

'Jon, come in. I was just explaining to DCI McCloughlin about how we're restructuring the investigation. He's kindly agreed to give us some officers to follow up the lines of enquiry created by Kerrigan's death.'

Jon eased himself into a chair, saying nothing.

'What were you about to tell us?' McCloughlin said, a look of amusement in his eyes.

Jon cleared his throat. Summerby's arched eyebrows indicated he should carry on. Self-consciously, Jon placed the A to Z on the table. 'There is something that links all three murders.'

Summerby leaned forward. 'What?'

With a glance at McCloughlin, Jon said, 'Rose Sutton died up on Saddleworth Moor. It's where various springs rise up, merge together and form the start of the River Medlock. The river then flows straight towards the city; Derek Peterson was found by Crime Lake which adjoins the Medlock valley. Trevor Kerrigan was killed on Brookvale golf course, which is bisected by the Medlock.'

The two men were staring at the map.

'Because of the very fact it's a river, the Medlock is bordered by uncultivated land. I looked down on it in the Daisy Nook Country Park. Wide, steep banks, covered with trees and bushes. What if Danny Gordon is using this cover to creep up on his victims?'

'So you're saying they are just random attacks?' Summerby murmured.

'Not necessarily. He could have been stalking them before the attacks, working out the best place to strike.'

'You make him sound like a predatory animal,' McCloughlin said.

The derisory note in his voice rankled with Jon. God, I'd like to lamp this arsehole. 'Maybe that's what he thinks he is,' Jon replied, looking at the map. 'Isn't that what the whole werewolf thing is about? People who believe so strongly they're a wolf, they start to behave like one.'

'So what does that make Danny Gordon, a werepanther?' McCloughlin smirked.

'Danny Gordon is obviously extremely disturbed, that much is obvious,' Jon replied. 'Who's to say he hasn't become delusional in his beliefs?'

'How does this assist the enquiry?' Summerby asked.

'If he's following the river, we could start searching the land bordering it at the very least.'

Summerby didn't sound convinced. 'Do panthers follow rivers? Working on your theory of Gordon pretending that he is one, we need to know.'

'I'd guess Jeremy Hobson could tell us that.'

'Get on to him immediately then.'

Jon left the room with the impression Summerby was humouring him. He could almost hear his senior officer's thoughts. If DI Spicer wants to relinquish his lead role and chase shadows, so be it. In the corridor he glanced at his mobile in the vain hope a message from his wife might be there. The screen was blank. He rang home. His mum picked up. 'Still no sign of her?'

'No.'

Jon weighed up his options. 'Are you OK to stay a little longer? I've got to nip out on a visit.'

She sighed. 'Go on then, but I can't just wait here all day.'

Five minutes later DCI McCloughlin walked back down the corridor to his office and shut the door. After sitting down he extracted a mobile from his pocket, leaving the desk phone untouched. After selecting a number from his phonebook, he swivelled round so his back was to the door. His call was answered immediately.

'Carmel Todd, crime desk.'

'Hello Carmel, can you talk?'

'DCI McCloughlin? Absolutely.'

'Good, I have something for your next edition.'

'Fire away.'

'You're aware another body's been found?'

'Yes. We just received a fax from your press office. Is there another panther out there? My editor is tearing his hair out.'

McCloughlin smiled. 'Just don't give the reward money out quite yet. This morning's victim was a loan shark operating in the Droylsden area, name of Trevor Kerrigan.'

'Any connection to Sutton or Peterson?'

'Unsure as yet. Which is no surprise given the way the investigation has been handled so far. You'll love the latest theory. I recommend you give it a "clutching at straws" kind of slant.'

'I'm all ears.'

'Plot the locations of the killings on a map and you'll see they've all taken place within the vicinity of the River Medlock. They're now wondering if a panther . . . '

'Hang on, I thought Danny Gordon is the prime suspect?'

'Yes. But now they think he believes he's a panther.'

A laugh of disbelief escaped Carmel. 'You're joking.'

'I wish I was. They're thinking Danny Gordon is creeping along the banks of the Medlock, using it as a kind of hunting territory.'

'Where does the river lead?'

'Look at your map, Miss Todd. Directly into the city centre.'

She let out a low whistle. 'Now that is a good story.'

'I thought you'd like it.'

'Can I ask you a question, DCI McCloughlin?'

'Yes.'

'Why are you doing this?'

'Doing what?'

'Feeding me this information.'

McCloughlin thought about how, until quarter of an hour ago, the biggest incident to hit Manchester in God knew how long didn't involve him. Worse than that, DI Spicer, a man who had defied his orders on two previous investigations, was heading it up. But now a new hand of cards had been dealt. He had been asked by Summerby to help out and Spicer was actually requesting a lesser role. Once the *Chronicle* printed the man's latest theory, he would be marginalised completely. 'Do you want this help or not?'

'Oh yes, don't get me wrong. I couldn't appreciate it more. It's confusing me, that's all. DI Spicer seems like a decent officer. He's doing his best. Surely these tip-offs just undermine all his efforts?'

'Miss Todd, don't you worry yourself with details like that. I suggest you get over to Buxton Zoo. That's where you'll find Spicer pursuing his half-crazed line of enquiry.'

Twenty-Eight

Jon slowed to a halt and examined the chunky wooden sign: *Deliveries and office building.*

He turned down the right-hand road and followed it to a low building that had been clad in rounded lengths of timber, giving it the appearance of a log cabin.

In the reception area was a massive aquarium that appeared to contain a sizeable chunk of the Great Barrier Reef. Brightly coloured fish darted in and out of the cliff face, unconcerned by the masses of bubbles spiralling up from the gravel bed. The woman behind the counter wore the same type of shirt Hobson had on in the police station at Mossley Brow.

'I need to speak with Jeremy Hobson please.'

'And you're from?'

Jon realised he'd forgotten to take out his identification. 'Sorry. DI Spicer.'

She looked down at her appointments book.

'He's not expecting me. If you could say it's me, he knows who I am. It's very urgent.'

'OK,' she said, glancing at her watch. 'He'll be over at the panther enclosure, preparing their feed.'

She entered a three-digit number into the phone and waited. 'Hi, it's Sally in reception. I have a DI Spicer to see Jeremy. He says it's urgent.' A short pause. 'Fine. I'll let him know.' She looked up. 'Someone is on their way over. Please help yourself to a tea or coffee.'

Jon stepped over to the machine, eyes settling on the button marked black coffee. What a win, he thought, reaching for a cup. Five minutes later a young man in a green fleece, khaki shorts and hiking boots walked through the double doors. Jon drained the last of his drink and followed him along the outside of the perimeter fence.

Through the metal links he could see crowds of people walking quickly along pristine paths punctuated by green litter bins. Beyond them a wire canopy reared up into the sky and Jon watched several monkeys swinging about in the branches of a tree contained within it, their mocking cries carrying across the zoo. But the crowds didn't seem interested: they were all heading straight past. I can guess where, Jon thought.

His guide reached a double gate and unlocked the padlock securing it. They stepped through and walked towards the rear of a large building made from giant breeze blocks. At the base of one wall was a row of old aquariums. Grass had grown up around them and each one was full to the brim with brackish-looking rain water. Obviously we're in an area not open to the public, Jon thought.

As they rounded the corner, an office that extended off the much higher main building was revealed. To the side of it ran an electrified fence that must have been at least thirty feet high. Its top part was angled inwards and Jon was reminded of the exercise area at Strangeways prison.

'He's in there.' The young man pointed to the door of the office and walked back the way they'd come.

Jon approached the building and stepped through the door into a kitchen area. Hobson was standing by the sink, cleaving lumps of red meat into smaller pieces. There were three metal buckets on the floor, two already full of flesh.

Jon met the other man's eyes and felt himself recoil slightly at their watery gaze. Hearing a radio playing in the office beyond, he said, 'Have you heard the news this morning?'

'No. Too busy running round.'

'We've found a third body. Same injuries as Rose Sutton and Derek Peterson.'

The meat cleaver froze half way through a downward sweep and Hobson looked over his shoulder, pale blue eyes wide open. 'Same injuries?'

'And a hair was recovered from the victim.'

The metal blade thumped into flesh and bone. 'My God, so it's not over. That means there's a second animal out there.'

'Or someone who's very good at staging attacks so they resemble those of a panther.'

Hobson swallowed. 'If you permitted me to see the body, I could tell you that. You told the papers I was advising on the investigation, after all.'

Not until I know what you're about, mate, Jon thought. 'Actually, I have a few questions to ask you about the hunting habits of panthers.'

'No problem. Do you mind if we talk as I prepare their meal?'

'Fine with me.' Jon skirted past Hobson and looked into the office beyond. On the wall above an untidy desk was a collection of panther photos. In the corner was a unit of grey lockers, name labels on each door. Next to that was a book case. He examined the spine of the largest publication.

Wild Cats of the World. Mel Sunquist and Fiona Sunquist.

Jon imagined the authors living out in secluded forests, waiting endless days for a glimpse of their subject. No wonder they wrote as a couple. His attention was drawn to a TV monitor. The view was of an enclosure with a bare tree trunk lying on its side.

Hobson's voice came from the kitchen. 'The red buttons let you switch between cameras, including the ones in their dens.'

'How many panthers have you got?' asked Jon, pressing each button in turn. The third view revealed a solitary animal asleep on a raised platform. The camera was looking directly down and any sense of perspective was impossible to gauge.

'Three. Mweru, a female, and her one-year-old female cub, Mara. Then there's Samburu, a fully grown adult male. The enclosure is divided in two. Samburu has one half, Mweru and Mara the other. Come on, you can meet them close up.'

Jon looked into the kitchen to see Hobson walking outside, buckets hanging from his arms. They approached a plain wooden door built in to the rear wall. Hobson placed the buckets on the worn grass and produced a set of keys from the pocket of his khaki gilet. He opened the door to reveal a narrow concrete strip, on the other side of which was a screen of heavy duty wire mesh and metal grates. A sharp smell immediately filled Jon's nostrils.

'Like all cats, they spray to mark their territory,' Hobson explained. He crouched down and pressed a palm against the concrete floor. 'Feel. This area has under-floor heating. It magnifies the smell.'

Jon pressed a knuckle against pleasantly warm concrete.

'You're welcome to come inside but please keep to the back wall,' Hobson instructed.

Jon did as he was asked. Examining the gloomy space beyond the wire, he realised he was looking into the dens he'd just seen on the CCTV screen. On each side of him were two more thick wire doors reinforced with metal struts. Beyond them were the main enclosures themselves. A row of windows stretched round the perimeter and Jon could see dozens of people looking through.

Hobson stepped in and clanged two metal pails together, which brought immediate movement from the right-hand den. A moment later a dark shadow moved up to the wire and Jon found himself looking at a pair of golden eyes. The animal, barely arm's distance away, regarded Jon for a second. He looked for any emotion, but the stare seemed neutral, bored almost.

'Ah, Samburu's in I see,' said Hobson. 'Hello big fella.' He placed the pails on the floor and moved to one end of the concrete strip. 'Don't be fooled by appearances. Docile but deadly is what I tell every assistant. He looks like he'd be nice to stroke but, give him half a chance, he'll have your hand off. First you'd know about it was when you realised your arm ended at your wrist. That's why I said keep to the back wall. Going too near only provokes him into making a lunge – and I don't want him snapping a tooth off on the wire mesh.'

Jon felt an uneasy thrill of excitement. Just a sheet of wire separated him from a creature that would kill him without any hesitation at all. Hobson had grasped a metal handle connected to a wire that ran up the wall and into the den. Another wire stretched from a large counterweight. As the counterweight lowered, the handle in Hobson's hand rose until he could secure it on a hook embedded in the wall. 'I've just lowered the trapdoor to his den. That keeps him inside while I put his food out. Now, where's Mweru and Mara?'

He picked up a bucket and ran it down the door leading into the other enclosure. Two panthers of almost equal size appeared from a thicket of bamboo. Lazily, they padded across the sandy floor and disappeared round to the front of their den. Next thing two more sets of yellow eyes shone behind the wire. Hobson stepped gingerly past Samburu's side and lowered the trap door to the neighbouring den. 'Right, all in.' He stood in front of the gate leading into the mother and cub's enclosure, then took his keys out once again. Fixed to a metal plate in the centre of the enclosure was a building site sign with a graphic of a head in a hard hat and a raised hand. *Danger: Keep Out.*

Hobson glanced up at a mirror high on the wall that let him see into the den. 'Check and double check,' he whispered, more to himself than Jon. Then he unlocked the gate's padlock, slid back two large bolts and shouldered it open. Next he picked up two of the buckets and walked out into the enclosure itself. Jon saw the spectator's faces begin to turn. Fingers started to point. Mweru and Mara paced back and forth across a patch of light, tips of their long tails twitching. Samburu was nowhere to be seen.

Hobson walked confidently over to a pole of wood and wedged a chunk of meat into the V at its top. You love this, don't you, Jon thought, beginning a quick tally of people watching. He gave up at the third window, having counted forty-eight faces.

His eyes returned to Hobson as he proceeded round, hiding bits of meat on various branches and ledges of rock. Two minutes later he returned to the side gate, both buckets empty, face slightly flushed.

He relocked the side gate then reached for the handle controlling the counterweight. 'OK ladies, give them a good show.'

The metal trapdoor scraped up and the two cats appeared in the open. Mweru made a beeline for the wooden pole. Rearing up on her hind legs, she sniffed the meat then, almost reluctantly, grabbed it in her jaws. Hobson chuckled. 'Beef.

They hate it. Chicken every day would be their choice. Right, now for Samburu.'

He lobbed the empty pails out on the grass, picked up the third one, then approached the side gate to Samburu's enclosure. The same procedure was repeated and Hobson strode out like a gladiator entering the ring. Jon glanced at the handle to the counterweight. You'd soon lose that swagger if I unhooked that counterweight, he thought, looking at the den before him. In its corner was a metal door with a small viewing window. 'You're hiding behind that aren't you?' whispered Jon, stepping up to the narrow opening and peering through.

An eye appeared, immediately followed by a snarl as several yellow teeth connected with the edge of the window. Jon actually felt the animal's breath on his face as he lurched backwards, the back of his head thudding against the wall behind. The panther appeared at floor level and pushed a huge paw at the gap below the wire mesh, cruel claws fully extended. All the while it stared at Jon in that same emotionless way. No hard feelings, the look seemed to say. But of course I want to eat you.

Jon looked at its slick coat, darker spots just visible in the glossy fur. But for a heavier bunching of muscles about its shoulders, the animal had very similar proportions to a domestic cat. It was just about twenty times larger and able to haul prey heavier than itself up a vertical tree trunk. Jon glanced at the height of the viewing window. Easily six feet up, he thought, and all you had to do was rear up on your hind legs to be the same height as me. He couldn't help smiling. 'You crafty bastard,' he whispered. 'You knew I'd eventually look through, didn't you?'

The cat moved away, apparently now bored with his presence. Jon glanced again at Hobson as he completed his circuit of the enclosure, pausing to actually bow to the watching audience. Suspicion blossomed in Jon's head. 'You like this too bloody much.' He looked at where Samburu had pawed the mesh. A few hairs were caught there. Jon reached in his pockets, pulled out a small evidence bag, then crouched down. Samburu was just visible at the other side of the den, sitting in front of the trap door, waiting to be released. Jon quickly extended a hand, plucked a few hairs from the wire and stood up. A swift check of the other den revealed a few more hairs on the wire there and he snatched those for his collection.

When Hobson reappeared Jon was at his designated spot, arms behind his back.

'That's them sorted,' Hobson announced, wiping his hands on his shorts then securing the gate to the enclosure and lifting the trap door to Samburu's den. 'What was it you wanted to ask me?'

They stepped back outside and Hobson locked the wooden door behind them. 'Are panthers known to follow rivers and streams? Perhaps to use as a hunting ground?' Jon asked.

Hobson paused for a moment. 'Yes. Especially in jungles. A river provides a natural pathway through thick vegetation.'

'Do they mind water?'

'They don't seek it out like tigers do, but they certainly don't mind swimming across a river if it cuts through their territory. More often a river probably acts as its edge. Delineating the border. Of course a river crossing point would also be a good place for a panther to ambush its prey.'

Jon nodded, satisfied the answer reinforced the Medlock theory.

'Why do you ask?' Hobson said, picking up the empty pails.

Should I tell him? Jon wondered. Yes, let's see how he reacts. 'This morning's victim was found within metres of the Medlock. The river also runs through Daisy Nook Country Park where Peterson was found. The Medlock rises at the foot of Saddleworth Moor where, as you know, Rose Sutton was killed.'

During his short speech Hobson's pale eyes flickered all around, never once settling on Jon. 'Interesting.'

'Isn't it?' Jon replied, now studying the man more carefully. He glanced towards the gates he'd come by. 'I'd better be heading back. Is the zoo always this busy on a weekday? There must have been a couple of hundred people watching just now.'

Hobson stacked the buckets into each other and led the way towards the reception building. 'Not usually, no.'

'Just since people started getting killed?'

'That's right. Some of the staff see it as macabre, but I'm trying to use it as a way of educating people about these magnificent animals. I've written a panther information sheet for staff to hand out. It encourages people to give money to conservation projects. Donations, I hear, have risen sharply.'

Jon wasn't surprised. People were so easily seduced by anything that slaughtered their fellow humans. Panthers, sharks, crocodiles, inmates awaiting execution on death row, Apache gunship helicopters. 'So must your takings at the gates.'

'True,' Hobson replied, eyes on the ground in front.

'How would you describe your relationship with Rose Sutton?'

Hobson glanced at him and Jon looked straight back with a steady gaze.

'We got on pretty well. A shared interest, I suppose. She was fascinated by the prospect of a panther roaming their land. Unlike the husband. He just wanted to kill it.'

'You spent a fair bit of time with her then? Up on the moors?'

'Not really. They'd lost maybe a dozen sheep over the last few years. Sometimes I wouldn't see her for months.'

'Ken Sutton suspected she was having an affair.'

Hobson was about to smile, then his face dropped. 'Hang on. Are we discussing the behaviour of panthers or Rose Sutton's personal life?'

'I don't know. They seem to be linked, at least in death.'

By now they'd reached the perimeter fence. Hobson put the buckets down. 'You said earlier the killing this morning could have been someone staging an attack to resemble a panther.'

Jon cocked his head to the side. Come on then smart arse, what was I implying? He watched as Hobson pondered what to say.

'I've been working for some time now on the theory that there is more than one Alien Big Cat living in the Peak District National Park. The locations and almost simultaneous killings of sheep, that sort of thing. I don't believe it's a human you're hunting.'

No, you probably don't, thought Jon, but that's not going to stop me searching. 'Thanks for your help.'

Hobson let him through the gate and he walked back to his car, got inside and rubbed his face with the palms of his hands. Come on Jon, think. What's going on? Should more of the investigation focus on Hobson? He removed the evidence bag from his pocket and held it up. The collection of hairs inside stuck to the plastic, some crossing over each other as if arranged in an archaic code. What will you tell me? he asked himself.

A car appeared at the edge of his vision, crossing the car park and coming to a halt in the far corner. Carmel Todd got out and set off for reception. What the fuck was she doing here? Is this a pre-arranged meeting or have you just received a call? He remembered the radio on in Hobson's office. The man could easily have heard the news and rung her. He waited until she'd gone inside, then started his car. His mobile went off. Eagerly he glanced at the screen, but his wife's name wasn't showing.

'DI Spicer here.'

'Jon, it's Rick. You need to get back here.'

'What's happened?'

'Danny Gordon has been found in a squat on the Oldham Road.'

'Yes! Is he being taken to Longsight?'

'No, the MRI's mortuary. Officers at the scene reckon he's been dead a good five days.'

Jon sat back in his seat. Five days? That meant it was impossible that his prime suspect was the killer. 'He's dead?'

'Suicide. There's a note with the body, it puts Peterson right in the shit.'

'Where is this squat?'

'Head towards the city centre on the Oldham Road, it's the last tower block on your left just before you hit Great Ancoats Street. You can't miss the place, it's a total eyesore.'

'I'm on my way.' As he dropped the phone on to the passenger seat behind him, the thought burrowed back to the front of his mind. Where the hell is my wife?

Twenty-Nine

Jon got there forty minutes later. A uniform waved him into a lay-by on the opposite side of the road to the ugly building. A barrier of blue construction site hoardings had been erected round the base of the derelict premises. Judging by the volume of graffiti covering them, they'd been there for quite some time. Rick stood waiting in the gap where one panel had been removed.

'You looked fucked, mate,' his partner cheerfully announced.

'Thanks.'

'How's Alice?'

Jon shook his head in reply. 'By the way, I've stepped down from trying to head up the investigation. Summerby's assuming responsibility.'

'Probably not a bad thing. You've got other things on your plate.'

'Yeah well, your position on the team is unaffected. I guess you're just lumped with me.'

'Perfect. We're still in the thick of it, but now the pressure's off.'

I wish, Jon thought, turning to the building that loomed over them. 'This looks a nice place to live.'

The overgrown grass surrounding the tower block was littered with debris. Segments of window frames, panels of formica, squares of plywood. Sprinkled over everything was a generous amount of broken glass. All the windows at ground level were covered by metal plates, those on the first and second floors by chipboard. But many had been kicked out and, from the third floor up, no windows or even frames existed.

Looking up, Jon could see the ceilings of the higher flats, only bare plaster and wires where lights had once hung. A sign on the side of the building announced, *If any incident occurs in connection to this property, call Secure Holdings.*

He read the phone number, wondering how long ago the company had gone out of business. 'People actually live in here?' he asked as Rick led him to a side door, the metal panel covering it bent back.

'Quite a few. They're all in the main foyer giving statements. According to the housing inspectors who found the body, the building was first taken over by a bunch of art students. There's no leccy or gas, but the water's still connected, so they weren't shitting in buckets. They held a few wild parties, then the local vermin cottoned on. It soon descended into crack dens and all the rest of it. The students were scared off a long time ago.'

'Where was Danny Gordon?'

'Sixteenth floor, corner flat. I don't think many could be arsed climbing up that high. The door to the flat was locked, but the smell gave it away.'

Squeezing through the gap between the door frame and protective panel, they entered a stairwell that reeked of urine. Jon was instantly reminded of the sharp aroma in the panthers' dens.

As they set off up the stairs Jon noted that the elaborate murals on the walls had been ruined by a covering of mindless graffiti. It was, he thought, a clear indication of the order in which the tower block had been colonised. Arty free-thinkers first, brain-dead no-thinkers second. As they reached each landing the view over the city became more impressive. To their right was Sportcity, site of the facilities built for the Commonwealth Games and now used by local teams, including Manchester City Football Club in the main stadium. He spotted the B of the Bang sculpture, a collection of metal spikes radiating outward from a central point that was meant to symbolise the explosion of energy from a starting pistol. Jon smiled when he thought of what the locals had named it: Kerplunk.

As soon as they stepped out into the corridor of the sixteenth floor the smell hit him. There it is, Jon said to himself. The unmistakeable aroma of rotting human. They paused at the door to flat 242 while Rick took out a couple of white face masks from the scene of crime bag kindly left at the door by forensics.

Jon was looking at the splintered wood a third of the way up the door frame. 'What went on here?'

'The housing inspectors kicked it open, reckoned the smell was dead pigeons.'

'They didn't have keys?' Jon asked, mask held to his face.

'Not for the lower lock. Looks like Danny Gordon had fitted that one himself.'

Jon stepped through the door and turned around. At the top of the door was a bolt. 'That wasn't drawn?'

'Suppose not,' Rick replied. 'Is that significant?'

Jon shrugged. 'If he took the trouble to lock himself in, why not draw the bolt across too?'

'You're thinking someone else locked him in, from the outside?'

'Maybe. No doubt it's suicide?'

'It looks more or less certain, though there is something odd on the suicide note.'

Rick walked down the bare concrete corridor and into the front room. In an attempt to reduce the draught that must have blown in, Gordon had tacked plastic sheeting over the window frame, reducing the light from the outside. A few packing crates stood in one corner, clothes piled untidily on top. In the middle of the room a fold-out table was covered in empty tins. Soup, baked beans, ravioli.

In the other corner Danny Gordon's corpse lay on a bare mattress. Decomposition was well under way, but even the patches of black blossoming under the waxy skin couldn't mask the obvious injuries to his face. He was wearing a T-shirt and shell-suit trousers. The trainer and sock on his left foot were missing and sticking out from between his bare toes was a tarnished syringe.

'Look at his forearms, completely fucked,' Rick said from behind his mask as the white-suited forensics investigator moved to the side.

Jon examined the thick peppering of punctures that ran along them. 'So you think he's been here a good five days?'

'Yes, that's a good estimate,' the woman replied.

'Which means, though it's possible he killed Rose Sutton, he couldn't have been responsible for Peterson and Kerrigan,' murmured Jon.

'Looking at those skinny arms, I doubt he could have inflicted much damage on anyone, male or female,' Rick added.

'Where's the note?' Jon said, turning away from the pathetic sight.

'Here,' Rick nodded to the table. 'He points the finger squarely at Peterson, describing the abuse that went on in the Silverdale. Says that Peterson destroyed him and he can't go on any more.'

Jon skimmed over the childish writing with its embarrassing amount of spelling mistakes. What a life, he thought. That it ended like this, in a squalid tower block flat on a mattress probably dragged from some skip, seemed depressingly inevitable.

Jon reached the end of the note. Below Danny Gordon's signature was a single word. Kuririkana. The writing shifted out of focus as Jon looked inwards, searching his memory. Where have I seen that before? He tried to replay his movements over the last few days. Bollocks, it was like searching for a needle in a haystack. 'Have you seen that word somewhere else? It looks familiar somehow.'

Rick shook his head. 'I thought you might know. What's that song the All Blacks do before rugby matches?'

'The Haka.'

'That's it. Could it be Maori? Looks like it might be to me.'

'You know, I've seen it performed so often, but I've no idea what the lyrics are.'

'DC Adlon has gone to the University, maybe they can help. Thing is, it doesn't appear to be Gordon's handwriting.'

Jon looked more closely. Rick was right. Though written with the same pen, the letters were regularly spaced and less spiky. 'Any sign of the pen?'

'No,' the woman in the white suit replied. 'Not so far anyway.'

Jon looked towards the corridor. 'Let's assume someone

locked Danny Gordon into this flat on their way out. Could it be the same person who wrote that word?'

'You're saying someone helped him kill himself?' Rick replied.

'Not necessarily. They could have sat with him while he did it. Or maybe just found him after the event.'

'You mean a mate of some kind?'

'It's the sort of thing a mate might do.'

'The only mate he seemed to have was this Jammer.'

'Exactly. Any black guys with dreadlocks downstairs?'

'Let's take a look.'

The screens covering the main doors had been removed and the doors themselves opened. Despite this, the smell of unwashed bodies and musty clothes filled the air. All the squatters had retreated from the patch of daylight shining in, preferring to sit or lie in the shadows beyond. There were about twenty of them, all waiting in silence as several clipboard-wielding officers worked their way around.

Jon started at the right-hand corner. His eyes had only passed over three faces before they connected with his younger brother's. He was staring back at him through a haze of cigarette smoke. Jon's immediate reaction was to move his gaze on, but his mind was suddenly racing. Jesus Christ, that was our kid. What's he doing here? Please God, don't let him be connected to this mess. His eyes slowly moved back. Dave's hair was longer, and though the face was thinner it only seemed to emphasise the square features of the Spicer family.

'No black guys,' Rick said at his side.

Without replying, Jon walked across the foyer. 'Has this man been statemented?'

The nearest officer glanced back. 'Yeah. Andrew Adams, no fixed abode. Fake name if I ever heard one.'

Jon motioned with his fingers. 'A word outside please.'

With a lazy grin, his younger brother got to his feet. As they headed for the doors, Rick started uncertainly over. Jon warded him off with a raised palm.

Once outside, Jon moved a good ten metres from the doors

before turning round. His younger brother was dragging on a roll up, the smirk still on his face. Jon looked him up and down. Dirty jeans and battered trainers. Beneath a shapeless top the bones of his shoulders stuck out too sharply. He seemed to have regressed back to his teenage weight. 'What are you doing here?'

'Sorry officer?'

Jon realised he'd snapped the question out. He started again. 'All right, Dave?'

'Yeah, Jon. Fine. Just been rudely awoken by your colleagues, but other than that, I'm good. You?'

Jon nodded. 'You living here?'

His brother turned to the building, took a last drag on his roll up and dropped it into the grass. 'Only recently. I've been up in the Lakes over the summer. Enjoying the country life.'

Enjoying some poor bastard's empty holiday house, Jon thought. 'Why haven't you rung Mum? She's worried sick about you.'

Dave shrugged. 'The old man still alive?'

'Course he is.'

'There you go then.'

'Why punish Mum because you fell out with Dad?'

'Fell out? He threw me out.'

'You—' Jon stopped. This was heading in the usual direction. Who said that, who did what. He took out his pack of cigarettes, flipped the top open and held it out.

'Naughty, naughty,' Dave smirked, taking one. 'You never kicked the habit?'

Jon slid one out for himself and lit both up. 'I did for a bit. Listen, just call her will you? Tell her you're OK.'

'You've seen me, you can let her know.'

'But that's not the same. You know that.'

'And you know she won't let me leave it at that.' He adopted a whining voice. 'What are you doing? Where are you living? Why don't you come home?'

Jon felt his shoulders tensing up. You're close to a fucking slap. 'What are you doing?'

Dave paused to drag on his cigarette. 'Meaning?'

Jon held a hand towards the tower block. 'This, for fuck's

sake. Kipping in derelict buildings with a load of addicts. I don't suppose you're working.'

His brother laughed scornfully and Jon felt his resentment of him increase. 'Nice going, our kid. Some fucking life you've got here.'

His brother's lips curled, the prelude to countless childhood fights. 'Unlike yours? Look at you, the system's sucking you dry, pal. You look fifty, slaving to pay off your mortgage, putting aside a few hundred each year for your tedious week in Spain. No fucking thanks.'

Jon drew the fingers of one hand along his jaw and imagined how exhausted he must look. 'We've got a kid.'

His brother blinked. 'No shit! You're a dad?'

Jon nodded. 'Holly. She's three months old.' He saw the half smile appear on his brother's face. So family did matter, at least a little. Jon seized the opportunity. 'Will you call Mum?'

'OK, I'll try. Holly? That's cool. What does she look like?'

Jon smiled back. 'Babies all look the same to me. Most people reckon she's got Alice's eyes in a Spicer face.'

Dave laughed. 'Poor bitch.'

They remained silent for a few seconds. Jon glanced again at the empty building. 'Did you know the guy who died, Danny Gordon?'

Dave crossed his arms. 'Only to chat to. He was pretty fucked up.'

'Did he ever show up with a black guy?'

'Jammer? Yeah, they were good mates.'

'Who is this Jammer? What's his real name?'

'Just know him as Jammer. He'd look out for Danny when he got aggressive. Saved him from getting a kicking.'

'Why'd he get aggressive?'

'Who knows. The guy was a head case. He'd flip out sometimes, especially after drinking.'

'When did you last see Jammer?'

'A few days back. Maybe five. He was looking for Danny.'

'Where was Danny?'

'I don't know. No one had seen him for a bit. How long has he been dead up in that flat?'

'Around five days.'

'That explains why no one had seen him.'

'Where'll you go now?'

'There are other places near here.'

'So you'll call Mum?'

His brother put his hands in his pockets and hunched his shoulders. 'Can you lend me some cash?'

I understand, thought Jon. You'll call Mum if I pay you to. He felt dismay at how cheaply his younger brother must value their family. Jon reached for his wallet, glancing at his brother's sleeves as if he could see through them for signs of drug use. How far was Dave from Danny Gordon's fate? He had a glimpse of being called out to some boarded-up house to identify his brother's body, lying in a back room surrounded by a puddle of its own fluids. Reluctantly he removed two twenties and held them out. Dave's hands stayed in his pockets, eyes still on the wallet. Jon slid out the final twenty and extended the notes at waist level as if paying for something illicit.

The money disappeared into Dave's pocket. 'Cheers bro.'

A minute ago it was pal, Jon thought bitterly. Wallet still out, he removed a business card and held it up. 'My mobile's on this. Keep in touch, yeah?'

Dave winked in reply, turned on his heel and slunk off towards the gap in the hoardings. The uniformed officer blocked his exit and Jon was forced to call over that it was OK. Dave held up a thumb and then was gone.

Jon took a last drag of his cigarette and let it fall from his fingers. As he crushed it angrily underfoot he heard Rick's voice.

'Who was that scuzz-bucket? A snitch or something?'

'Yeah, something like that,' Jon sighed.

'Well, no one in there has seen Jammer for a few days. We'd better head back to Longsight I suppose. Summerby's called a briefing for five-thirty.'

They were crossing the road when Rick's mobile rang. 'DS Saville. Ah, excellent. Really? OK, thanks for letting me know. See you back at the station.' He rung off and looked at Jon. 'That was Joe Adlon. The word at the bottom of the suicide note means, "remember".'

'Remember?' Jon mused. 'Why write the word remember?'

'You remember something that's been done in the past. Peterson's abuse of Danny Gordon?'

'But if someone else wrote that, what were they saying? I remember what he did to you. Some sort of a tribute or acknowledgement?'

'Or it's an instruction. To whoever finds the body.'

Jon pulled his car keys out. 'Summerby will need to get Dr Heath's opinion on this. Too psychological for me. Anyway, did he say what language it was in?'

'Yeah. A tribal dialect from Kenya. Kikuyu.'

'Kenya?' Jon said, immediately conducting a mental check of any previous time the country had cropped up in the investigation. His mind halted at an image of Jeremy Hobson describing how he'd seen a leopard dragging the carcass of a young giraffe up a tree in Kenya. He removed the panther hairs from his pocket. 'We need to get a DNA test done, and fast.'

Thirty

As they walked into the incident room Jon scanned the faces inside. From the way most officers avoided his eyes, he knew news had leaked out that Summerby had taken charge of the investigation. Keeping his chin up, he went over to his desk and picked up the phone. 'Hi, Nikki, it's Jon here.'

'What's making me think you need a really urgent favour?'

'You've got me sussed. That DNA test kit you mentioned. Will it work on a few more hairs I've got?'

'Only if there are follicles attached. I haven't got the facilities to test off keratin alone.'

Jon examined the bag. 'There are. On most of them anyway.'

'I'll try then. Send them over to my office.'

'Don't you want to know what it's about?'

'Jon, I'm sitting outside a courtroom and they're calling me in at any moment to give evidence. Just send the things over and I can ring you back. It'll be early evening though.'

'Cheers Nikki, they're on their way.'

He checked his message inbox yet again. Still nothing from Alice. This was getting ridiculous. He tried her number again. Bastard answerphone. 'Ali, it's me at three twenty-five. Call me when you pick this up, I don't know where you are.' He pressed red, then immediately called home. When the phone was answered it was Alice's voice that came down the line.

'Alice!' He sat back. 'Thank God for that. Where've you been?'

'The library.'

'All day?'

'Yes, I've just walked in.'

'I've been trying to call you on your mobile . . . ' He stopped, realising why it had been turned off.

'Oh, I must have forgotten to turn it back on when I came out. You've been leaving messages?'

She sounds really upbeat, Jon thought, finding her shift in mood confusing. 'A couple. I didn't know where you were.'

'But I couldn't have it switched on in there.'

'I realise. What were you doing anyway?'

'Researching the Iraqi civilian death count.'

Oh no.

'There was an article I needed in a back issue of the *New Statesman*. Honestly, the whole thing is . . . scandal isn't strong enough. It's an—'

'What did you do with Holly?'

'What?'

'Holly. Where has she been all day?'

'With me of course. I took everything I needed down to the basement café. No one minded me breast feeding down there.' She dropped her voice to a whisper. 'You realise your mum's here? She's fussing around in the kitchen.'

'I know. I asked her. Alice, I didn't know where the hell you were. I was really worried, to be honest. You just disappeared.'

'Oh, so you sent her round?'

Irritation had crept into her voice.

'Not to check up,' Jon protested. 'Just see if you were OK. Anything could have happened. You might have slipped in the shower.'

'But you couldn't find the time to check yourself?'

'Not this morning. There was another body found—'

'You're still on that case.'

'In a supporting role, yes.'

Silence.

'Ali, I couldn't just pack it in completely. Listen, I'll be back soon. I'm waiting for the results of a couple of tests.'

'Fine. That's fine. Is your mother staying here until then or am I safe enough to be left alone with my baby?'

'She's only trying to help.'

'Holly's ready for a feed. I'd better go.'

'Can you put Mum on then?'

He heard Alice walking away. 'Mary, Jon wants a word.' Her voice grew fainter with each step.

A few seconds later his mum came on the line. 'Hello, Jon.'

Do I mention seeing Dave? Or would it be better if he rings. Unsure of the best option, he decided not to mention it. 'Thanks for sticking around, Mum.'

'No problem. I've done some cleaning up.'

'Is Alice in the front room?'

'She is.'

'How does she seem to you?'

'Grand. A bit confused to find me here though.'

'And Holly?'

'The little poppet's fine.'

'Are you staying? I should be home soon.'

'Well.' She sounded uncomfortable. 'Your dad's expecting me back. I've put on another casserole for you two. I don't want to get in the way.'

'I know, Mum. But I'm worried about Alice. Does she really seem fine?'

'Absolutely. Jon . . . this is very awkward.'

He nodded, suddenly aware of the position he was putting her in. 'Sorry. You head off then. I shouldn't be long.'

He kept the receiver to his ear despite the fact his mum had hung up. Could Alice have turned a corner? OK, the object of her enthusiasm wasn't exactly healthy, but at least she was sounding happier in herself. Yes. Perhaps she just needed something to occupy her mind. He replaced the phone, trying to ignore the part of him that was totally unconvinced.

'Everything OK?' Rick asked from the next desk.

'That was Alice. She sounds like her old self. Well, not totally. But miles better.'

'Really?'

'Yeah.' He shook his head. To think it occurred to him that she and Holly could have been in danger. He glanced at Rick, wondering whether to ask if his sister had ever considered harming herself, but it wasn't the right time or place. And besides, asking the question implied he was concerned Alice might – and that was ridiculous. 'She's been out with Holly in town. You could hear the energy in her voice.'

Rick looked relieved. 'Fingers crossed then.'

For the next hour and a half they typed up reports for the indexer, their bursts of conversation eventually broken as the doors opened. A couple of officers entered the room with the first items recovered from the scene of Trevor Kerrigan's death. A large plastic evidence sack with his golf bag and clubs inside was propped in the corner, followed by the files from the boot of his car. Another handed the indexer a bag containing his keys, mobile phone and wallet. Jon turned back to his computer, thinking of the team that would be in Kerrigan's house questioning the wife about his enemies.

A couple of officers had sauntered over, eager to see what had been left behind at the scene of the latest murder. Jon heard plastic cracking as one lifted the golf bag up for closer inspection. 'Callaway, Terra Firma. Very posh. What did this guy do for a living?'

'Moneylender apparently,' someone else replied. 'Could it have any more pockets?'

The other officer laughed. 'This is top notch. Look, an insulated pocket for your drinks.'

'Nice touch. What's that scratched in the leather?'

'Where? Oh yes. Kuri . . . kuriri . . . what does it say?'

In his mind's eye, Jon suddenly saw the word. It was scrawled on a notice board, nestled amongst other signatures. There were trees behind it and through them, the shine of water. Was it Crime Lake? The car park where Derek Peterson was found? He stood up and said loudly, 'Kuririkana.'

Rick's hands were frozen above his keyboard. 'The word on the bottom of Danny Gordon's suicide note.'

Everyone turned to look at them. Jon pointed to the officers with the golf bag. 'Is that what it says?'

One leaned down. 'It does.'

He began to click his fingers. 'That's not the only place I've seen it. Crime Lake. I think I spotted it there.'

'Crime Lake? Whereabouts?' Rick asked.

'I'm not absolutely sure. It's just an image that flashed in my head, but it could have been on the notice board in the car park where Peterson was found.'

'It's the killer. It has to be. Why leave evidence like that at each crime scene?'

'He's making a point, telling us something. And it's so important to him, he doesn't care if it gets him caught.' As he grabbed his jacket he saw Rick getting up too. 'Don't worry mate, I may be wrong. There could be fuck-all there. You finish up your report, it's best you're here when Summerby comes downstairs to hold the briefing.'

'You sure?'

'Yeah, I'll ring you if I find anything.'

Rush hour traffic was beginning to build on the M60 and Jon resorted to the siren a couple of times to shift cars out of the way. By the time he reached Crime Lake, dusk was beginning to fall. Jon found his eyes dragged towards the distant moors, mere shadows in the rapidly gathering gloom.

As he pulled into the car park, he looked around. He always found it slightly unsettling to return to a murder scene and find everything normal once again. It seemed like the violent death of a person should have some permanent effect on the surrounding area. But what? A withering of the undergrowth, a gnarling of the trees, a crumbling of the earth itself? He knew it was absurd. By that logic, the whole country would be dotted with barren patches. Once in France, he and Alice had made a detour to the Somme. The pleasant rolling fields were almost disappointing. Only the silence let you imagine the carnage that had once occurred.

He put the headlights on full and the notice board at the top of the car park shone bright in the beams.

Crime Lake. No Motorbikes.

Already certain the word would be there, he opened the car door and got out, leaving the engine running. The edges of the notice board were covered by a mass of signatures. Wozza. Ruhul. Amie and Jade. Ashif. He worked his way through them quickly, and spotted the word he was looking for in the top left hand corner: Kuririkana.

What did it mean, he asked himself, stepping out of the headlight's glare. Remember. Remember what? The word had now been found at the site of a suicide and two murders. His head turned and he looked towards where he knew the moors lay. What was the betting it was somewhere up there, in the vicinity of where Rose Sutton's body had been found?

He pictured the murder scene, the bare peat earth, stunted gorse and scattering of giant rocks. The rocks. If it was anywhere, it would be scratched or written on them.

His mobile rang, causing him to jump. Nikki's name on the screen. 'Hi there. Still in court?'

'No, you're in luck. The defence had something new, so the judge adjourned it until tomorrow. I'm back at the office. These hairs you sent over aren't human.'

'No, I swiped them from the panther enclosure at Buxton Zoo.'

'And you want me to compare their DNA with the samples on the system.'

'Yes please. But – and you're going to kill me for this – can you put the test on hold? Something else has cropped up.'

'What?'

'Any chance of you coming over here with that special light you use for picking out stains and other stuff?'

'The Portascope. Why?'

'I need to recheck where Rose Sutton was killed. I think we missed some evidence. A word, written somewhere near where her body was found.'

'You want me to go tramping round on those moors now? Jon, I can't see out of my window any more. You know why that is? It's dark.'

'Right. Which is the best time to use that light.'

'You're serious, aren't you?'

'You don't have to come with me. I just want to borrow it.'

'Good. Because aside from that animal, who knows how many madmen with rifles are prowling around up there.'

'So you can bring it over?'

She sighed. 'Give me the directions.'

Thirty-One

When her BMW Mini pulled into the car park Jon was sitting in his vehicle, the ordnance survey map for the Dark Peak spread out across the steering wheel and dashboard. The interior light of his car was weak, causing him to squint as he studied the faint lines on the paper.

Holding a hand out of the open door, he waved a greeting to Nikki and sat back. She parked alongside him and climbed out, pausing at the boot to remove an aluminium carry case. 'I can't believe you dragged me out here,' she announced, placing the case on the tarmac.

At just over five feet tall, Jon didn't need to look up much to meet her eyes. She was still wearing her outfit for court, a tailored black trouser suit over a crisp white shirt, collar overlapping the jacket's lapels. Her dark brown hair had grown longer since he'd last seen her, and the style had evolved from tousled to wavy. She pushed some strands away from her face and smiled. 'What?'

Jon's eyes flickered momentarily to the side. Shit, I was staring. 'Thanks for coming out so fast.'

'Yeah well, you're lucky I didn't get lost. I'm not used to leaving the city centre.'

He wondered if she still had the little loft apartment in the Northern Quarter. He remembered her description. Exposed brick walls, steel girders and floor to ceiling windows with views out over the city. It sounded a nice pad. And with her determination never to have kids, why sacrifice it for some cramped semi in the suburbs?

She pointed to the map. 'Are you really going up there alone?'

He nodded. 'Everyone else is back at Longsight in a briefing.'

'Do you know the way?'

'Kind of. There's a track branching off the A6024 near the top of the moor. It leads towards Black Hill. Rose Sutton's body was found in a gully just a short walk from there.'

'What's wrong with getting an officer from Mossley Brow to show you the way? Surely they'll be familiar with the area?'

Jon thought about how Clegg was hiding something. 'I don't trust the officer in charge.'

Nikki arched an eyebrow. 'So why not Rose Sutton's husband? He must know the moor like the back of his hand.'

'Same reason.' Jon looked at the carry case. 'So, how does this work?'

Nikki crouched down and popped the clips. Inside was a layer of high density foam. Securely nestled in precision-cut cavities was a collection of items. She placed a finger on the largest, a black box with an empty bulb socket at the front. 'This is the Portscope, a handheld forensic light source.' She touched a smaller black box alongside. 'Twelve-volt battery, fully charged. Here's the bulb, it screws into the front. These are your filter covers. Different things show up under different wavelengths of light. UV light, which is less than four hundred nanometres is good for certain powders, inks and dyes, though not gunshot residue. Violet light illuminates blood stains, blue light shows up most other bodily fluids, blue green and green are best for fingerprints.'

'OK, where's the switch for the wavelengths?'

'It's not that simple. You need to tune in the lamp to the different colour bands, then fine tune it with the filters. You're scanning grass and earth right?'

'And rocks. Grit-stone boulders.'

'OK. There's a good chance the rocks will create background interference. They may glow or darken under certain wave-lengths, so you'll need to eliminate that . . . ' She paused. 'I'm going to have to come, aren't I?'

'No,' Jon said, folding the map over. 'Just talk me through how to do it.'

'Pissing hell!' She stood up. 'Why did I ever think I could explain how to use this in five minutes? It takes an entire training course to learn how to use it properly.' She walked back to the boot of her car, opened it and removed an industrial sized torch, Wellington boots and a big red quilted ski jacket. 'We go in your car though. I'm not driving Mojo down any farm track.'

'Mojo?' Jon replied with a grin.

'What's wrong with that?' She smiled back, flicking a black shoe off.

As they followed the road to Hollingworth, Nikki produced a purple hair band and started tying her hair back. Jon watched her from the corner of his eye, always impressed at how she never shied away from a challenge.

'How's home life?' she asked, face obscured by her raised forearms.

Jon stared at the road in front. 'Not bad. Holly's three months old now. She's doing fine, feeding really well. Actually, she can be a bit awkward at night.'

Nikki grimaced. 'The thought of feeding a baby every two or three hours round the clock. I don't know how you do it.'

'Well, I get the easy deal. Alice is breastfeeding. I normally just give Holly a bottle of formula last thing before bed. Maybe the odd night feed if Alice is really knackered.'

'All credit to her, that must take some willpower.'

She looked out of her side window and Jon could see the tension in her neck. The silence began to grow heavy and he searched for something to say. 'So, are you seeing anyone at the moment?'

Still looking away, she shook her head; Jon noticed the stubby ponytail shake. 'Nah. Spending too much time doing this bloody job.'

The comment was meant to be light-hearted, but she didn't quite pull it off.

He tapped the edge of the steering wheel with his forefingers. 'No sexy lawyers caught your eye recently?'

She quickly turned her head, eyes searching out his, checking the comment was meant in jest. 'Oh yeah, some smooth-talking guy in an even smoother suit. Just my style.'

'What about judges or magistrates then? Let one be your Sugar Daddy.'

She was looking back out the window. 'Just drop it, Jon. You're safely wrapped up in your idyllic family life. It's easy for you to take the piss.'

Yeah right, he thought. Idyllic is one way of describing it. 'I wasn't taking the piss.' He stopped, aware the conversation had dwelled too long on their relationships. They drove on in silence, the subdued light of Tintwistle's cottages fading away behind them. Soon they were surrounded by darkness, his car advancing into the ever-receding tunnel of light cast by its headlamps.

Nikki pressed her nose to the glass and cupped her hands to the sides of her face. 'There's nothing out there.'

'Wait until we get to the top.'

The turn-off for the A6024 soon appeared on their left and the sound of the engine dropped as he slowed down to take it. Moving into second gear, he eased his foot off the clutch and the engine's noise returned, now revving much higher as they started climbing the steep road.

He saw Nikki's shoulders shudder as she crossed her arms. 'You still happy to do this?'

'Of course. What's that light up ahead?'

Hanging in the darkness above was a red glow. 'It's the top of a radio mast. We'll use it to guide us back to the car.'

As they completed the ascent, the light seemed to float in the air like a crimson will-o'-the-wisp. Resisting the temptation to stare at it too long, Jon kept his eyes on the road. When its glow was almost above them he slowed to a crawl. There was the mouth of the track, base of the mast just visible as they turned down it.

The vehicle began to bump and lurch as they rolled slowly along. After thirty metres a large pothole appeared in front of them and he brought the car to a halt. 'I'm not risking that.'

'Right,' said Nikki in a businesslike voice. 'Let's get this done.'

Jon killed the engine and blackness flooded the vehicle. He quickly reached up a hand, flicked on the interior light, then spread the map out. 'OK, so we're here.' He slid his forefinger over the paper, aware of the eddies of wind nudging the car. 'There's Black Hill.' He nodded at the windscreen and then looked back down. 'A kilometre that way, maximum. At the top is a cairn of rocks, so we'll know once we reach it. The gully Rose Sutton was killed in is just nearby.' Squinting, he focused on a series of V-shaped kinks in the contour lines. 'Must be one of these. Grouse Clough I should think. Are you ready?'

'Ready.'

Their doors opened simultaneously and a rush of cold air whisked through the vehicle, almost flipping the map from his hand.

'Bloody hell,' Nikki said, climbing out and shutting the door. The turbulence instantly vanished and Jon folded the map so the section they were on was uppermost. Outside he looked about, the wind moaning as it passed through struts of the radio mast. Thanks to a faint glow where the moon was trying to shine through a thin layer of cloud, he was able to make out the dark terrain stretching out all around them. He peered ahead, just able to make out a lump that stood fractionally higher than its neighbours. 'Black Hill, straight in front.'

'Good,' Nikki replied. 'You can carry the Portascope and lead the way.'

She turned her torch on and shone it downwards, creating a circle of light around her feet. Its brightness only seemed to emphasise the darkness surrounding them. Leaning down, Jon curled his fingers round the case's handle, surprised at how heavy it was. No problem, he thought. Ten minutes to the gully, half an hour to search the rocks, ten minutes back. Less than an hour. Piece of piss. He skirted to the side of the pot hole, glad he hadn't tried to drive over it.

After another hundred metres the track ended at a shallow ditch. He stepped over it, feet sinking into the soft turf beyond. Turning round, he held a hand out to Nikki. Small fingers that were colder than his gripped his hand and she jumped across. As she landed on the other side her momentum carried her forwards into Jon. Their bodies were up against each other as she gripped his elbow with her other hand to stop from falling backwards.

Jon felt her stomach as it pressed against his groin. The blood surged in his chest. Do not go there, he said to himself, stepping back. 'Close one. You nearly went in there.'

'Yes,' she replied in a voice charged with emotion.

The torch picked out a narrow path through the clumps of thick grass. 'Sheep trail,' said Jon. 'We'll follow that.'

With Nikki walking behind him, they followed the route carved by the animals. Every now and again Nikki directed the beam off to the side to reveal shimmering ponds of black water, their surfaces silently rippling in the stiff breeze. Other times the beam of the torch picked out bushes of gorse, each branch and twig brought into sharp relief against the infinite darkness behind. They resembled exotic plants glimpsed on the seabed, twisted and bowed by the weight of water pressing down from above.

Jon pushed on, pausing every now and again when an alternative path branched off. By keeping the red light of the radio mast directly behind them, they made their way slowly across the moor. After twenty minutes Jon became aware that there was higher ground before them. 'Shine the torch ahead will you? I think this is Black Hill.'

'I bloody hope so.'

The beam lifted up and there, at the top of the slope in front, was a pile of stones.

'That's the cairn!' Jon said.

He felt her hand slap him on the back. 'Good going.'

'The gully is just on the other side.'

They passed the stones and tramped down the opposite slope, high stepping over branches of heather before finding a sheep trail that led in the right direction. Jon could feel they were descending and, when he looked back, he saw the red light was now only just visible above the curve of the land. A few dozen steps later and it had disappeared completely. He hesitated. This is bloody stupid, he thought, uneasy now there was nothing to keep his bearings by.

'What's up?' Nikki asked behind him.

Come on Jon, you're nearly there. 'Nothing. It's somewhere here on our left. Have a look down there.'

261

Nikki shone the torch in the direction he was pointing. A narrow gully was revealed. Jon stared down into the gloom. It didn't seem right. 'Must be the next one.'

'How can you tell?'

'I'm not sure, it just doesn't feel familiar.'

He heard her sigh. 'Go on then.'

Uncertain now, he carried on until he heard the sound of running water. Another gully had to be on their left. 'Try shining it again.'

The beam swept down, immediately picking out the cluster of rocks. Thank God for that, he thought. 'This is it.'

The little stream had died to a trickle and they were able to pick their way down the slope with relative ease. Within twenty metres of the rocks, Nikki shone the torch forwards again. Four ghost-like forms suddenly broke away from the boulders. She quickly cut off her cry of alarm. 'Jesus, they made me jump,' she giggled as the sprinting sheep disappeared beyond the range of the beam.

'I'm glad you're nervous too,' Jon said. 'I nearly pissed myself.'

They both laughed out loud as they approached the rocks. Jon put the Portascope down, rotating his shoulder back and forth to relieve his aching muscles. 'She was lying right here,' he said. 'The theory is whoever jumped her was using the rocks for cover.'

'Whoever or whatever?'

'Whoever,' Jon stated firmly. 'Let's not shit ourselves up any more than is necessary.'

Nikki shone the torch around, picking out strands of white fleece on the black soil. 'What a grim place to die.'

'Yup,' Jon replied. 'What do you reckon our chances are of finding anything?'

'Minimal. These rocks are our best bet.' She handed the torch to Jon, opened the case and took out the main unit. After screwing the bulb in, she selected a filter cap. 'We'll start with UV.' She attached the battery pack and put her finger on the switch. 'You can turn the torch off.'

As Jon did so he heard the Portascope click on. An eerie halo of blue light bathed the area before them. Holding it at waist height, Nikki started to sweep the rocks. Lichen and moss shone white in its unearthly glow and once again Jon felt like he could have been on an ocean bed.

Nikki worked her way along the semi-circle of rocks. 'Nothing ink based,' she said, removing a filter and releasing a burst of white light. 'Let's go to violet.' A new filter was attached, which turned the glow a soft reddish colour. Nikki began to sweep again. Now the lichen was hardly visible, though scratches and irregularities on the rock's surface suddenly were. Jon was glancing uneasily into the darkness behind him when he became aware that the glow had stopped moving.

'Got something?'

'I'm not sure. Is this a letter? It is! That's a K, or what's left of it.'

Jon looked over her shoulder. Just visible on the pockmarked surface was a darkish stain in the shape of a ragged K. 'Go to your right.'

Nikki swept the light across, and a faint U, R and I were revealed. 'Does that say Kuri?' Nikki asked.

'Go to the next rock, you'll find more letters there.'

She stepped sideways and the rest of the word appeared. 'Kuririkana. What does that mean?'

'Remember,' Jon replied. 'What do you think it's written in?'

'There's only one substance that glows black under violet light, and that's blood.'

Jon felt as though a cobweb had just caressed the back of his neck. He briskly rubbed at the spot with one hand. 'Can you take a scraping, for DNA?'

Nikki waved a hand. 'Problem is the cleaning agent, whatever it was.'

'Cleaning agent?'

'Someone's tried to rub this off. In fact, they probably believed they did remove it. In daylight, this would be invisible. Luckily, blood is one stubborn substance to remove completely, especially from a surface like this.'

Who could have tried to remove it? Jon ran through the list of people who'd visited this spot. Ken Sutton, Adam Clegg . . .

Jeremy Hobson. Had his alibi been checked for the night of Rose Sutton's death?

Nikki had removed a pot from her jacket and was scraping at the rock when the noise cut through the night. He saw her back stiffen and when she looked round at him, her eyes were wide with fear. 'What was that?'

Jon had to swallow before any words would come. 'Screech owl?'

Nikki was still crouching, eyes now shifting to Jon's side and the blackness beyond.

What? He wanted to shout as his pulse rocketed away. Is there something behind me?

'That was not a screech owl.'

Keep calm, Jon told himself. Do not let her see you're scared. 'A sheep then. They make pretty weird sounds, coughing and all sorts.'

'Jon, that was a snarl. Sheep do not—'

The noise came again, carried on the wind from somewhere further down the ravine. It was a throaty sawing sound, like air going in and out of a large pair of bellows. So that's what it feels like to have your hair stand on end, Jon thought as his scalp contracted against his skull. Casually he flicked the torch on and shone it down the slope. He may as well have tried to illuminate an aircraft hangar with a candle. 'Or a deer. A stag. You get them up here.'

'At night?' Nikki plucked the lens off the Portascope and began using the white glow to put the lenses back in the case. She slid the battery into its slot, then the torch, turning it off only when it was in place. She stood up. 'You can carry that. Fucking hell, Jon, it wasn't a deer. It was not a deer.'

A sharp odour caught in Jon's nostrils. Run! Just bloody run, his instincts screamed. 'Come on then,' he replied calmly, knowing how panic could pass between people like an airborne infection. 'We may as well head back. You lead the way, I'll be behind.'

'Too pissing right you will be. You got me out to this godforsaken place.'

They both started making their way up the ravine, neither

now trying to step carefully over the boggier patches. Looking up, Jon was just able to make out where the slope ended and the sky began. 'Not far to the top,' he murmured, weighing up the case in his hand and wondering whether it would be better to swing as a weapon or clutch as a shield. He remembered the size of Samburu's claws. Jesus, calm down. You are not about to be attacked.

At the top of the slope Nikki paused, her breath coming in shallow gasps. 'Which way?'

'Right. We're heading towards that lump of land, see? At about two o'clock.'

'There are two paths, which one?'

Jon shone the torch ahead. Bollocks, she was right. 'OK, the right hand one. The other cuts away too—'

The noise came again. It now sounded level with them, somewhere off to their side. Nikki grabbed Jon's arm. 'What is that? Oh, please God, this isn't happening. Please tell me . . . ' He felt her grip starting to shake and her words dissolved into a single sob.

'Keep going, OK?' He pushed her down the right hand path, and as they made their way along, the only sound was the heather rasping against their damp legs. Just a walk in the park, Jon thought to himself, suppressing the flickers of panic threatening to catch fire in his brain. A nice walk in the park, tra la la la, that's all this is. A nice walk. Where've I got that line from, he wondered, guessing it was something he'd heard in a film. With a jolt he realised – *American Werewolf in London*. The scene where the beast attacks the backpackers out wandering on the moors. That bloody film, I wish I'd never seen it.

The noise came again. An urge to change direction away from it overwhelmed him. A trail opened up on their left. 'Take that one,' Jon snapped.

The terrain started rising and, to his immense relief, the red light at the top of the radio antenna bobbed into view. 'Keep going, Nikki. That's good. Keep aiming for that light.'

They skirted round the cairn at the top of Black Hill and marched down the other side without pausing for breath. Now on the plateau at the top of the moor, their stride lengthened. All the while Jon kept his head cocked to the side, listening out for the sound of anything pursuing them. After another five minutes he let the torch beam swing up. Dull metal glinted at the outer edge of the beam.

On seeing the car Nikki broke into a jog. They hopped over the ditch and on to the track. Somehow just being on a man-made surface was reassuring. Five metres from the car Jon said, 'It's not locked. Jump straight in.'

He opened the rear door, slung the case on to the back seat, opened the driver's door and got in. Nikki was in the passenger seat, her legs shivering violently.

He shut the door and started the engine, flicking the central locking on as he did so. Then he put the vehicle into gear and reversed as fast as he dared up the track, not giving a toss what happened to the car's suspension.

Thirty-Two

Jon nudged the car up his drive, bringing the front bumper to within inches of his house before pulling the handbrake on. He sank back in his seat. Thank Christ to be home. His mind was still twitching, settling momentarily on one aspect of what had happened on the moor before springing to another. When they'd got back to the car park at Crime Lake not a single word had passed between them. During the drive down off the moor Jon had glanced across at Nikki several times. She was hunched in her seat, knees, shoulders and elbows drawn in as she nibbled on the tip of a thumbnail. Occasionally the hand moved upwards to brush a tear from the corner of her eye.

He parked next to her car and she immediately got out, stepped over to the driver's door and got inside. The engine started and he had to quickly climb out and knock on her window. The noise startled her. 'Hang on, Nikki. I've got the Portascope.'

She nodded, then gestured to the back seat. As he placed the case inside, he quietly said, 'Do you want to talk about this?'

She shook her head, hands clamped on the steering wheel.

'Nikki,' he watched her ponytail trembling. 'Maybe we should take five minutes to calm down.'

'Fuck off.' She was still staring ahead. 'You had no right to take me up there.' She shuddered. 'Just shut the door. I'm going home.'

He straightened up, then ducked his head back in for one last try. 'Nikki, I don't know what it was up there, but . . . '

The vehicle started to move and he had to step forwards to swing the door shut. She had accelerated down the road before remembering to turn her headlights on.

With a sigh, Jon looked at his house, hooking a finger into the inner curve of the steering wheel. He'd ring her tomorrow. What had really occurred up there? The primal terror that had come so close to engulfing him was skewing his perception of events. He tried to analyse things objectively. They'd heard a strange sound. In the darkness, their imaginations had supplied the image of what had made it. A huge black beast, a monster moving stealthily forward, yellow eyes able to see them clearly in the night.

But it was only a noise and, at one point, the faintest trace of a smell. It could easily have been a stag, a badger, someone with a tape of a big cat. The headrest seemed to be curling about his ears, gently cupping his skull. A tape recording. The sort of thing to scare off unwelcome visitors. Hobson. He could have recorded any number of those noises. Yeah, that wouldn't be any problem at all. An impact in his lap brought him awake. His hand had dropped off the steering wheel as sleep had relaxed his grip. With itchy eyes he regarded the glow at his front window. Hopefully she's relaxing in front of the telly, he thought.

He opened the front door to hear the tapping of computer keys. She was sitting at the computer in a tracksuit with an old cardigan over the top. Her hair was tied back in a loose ponytail. Strands bulged out at the side of her head, increasing her dishevelled look. He glimpsed a Portcullis logo at the top of the screen.

'Sorry I'm late back. I got delayed.'

'I didn't think you'd be home any earlier.' She didn't turn round.

'What are you up to?'

'There's these things called Hansard documents which let you see what's been debated in the House of Commons and I've been on Number Ten Downing Street's site. I can't find anything on civilian deaths in Iraq and I've been here for bloody hours.'

For fuck's sake, he thought, put another bloody record on will you? He knelt down and looked at Holly on her play mat. 'Hello, princess, how are you doing?'

Her head jerked at the sound of his voice and her arms began to wriggle back and forth. 'Daddy's home. You coming for a cuddle?'

He slid a hand under her nappy to lift her up. 'Ali, she's soaking wet.'

No reply.

He unbuttoned the base of her babygrow and was hit by a cloying smell. Brown stains were leaking out from the edge of her nappy. 'She's filthy. How long has she been lying here?'

He spotted the shadow of a frown as she glanced with tired eyes at their daughter. 'Well, change her then.'

'I will. But I'm asking how long she's been left here.'

'Since her last feed. I'm not sure. She wasn't crying.'

'Surely it's not a good idea for her to be lying in her own shit?'

The comment was intended to goad her, but all it provoked was another backward glance. 'When's the last time you changed her nappy?'

He opened his mouth, but said nothing.

'Exactly,' she answered, eyes on the screen once again. 'Do your fair share before having a go at me.'

But that's not the point, he thought. You should be concerned that Holly was being neglected. She clicked the mouse and another text-heavy page filled the screen. There was a detached air about her, as if attending to Holly was just another household chore. You're using this Iraq thing as a way to screen her out, he thought, remembering something about depressed mothers being unable to connect emotionally with their babies.

'Come on then, you,' he whispered, carrying Holly upstairs to the nursery. After bagging up the dirty nappy and wiping her clean, he wrapped a fresh nappy around her. 'We don't want a dirty bottom, do we?' he whispered. She grinned at the sensation and he wondered whether to call down that their daughter had just produced her biggest smile yet. Then he changed his mind, afraid Alice would just grunt a reply back up the stairs.

He gazed down at the tiny human before him. So totally helpless. She stared back, eyes fixed on his. He actually felt something shift in his chest as the realisation suddenly hit him. You're ours. Ours. The word was filled with new significance.

No one else will care for you in the same way because no one else is responsible for you in the same way. We created you. But now your mum doesn't seem able to cope with you. Which leaves me. I've got to take care of you until Alice is better.

He leaned down and brought his face so close to hers he could see his entire head captured in her unwavering pupils. There he was, as much a part of her as she was of him. He picked her up and held her close, waves of emotion flooding out. Then he bowed his head and held a kiss to the top of her skull, drinking in the delicious warmth coming from her soft skin.

The voice came and went, music drifting lazily over it. Then someone spoke over an urgent drumming. Words caught in Jon's semi conscious mind. Key 103 bulletin. Dramatic new theory. No official comment. River Medlock. Other world news. Attack on the Rashid Hotel, Baghdad. Paul Wolfowitz narrowly escapes.

He struggled to bring himself awake, eyes opening just as the newsreader announced, *And now to our main story. This morning Manchester awakes to a dramatic new development in the hunt for the Monster of the Moor.*

Jon looked to his left. Alice was sitting up in bed, Holly silently feeding at her breast.

Analysis shows that all three victims were attacked within a short distance of the Medlock, a river that rises on Saddleworth Moor and runs into the very heart of the city. What worries experts is the possibility that, if the Monster is following the river in its hunt for new victims, it will end up in the centre of Manchester itself. So far, no one from Greater Manchester Police has been available for comment.

'Christ!' He kicked the duvet off and looked at the clock. Seven. He should have been up an hour ago. Flipping open his mobile, he scrolled through to Carmel's number and pressed connect. 'Who fed you that information?'

'Sorry, is that DI Spicer?'

'Who was it? Do you realise the shit this story will stir up?'

'You know I can't tell you that.'

'No?' He stood up, walked over to the window. Grey drizzle

was falling outside. 'You don't need to. I saw you yesterday at Buxton Zoo. It was Hobson.'

'You're wrong actually.' Her voice had softened. Was it sympathy he heard? 'You need to look closer to home.'

Jon glanced at Alice who was staring back at him. He turned away. 'Piss off, Carmel.'

He threw the phone on the bed and set off for the shower. Alice's voice stopped him in the doorway. 'So much for keeping work and home lives separate.'

'Yeah, sorry,' he mumbled. 'What time did you come to bed last night?'

'Around midnight. You were fast asleep with Holly on your chest.'

'Was I?' Jon looked at his side of the bed. 'I remember changing out of my work clothes and then lying down with her. She was asleep?'

'You both were. They don't recommend it. If you'd rolled over—'

'I didn't mean to – Christ. I must have just nodded off. Did you sleep OK?'

'So-so. She needed feeding at around two, then again at four.'

'God, I didn't even hear that. You should have woken me, I could have given her a bottle.'

'I tried to. You were dead to the world.'

He felt a pang of guilt at having left his wife to get through the night feeds on her own. 'How are you feeling?'

'Fine.'

Jon tiptoed through his next comment. 'You seem so wrapped up in this research thing. I don't want you getting upset about it.' He lightened his tone and smiled. 'Don't forget we've got a little girl to look after too.'

She looked down. 'I'm feeding her now, aren't I?'

Yes, but that's about all you're doing with her. 'True. But go easy. The last thing you need to do is exhaust yourself stressing out over what's happening in Iraq.'

'Do I look tired?'

He nodded.

She smiled. 'Well take a look at yourself. You're a complete wreck.'

Yeah, Jon thought. Nine hour's sleep and I still feel like shit. He grinned back, 'I'd better grab a shower then and make myself look beautiful.'

Summerby, McCloughlin and most of the incident room team were surrounding the centre table when Jon walked in. He spotted several copies of the *Manchester Evening Chronicle* dotted about.

'Morning, Jon, nice that you made it in,' Summerby said, before looking back at the front page. 'Just what we didn't want to happen.'

The photo was an aerial view of the Greater Manchester area, the route of the Medlock highlighted in a lurid red. Big crosses marked where all three victims had been discovered, next to each was a panel giving estimated time and date of death. Hovering over the city centre itself was a large red question mark.

The headline read, *River of Death*.

Jon sat down. 'I know where this has come from. Hobson, the big cat expert at Buxton Zoo. I saw the crime reporter from the *Chronicle* arrive there yesterday for a briefing. The bastard is using this whole thing as a business promotion.'

DC Adlon spoke up. 'I didn't have time to find much on the bloke, but a company search threw up something interesting. Buxton Zoo is a public limited company and Hobson is the majority shareholder.'

Summerby sat back and looked at Jon. 'I gather the reason you missed my briefing yesterday was because you were back at Crime Lake.'

Jon nodded. 'The word Kuririkana is written on the notice board at the top of the car park and on the rocks by where Rose Sutton was found.'

'You've been up on the moors too?' Summerby demanded.

Catching Rick's look of surprise, Jon coughed awkwardly. 'I went straight up there after I found the word on the notice board in the car park. It had been daubed on the rocks in blood.

Rose Sutton's at a guess. Someone had then done their best to remove the word. Only a sweep with a Portascope showed it up.'

Summerby stared back at him. 'What's your conclusion then?'

'I'm not sure. I know Jeremy Hobson has spent time in Kenya though, he told me himself.'

Summerby mulled on the conversation as officers began to speculate in whispers. 'Right, we'll come back to that. In the meantime, Gavin Edwards has some other developments you should all know about.'

The press officer ruffled his copy of the newspaper. 'I have a contact on the features desk at the *Chronicle*. They're doing an interview with a man who's booked into the Royal Hotel in Buxton for the next twenty-one days. He says that's how long he'll need to trap and kill the panther.'

'Who is he?' Jon asked.

'He runs an agency that organises bear shoots in Eastern Europe, among other things. Quite a character apparently.'

Jon rolled his eyes. 'Where's he from?'

'He's British.'

'And I presume he's armed with some sort of a weapon?'

'Yup. It's got a scope on it that would put a paparazzi photographer to shame. I understand they've already done a photo-shoot in the grounds of the hotel. He even wears a hunting hat with game feathers in it.'

Jon looked at Summerby. 'This is getting like the wild west.'

'Agreed. I've been on to the Chief Constable of Derbyshire. This hunter fellow's firearm certificate is up to date, so all they can do is warn him not to discharge it in unauthorised areas. If the farmers allow him on to their land, we can't stop him.'

'There's more from the local papers,' Edwards said reluctantly. 'I just heard a black Labrador was shot and killed early this morning in Tandle Hill Countryside Park near Oldham.'

'Shot with what?' DC Gardiner asked.

'A bolt from a crossbow. The owner said the animal was retrieving a ball from undergrowth. He heard a yelp and when he went to investigate he saw a person in full camouflage gear standing over the dog. He turned the dead animal over with his foot, then casually walked away.'

'Once he realised it wasn't a panther,' DC Gardiner concluded.

'How many panther sightings have we had from Saddleworth since news of Kerrigan's death broke?' Summerby asked.

'Twenty-seven at the last count,' Edwards replied. 'And not just Saddleworth. There's been calls from Stalybridge, Ashton-under-Lyne, Glossop, Whaley Bridge. Even Bury.'

'Bury?' Jon said. 'That's nowhere near Saddleworth.'

'People are terrified. It's certainly not a good time to be a black cat. The RSPCA have reported another one being killed in Levenshulme. Uniforms also recovered a carcass of one from a lock-up garage in Cheetham Hill. It had been clubbed to death. There are even reports of someone in a tower block in Gorton shooting crows with an airgun.'

'Crows? Why?' DC Gardiner asked.

Edwards shrugged. 'They're animals and they're black?'

Jon saw he was serious. 'God, he's probably right.'

The phone on Jon's desk rang. Rick reached over and picked it up. 'DI Spicer's phone. Yes he is.' He held the phone out. 'Nikki Kingston. She says it's urgent.'

Jon walked over. 'Nikki, it's Jon here.' He turned slightly from the mass of listening officers. 'Everything all right?'

'I've got something important for you.'

Keeping it strictly business then, he thought. 'Go ahead.'

'I did the DNA test on those hairs you gave me. The ones from Buxton Zoo.'

'What did you find?'

'I'm still bloody furious with you. Do you realise that?'

'I was hoping we might talk . . . '

'Save it. I don't want to hear your bullshit apologies. The hairs from Rose Sutton and Derek Peterson match some of the hairs from the sample you gave me. There was a Y chromosome present, so it came from a male animal.'

Jon felt his grip on the receiver tighten. Samburu. 'You're certain? No chance of it just being the same species or something? How big is the gene pool for panthers? There could be—'

'Don't try and lecture me on DNA analysis, Jon. It's a match. Now I'm sending you the hairs back. You'll need a proper lab test to make it official.'

She hung up without another word. Jon cradled the handset in his palm, eyes on the floor.

'Well? Don't keep us in suspense man.'

Summerby's voice. Jon replaced the phone and turned to face him. 'I think we have a breakthrough. The hairs from Sutton and Peterson belong to a male panther called Samburu. It currently resides in the enclosure at Buxton Zoo.'

Gavin Edwards frowned. 'I don't understand.'

'I believe Jeremy Hobson killed all three victims and left the hairs to whip up this frenzy about panthers.'

'Here we go,' McCloughlin muttered. 'Spicer going off with all guns blazing. Why would he do that?'

Jon shrugged. 'The usual. Money. Possibly revenge in the case of Rose Sutton. It's likely they were having an affair.'

McCloughlin scowled. 'Couldn't any visitor in the zoo grab a few hairs from the bars of the panther's cage?'

Jon shook his head. 'You can't get anywhere near the animals. The viewing gallery is made up of plate glass windows and the outer part of the enclosure is double fenced. There is no way a member of the public can get within touching distance.'

'How did you get the hairs then?'

'Hobson let me watch him putting their food out. I got the hairs from the point staff get access to the enclosure.'

'So any staff member could have taken them.'

'Possible, I suppose. But who else has got the motive apart from Hobson? Plus he has the know-how on a panther's attack techniques. He'd be able to stage it so the injuries were convincing.'

Summerby laced his fingers. 'I'm not convinced, Jon. But bring him in for questioning. God knows we need this thing wrapped up before all hell breaks loose.'

Jon and Rick clicked through the zoo's turnstile, warrant cards still in their hands. The zoo seemed quiet, just a young boy with a bunch of balloons standing in front of the monkeys' cage.

'I know where everyone will be.' Jon led Rick towards the panther enclosure. Despite the droplets of rain carried on the chill breeze, a large crowd was gathered at the railings to the outer part of the enclosure. Hobson was in the centre of the throng, midway through one of his lectures. A young male assistant stood to his side.

'Look at him,' said Jon, coming to a halt. 'I said he was loving this.'

'So this is Samburu, a fully grown adult male,' Hobson announced. He'd placed a foot on the lowermost rail and was resting his forearms on his knee. It looked like he was posing for an imaginary camera. Below him, Samburu paced impatiently to and fro.

'How heavy is he?' asked a man with a toddler perched on his shoulders.

'Just under ninety kilos.'

'What's that in stones?'

'Fourteen.'

'Jeez, that's more than me,' another man said to the woman at his side.

'Do they like water?' someone else asked.

'They don't mind it at all. Here, I'll show you.' Hobson lifted out a hunk of pork and tossed it into the shallows of the muddy brown pond in the corner. Samburu shot him a baleful look before gingerly stepping in and sinking his head below the surface. His face reappeared, meat held firmly in his jaws. The crowd clapped as he turned and waded out. After flicking his paws dry, he walked behind a clump of exotic looking grass.

I don't blame you, thought Jon. It can't be fun being made to perform for this bunch of idiots.

'He always eats there,' Hobson continued. 'Now, I'll be feeding Mara and Mweru next.' He picked up the empty pail and began to make his way through the audience, nodding to appreciative comments as he went.

Time to burst your bubble mate, Jon thought, stepping forwards to block his way. 'Mr Hobson. Could I have a word?'

Hobson tried to step past, chest still puffed out. 'Certainly. After I've fed the other two cats.'

Jon leaned a shoulder in his way. 'Now. If you don't mind.'

Irritation showed in Hobson's eyes. People at the outer edge of the crowd were turning round, sensing a more interesting spectacle unfolding behind them.

'Detective, I have work to do. Now, I'm willing to assist you, but you'll have to wait.'

'It's Detective Inspector, Sir, and I'm afraid we can't wait. You'll come with us now.'

Hobson's pale eyes shifted to Jon's side as Rick stepped forwards too. The bluster disappeared from his voice. 'What's this about?'

'Guess.'

Hobson turned to his young assistant. 'Martin, get Mr O'Brien to feed Mara and Mweru.' He handed the empty bucket over. 'Don't forget their vitamin supplement.'

Once they were out of earshot of the crowd, Hobson said, 'Am I under arrest?'

'No,' Jon replied. 'But you would have been if you didn't agree to come with us.'

'I don't understand. This is to do with the attacks, isn't it?'

'Let's just leave it until we get to the station.'

With Hobson in the back of the car, they set off for the A624, aiming for the motorway back into Manchester. Jon kept an eye on Hobson in the rear view mirror. The man was silent. Too silent. He's thinking through his options, thought Jon. Suddenly he wanted to get the interview going. A traffic bulletin announced big delays on the M67 so Jon turned towards Mossley Brow instead. Ten minutes later they were escorting him into the station's reception.

'Is Inspector Clegg here?' Jon asked. 'We need an interview room.'

Clegg appeared seconds later, shock showing on his face when he spotted Hobson. 'DI Spicer. You need an interview room?' He glanced at Hobson again.

'Yes, thanks. Where can we go?'

He led them through into the corridor and opened the first

door they came to. Jon ushered Hobson inside then said to Rick, 'Stay with him, I'll be two minutes.'

Once the door was shut, he turned to Clegg. 'We'll need blank tapes.'

Clegg looked at the door. 'Why have you brought him in?'

'There's a lot of circumstantial evidence tying him in with this whole mess.'

'He's a suspect?'

'More than that. I think he could be our man. I'm keen to get the interview started as quickly as possible.'

Clegg lumbered off to his office, returning with two blank tapes. 'Mind if I sit in?'

'Be my guest,' Jon replied, peeling the cellophane off. Once the machine was recording, Jon explained to Hobson he wasn't being formally charged with anything but, in the interests of the investigation, it would be helpful if he could clarify a few points.

Once Hobson gave his assent, Jon leaned forward. Rick was sitting on one side while Clegg leaned against the wall in the opposite corner. 'Where were you between six and ten last night, Mr Hobson?'

'At home.'

'What were you doing?'

'Watching telly.'

'What did you watch?'

'The usual stuff. A few soaps. There was a film on with Sean Connery. The one about the prison where he has a white wig.'

Fine, Jon thought. You've got last night's television schedule worked out. Doesn't mean you weren't up on that moor with a tape recorder. 'And the morning of Trevor Kerrigan's death?'

'That was yesterday?'

'Correct.'

'I was opening the zoo up.'

'At dawn?'

'Well, I usually get up at six-thirty and sign for the food delivery at the main gates at seven-thirty.'

'Anyone help you with that?'

'Yes, Mr O'Brien. He is often there before me.'

'You saw him yesterday morning?'

'Yes, he was there.'

'And that was when?'

'I said. Seven-thirty, maybe just after.'

Kerrigan was found just before seven. Could Hobson have made it from the Brookvale golf course to his zoo in half an hour? If the roads were quiet, yes. But he would have also needed to remove a lot of blood from his person before signing for any deliveries of meat. 'Tell me a bit about your time in Kenya.'

'Sorry?'

'You mentioned to me that you'd seen a leopard drag the carcass of a baby giraffe up a tree in a Kenyan game park.'

'Oh that. Yes, I've been to Kenya on three occasions.'

'Holidays?'

'And research. I stayed for a few weeks each time.'

'Does everyone speak English over there?'

'Mostly, yes.'

'What do they speak if it's not English?'

'There are a variety of tribal dialects. I'm not sure what they are.'

'You've no idea at all? Surely it helped to have a few words? Please, thank you, that sort of thing.'

'Afraid not.'

Jon regarded him, wondering if it was a mocking look he'd caught in those pale blue eyes. 'I take it you've seen the papers this morning?'

'Yes. I was surprised you released the story about the Medlock. Won't that cause a fair amount of alarm?'

'It already has. And I didn't release that information. Someone else did.'

'By the way you're staring, I take it you think it was me?'

'Do you ever have dealings with *Manchester Evening Chronicle* reporters?'

'No. Other than with people in their promotions department, or if we have any interesting new births to report.'

'No one in their crime section?'

Hobson blinked, white lashes creating a haze at the edges of his eyes. 'Someone did come to visit me yesterday. She was asking about panthers. In fact, she was asking about you, DI Spicer.'

'How do you mean?'

'She wanted to know if I'd spoken to you. She seemed to have caught wind of the river theory. I suggested that she contact you directly.'

Something niggled at the back of Jon's mind. How did Carmel know he'd be there? His visit was unannounced, so Hobson didn't know he was on his way. Jon laid his palms on the table. 'When I last saw you, we spoke briefly about your relationship with Rose Sutton. I'd like to ask you a few more questions about that now.'

Hobson remained still, but Jon saw Clegg shift as he transferred his weight to the other foot.

'You're a bachelor, Mr Hobson?'

'I am.'

'Could I ask if you're romantically linked to anyone?'

'You mean girlfriends?' he asked in a patronising tone.

Jon nodded.

'No.'

'Boyfriends then?' Jon watched Hobson with amusement. He'd thought that that would wipe the smile off his face.

'I'm not a . . . I'm not interested in other men.'

'As I mentioned before, Ken Sutton seemed to believe his wife was having an affair.' From the corner of his eye, he saw Clegg raise a hand and adjust his collar. 'Were you seeing her in that context?' he continued.

Hobson crossed his arms. 'I told you I wasn't.'

Jon tapped a forefinger against his chin. 'Thing is, Mr Hobson, some of her friends say she spoke very highly of you. Almost like she was a little bit in awe. You obviously shared an interest in panthers.'

'So therefore we were frolicking together amongst the heather?'

'She was seen once or twice crossing fields to a car park at the edge of Holme. No one was quite sure what she was up to.' Clegg fidgeted again and Jon almost asked him if he had anything to say. 'In my experience of murder cases, sex usually plays some sort of role. Especially when the victim is a woman.'

'I've had enough of this,' Hobson said, getting to his feet.

Clegg extended a hand. 'Jeremy, sit down. DI Spicer? I need a word outside.'

Jon looked up, clocking the pained expression on the Inspector's face. 'OK. DS Saville, can you turn the tapes off while I consult with my colleague outside.'

Jon moved down the corridor before saying, 'You better have a damn good reason for butting in like that.'

The colour had risen in Clegg's cheeks and he struggled with his words. 'Hobson wasn't seeing Rose Sutton. I was.'

'Say that again.'

Clegg looked down, suddenly interested in the nails of his beefy hand. 'Rose and I had been seeing each other for the last few years.' He looked up. 'It was the extension of a friendship that went back ages. Far longer than Ken Sutton had known her.'

Jon stepped forward and thrust a finger into Clegg's face. 'I asked you that time at the top of Sutton's drive to come clean.'

Clegg's eyes flashed and he raised a hand to brush Jon's finger away.

Go on, you fat fuck, Jon thought, I'll drop you, whatever your size. Their eyes connected and Clegg changed his mind. He stepped back and his hand lowered. 'How could I ever have known it would escalate into this?'

'Maybe it wouldn't have if you'd been straight with me,' Jon muttered, turning away. Shit! He tried to integrate this new piece of information into the scheme of things. His immediate thought was that it placed Clegg firmly on the list of suspects. And Sutton. The farmer's suspicion about his wife were correct. Had he come across actual proof and killed her as a result? Glaring at Clegg, he said in a little more than a growl, 'What sort of a man is Sutton?'

'You mean, could he have killed Rose?'

'Full marks for intuition.'

'He didn't know about us.'

Jon slammed a palm against the wall. 'That wasn't my fucking question! Besides, how do you know he didn't find out?'

'Because he would have come for me. There's something in him. Something cold.'

Jon felt his fingers curling up. I would so love to throttle you. 'You didn't tell me this because you were afraid of what Sutton might do? Don't you think your opinion of Sutton would have been of some use earlier in this investigation? Why is he so cold? Give me an example. Did he treat Rose badly?'

'Not physically, but emotionally. There was no affection, no love. It was just a partnership. They ran the farm together, that was it.'

'Why does that make him capable of violence?'

'It doesn't. That dog he shot. The one that was worrying his sheep. He didn't shoot it once. He winged it with one barrel, then emptied the other into it at point blank range. After that, he tied it to the rear bumper of his Land Rover and dragged its carcass across the field to the couple. I could tell he'd relished it. There was something in his eyes as he described doing it, a sadistic look. I thought, you could do that to any living thing, animal or human.'

Jon also remembered the cruel delight in Sutton's voice as he'd recounted the event. 'And you approved his application for a high-powered hunting rifle. I can't believe you kept all this back. You're off the investigation, you understand? And I want a statement from you about all of this, along with your where-abouts on the night of each murder.'

'On the night of each murder?'

'Think about it, Clegg, you're right in the shit over this one. Now, where's your senior officer? You're going to tell all this to him.'

On the way back down from the Superintendent's office, Jon ran over Clegg's admission. It still didn't seal things up. Sutton had moved up on the list of suspects, true. But he'd a seemingly sound alibi for the night Rose died. In his gut, Jon didn't think Clegg could have done it either. The man had immense physical power, no doubt about that, but there was no motive Jon could think of for killing Peterson and Kerrigan too.

Hobson? Still in the picture, no doubt about it. But what was his connection to Peterson and Kerrigan? And how could he have known Danny Gordon? That would be a good place to start. He opened the door to the interview room and got an impatient glance off Rick.

'Sorry for the delay. Some new information just came to light.' He flicked the tape back on. 'Interview resuming at ten forty-six, now present in the room, DI Spicer, DS Saville and Jeremy Hobson.' He removed the photo of the Silverdale five-a-side team from his folder and slid it across to Hobson. 'The youth in the middle of the football team. Have you ever seen him before?'

Hobson regarded the photo for all of a second before looking up. Here we go, thought Jon. Never seen him. To his surprise, Hobson nodded. 'He worked briefly at the zoo.'

'Danny Gordon worked at your zoo?'

'That's Danny Gordon? My God, I didn't realise that was his name. As part of our community involvement, we accept lads from the Silverdale facility on work placements. The one helping me today, he's from there.' He turned to Jon. 'Only a fraction of any zoo staff are permanent. During holiday periods we need to double our numbers, so we take seasonal staff from many places. Students of zoology, animal behaviour and veterinary sciences, along with more casual workers.'

Jon glanced at Rick, who was looking equally surprised. Rick turned back to Hobson. 'So Danny Gordon did a stint at your zoo. When?'

'A few years back.'

'Doing what?'

'Cleaned tables in the café. I offered to let him help with the animals, but he obviously didn't enjoy it. City lad through and through.'

Jon thought about how Samburu's hairs had turned up on all three victims. 'Did he ever help out with the panthers?'

'Once. He hated the smell though. Unlike his friend. He took a real shine to them.'

'Who?' Jon asked.

Hobson placed a finger over the head of James Field. 'Him. They arrived together. He was called James, I think. Far more enthusiastic. In fact, he was one of the best workers the Silverdale ever sent.'

Jon felt light-headed. He didn't know how it fitted together, yet, but he knew this was it. 'You're saying James Field had plenty of contact with the panthers?'

'Oh yes. I trusted him to feed them, clean them out. He took to studying their behaviour, learning their natural history, everything.'

'Hunting techniques?'

'Yes. I expected him to apply for a full time job to be honest. I would have taken him on too.'

'Gordon and Field were good mates?'

'Absolutely. They stuck together each break time, shared those roll-up cigarettes they all seem to smoke. James was stronger, more mature. I got the impression it was almost a big brother, younger brother kind of thing between them.'

Jon took a deep breath. Slow down, he thought. Keep your head clear. All that stuff James Field had said about hardly knowing Danny Gordon. What bullshit. 'Right, I'm concluding this interview at ten-fifty.' He clicked the tape off and looked at Hobson. 'One minute please, Rick and I need to talk.'

Out in the corridor he had an almost overpowering urge to leap into the air. 'It's Field. Am I right?'

Rick's eyes shone with excitement. 'How does it work? Field killed Sutton, Peterson, Kerrigan and his best mate?'

'No, Danny Gordon killed himself, unable to take it after Peterson humiliated him all over again. Field found his friend's body and decided to settle things with Peterson himself. He added the word to Gordon's suicide note. Simple revenge. Kuririkana. Remember. It was payback for what happened in the past.'

'So how do the other deaths fit in?'

'We'll find out soon. We've been concentrating on Danny

Gordon. But if it's Field doing the killing, there's no wonder we haven't found any links between the victims. We need to get over to that garage straightaway.'

Thirty-Three

The side street was still clogged with cars. Droplets of rainwater were clustered on the windscreens, drips slowly fell from dented bumpers, pooling in the oil-stained puddles. A train rumbled by overhead, wheels screeching on the steel tracks.

Jon and Rick hurried along the narrow street, halting at the door to 'A and L Repairs'. Sensing Rick was hanging back, Jon looked over his shoulder. 'What?'

'I just thought, shouldn't we get back-up? If it's him, he's got one evil weapon on him.'

Jon paused, realising his eagerness had got the better of him. 'There's no back way for him to get out by. We can call for help once we know he's inside.'

He knocked on the door before pushing it open and stepping into the dingy interior. A Vauxhall estate was up on jacks, the legs of a dirty pair of overalls poking out from beneath. 'Hello there,' Jon announced.

The legs twitched and the garage owner wheeled himself out from beneath the vehicle, the body board he was on completely obscured by his bulk. 'Yes gents?'

Glancing towards the shadows at the rear of the garage, Jon said, 'Is James Field about?'

The man sat up and, still holding a spanner, wiped a cuff across his forehead. 'Nope. He's not turned up since you were last here.'

'Got a home address or phone number for him?'

'Yeah, I've tried ringing. He's not answering. Tell him he's sacked when you catch up with him.'

'What's his address? We'll pop round.'

With a grunt, the man got to his feet. He led Jon and Rick to the rear of the garage and opened a dirty address book. 'There you go.'

Jon took out his notebook and jotted it down. 'Can I take a look in his locker?'

'Padlocked.'

'Maybe you decided to break into it? It's your locker, after all.'

The man nodded. 'I suppose I could have.' He picked up a stout screwdriver off the workbench and positioned the end of it beneath the metal plate on the door. Two sharp yanks and the piece of metal flew off. He headed back to the Vauxhall.

Jon swivelled the reading lamp so its beam shone inside. On top of a pair of overalls was the book James Field had been reading.

Secrets of the SAS – Survival and combat techniques for the world's harshest environments.

Jon pulled on some gloves and opened the book to reveal a section on camouflage and ambush. 'Oh bollocks,' he said, putting it on the table, then gently lifting out the overalls. Beneath them was a box file. He placed the overalls on the workbench and with the tip of a finger, lifted the file's lid. Inside was a large piece of folded paper. Jon lifted it out by its edges and gently shook it open.

'Sweet Jesus.' At first he thought it was a diagram for a particularly brutal looking garden fork. Thin lines next to it gave measurements in millimetres. The handle, little more than a tube with a splayed base, measured one hundred and forty. It then merged with an oval shaped piece of metal with four bumps running across the top. From each one there emerged an evil looking hook, each one measuring forty millimetres. Further round the oval was a barb-like fifth. 'The dew claw,' murmured Jon. 'He's replicated a panther's paw.'

'My God,' said Rick. 'It's the murder weapon.'

'Or weapons,' Jon replied. 'One for each hand.'

As Rick returned to the car for evidence bags, Jon addressed the garage owner once again. 'Did James show any interest in welding?'

He slid back out from under the vehicle. 'Yeah. He was making garden ornaments. Don't know what. I'd leave him to it, let him lock up at night.'

Jon looked at the acetylene tank and blowtorch to his side. Garden ornaments, my arse.

It was a short drive to Field's place in Ryder Brow. The flat was located on the ground floor of a three-storey 1970s building. The armed response unit showed up ten minutes later, shortly followed by the call from the Detective Super giving them permission to enter the flat.

Jon and Rick watched from down the street as the building's residents were quietly ushered away. Once the area was clear, the team went in. The communication officer's helmet mike sounded seconds later. 'No one in.'

Jon and Rick ducked under the cordon tape, reaching the doors to the building as the armed officers began filing back out, Heckler and Koch MP5 carbines held across their chests. The front door to Field's flat had been smashed off its hinges and they had to step over it to enter his property. An armed officer appeared from the front room, removing his earpiece as he did so. 'One of you DI Spicer?'

'Me,' Jon replied.

'You've got a letter.' He jabbed a thumb over his shoulder. 'In there.'

The front room was sparsely decorated with second-hand furniture. A sofa was positioned against the back wall, an African-style throw failing to conceal the battered upholstery at its base. Mounted on the wall above it was a wooden face mask, splashes of red surrounding the jagged eyes, lines of dots running across the forehead and cheeks.

'Something gives me the feeling that's from Kenya,' Rick commented.

Jon turned to the note on the table.

To DI Spicer,

  If you're reading this, you've worked it out.

  Once you turned up at the garage, I knew it wouldn't be long before you came back. After Kerrigan I rechecked Danny's place and saw all the police cars outside. I knew then it was time to go.

You won't find me now. I'm a shadow in the night, the darkest part of your fears, the stuff of nightmares.

There's one more place I'm going to visit, then I'm done. Death doesn't scare me. My life never began and what little of it remains will be spent putting this final wrong right.

Kuririkana.

The words set a hoard of terrible images swirling in Jon's head. Snippets of the moor at night, the red light floating in the blackness above, the fragment of sheep's fleece snared on a spike of gorse, crows sweeping low across the dead sky, the gaping throats of Sutton, Peterson and Kerrigan, dark clouds spreading across the land. And behind it all that low throaty rasp, as if conjured from the pit of hell itself.

'He doesn't sound like a happy bunny,' the man with the firearm announced.

Jon's mind snapped back to the present. 'He's after one more person. Rick, get on to Summerby, we need to find every detail from this bloke's miserable, fucked up life.'

Rick had just got through to their senior officer and was reading James Field's note out when Jon's phone went. He glanced at the screen. Mum. 'Hi, can I call you back?'

'Yes, OK. But is Alice with you?'

Jon blinked. 'No. She said she'd be at home.'

'Well, I'm on your doorstep and she's not answering again. I've brought you another pie.'

'Have you got your key?'

'Yes.'

'Go ahead and open the door. I'm sure she'll be in there.'

He listened as she unlocked the door. 'Alice? It's me, Mary. Are you in?' A second's silence. 'No, it's empty.'

Jon breathed in sharply through his nose. 'Hang on. I'll try her mobile.' He pressed the speed dial, listened as the phone started ringing. Thank God, it's not on answer phone.

'It's me.'

'Mum?'

'Yes. Alice's phone is in the kitchen.'

Fuck, she never goes anywhere without it. 'Mum, can you stay there until she gets back?'

'Again? OK, I'll hang this washing out.'

He returned the phone to his pocket. Was he panicking over nothing? Yes. She hadn't cracked up. Jesus, he'd attended enough incidents where someone had. She wasn't even close to the mental state of those poor bastards.

'Problem?'

Jon looked at Rick. 'Alice has disappeared again.'

'Again?'

'Yeah, she went off to the library yesterday. She'd switched her phone off.'

'And today?'

'She's gone off somewhere with Holly and left her phone at home.'

'Do you want to go back to your place?'

Jon weighed it up. 'No. Mum's there. We'll only do each other's heads in if I'm waiting there too. She'll have just popped out to the shops or something.'

Rick shrugged. 'If you're sure. Summerby's putting everything into finding James Field. There's a team heading over to the Silverdale as we speak, another has gone to find his probation officer and they're trying to trace his social worker too.'

'What about us?'

'He says to start going through this place. A car's on its way to help.'

Jon looked around. 'Let's do it then.'

Thirty-Four

They started going through the front room, pulling out drawers, leafing through papers, searching for any clues as to what James Field might be planning next.

Rick went over to the answer phone and pressed play. Three messages from the owner of the garage asking where he was. They'd moved to his bedroom when Jon heard Rick announce, 'This is weird.'

Jon paused at the open wardrobe and glanced over his shoulder. Rick was on his knees, bent almost double so he could see under the bed. 'What is?'

'There's nothing of a personal nature. I was expecting some porn hidden in here at the very least. Would you have any meaningful idea of who lived in this flat if we didn't know already?'

Jon bowed his head in thought. Rick was right. The flat was missing the usual items that made it someone's home; photos of friends and family, phone numbers on scraps of paper, even documents such as phone bills, bank letters or nectar card statements. James Field had left as much trail as a ghost.

He turned the wardrobe inside out. Old trainers, battered jeans, a hooded top. The bathroom bore even less fruit. No bottles or pills bearing a GP's label or a pharmacy's price sticker. Jon slammed the cabinet shut. 'There has to be something in this place.'

They pulled up carpets, tapped for fake floorboards. Nothing. 'Right,' said Jon. 'The bastard thinks he's clever. Let's check outside.'

They went to the walled off area containing the residents' bins. Green containers were lined against the wall, each one bearing the number of a flat. Jon zoned straight in on number three, flipping it over and dragging out a single bag of rubbish. He ripped it open, spilling potato peelings, blackened bananas and several empty pots of yoghurt, green mould ringing their rims. 'Let's check the rest.'

They started tipping over the others and hauled out rubbish sacks, the sweet smell of putrescence filling the air. Scrunched up letters, pizza boxes, clumps of hair, empty wine bottles, used tampons, plastic containers, lumps of festering chicken, crumpled tins and cans.

'No wonder the country's landfill sites are overflowing. Have this lot heard of recycling?' Rick muttered, crouched before a knotted bin liner. He pulled the plastic apart and his hands stopped. 'Jon.'

Jon turned. A shoebox was at the top, its lid slightly off. 'Lift it out, carefully.'

Using the tips of his gloved fingers, Rick lifted the object clear of the debris surrounding it. The layer of grey dust covering the lid had finger marks in it. Rick flipped it off and they stared at the pile of letters inside. The address on the uppermost envelope read, *James Field, Flat 3, Oakdene Flats, Thomas Street, Ryder Brow, Manchester.*

'Gotcha,' Jon grinned.

Back in James' flat, they started laying the letters out on the living room floor. Most of the envelopes were written in a childish style. 'Danny Gordon's writing,' Jon said. The remainder of the envelopes were written in a neater hand. At the bottom of the shoebox was an envelope with Kenyan stamps on it. No letter was inside, just the stubs of two plane tickets. 'He flew to Nairobi on the fifth of March, two thousand and one, returning on the twenty-sixth.'

Rick had slid a letter out from one of the envelopes bearing the childish writing. 'You're right, it's sent from Strangeways. Jesus, Danny Gordon couldn't have been awake in many of his school classes, the spelling is atrocious.'

'What does it say?' Jon asked, picking up a letter with the neat handwriting.

'Just going on about being bored. Slagging off his padmate, talking about what they'll get up to when he gets out.'

Jon unfolded his letter, a frown slowly appearing on his face. 'It's from a Pat and Ian Field.'

'His parents?'

Jon read the letter in its entirety. 'They adopted him.' He turned the letter over, glanced at the date at the top. 'This was written after James returned from Nairobi. They're asking his forgiveness for what happened, saying it wasn't their decision about his name. They tried to do what was right and they still love him as their son.' He looked at Rick. 'Are you thinking what I'm thinking?'

Rick looked at the note James had left for Jon. 'The one more place he has to visit. Surely not?'

'I don't know. I hope not, but . . . Christ, they obviously infuriated him.'

'Is there an address or phone number?'

'Both. They're asking him to at least call them. I've got a really bad feeling about this.' He took his phone out and entered the number.

A woman answered. 'Yes?'

'Pat Field?'

'Yes, who is this speaking?'

'My name is DI Spicer. I work for Greater Manchester Police.'

'Oh.'

'Mrs Field, is your husband there?'

'Yes.'

'With you in the house?'

'He's out raking leaves off the lawn.'

'Is anyone else with you?'

'No. Detective, your tone of voice. Is this bad news?'

Bad news? You could say that. 'I don't mean to alarm you, but can you get your husband inside the house and then lock the doors?' He paused, wondering whether he should say any more. You've no choice, he thought. He could be in their garden right now. 'Do not allow anyone inside, unless they're a police officer. I'll send a patrol car round and I'll be there soon.'

'What is this about?'

'Mrs Field, this concerns James. Do not let him in, do you understand?'

'James.' There was a note of resignation in her voice. 'What's he done?'

'There isn't any time. Just get your husband inside, we'll be there soon.'

He hung up, eyes still on the letter. 'Bollington. That's about forty-five minutes away.'

They were on their way out when the support car arrived. 'Seal the flat,' Jon barked, handing the letter to the officer in front. 'And contact the police station nearest to this address. Get them to send a patrol car round, it's where James Field might be heading. Tell Summerby we're on our way there.'

They passed the *Welcome to Bollington* sign forty minutes later. The sky resembled an old sheet, dull white as far as the eye could see, bare twigs on the trees outlined sharply against it.

The narrow high street ran on and on, leading them past several pubs. At an aqueduct a lane led off to the left. 'That's it, Owen's Lane,' Rick said, an A to Z open on his lap.

Jon took the turn and the car bumped over rough cobbles. Waterview was the fourth cottage they reached, ivy creeping over stone walls. A patrol car was already outside, a uniformed officer leaning against it.

'Thank God there are no ambulances,' Jon said.

They parked behind the vehicle and jumped out. 'DI Spicer and DS Saville. Your colleagues are inside?'

'Yes, Sir,' the officer replied. From his expression, Jon could see he was dying to know what this was all about. 'Keep in your vehicle and lock the doors. Maintain contact via your radio.'

The young man began to smile.

Rick stepped forward. 'The guy we're after? He's a total fucking head case.'

The officer's expression dropped like a stone when he saw they were serious. Quickly he clambered inside.

Jon and Rick strode up the short path and knocked on the wooden door. Movement behind the frosted glass and the door opened. 'Don't do that again,' Jon said to the officer, voice low. 'You ask the person to identify himself first, understand?'

The man nodded. 'Sorry, Sir.'

Jon and Rick stepped into a low hallway lined with watercolours of the local area. Lyme Park, Kinder Scout, Fernilee Reservoir.

'They're in the front room, Sir.' The officer pointed to the left.

Jon was surprised to see that the couple were both white. He was completely bald, she had grey hair tied back in a bun. He guessed they were in their late fifties. They were sitting side by side on a floral patterned sofa, their hands clasped together. Mrs Field wore slippers and the husband an old pair of mud-caked shoes. Bits were on the cream carpet. 'Mr and Mrs Field, I'm DI Spicer. Sorry for all the commotion.' He looked at the wife. 'We spoke just earlier?'

'Yes,' she replied nervously. 'What happened?'

Jon took a seat opposite them. Where do I start, he wondered, extracting his notebook to give him a few seconds. 'It's about James. Your adopted son?'

They both nodded in perfect unison, the action of lifelong partners.

'Why all this?' The husband's voice was deep. He waved a hand at the mullioned window and the patrol car outside.

'I'm afraid it appears James is involved in a couple of incidents that have involved the use of violence.'

He watched as they turned to each other. Tears had sprung up in Mrs Field's eyes and her fingers tightened on her husband's. 'Oh Ian.'

Mr Field put an arm round her shoulders and cleared his throat. He looked at the wall to his side. 'We were afraid something like this would happen.'

Jon followed the direction of his sad gaze. The framed photo above the fireplace was of a young boy running through a carpet of bluebells. The shattered hopes of proud parents.

'Was it robbery?' Mrs Field asked.

Jon didn't reply. How can I tell them? It wasn't possible. Instead he dipped his head as if in agreement, unable to actually say yes.

'Armed?' Mr Field asked.

Oh shit, thought Jon. Now I'm getting dragged in deeper. He

dipped his head once again. 'Could you tell me about James? We need to know as much about him as possible.'

The couple's eyes met once again and he could see Mr Field was waiting for his wife's assent. Jon was suddenly aware of a clock ticking in the room. Finally she gave a single, reluctant, nod.

With a sigh, Mr Field began. 'We adopted James when he was six. He was an orphan and had spent all his life inside children's homes. He'd never known anything else. Pat and I couldn't have children. This was in the early eighties, before they tightened the rules about white parents and different race children.'

Jon nodded, aware of how the adoption agency had altered its policy in the light of problems arising from Vietnamese, then later, Romanian adoptions.

'We were living in Manchester at the time. Near Prestwich. James was a very intelligent child, but restless, insecure. He couldn't understand so many things when he first moved in. How we would trust him.'

'Like money,' Mrs Field explained in a tremulous voice. 'The way we didn't lock away our cash. He would steal it at first, hoarding it in places round his bedroom. It took a while before he realised there was no need. School was where the real problems started.'

Her voice fell away and the husband took over once again. 'Kids — and some adults I regret to say — couldn't understand how a black child could be dropped off by a white mum. Pat got some comments, but nothing, I suspect, to what James suffered. He became rebellious, that old streak re-emerging. Fights. He's a powerful lad and soon no one was prepared to take him on. The bad elements accepted him into their group. We found it harder and harder to control him. He was arrested for stealing from cars. Then he started taking the cars themselves.'

Jon noted it all down, the familiar path leading to prison opening up before him. An image of his younger brother crossed his mind.

'He was sent to a young offender's facility called the Silverdale when he was fourteen. School had expelled him already. That was for eight months and he returned worse than ever. Now we

296

did have to lock up our money. He'd made new friends in that place. At sixteen he was able to give up on education completely. His home tutor was glad, scared of him in my opinion. Anyway, we saw less and less of him after that. He was back in the Silverdale within months – joyriding and assaulting a police officer – and the few times he did return home, he kept asking about his real parents. The issue became more and more important to him.'

Jon looked up. 'Who were they?'

'We only had limited information, and that's because the authorities didn't know that much either. His mother, we gathered, was of Kenyan descent. She was from a tribe called the Kikuyu, but she had also been brought up in this country by a white couple. She died giving birth to James.'

'And the father?'

'No one knew who he was. Although James looks more black than white, he is mixed race. So we knew the father was white.'

Jon thought about the letters. 'We found some correspondence in James's flat. You had written to him there.'

Mrs Field's chin went up and she wiped a tear from her eye. 'He'd kept those letters?'

'Yes,' Jon answered, not mentioning that they'd been dumped in a neighbour's bin. 'You were talking about his real name. We didn't understand.'

Mr Field glanced up at the ceiling, as if to gather strength from above. 'On his eighteenth birthday, James exercised his legal right to see all his documents held by the adoption agency. He came to see us immediately afterwards. The lad was very upset, angry even.'

The lad, Jon thought. No longer your son by this time. 'What had he discovered?'

'He wouldn't show us. But he'd learned that, although his mother was called Mary Sullivan, her real surname was Gathambo. As I mentioned, she died giving birth to James. Twenty-sixth of November, nineteen eighty-two, the Wythen-shawe hospital. She had turned up there pretty much destitute, her few personal effects had been retained by the adoption services and given to James all those years later.'

Jon sighed. Things were opening up. Past deeds, motives for revenge. 'Go on.'

'There were letters from other members of the Gathambo family still in Kenya. She must have made contact with them. She was, James told us, planning to return to Kenya and live with them, but then she fell pregnant.'

'I don't follow,' Rick said. 'The mother was brought up by a white couple with a surname of Sullivan, yet she had real family in Kenya?'

Mr Field ground his teeth together. 'We tried to work it out too. James was . . . distraught. I don't know anything more about his mother's adoptive parents. It was never mentioned to us.'

'But James flew to Kenya?' Jon asked.

'Yes,' Mr Field replied. 'One of the letters from his cousins, or whatever they were, mentioned his mum's pregnancy. They'd told her to be strong, once she got to Kenya, they'd help with the baby. He wanted to meet them.'

Jon circled his pen to form the dot of a large question mark he'd drawn on the page. What the hell was this all about? 'Going back to James's name. Why were you saying sorry?'

'The last letter his mother sent to Kenya, she'd obviously mentioned in it what she was going to call the baby if it was a boy. James was furious her wishes hadn't been followed. But it wasn't our choice, someone at the hospital made the decision.'

Jon's pen stopped its revolutions. 'Field?'

'No, his Christian name. James was just the nearest English equivalent they could think of. He should have been called Njama.'

Rick sat back. 'Jammer.'

Mr Field looked at him. 'No, you're meant to pronounce the N at the beginning. Anyway, we did what we could to help. The flight for instance. We paid for him to go back and meet his relatives.'

'And he was gone for three weeks?'

'About that, I think. He came back a very different person though.'

'How do you mean?'

Mr Field turned to his wife. 'Pat?'

'We picked him up at the airport,' she said. 'He was quiet, brooding. Whoever he had met in Kenya had had a very profound effect on him.'

'Was he happy to have gone?'

'No, not in my opinion. I believe they'd radicalised him.' Bitterness made her words sour.

'Sorry?'

'That's the word they use nowadays isn't it? They'd radicalised him over the history of Kenya. Tell me, what is your impression of the Mau Mau?'

Jon stared back, feeling like a schoolboy caught out in class. To his side, he saw Rick shift in his seat, and to his relief, his colleague began to speak. 'The Mau Mau was a terrorist organisation which sought to overthrow the British government in Kenya. They would emerge from the jungle at night to butcher white farming families. Their attacks were particularly savage, linking into some sort of primitive oath they'd taken to kill all whites. I think they may even have eaten parts of their victims, that sort of thing. I know the British authorities had a really tough time containing the violence.'

Mrs Field nodded. 'But not according to James once he came back from visiting his relatives. According to him, they weren't bloodthirsty terrorists who hacked innocent civilians to death. No. They were freedom fighters nobly trying to reclaim their land from an occupying force. They weren't even Mau Mau, they were the Kenyan Land and Freedom Army. They'd filled his head with all this stuff about British penal camps. How our troops tortured Kikuyu suspects in their thousands. Terrible stories, not like anything I've read in any history book.'

'What had that got to do with James's past?' Jon asked, trying to keep up.

Mrs Field waved a hand, voice stronger now she wasn't talking about the boy they'd tried to raise. 'Who knows? He wouldn't let us in on that. We were now part of the problem, part of the system that had ripped him from his true past. I could see that was what he thought. I shudder to think what part his relatives over there had played in the uprising.'

Jon stared down at his notes. He was fairly certain Peterson was killed because of what he'd done to Danny Gordon. But what linked Rose Sutton and Trevor Kerrigan? Why had they died? And who was the last person James Field was after? Was it his adoptive parents? It could be anyone from the staff on the maternity ward at the Wythenshawe to the members of the social services team who decided to name him James. Too much was being revealed too fast. How could they possibly trace and protect all these people before James made his final attack?

His phone started to ring. 'Excuse me,' he said on seeing Summerby's name on the screen. He got up and walked through to the kitchen. 'Yes, boss?'

'Jon, what have you got?'

'Loads, Sir. I think we'll have to come back in to discuss it all.'

'Exactly my sentiments. The team sent back to the Silverdale have also called; they're returning here with some vital evidence.'

'Sir, I think we should place the staff there under guard.'

'Don't worry. Uniforms are on the doors.'

'We also need to trace the hospital staff involved with James Field's birth at the Wythenshawe. And the social workers involved with the adoption. They may be in danger too.'

'OK, I'll get some people on it. Are you ready for this? The DNA test on the skin caught on Kerrigan's ring has finally come back. Forensics thought the sample had been contaminated, hence the delay. It matched James Field's sample taken after his arrest for ABH in nineteen ninety-nine.'

'That caused confusion?'

'No, this did. Trevor Kerrigan was James Field's biological father. He ripped his own dad's throat out.'

Thirty-Five

They arrived back at Longsight early in the afternoon. The incident room was alive with activity, everyone skirting past the table in its centre. Sitting in silence down each side were several members of the Outside Enquiry Team. At the top of the table Summerby and McCloughlin were conferring over a raft of reports.

Jon looked at the top of McCloughlin's head and felt his hackles rise. 'I forgot that bastard had wormed his way on to the investigation,' he whispered to Rick.

Summerby beckoned. 'You two, take a seat. Gardiner and Murray are on their way back from the photocopier.'

Jon and Rick had just squeezed a couple of chairs in at one corner when the two officers hurried into the room, a pile of paper in Murray's hands. Once they were seated, Summerby nodded. 'Let's hear it then.'

Murray took in a breath. 'The director at the Silverdale called any staff that had dealings with James Field. There's this retired teacher who goes in and tries to get the kids going with academic work. He said he had something very interesting. Apparently James Field had turned up at his house quite a while after leaving the Silverdale. He wanted the teacher's help in making a project.'

'When was this?' asked Jon.

'Summer of last year.'

After he'd returned from Kenya, thought Jon.

'The tutor said Field had got all this stuff with him, letters, bits of library books, photocopies of pamphlets, all sorts. He said James was by far and away the most naturally intelligent offender he'd ever dealt with. He didn't mind helping him turn it into a coherent project. This is a copy of what they produced, the tutor kept it to use as an example for other offenders of what could be achieved with a little effort.'

The two officers began to distribute stapled batches of A4-size paper. As Jon picked his up he could feel they were still warm from the photocopier. When he saw the writing on the front cover, he felt the blood slow in his veins.

'Field titled it, "Kuririkana",' Murray announced. 'As we all now know, it means "Remember" in Kikuyu, an African dialect.'

McCloughlin whistled. 'Talk about incriminating yourself. He may as well have just signed his own life stay in Broadmoor.'

Murray smiled grimly. 'The tutor took us through the project. It's heavy stuff but, according to him, genuinely researched. If you look at the contents, you'll see it starts with a chapter called Repressed People, you've then got Shoot to Kill, Breaking Resistance, Murder Camps and lastly, State Lies.'

'We can all read, DC Murray,' McCloughlin butted in. 'We're also in a bloody hurry here. So just one thing. What the hell has this got to do with finding James Field?'

Murray looked uncomfortable. 'I don't know how it links to the killings so far. It's about the Mau Mau uprising in Kenya during the late fifties.'

'Try and give us a quick summary and we'll see if it rings any bells with what anyone else has got,' Summerby instructed.

'Right,' Murray replied. 'Repressed People is all about how the British claimed to be on a civilising mission when they invaded Kenya. In reality they were after its natural resources. They declared all of its land . . . erm, I forget the phrase.' He turned a couple of pages and his finger started tracing down. 'Here we go. Crown Land. Basically the Kikuyu and other tribes were shunted into reserves while fertile areas were given over to white colonists. These became known as the White Highlands. Most of it was the ancestral lands of the Kikuyu tribe. Eventually, they were allowed back on to farm it, but were paid a derisory amount and taxed on their huts. It was essentially a feudal system, not seen in Britain since the Norman Conquest almost a thousand years ago.'

'So the Empire sucked,' interrupted McCloughlin. 'Is this relevant?'

Jon glanced at Summerby. Come on, Sir. Don't let him start to take things over.

'Bear with us,' DC Murray replied. 'After World War Two, the Kikuyu started forming organisations to lobby for the return of their land. In nineteen fifty the authorities responded by arresting the leaders and banning many of the groups.'

McCloughlin sighed. 'In nineteen fifty. That's the last bloody century.'

Summerby's head jerked with irritation. 'It somehow connects to what we're dealing with today. Will you let my officers speak?'

Jon kept looking at Murray, but a small smile escaped him. About time, boss, he thought.

Murray looked back down at the page. 'The tutor underlined this bit, said it's quite pivotal.' He began to read. ' "The Kikuyu grew ever more rebellious and in October nineteen fifty-two a State of Emergency was declared. Thousands of British soldiers were brought in. When leaders such as Jomo Kenyatta were arrested, hundreds of Kikuyu nationalists fled for the forests of Mount Kenya to establish a resistance movement. They formed themselves into the Kenyan Land and Freedom Army. Members who'd fought with the British during the World War organised them into units, even allocating ranks including General." ' Murray glanced up. 'They began attacking white property, then the settlers themselves.'

'Mau Mau. You're talking about the bloody Mau Mau, not a real army,' Summerby said.

'Sir, I'm only recapping what's in here,' Murray answered, beginning to sound exasperated. 'If you go to the last chapter called State Lies, you'll see that the jungle fighters never called themselves Mau Mau. No such word exists in the Kikuyu language. According to this, Mau Mau was a propaganda myth created by government press handouts devised in London. They depicted the insurgents as anti-European and anti-Christian, saying they were determined to seize power in Kenya. Mau Mau was meant to play on Western prejudices about witchdoctors, mumbo jumbo and jungle savages. Read it for yourself.' He turned to the last pages. 'Press releases talked about, "the bestial wave of Mau Mau", murders were committed by "terrorists insatiable for blood". The British press fell in line with the Government's stance, using words such as dark, satanic, fanatical, merciless, evil and primitive to describe them.'

McCloughlin shook his head. 'I think we're wasting valuable time with this . . . this version of history.'

Jon stirred in his seat. *Time to shut you the fuck up.* 'Actually, James Field's adoptive parents described how he flew back to Nairobi to meet members of his estranged family. That was in March two thousand and one, a year before he went back to his old teacher to write this project. We don't know much about his natural family, but his mum's surname was Gathambo. She was from the Kikuyu tribe. Somehow she ended up in this country, brought up by a white British couple called the Sullivans.'

Summerby's head went up and he shouted over to the office manager. 'Where's Adlon with the stuff from the social services? We need to know who the blazes James Field's real mother was.'

The manager held up a hand. 'He just rang in. They're down in the archives now. The records are being dug out as we speak.'

Jon sat back, glancing to his side as Rick let his copy of Field's project fall open at a page of images. 'Jesus Christ.'

'What?' said Jon, looking down. At the top were a couple of crude looking firearms, toy-like in their clumsy simplicity. The caption below read, '*KLFA weapons, from a display at the Imperial War Museum where they're referred to as Mau Mau rifles.*'

Next was a photo of a black man lying on a blanket. The caption read, '*Field Marshal Dedan Kimathi, leader of the KLFA. Executed, February 19th 1957.*'

Alongside was a photo of the side of a plane, a line of little men with spears drawn on the fuselage. '*RAF decals during the war.*'

Below that was an illustration of a naked man leaping through the air, deep shadow tactfully concealing his groin. Covering the top of his head and flapping outwards from his back was the pelt of a black panther. The animal's gaping mouth framed the man's face which, in turn, was midway through a fearsome looking shriek. Clutched in each hand was a terrible claw-like weapon. *'No act of savagery is beneath the bestial Mau Mau.'* In the very corner of the picture was a grouping of five letters. *H.M.G.P.O.*

'What is it?' Summerby demanded.

Rick's shoulders shivered momentarily. 'The weapons he's holding. They're identical to the ones James Field made.'

'Which weapons?'

'The ones from the garage he worked in. We radio'd for a car to bring over the plans he'd drawn before we drove down to Bollington.'

McCloughlin stood up. 'What's the name of the exhibits officer?'

'Sergeant Sheehan,' someone murmured.

'Sheehan, you fucking half wit. Anything interesting you'd like to share with us?'

An officer with tight wiry hair turned to a stack of evidence bags on his desk. 'Sir? I'm getting buried here, can you be more specific?' His cockney accent sounded out of place in the room.

'A big piece of paper. Like the ones you'll be doodling on down at the job centre.'

He shuffled through the pile, eventually pulling a bag out. 'This?'

Jon stepped over to the desk. 'Don't mind the arsehole,' he whispered, taking it from the other man. 'And we'll need that one with the book in too.'

After placing the two bags in the centre of the table, Jon sat back down. 'James Field, or Jammer as he was known to his associates, has recreated the weapons in this illustration of a Mau Mau terrorist. It's all about revenge. We also found this book about SAS camouflage and ambush techniques. He's probably dressing himself up in combat clothing, then jumping out on his victims and ripping them apart the same way Mau Mau terrorists ripped open theirs. After that, he's planting hairs from the panther at Buxton Zoo on the bodies.'

There was silence for a couple of seconds. Summerby turned to Murray. 'You'd better tell us what's in those other chapters.'

Gardiner held up her hand. 'Sir, I went through the last parts while DC Murray was driving us back here. Chapter Two,

Shoot to Kill, goes on about the colonial government's policy of opening fire on any person seen in prohibited areas. Militia groups formed by the white settlers started using it as an excuse to try and wipe the Kikuyu, or Kukes, out. Those living on isolated farms with no phones brought in bounty hunters who were paid twenty shillings for every suspect they killed. British Army units set up scoreboards, officers paid a bounty for each company's first kill, usually five pounds. The soldiers would cut off the hands of any suspect they shot and carry them back to the camp to prove someone had been killed. The RAF took to decorating their planes with silhouettes of an African holding a spear for each kill they made.'

Several people's eyes were still on the page of images, including the photo of the plane with its line of little men drawn on the side. Jon couldn't quite believe what he was hearing. They really just opened fire on anyone they saw?

'Next chapter is called Breaking Resistance. This describes how, to stop the supply of food, ammunition and medical supplies to the KLFA, the British started rounding up the Kikuyu and placing them in what were officially called protected villages. Surrounded by barbed wire, watch towers, armed guards and dogs, these prison camps lacked sanitation and were horribly overcrowded.'

'Why? How many people did they put in them?' someone asked.

Gardiner leafed through her copy of the project. 'It says somewhere. Ah, here it is. "By nineteen fifty-three over one hundred thousand Kikuyu had been evicted from their homes. In Operation Anvil, in nineteen fifty-four, soldiers rounded up the entire Kikuyu population of Nairobi. Twenty thousand were interned without trial. By the end of nineteen fifty-four tens of thousands were behind barbed wire."'

McCloughlin's head was down. 'I still don't see where this is going.'

Gardiner shot the thinning hair on top of his head a withering look. 'Murder Camps describes the process of dealing with Mau Mau suspects. Anyone arrested by the security forces – men, women or children – was screened to see if they'd taken the oath of Mau Mau allegiance. Screening was another word for interrogation. It involved beating and—' Her eyes flicked downwards in embarrassment '—other forms of torture. The aim was to get a person to break their oath by confessing to have taken it. Then their rehabilitation through increasingly less secure camps – or the Pipeline as it was called – could begin. However, typhoid outbreaks started to occur.' Again she started reading from the page. '"Interned people slept in the same rooms as their toilet buckets. Bed bugs and lice infested them, rats were killed for food."'

'Maybe we have dwelt on this long enough. How did it all end?' Summerby asked quietly, eyes on the table.

'News of the atrocities started leaking out back in Britain. Questions were asked in Parliament, though the government of the day did its best to deny everything. Also the Mau Mau had been bombed out of existence by the late fifties; the RAF dropped over fifty thousand tons of ordnance into the jungles during the conflict. Keeping the Kikuyu in prison camps started to become an expensive political liability. By nineteen fifty-seven, two thousand prisoners were being released back on to the reserves every month. When a cover-up of an inmate massacre at the Hola detention camp was exposed in nineteen fifty-nine, it was the final nail in the coffin for the Pipeline. The British withdrew and the country was independent a few years later.'

A few people fiddled with their photocopied sheets in the silence. Summerby looked around, then stood up, yanked the map off the whiteboard behind him and grabbed a marker pen. In the middle of the empty board, he wrote *James Field/Jammer*. He drew a vertical line above it and turned to Jon. 'What was his mother called?'

'His birth mother was Mary Gathambo. His adoptive parents are called Pat and Ian Field.'

Summerby wrote the names down. Next to James Field he drew a horizontal line and wrote *Danny Gordon*. Above that he wrote *Derek Peterson*.

'So, given that Danny Gordon was dead before Peterson was murdered, we're assuming James Field killed him as payback for his mate's suicide.' He picked up a red pen and connected Field's and Peterson's names. Switching back to blue, he then wrote *Trevor Kerrigan* next to *Mary Gathambo* connecting it to James Field with a blue and then a red line. 'James Field also killed his birth dad, for reasons as yet unkown.'

To the side he then wrote out *Rose Sutton*, connecting it to James Field with another red line. 'His first victim, again, killed for reasons as yet unkown.' Below Sutton's name, he jotted down a question mark. 'And the final person or persons he's after. Who might it be?'

'If he killed his own dad, maybe he'd kill his mum's adoptive parents, they abandoned her after all,' Gardiner said.

Summerby looked at the board. 'You're right.' Above Mary Gathambo's name he added two more vertical lines, topping one with a question mark and the other with *Sullivans*. 'Mary's mum and dad, adoptive and natural, we need to know all of their whereabouts. OK, who else?'

Rick briefly raised a hand. 'Whoever changed his name from Njama to James. Midwife at the Wythenshaw, the doctor who delivered him, the social worker. Could be any number of people.'

McCloughlin crossed his arms. 'What about the Silverdale? Maybe there was more than one kiddy fiddler on the staff. Perhaps we should be thinking about that tutor who helped him produce this load of shite.' He tossed his copy of the project to the side.

Summerby added *Tutor* to the growing list by the question mark. 'Who else?'

Jon interlaced his fingers. 'Someone tried to scrub the word 'Kuririkana' from the rocks on Saddleworth Moor. Clegg has been hiding information from the start of this thing.' He thought about the Inspector at Mossley Brow. Suspended from duty, his sister dragged in and cautioned. 'The bloke was banging Rose Sutton. Maybe he's on the hit list.'

'And Hobson,' added Rick. 'He's had dealings with Field too.'

As their names went on the board, the office manager called over. 'Boss? DC Adlon's on the line with that information.'

Summerby pointed to the phone on the desk. 'Put him through to here, I'll switch to speakerphone.'

McCloughlin jumped to his feet. 'Silence in this room!'

The buzz of the civilians' voices manning the phones evaporated. A high-pitched version of Adlon's voice emerged from the unit's base. Jon wasn't sure if the squeak was due to excitement or the loudspeaker. 'Boss? Are you there?'

Summerby nodded. 'Go ahead, you're on speakerphone.'

'We've got the records. Copies of all this stuff were taken by James Field back in two thousand. It's a sad bloody story. No wonder the lad flipped out. James Field's birth mother was Mary Gathambo. She was brought up by the Reverend William Sullivan and his wife, Emily. They lived in a vicarage just outside Warrington. The Sullivans were Mary's legal guardians, not adoptive parents. They returned from Kenya with Mary when she was eleven months old.'

'So who are her birth parents?' Summerby asked.

'Mary was an orphan. Apparently her mother died in a place called the Kamiti detention camp. Medical complications after the birth.'

'Have you got contact details for the Sullivans?'

'They're dead. Both were killed in a car crash in nineteen seventy-nine.' Summerby reached out and crossed their surname off the list as Adlon continued. 'Mary was eighteen at the time. It seems they'd not written her into their will. None of the relatives were interested so she was basically left to fend for herself. Details are sketchy from that point on, just stuff she was prepared to tell the hospital staff. She moved to Manchester and lived in bedsits for a while, but by the time she turned up at the hospital she'd been sleeping rough.'

'Sleeping rough while pregnant? Why do that?' Summerby asked.

'No explanation. Fell behind with her rent?'

Jon's mind was turning. 'Kerrigan started out in the property game, bedsits and the like. What if Mary was a tenant he took liberties with? It would explain how she ended up preferring to sleep rough.'

Summerby's eyes were on the board. 'You mean he raped

her. That's why Field killed him. But how did he find out who his father was?'

'Sorry. You talking to me, boss?' Adlon's voice buzzed.

'No, rhetorical question. What were the Sullivans doing in Kenya?'

'He was the chaplain for the Kamiti area. Left in the late fifties just before the country got its independence.'

'With an orphaned Kenyan baby?'

'There are notes from the social worker who initially dealt with the Sullivans on their return to Britain. Apparently Kenya was in chaos. There'd been this armed uprising by the Mau Mau, thousands had been locked up in specially built camps. Then the decision was made to release them all. It seems in all the confusion many orphaned babies were left behind. Convents took in some but the Sullivans took in Mary Gathambo.'

Rick coughed. 'Before the Sullivans died, we know they told Mary all about where she was from, including her family name. She'd obviously contacted members of the family back in Kenya. James Field had the letters they'd sent her. She was planning to return to the country when she fell pregnant by, we now know, Kerrigan. We also know James Field made contact with the relatives and flew out there to meet them in March, two thousand and one. He came back a different person, knuckled down in a job, kept out of trouble and quietly planned all this.'

Summerby slapped the end of the marker pen against his palm. 'We're no nearer to working out who he's after next. DC Adlon, bring everything you've got back here.' He cut the connection and turned to the table. 'We need to re-question every offender who was in the Silverdale at the same time as Field. And go round the squats, pull in everyone who knew him as Jammer.'

A phone rang and was swiftly answered. 'Is there a DI Spicer here?' a female civilian called out.

Jon turned to her, instantly clocking her worried expression. 'It's Sergeant Innes in the radio room. He's got a message about your wife.'

Thirty-Six

Jon got to the woman in three strides and took the phone from her outstretched hand. 'Sergeant?'

'Jon. This might be something and nothing. Your other half, is she called Alice?'

He felt a plunging sensation, as if he was in a lift that had unexpectedly started to go down. 'Yes. What is it?'

'You know the Liberal Democrat constituency offices in Cheadle Hulme? On Gill Bent Road?'

'Yes.'

'We've just received a call about an incident there. A woman turned up, er, in a bit of a state. Complaining. Apparently about the war in Iraq.'

He knew instantly it was his wife. Please let her be OK. Oh God, what about Holly? 'Is there a baby with her? Does she have a baby?'

'Yes. A girl. The staff are caring for her.'

'The staff? What's Alice doing?'

'The caller described her as extremely agitated. I'm sorry, Jon.'

He lowered the handset and stared at the wall. Rick's voice sounded behind him.

'Jon, what is it? Is Alice OK?'

He hung up. 'I've got to go. Alice isn't well.' He was in a tunnel, the only visible things were the doors he was marching towards. Voices were around him, exact words unintelligible. He was about to grab a door handle when he realised he didn't have his car keys.

Summerby collared him as he returned to his desk. 'Jon, is there a problem?'

'It's my wife. I have to go.'

Summerby clicked his fingers. 'DS Saville, go with him.'

Jon waved a hand. 'It's all right.'

Footsteps followed him down the corridor. He glanced over his shoulder to see Rick, his mouth beginning to open. 'Come on mate, I'll drive you.'

'It's all right, honestly.'

'Jon, just let me drive, OK?'

Anger flared and he started to turn. But as he did so a sense of nausea welled up. He wanted to sit down. 'All right,' he swallowed.

Once in his partner's car, Jon leaned back in his seat. What has happened? Has she gone mad? Have I lost her forever? He saw Alice in a white hospital gown, rocking back and forth. Oh no. Gritting his teeth, he got out his mobile and phoned home. 'Mum, I'm picking Alice up. Bringing her home.'

'Where is she?'

'I'll explain later. Please, stay there just a little bit longer. Thanks, Mum.'

He flipped the phone shut, then directed Rick to the Liberal Democrat's office. When they pulled into Gill Bent Road ten minutes later they immediately saw two patrol cars, blue lights flashing in the dimming afternoon light.

Oh my God, what has she done, he thought, opening the car door before it had rolled to a stop. He approached the office, holding up his badge to the uniform standing there.

The constable looked surprised. 'Didn't expect you guys to come out to this. It's only some hysterical witch.'

Jon had him pinned against the doorframe before he knew what he'd done. His voice came deep and low. 'That's my wife.'

The officer's eyes were bulging in his head, skin going rapidly purple. Jon released his grip on the man's throat and entered the building. Staff had gathered in the corridor, nervous whispers rippled around him.

In a side room a woman was crouched by their buggy. Holly was inside, a little hand wrapped round the woman's finger. From the end of the corridor he heard a strained moaning, as if someone was struggling with a heavy weight.

With a sense of dread he set off towards it. As he got nearer to the open door he could hear a man speaking, effort twisting his voice. He entered an office strewn with papers. Alice was face down on the floor. A female officer was sitting on her legs, hands clamped over her ankles. A male officer with black hair was crouching at his wife's side, one knee in the small of her back. Alice's arm was bent backwards by his grip, her face pressed into the carpet, strands of hair around her head. 'It's simple, love. You calm down and I'll release my grip. Or do you want us to spray you again?'

Jon felt his vision tunnel again. He grabbed a fist full of the male officer's hair and bent his head back so their eyes met. 'Get your hands off my wife.'

Noise to his side. He turned his head. A third officer. He was lifting an arm, bringing a small can up towards Jon's face. He shot out the heel of his hand. It connected with the man's chest and he flew backwards over a desk. Rick's voice. 'Easy! Easy! We're police officers. Jon, let go. Let go!'

He looked down, saw the officer's face screwed up in pain. He unclenched his hand, strands of hair falling from his fingers as the man sank to the floor. The female officer moved warily back and Alice scrabbled to a sitting position.

With streaming red eyes, she looked round the room. 'Jon? Jon? Is that you?'

He held out his hands and knelt down. 'Shush, Alice, it's OK.'

Her face softened and he wrapped his arms about her, taking her weight as she collapsed against his chest. He heard Rick's voice again. 'You OK, mate? Can you stand? Good.'

Jon turned to see the officer he'd slammed over the desk getting back on his feet. Keeping one eye on Jon, he leaned down to retrieve his can of pepper spray from the floor. 'You're well out of order. That . . . that was assault. I'll report this.'

Jon looked at his face. He was in his early twenties, outrage all over his young features. 'Piss off out of it.' He swept his eyes over the other officers. 'All of you. Fuck off.'

The black-haired one got up, massaging his scalp with the fingertips of one hand. 'She had flipped out. She was wrecking the place.'

'So you fucking pepper-sprayed her? Get the fuck out.'

Rick stepped forward. 'It's OK you lot, we'll take it from here. Everything's cool.' He guided them from the room and as they went down the corridor, Jon heard the female officer say, 'Was that his wife?'

The door gently shut and Jon lowered his head, pressing his cheek against his wife's hair. 'Alice? Are you OK?' he whispered.

She didn't answer. He continued to cradle her, listening as her breathing began to slow. The office was a total mess. Files were pulled from shelves, sheets ripped from the binders. What the hell had she been doing?

There were footsteps outside and the door half opened. Rick looked in. 'She OK?' he whispered.

Jon shrugged.

'Holly's down here. I think she's hungry. What can I do?'

'Is there a red bag by the buggy?'

'Yes.'

'There'll be a half full bottle in there and a little pot of formula. Tip it in and heat it in a microwave. About ten seconds, just so it's lukewarm. Got that?'

Rick nodded.

'And you've got my home number in your phone?'

'Yes.'

'Call it. My mum's there. Tell her to ring Doctor Shaw and ask her to come round to our house.'

Jon looked up from his armchair as Dr Shaw entered the room. His mum and younger sister Ellie were on the sofa, Rick was half sitting on the windowsill, sipping from a cup of tea. The curtains were open and the glass in the windows shone black.

Jon started to get up, but the doctor gestured to him to sit down. 'I'm fine.' She placed her bag on the floor, strands of long brown hair falling over her face as she did so. With the tip of a thumb, she pushed them behind one ear. 'You should have rung me weeks ago.'

Jon felt a blush rise in his cheeks. 'I couldn't work it out. She insisted she was just tired. I wasn't sure . . . is she awake?'

'No. I've given her some sleeping pills. She'll be out until the morning.' Her eyes turned to Holly, who lay in Jon's lap. 'Your baby will have to make do with bottles of formula. I wouldn't normally advise this, but it may be better if Alice gives up breastfeeding all together. She really needs total rest.'

'What about medicines?'

'Well, I think it's best I come back to see her tomorrow. If she needs something to calm her nerves, that's not a problem. As regards anti-depressants, let's talk first. There are many other options before we turn to pills.'

Jon caught a glimpse of his sister's face. Seeing her on the verge of tears brought a lump to his throat.

'Now,' the doctor continued. 'You take care of that gorgeous little girl. I'll be back tomorrow, ten o'clock.'

'Thanks for coming out.'

'No trouble.'

Jon handed Holly to his mum and showed the doctor to the door. When he walked back into the front room, the others were talking. Jon looked at his sister and suddenly thought about his brother, Dave. 'Mum, did anyone else call you today?'

She looked up. 'No. Should anyone have?'

That little bastard, Jon thought. 'No, I just wondered if Dad was OK.'

'Oh, I've talked to him. He's coming round with fish and chips.'

Jon nodded. 'I'll brew up again.'

He wandered into the kitchen and flicked the kettle on. The appliance began to tick as electricity warmed the element inside. Soon it began to rumble quietly, the bubbling sounds picking up in strength to something that resembled a roar before the kettle turned itself off. The noise he'd heard on the moor came back to him and he couldn't keep thoughts of the case from his head. Had it been Field making the sound? He must have written the word Kuririkana on the rocks, but who had scrubbed it off? Sutton? Surely, if he was first to have discovered his wife's body, the letters would have been plain to see? Something was going on at that farm, no doubt about it.

As Jon poured fresh water into the pot the conviction grew.

'Field killed Sutton's wife? Why? The affair? That was of no concern to Field. His motive is revenge for past wrongs.'

'Talking to yourself, Jon?'

He turned to see Rick standing in the doorway.

'Did I say that out loud?'

Rick nodded. 'You know what they say about that. First signs of . . . ' His words dried up.

'What if Field killed Rose Sutton to get back at the husband? The message on the rock was for him, that's why he scrubbed it off.'

Rick shook his head. 'Leave it, Jon. There's dozens of officers tracking down Field. Talking of which, I'd better report back too, Summerby will be wondering where I am. Shall I call you tomorrow?'

'But we overlooked Sutton. Did his name go up on that whiteboard?'

Rick said nothing.

'It didn't. Listen Rick, I think the man could be the key to this. He's hiding something, I'm certain.'

Rick sighed in frustration. 'Jon, drop it. Enough's enough. Your wife is upstairs, remember?'

'Ten minutes with Sutton. That's all I need.'

Rick held up a hand. 'Jon, you've been going on about your wife being exhausted and obsessed. Look in the bloody mirror. You're on your last legs and you're still harping on about the case. That doctor should have been giving sleeping tablets to you as well.'

Jon looked into the other man's eyes. 'I can't drop it.'

'You don't have a choice.'

Jon put the teapot back down. 'I've got a feeling about this, Rick.'

He pushed past his partner and walked into the front room. Holly was fast asleep in his mum's arms. 'Mum, can you give Holly her next bottle? I need to pop out.'

'Pop out? Where?'

His mum and sister were staring at him in disbelief.

'To see someone. I'll be an hour, two at the very most.'

'But Alice is—'

'Alice is asleep, Mum. She won't stir until the morning, you heard Doctor Shaw.'

Ellie's face was showing anger. 'Jon, get a bloody grip. You can't be serious.'

'Listen to her, Jon. She's right.' Rick's voice, behind him.

Jon felt his resolve falter. He crossed the room and sat down. They're right, what was I thinking? But then he caught sight of the windows and the darkness beyond. This thing started on the moors and that's where it'll end. He got back up. 'Two hours. I'll be back in two hours.'

Silence as he crossed the room.

'You coming?' he asked Rick as he reached for the keys to Alice's car.

His partner shook his head in reply.

Fuck you then, Jon thought, slamming the door behind him. Outside he paused. If you're going to feel like shit, you might as well do it properly. He reached for his cigarettes and jammed one into his mouth. After reversing out on to the street he pushed the dashboard lighter in and hit the accelerator.

The traffic was light as he turned on to the main road. He glanced at the clock. Jesus, ten past seven. The M60 came into view, a trickle of cars gliding along in its orange glow. Jon steered off the slip road and rapidly cut across to the fast lane. Smoke curled up from the cigarette held in his right hand before being sucked out of the crack in the side window.

He kept his thoughts on Sutton, knowing if he didn't guilt would force him from the motorway and back to his house. The turn off for Bredbury shot past and his phone started to ring. Rick's name on the screen. Jon toyed with ignoring it, sure it would only be his partner having a go. He dragged deeply on the cigarette and flipped the phone open.

'Jon, where are you?'

'M60, just past Bredbury.'

'I just got a call from the station. Some uniforms patrolling the banks of the Medlock spotted something on the edge of Oldham Golf Course.'

'Something?'

'They're not sure what. One thought it was a person. The

other reckons it was a big cat. He swears it had a tail. Anyway, whatever it was, it raced off across the fairway. The helicopter's been called out, dogs, armed response. Everyone's heading over there.'

Jon kept his foot on the accelerator. The turn-off leading to Saddleworth Moor was up ahead. 'I'm carrying on to Sutton's farm.'

He hung up before Rick could respond.

Thirty-Seven

As he reached the top of the empty moor, the red light of the radio mast came into view. In the blackness behind it a pale light glowed in the sky. Dark clouds slowly shifted and a ghostly moon was revealed. At least it's not full, he thought. Faint light seeped down, coating the moor in a silvery sheen and emphasising the shadows pooled in every dip of the wild landscape.

He pressed on, reaching the other side of the plateau a few minutes later. The road curled down towards Holme and soon the track to Sutton's farm appeared on his left. Jon bumped along it before swinging the vehicle round to the farm buildings. A fence, topped with barbed wire, blocked the way into the courtyard. As he came to a halt, security lights mounted high on the walls switched on.

He got out of the car, immediately aware of the sounds of sheep in the barns. Several lights shone in the farmhouse itself. A gate was built into the fence and an open padlock was hanging from the links. Cautiously, he swung it open. 'Hello? Mr Sutton? DI Spicer, Manchester Police.'

As he rounded the corner of the farmhouse Sutton's Border Collie, Chip began to bark, a chain tying it to the kennel behind. More security lights came on to reveal Andrew Du Toit. He was standing in the doorway to the farmhouse, a rifle levelled at Jon. 'Fuck, didn't know who you were. We're just locking up for the night.'

As he lowered the weapon, Jon breathed out. Anger replaced his feelings of shock. 'You always walk round with a loaded gun?'

'Mostly.'

'Is Ken here?'

'Inside.'

As Jon walked across the courtyard he noticed that each barn was full of sheep. Fencing had been erected in the gaps between the buildings, barbed wire snaking along the top. This isn't to keep the sheep in, Jon thought. It's to keep something out.

The kitchen was the same as before, except for some sort of monitor set up next to the pair of walkie-talkies. Jon carried through into the front room, the mounted heads of dead animals staring down at him from every wall. Sutton was in the chair by the fire, a rifle with telescopic sights leaning against the wall. His gaze shifted briefly to Jon then returned to the flames. His eyes seemed almost to shut and Jon thought he looked more gaunt and strained since the last time he saw him in that chair.

'Mr Sutton, we need to talk.'

The man didn't answer.

Jon sat down opposite him. 'You know more about these killings than you've admitted. I need to know the truth before someone else dies.'

Sutton snorted as Andrew moved across the room and settled on the sofa. Jon pondered which angle to take. There wasn't a lot he could do if Sutton chose to stonewall him. He needed to provoke a reaction. 'Why did you remove the word Kuririkana from the rocks by your wife's body?'

Sutton's half-closed eyelids moved slightly.

'You won't realise this, but the same word was written at the scenes of Derek Peterson's and Trevor Kerrigan's murders. It also appeared at the bottom of a suicide note left by one Danny Gordon.'

Sutton remained impassive.

Jon sat back, injecting a more casual note into his voice. 'Why all these security measures? Shouldn't the guns be kept in their locker when not in use? Are you frightened of something, Mr Sutton?'

His head moved a fraction. Obviously unsettled by Sutton's silence, Andrew Du Toit said, 'We're taking extra precautions because of the animal out there.'

Jon kept his eyes on Sutton. 'Animal or person?'

Du Toit looked confused. 'What do you mean?'

Jon saw a chink in Sutton's defence. His nephew didn't know what was really going on. 'Your uncle has reason to fear a person, not an animal. These killings are to avenge past wrongs aren't they, Ken? That's why you scrubbed the word off the rock. You knew its significance. Do you speak Kikuyu then, Mr Sutton? Have you ever been to Africa?'

Du Toit sat forwards. 'Uncle? What's this about. Tell the policeman—'

Sutton's head whipped round and spit flew from his mouth. 'Say nothing!'

His nephew flinched backwards.

That's better, thought Jon. Now we're getting somewhere. The dead animals were staring down and Jon glanced up, as if by glaring back he could force their heads to turn. A stag, antlers branching out high from its head. Several foxes, their mouths partly open as if panting for breath. Deer, sharp horns spiralling up a good two feet. Jon's eyes narrowed. Those weren't deer, they were impala. He ran his eyes along the walls, identifying the head of a warthog in the corner.

'You lived in Kenya, didn't you? When was it?' He began working out the dates. Sutton was about seventy. During the fifties, he would have been in his twenties. He married Rose Sutton late. What had Clegg said? When he was well past forty? Was that because he didn't live in Britain during the fifties?

'James Field.' Jon said the words slowly. 'Njama Gathambo.'

Sutton's head turned and Jon saw the fury in his eyes.

'That name means something to you, doesn't it? Njama Gathambo's mum was called Mary.'

Sutton kept his silence. Keep going, Jon thought. You'll hit a nerve soon.

'She was orphaned during the Mau Mau uprising in Kenya. Her mother died in a British detention camp at Kamiti.'

Still he kept his mouth closed.

'Njama has made two metal panther claws. He used them to kill your wife and then he daubed the word "remember" on the rocks with her blood.'

Sutton's fingers dug into the arms of his chair. 'The savages. The filthy, bloody savages. I knew that evil would never die.'

'Uncle, what's he talking about?'

'What did you do in Kenya? Were you in the army?'

Sutton shook his head. 'I was a farmer, one of the dozens who the Government encouraged to go out there and make something of that land. We transformed the country, made it a success. But the bloody Kukes weren't happy. They wanted what we'd created. They formed that barbaric sect and started attacking us, creeping out of the jungles, smeared in blood and entrails. Eating their victims.'

Jon sat forwards. 'You fought the Mau Mau?'

'It was a fight to save civilisation itself. And people get hurt in fights. I joined the Kenya Regiment. Later, when the detention camps were built, I worked in one of those.'

'Kamiti? You worked there?'

Sutton raised a finger. 'That was for bloody women. The ones who'd hide bullets in their baby's blankets, then smuggle the ammo to the animals hiding in the jungle.'

'Where did you work then?'

'Hola.'

'The site of that massacre? You tried to deny it ever happened.'

'Massacre?' Sutton gave a cruel smile, eyes glinting in the light from the flames. 'We only killed ten of them. They were the hardcore, the lowest of the low, the ones who wouldn't confess their oaths, no matter what we did.'

'And you did plenty, didn't you?' He looked into Sutton's eyes and saw only malice. You cruel bastard. He wanted to wipe the look from his face. 'Well, the grandson of one of those men you killed is coming for you, right now.'

'We built that country. And the Government in London sold us down the river. When they decided it was all an embarrassment, they washed their hands of us. They even let out Kenyatta, the biggest terrorist of all.'

'So you moved back here?'

'Before they handed power over to those bloody savages, yes. We had to leave that farm behind and start again. My sister, Andrew's mum, went to South Africa.'

Du Toit looked up. 'Hang on, this is all about a kaffir? You're saying my Aunty Rose was killed by a fucking kaffir?'

A beeping noise sounded in the kitchen. Du Toit's head snapped to the side. 'Something's triggered the sensors in the top field!' He jumped to his feet, grabbing his gun as he did so.

Sutton struggled to get up. 'No! Andrew, stay inside.'

Jon was on his feet. 'I'm calling for back-up. Everybody sit down.'

'Bullshit,' Andrew replied, hurrying into the kitchen.

Sutton was reaching for his gun.

'Stay where you are,' said Jon, pulling his mobile out. One bar of signal flickered on and off. He tried to dial Longsight, but the call was dropped after two shaky rings. Bollocks! Du Toit reappeared in the doorway and threw a walkie-talkie to Sutton. 'I'm going out. Keep this turned on.'

'Andrew, don't!' said Jon, grabbing Sutton's arm as he too made for the door. 'Where's your bloody phone?'

Sutton struggled to get free. 'There, by the gun cabinet.'

Jon bounded over to it. 'How does it work? I can't get a dial tone.'

Sutton turned in the kitchen doorway. 'The green button. Press it.'

'I have! There's nothing.'

Sutton walked stiffly over, listened to the phone, jabbed at the green button and lifted it to his ear once again. 'He's cut the wires.'

Jon remembered the line from Field's project. The Mau Mau chose isolated farms with no phones. Think. There must be some way of getting help.

Sutton returned to his armchair and sat down on the edge of it, rifle in one hand, walkie-talkie in the other. Low static emanated from the speaker.

'We should go and get him back,' Jon said, peering through the tiny windows set into the thick walls.

'He knows what he's doing,' Sutton stated, before adding, 'Kill the bastard, Andrew.'

Jon paced up and down. Text messages! Don't they require less signal to get through? He started typing, *Suttons farm.*

The walkie-talkie came to life. 'He's here, on the track. Climbing down one of your telephone posts. Looks like he's wearing an animal skin.'

Sutton pressed the transmit button. 'Kill him! Kill the bastard!'

As Jon tried to grab the walkie-talkie it emitted a sharp burst of static. An instant later the sound of a gunshot rolled across the fields outside. 'I think I winged him! He's running back to the top field.' The words came in broken snatches. 'He's fast.'

Ken stood up. 'Now we'll show him who's boss.'

Still trying to type the message, Jon made a grab for him. 'Sutton, do not go out there!'

The older man yanked his arm free, the walkie-talkie falling to the floor.

'Jesus,' cursed Jon. Quickly he completed the message. *Jammer here. Send help.* He brought Rick's number up and pressed send. The little envelope on his screen folded itself over and flew off. A second later the words, *Message Sent* appeared. 'Thank fuck for that,' Jon said.

Outside the quad bike roared to life. Jon got to the front door just as Sutton zoomed past, his rifle jammed into a gap behind the seat. The red lights bounced away down the track, Chip barking manically at them.

Jon looked at the dog. 'This is a fucking nightmare.' He went back into the kitchen. What the hell do I do now? Inside the front room, the walkie-talkie continued to buzz. Jon went though, picked it up and pressed the transmit button. 'Hello? Andrew, can you hear me? Andrew?'

He crossed the room and looked into the gun cabinet. Sutton's single shot .22, used for killing rats. Better than nothing. As he pulled it from the rack the walkie-talkie sounded again.

'I'm near the wall. The sneaky bastard, I think he's doubled—'

A burst of noise like a hurricane, punctuated by gasping screams. Silence.

Jon pressed the button. 'Hello! Andrew! Can you hear me, Andrew!'

He let his finger off and now heard the sound of an engine getting louder and louder. The noise died down and, as Jon stared into the fire, he heard Sutton's voice. 'Oh Andrew. Oh sweet Jesus Christ. Andrew can you—'

A loud snarl. The start of a shout, abruptly cut off. Jon threw the walkie-talkie on to the armchair and ran from the room, the rifle in his right hand. Images seemed to register in freeze frames. The red light on the monitor in the kitchen flashing on and off, Sutton's cat staring smugly at him from on top of the Aga, Chip barking loudly and throwing himself against his chain, sheep in the barns with mouths open as they bleated in fear.

He ran down the track, all the while glancing through the low hedge into the top field. The headlights of the quad-bike came into view. The vehicle was motionless on the far side of the field. Jon squeezed between the thorny branches and began jogging across the lumpy grass, all the time trying to scan the darkness before him.

The headlights shone towards the dry-stone wall, just illuminating the beginnings of the moor as it loomed up, blotting out a good part of the night sky. Within fifty metres of the still idling vehicle he stopped. Two bloody forms were visible in the outer reaches of the quad-bike's beam, steam rising from their wounds. They were lying almost at the base of the dry-stone wall. Jon fought the urge to turn and run. Instead he began a slow circle round, trying to get a better view. Fuck this, a voice screamed. Get back to the farmhouse and lock yourself in. One of the bodies moved, a hand fluttered weakly in the air. Shit, Jon thought, drawing closer, gun held before him.

Now he could see them better. Andrew Du Toit was on his side, a gory mess below his chin. His unblinking eyes stared at the grass and Jon knew he was dead. Next to him Sutton lay on his back, a hand still waving weakly in the air. Along with the steam rising from his gaping chest, Jon could see breath curling from his open mouth. He crept forwards. No sign of the killer. Maybe hiding on the other side of that wall? He knew that helping Sutton meant entering the beam of light and exposing himself to view. His heart was like a drum beating in the night. Do it. Go in fast, get him on to the quad-bike and drive for the main road. Don't! Just turn around and get away from here! He extended a foot, then brought it back. He took several quick breaths. 'Come on Spicer, go, go!'

Keeping low, he ran across the grass and entered the bright glare. As he knelt down, he looked for their weapons. All he spotted was the other walkie-talkie by Sutton's leg. Quickly he jammed it into his pocket. Then he tried to hook an arm under Sutton's. The man was like a sack of coal. Jon looked at the rifle in his hand. Do I put you down? No fucking way. He grasped Sutton's collar and started trying to pull him through the long grass towards the vehicle. The lamp shone directly into his eyes and slowly he started to stagger towards it.

Something black passed across the beam of light, a long tail trailing behind it. Jon squinted, just able to make out movement behind the vehicle. The engine abruptly died and with it the light. Jon blinked, suddenly unable to see a thing. At his feet Sutton let out a shuddering sigh then stopped breathing. Jon opened his eyes as wide as they could go. But all he could see was churning clouds of bright colours, his night vision ruined by looking into the headlight. Shit, shit, shit. From the darkness in front came a low rumbling snarl. Ice blasted through Jon's veins and he let Sutton's corpse sink to the turf. Hands shaking, he brought the weapon up, desperately trying to hear if something was running at him. He felt tears brimming in his eyes. Alice, I'm so fucking sorry to leave you like this.

The noise came again, closer this time. Jon felt his last bit of self-control give way. Pure terror flooded him. His legs began to pump and he realised he was sprinting blindly across the grass. Pain exploded up from his left ankle and he pitched face first into the ground. He got back on his feet and tried to put some weight on his twisted ankle. An agonising stabbing carried right up his leg, countering the waves of panic, clearing his head. The dipping sheds, he thought, somewhere to my right. He started to hobble in what he hoped was the right direction. He became aware of the wall at his side. There was light above. The moon. It had come out. He was regaining the ability to see. Turning round he searched the field, just able to spot a dark form in the silvery light. It was zigzagging across the grass towards him, pointed ears sticking up from its head.

Lights on the track, flashing blue. Lots of them. The procession of vehicles was speeding towards the farm. 'Here!' Jon yelled, waving his arms. 'I'm here!'

The police cars didn't slow. He pointed the rifle upwards and pulled the trigger. A weak pop and the procession continued past. From the corner of his eye, Jon could see the black shape was now less than thirty metres away. He turned in the other direction. The sheds were just ahead. Half running, half hopping, he set off, the anticipation of the claws sinking into his back increasing with every step. Into the courtyard, railings lining the edge of several deep trenches. He thought of hiding in one, then imagined being trapped down there as the creature, with claws extended, dropped into the other end. A wooden door led into the shed on his right. Please. Please God you have to be open. Gasping for breath, he yanked the handle. Locked. He rammed the tip of the barrel into the gap between the edge of the door and the frame, started levering it violently back and forth. The barrel suddenly snapped with a loud crack. As the broken halves dropped to the ground he looked wildly around. There was one other door in the far corner of the courtyard. Knowing it was his last chance, he hobbled towards it, curled his fingers round the rusty handle and pulled. No! It wouldn't budge. As he sank against the wooden surface the walkie-talkie sounded in his pocket.

'Hello? Can anyone hear me? Jon, are you out there?'

Fresh energy exploded inside him. A chance to survive, however slim. He pulled the handset out. 'Rick! I'm in the field above the house. There's some sheds on the other side. For fuck's sake, hurry!'

At the edge of his vision a black form slid round the corner of the wall. His sense of elation vanished as he slowly turned his head. Holy Mother of God. The panther's pelt was dripping with gore, the fur matted together in stiff clumps. Beneath it he could make out a human form, totally soaked in blood. The cruel hooks of the weapons clinked against the concrete as the person lowered himself onto all fours and began crawling towards Jon, long tail dragging behind.

Jon sank to the ground, drew his knees up and held his palms out. 'Please, please, don't do this. I have a baby. I have—' Snot broke from his nose. His eyes filled with tears once again and he choked on his words.

Snarling quietly, the creature drew closer and a sour stench filled the air. The lower jaw of the panther had been removed and the upper part of the animal's head sat snug on the person's skull, long teeth curling down over his forehead. Now within striking distance, he sank on to his haunches and the low snarling stopped.

Pressing himself back against the door, Jon's breath came in short snatches through his nostrils. The head lifted up and he found himself staring into James Field's eyes.

'I remember you.'

Jon blinked. Terror had robbed him of the ability to reply.

'DI Spicer, isn't it?'

He raised himself up a little and wiped the snot from his lips.

'You offered me your card, tried to help me with a job. You have a good heart.'

Jon cleared his throat. 'Are you going to kill me?'

Field shook his head. 'One more person will die tonight, but it won't be you.'

Jon felt some of the elation return to mix with his sickening fear. He looked at the blood and dirt smeared on the other man's face.

'I disgust you. I can see it in your eyes.'

Jon swallowed. 'You . . . your appearance. It's shocked me.'

Field glanced down at his own body. 'I've been sleeping in ditches, fields and woods. Living off whatever I could find, washing in that river.'

'You were following the Medlock?'

He nodded. 'Since Kerrigan.'

Unsure if Field would strike, Jon slowly lowered one knee, the ankle throbbing with pain as he slid his foot outwards. 'Following it back here to Sutton?'

'Not Sutton. Kiboroboro. The killer. That's what the prisoners at Hola knew him as. They never found out the names of their mzungu guards, so they gave them nicknames instead.'

'I read your project about Kenya.'

Field smiled. 'Good. I knew you'd come across it sooner or later. The project you read – the original – has gone to the *Manchester Evening Chronicle*. I sent it to the crime reporter there. Once tonight is over she will have to tell the truth.'

'It was terrible, what happened there.'

Field raised a bloody claw and used it to scratch at his head.

'You shaved your dreadlocks off.'

'Yes, I think this pelt has given me lice.'

'Where did you get it?'

'The Burma market in Nairobi. You can buy anything there.'

'When you met your relatives?'

'Yes. You know Trevor Kerrigan raped my mother when she couldn't pay her rent?'

'We'd guessed as much. How did you learn that?'

'The letters she sent to our relatives in Kenya. In one she mentioned his surname. It was easy to track him down when I returned to Britain.'

'And Peterson?'

'You know why. For pushing Danny into killing himself.'

'Rose Sutton?'

Field shrugged. 'If he'd had any children, I would have killed them too. He destroyed my family. You've read my project, but you won't know what men like Ken Sutton did. You should know. Everyone should know.'

He sat down and crossed his legs, never letting go of the weapon in each hand. 'My grandfather, Magayu Gathambo, was an educated man. He went to the Tumutumu Presbyterian Mission in Nyeri. He worked as a clerk for a lawyer in Nairobi, then joined the British Army when World War Two broke out. When he returned home his family were living in squalor. But he refused to join the men who whispered about ending white rule. He still believed in those British values of decency and fair play, hoping they might be applied to black people too. When the soldiers drove into Nairobi in their Land Rovers, loud speakers blaring, ordering all Kikuyu to pack one bag and leave their homes, he cooperated.'

'Operation Anvil,' Jon whispered.

James inclined his head. 'Correct. At the screening centre in

Subuku they tied him to a chair and extinguished cigarettes on his back. They shocked him with electricity and forced hot eggs into his anus. My grandmother, Muringo, had her breasts squeezed with pliers and banana leaves rammed into her vagina. They didn't confess to the oath because they hadn't taken it. But once they were set free, they took it straightaway. Muringo remained in Nairobi, Magayu left for the forests of Mount Kenya to join the KLFA. He fought for three years, living as I have done, before he was captured on a return visit to see his wife in Nairobi. They were both immediately put into the Pipeline.'

Beyond the courtyard Jon saw the glow of torches starting to bob across the fields. He heard dogs whining and snatches of speech on the breeze, orders being given in low voices.

James cocked his head to the side, eyes staying on Jon. 'Time is running out, your reinforcements will be here soon. When Magayu arrived at his camp the doors to his cattle truck were thrown open. They ran a gauntlet of whistle-blowing guards and barking Alsatians. Officers screamed, "Piga! Piga sana!" Beat them, keep beating them! They were stripped naked and forced into a cattle dip of disinfectant. Some drowned in the stampede. He was issued with a pair of yellow shorts, two blankets and a wristband with a number. The few possessions he had were stolen, his clothes burned on a bonfire. He was graded as a black suspect, the ones most dangerously committed to independence. He was moved from camp to camp in shackles, forced to work laying roads, digging trenches, even building the runways for the international airport outside Nairobi. Many died on that project, but still he refused to confess the oath. He was eventually classed as hardcore and sent to Hola for breaking there.'

Now Jon could see the lights had split into two groups. From somewhere in the black sky came the chopping sound of a helicopter. 'I don't know what to call you.'

'Jammer. I'm neither James nor Njama.'

'Well Jammer, we need to discuss what's about to happen. That's an armed response unit coming across the fields.'

Jammer raked a claw across the concrete. 'It's not important. Just listen. Magayu survived the beatings and torture at every camp, but nothing could prepare him for Hola and the rule of Kiboroboro.'

'Sutton was the camp commander?'

'He had many ways of trying to make prisoners confess. Sometimes he'd put them in coils of barbed wire and kick them round the central square. But his speciality was his Land Rover, Gitune. That means Big Red. The prisoners called it that because it was so covered in blood. Kiboroboro would tie an inmate to the rear bumper by his ankles. Then he'd say, "Last chance to talk, Nugu." That means baboon. If they didn't, he'd drive round and round the camp perimeter until the body was just pulp.'

Jon remembered Clegg describing how Sutton had dragged the carcass of the dog back to its owners in the same way. Behind Jammer heads began to peer round the corners of the courtyard. They disappeared for a moment. Then armed officers ran out, forming a line. An amplified voice boomed out. 'Drop your weapons and move away from the officer!'

Jammer crouched lower. 'Because my grandfather was literate, he was given basic tasks in the camp office. He learned Kiboroboro's real name from memoranda he saw there. He also stole paper and smuggled out letters detailing the atrocities. They went to people in authority, both in Kenya and here, in Britain. He knew the letters reached their intended recipients.'

'How?'

'Because the people he wrote to returned them to the camp, demanding to know how such letters had leaked out. The treatment of prisoners was sanctioned at the very highest levels. They signed his death warrant. Kiboroboro tied him to the back of Gitune.'

'Jon, are you injured?'

He glanced over Jammer's shoulder, saw Rick by the left hand wall. He gave a slow shake of his head. 'It's OK. We're talking.'

The same loud voice again. 'I repeat, move away from the officer!'

'Shut up!' Jon shouted back. 'Listen, Jammer, we can talk about all this later. At this moment in time, it's more important you don't get shot.'

Jammer smiled. 'I said in my letter that death doesn't scare me. You know, when I met my relatives in Nairobi, I realised they were from a different world. Thing is, I don't belong here either. Children's homes and white parents. All my life I wondered about where I was from, who I was. My eyes, my nose, my hair. My anger. Where did it come from? On Sundays in the children's home I would hide when other kids' parents came to visit. I was so jealous. And when I found out the truth, it made me even angrier. Kerrigan raped my mother, but it was people like Sutton who really created me. You know what my grandmother's work detail in Kamiti was? Burying dead bodies, even though she was pregnant. They brought them to Kamiti by the truckload from surrounding camps. She gave birth to my mother, then bled to death in the bunk house. The guards' first question when they unlocked the doors each morning was always, "How many have died?"'

The sound of the helicopter had been growing steadily louder and suddenly the courtyard was lit by a brilliant white light. Jon counted fourteen armed officers forming a cordon across the top of the courtyard. 'Jammer, let's just stand up slowly and walk out of here.'

The other man raised his voice to be heard. 'The West always uses the same excuse when it invades a country of dark-skinned people. As it occupies their land and steals their resources you say you're there in a civilising role. Helping the people to shake off cruel rulers, bringing freedom and democracy. Benevolent, kind. But then some of the people you came to save start to resent your presence. They fight back with bombs, ambushes, booby traps. They strike quickly and melt into the crowds. And when your soldiers look to see who attacked them, there are only people in strange clothes looking back. Kukes, gooks, ragheads. So the soldiers vent their anger on them. And what has your civilising army become now? It can't be savage or barbaric. No, because they invaded to eradicate such things. But the evidence is there. Villages ransacked, homes burnt, old men, women and children murdered. The ones who invaded my country ended up massacring the people in their thousands.'

'White settlers died too.'

Jammer thrust a claw into Jon's face. From beyond those curved spikes officers tightened their grips. 'How many white settlers died? Do you know?'

Jon shook his head. 'Hundreds?'

'Thirty-two. More were killed in traffic accidents in Nairobi during the war. How many white members of the security forces died? Sixty-three. Freedom fighters? Eleven thousand, five hundred and sixty-three.' He paused. 'You think the KLFA were terrorists, not freedom fighters? I can see you do. The president of Kenya announced this year that the body of Field Marshal Dedan Kimathi, leader of the KLFA, will be exhumed and given a state funeral. And the number of Kikuyu people who died through internment, starvation and disease? No one knows, because the normally meticulous colonial government didn't keep count.'

Jon lowered his head as he thought of Alice's obsession.

'Kenyans have estimated over one hundred thousand Kikuyu died during the emergency. Some think double that. Once the Pipeline was closed down whole villages remained empty, the inhabitants simply never reappeared. Always the same story. The French in Algiers, the Belgians in the Congo, the Americans in Vietnam. Whites killing in the name of civilisation.' He inclined his head slightly to the side. 'How many of the soldiers pointing rifles at me are black?'

Jon didn't look. 'They're not soldiers, Jammer, they're police officers.'

'They represent the same thing. How many are black?'

Jon glanced beyond Jammer's shoulders. 'I don't know, they're wearing balaclavas.'

'We both know the answer.' He looked down at the claws. 'This thing that I've become. It was invented by the Government's press office in London. I became it to show that any heart of darkness in Kenya was created by the British. If anything threatens your way of life, you hunt it down and destroy it without mercy. Look at the hysteria I've created and think about how you've responded. The cats and dogs that have died, the number of officers sent to deal with me. Now it's time to end this.'

Jon saw the claws were trembling. He looked into Jammer's eyes. Fear shone there. 'Don't do this.'

'It can't end any other way. Just keep low.'

Jon leaned to the side and shouted. 'Don't shoot. Do not open fire!'

Jammer stood and from the line of armed officers a voice barked, 'Drop those weapons, now!'

Jon saw Jammer's eyes were shut as he raised his hands high above his head.

The rifles erupted, multiple flashes still visible even as Jammer's body was thrown against the wall. It connected with a wet thud before sliding down on top of Jon.

Epilogue

Summerby's office was pleasantly cool as Jon sat down. In the seat next to him was McCloughlin, who had moved his chair to the corner of the desk. Just to make sure we all know you're not on my side, thought Jon. Summerby was asking for his calls to be put on hold. 'So Jon,' he said, replacing the phone. 'There's a rumour going round that you're thinking of contacting the Manchester Police Authority.'

Jon nodded and Summerby's eyes instantly connected with McCloughlin's. When his senior officer spoke again his voice was devoid of any warmth. 'What are you thinking of saying?'

'I think you know. It was in my report that went into the log book.'

'DI Spicer, the Independent Police Complaints Commission has conducted a full investigation. It has found that all procedures were correctly followed.'

'That's bollocks, and you know it. For a start, the entire Armed Response Unit was briefed at the scene on what to say before the Assistant Chief Constable arrived. That's not according to protocol following a firearms incident.'

Summerby sighed. 'As I said, the IPCC is satisfied there is no case to answer. The Director of Public Prosecutions has signed it off.'

'It's a stitch-up. My report clearly stated that I'd instructed the Armed Response Unit to hold their fire.'

'Your words obviously weren't heard by the officer in command.'

'DS Saville clearly heard them.'

McCloughlin uncrossed his legs. 'Maybe he wasn't standing so close to the helicopter. I gather it was a bit noisy.'

Jon glanced at him, saw the mocking look in his eye. One

day, pal, one day I'll fucking have you. He looked back at Summerby. 'James Field stood up and raised his arms.'

'To strike you with those claws,' Summerby replied.

'How do you know it wasn't to surrender? They just opened fire on him.'

McCloughlin leaned forward and pointed a finger at Jon. 'To protect you, sonny. They were there saving your ungrateful life. I think you need to consider just whose side you're on here. If you contact the MPA over this, count your career as over.'

Jon looked to Summerby for his reaction. His senior officer crossed his arms. 'I think you need to consider your priorities extremely carefully.'

Fuck you all, Jon thought, standing up and walking from the room without another word. Half way down the stairs, his phone went. 'Carmel, what's happening with that story?'

'I'm sorry, Jon, they're not going to print it.'

'What do you mean? You're just leaving it with the young offender turns psycho story?'

'I've been to see my editor. I took the project Field sent me. He said the claims can't be substantiated. It's too inflammatory.'

'What about the colonial government's records? They must back it up.'

'I've looked into that. Everything, and I mean everything, was destroyed before they handed power over. No one even knows how many detention camps were built.'

'The relatives in Kenya then. There are survivors who witnessed everything, it's how James Field got all his information.'

'They could be after compensation. There are several groups still trying to sue the British government.'

'So you're burying the story.'

'It's not being buried, Jon, it's just too sensitive. I don't know. The decision came from the top, the big cheese himself.'

As footsteps started coming down the stairs behind him, a phrase Alice had started to use came to mind. 'It's censorship through silence. You call yourself a journalist?'

Carmel sighed. 'I did once. Jon, what do you think newspapers are? Who do you think owns them? Institutional shareholders, that's who. We have them to consider. Nothing could be achieved by running a story that attacks Britain so forcefully. Sales could go down, advertisers might desert us. The shareholders will call for heads.'

'And I thought it was about reporting the truth.'

'So did I when I started out in this job. Listen, you know when I mentioned who my source was on this story?'

The footsteps were almost behind him now. 'Yeah. You said I needed to look closer to home.'

'That's right. Just watch your back, Jon. At work.'

'Someone here was tipping you off?'

'That's all I can say, Jon, there's another call waiting. I've got to go.'

As she hung up he turned around. McCloughlin was about to step on to the landing, a mobile phone pressed to his ear. Suddenly it all clicked. Next thing he knew McCloughlin was lying on his back, blinking at the ceiling, blood running from his nose. Jon looked down at his fist. Oh fuck. McCloughlin's phone was on the third step. He picked it up and heard a voice saying, 'Hello? Is that you, DCI McCloughlin?' Carmel's voice. He dropped the phone on to McCloughlin's chest and carried on down the stairs.

Back on his drive, he locked the car and walked up to the front door, briefcase in his hand. He paused there, wondering if Ellie or his mum were inside visiting. Even though a few weeks had passed, they still hadn't fully forgiven his actions that night. Deserting his wife when she was so in need of his support. He didn't like to think about it himself. Fortunately Alice was able to accept how his mind worked. How he just could not let go of a case. She didn't like it, but she realised he could no more change his methods than he could the colour of his eyes. You're one lucky bastard, he thought, turning the key and pushing the door open. Punch's squashed snout appeared from the front room. His dog gave a snort of delight and bounded down the corridor. Jon went down to one knee and curled his free arm round the animal's neck, turning his face away as a wet tongue lapped at his ear.

'That's horrible.'

Jon stood up and looked at Alice. She was standing in the doorway to the front room, her eyes bright and clear, though whether from the anti-depressants or genuine emotion, he still couldn't be sure. Holly was cradled in her right arm, her little legs kicking with excitement. Jon walked towards them and took his daughter. Dragging his eyes from Holly, he kissed his wife. 'You're looking good.'

Alice nodded. 'I feel it. It seems so much easier now Holly is sleeping through.'

Jon's eyes went back to his daughter, who gazed up at him with a crooked smile. 'Yeah, sleep. It's the key to everything.' He didn't mention the dream that now haunted him. Curved teeth and sharp claws slashing at his face. How it always tore him from sleep at three in the morning. 'I just decked McCloughlin.'

Alice stared at him, lips slightly apart. 'Oh Jon! Please tell me that you're joking.'

He looked at the back of his hand, examining the angry red knuckles. 'Wish I was.'

Alice's voice dropped to a whisper. 'Well, that's it then. You'll be fired.'

Jon glanced up, a grin on his face. 'No I won't. It was in the stairwell at Longsight. There were no witnesses. McCloughlin was the one leaking stuff to the *Manchester Evening Chronicle* – and I know exactly which reporter he was tipping off.'

Alice's expression lightened slightly. 'So he won't take action against you?'

'Not if he wants me to keep quiet about what he was up to.'

'Did he actually tell you he won't?'

'No need. A weasel like McCloughlin? He'll have worked out the angles before I'd reached the bottom of the stairs. He won't say a word. Trust me.'

A smile of relief appeared on her face. 'Still, you shouldn't go round punching your senior officers.'

Jon paused, pretending to consider her comment. 'Yeah, you're right. I won't make a habit of it. So, what have you been up to?'

'There's some interesting stuff that came out today. *The Lancet* has published a survey on how many Iraqis have died since the invasion began. One hundred thousand, minimum.'

Jon stepped into the front room and looked at the computer with its piles of paper surrounding it. 'You really enjoy this, don't you? Writing to MPs, sending letters to newspapers.'

Alice sat down on the swivel chair. 'It needs to be done. We can't let the people at the top get away with it. Funny, but I hated politics before. This disastrous war has opened my eyes to so much.'

Jon studied his wife as she picked up her latest print-outs and squared them off. He could see how she was in her element. Always feisty, she'd never been able to sit in silence if she thought somebody was a liar. Now she had something to get her teeth into and the therapeutic value was obvious. He looked down, always amazed at how Holly could fall asleep with such speed. Placing her gently on the mat, he watched as Punch wriggled closer to take up his customary position guarding her. 'Well, I've got something else if you're interested.'

He opened his briefcase and took out his copy of Jammer's project.

'What is it?' Alice asked, hands already out.

'Read it. Let's just say it's not something that's likely to be reported in any of our newspapers. But you might find a few interesting comparisons with what's going on today.'

Alice was already bowed over the photocopied sheets as Jon turned to his dog. 'Hey Punch, fancy coming for a run?'

Author's Note

It would be nice to say the descriptions of Britain's colonial rule in Kenya were a figment of my imagination, but sadly they're not. For full details of that very hushed-up episode in our history, I used Caroline Elkins' excellent book, *Britain's Gulag: the Brutal End of Empire in Kenya*.

For shorter, but very good summaries, go to:

www.troopsoutmovement.com/oliversarmychap6.htm

www-personal.si.umich.edu/~rfrost/courses/ArchivesSem/papers/RobbieBolton.pdf

As for the invasion of Iraq, the history books have yet to be written.

The mystery of Britain's alien big cats remains unsolved. The bulk of this book was written in 2006 – during which time several more sightings were reported. There are many useful websites out there, especially that of the Scottish Big Cat Trust.

Acknowledgements

Once again, huge thanks to my editor, Jane Wood, who, after hearing a very jumbled plot description back in Harrogate, 2005, simply narrowed her eyes and said, 'I like that.'

The following (in no order of preference) were also essential in getting this book done:

Emma, Jane and the crew – for your enthusiasm and support

Nessy – for being such a swot. What's your rank now?

The Suppens – for the tour of your sheep farm on Werneth Low

Nicola – for the insight into crime reporting in Manchester

James – for taking me behind the scenes at Chester Zoo's jaguar enclosure

Senior – for being an old git.